He didn't reply. Instead, he held her gaze, leaned closer and brushed his lips against hers. Soft. Warm.

Heavenly.

Her eyes fluttered closed and she clamped down on the impulse to drag him toward her and grind her mouth against his the way her body craved, fearing what might happen if she took even one tentative step down that slippery slope.

Instead, she let herself glory in the moment. Finally! Here! Today was the day Carter McIntyre kissed her again! Had she imagined it like this? His lips so incredibly warm? His breath melding with hers as his mouth parted ever so slightly? *Journey* playing 'Open Arms' in the background?

Okay, maybe there wasn't a rock ballad playing on cue, but she made up for it by humming a soft moan of pleasure somewhere in the back of her throat as she let herself sink into the pleasure of this one, perfect kiss.

Just like the first time...

Who said coming home is easy?

Stacking
the Deck

Cheri Allan

~ Book Two ~
A Betting on Romance Novel

Five Oaks Books

This is a work of fiction. Names, characters, places and incidents are either the product of the author's imagination or are used fictitiously, and any resemblance to actual persons, living or dead, business establishments, events or locales is entirely coincidental.

Stacking the Deck

Editing by Orchard Edits
Cover Image Credits:
House porch with flowers & logo © Elena Elisseeva | Dreamstime.com
Apple blossoms © Soyka | Dreamstime.com
Garden gnome © Dave Bredeson | Dreamstime.com
Happy face yellow smileys © Miramisska | Dreamstime.com

Publishing History
First Five Oaks Books Edition, 2014
Print ISBN: 978-0-9904815-3-9
Digital ISBN: 978-0-9904815-2-2

Published in the United States of America

Acknowledgements

Books don't simply emerge fully-formed from the imaginations of the author. They are pulled into the world kicking and screaming (and sometimes demanding boxed wine) where they must be shaped, chiseled and buffed into respectability.

And so, I must acknowledge my debt to those who helped make *this* book worthy of you, dear reader.

My husband and children who, in the name of writing, withstand dust bunny storms and thrown-together meals that would make Julia Child cringe, and who understand what I mean when I ask: "Are you bleeding? Vomiting? How big a flame are we talking?" because the creative mind does not take interruptions lightly.

To the dear ladies of NHRWA who cheer so supportively and are a generous and knowledgeable resource for every writing-related issue. And when they don't have the answer, bless them, they have chocolate.

As always, I thank the Plotbunnies for hashing out plots and conflicts and inspiring and challenging me with "what if...."

I thank Charis, my editor. You always seem to know the story I meant to write. Thank you for keeping me on track.

A huge thank you to my beta readers for raising their hands and being willing to read on short notice. I owe you each a giant Whitman's Sampler!

And, because I know you are not a figment of my imagination, I thank my readers for taking a chance on this new author and then (Squee!) asking for my next book. Here it is. Just for you!

~ Cheri

For my dad,

*I'm so glad you were here to see my
happily ever after come true.*

~ Your Chickie

CHAPTER ONE

Twelve years earlier...

SHE'D NEVER FELT MORE EXPOSED.

Beth tried to focus, but her brain was misbehaving. As in not working. Instead, she was acutely aware of the creaking of his aged leather jacket, the heat radiating from his lean, muscular, oh-so-swoon-worthy body and the knowledge that she was going to have to give Mrs. Peabody, the school guidance counselor, an extra-large Whitman's Sampler at Christmas this year for the gift of assigning her to tutor [insert choirs of angels singing here] Carter. McIntyre.

"Twizzler?"

Beth started and realized Carter was looking at her expectantly. "We're not supposed to have food in the library," she blurted.

Stupid! What was she saying? Everyone ate in the library! You just couldn't get *caught* eating in the library!

He shrugged and snagged a long, strawberry-scented strand from somewhere in his backpack and took a bite. She watched as if in slow motion. He had good teeth. Not that he was a horse or anything, but they were nice and straight without being perfect-straight like all the girls that went to Dr. Lewalski's Orthodontics in the old mill building. She didn't think Carter ever had braces. That's how perfect he was.

Perfectly unattainable.

Beth licked her lips and frowned hoping she wasn't having a reaction to the new lip gloss she'd bought just for this occasion. Like he wanted to stare at inflamed lips for an hour. The thought made her stifle a nervous giggle.

She shouldn't be nervous. She could do this. She'd had two full days to prepare for this moment, and even the weather gods were on her side, for Pete's sake. There wasn't a hair-frizzing storm cloud in sight.

It was a picture-postcard late September day. The leaves of the giant sugar maple outside the library rustled softly, and a light breeze drifted through the open window, carrying with it the scents of leather, Twizzler and something intangible, hopeful and slightly wild.

Beth held her breath in her lungs and pressed her hands down her thighs, willing herself not to fidget. She wasn't prone to fidgeting as a rule, but she'd never been this close to Carter McIntyre before either. And he was here. Next to her. Talking to her. Asking her, God help her, questions...

"So, ah, do you tutor a lot?" Carter waited for her to answer, his lips tilting in that slight, irresistible, not-quite-a-smile way that made every sophomore girl's heart beat like a chipmunk's. He swallowed his bite of Twizzler, his long, tanned throat working. Beth glanced up at his eyes, then away again. My God. His eyelashes were to die for.

"Um. No. You're my first," she murmured. Then she froze.

Oh God! That sounded so...!

"I'll try not to be hard on you."

She flushed, a tidal wave of awareness and shock flooding up her neck and into her cheeks. Ohmigod, she did not do innuendo! She dove for her backpack on the floor to avoid looking at him and pulled out a highlighter as if it were a vital piece of tutoring equipment she'd nearly forgotten.

His leather jacket creaked as he moved restlessly in his chair. "I meant, I'll try not to make it hard. Tutoring me. Shit." He muttered that last word softly, and Beth realized with a start that maybe they were both uncomfortable. Obviously him for other reasons than that he was intensely, madly crushing on her, but still.

She cleared her throat and busied herself tidying the books and notebooks on the library table in front of them. "Of course! " she said, not quite sure whether to believe him. One never knew what to believe where Carter McIntyre was concerned. Rumors followed him around like swooning girls and the smell of freshly-applied Lip Smackers.

She set the highlighter parallel to her notebook and tried to breathe through her nose, quietly and calmly. How could she find his mumbled swear a turn-on?

She would not survive. This guy was so hot, so unsettling and so out of her league, she'd burn to a teenaged, hormonal crisp by the end of the quarter, for sure. They'd find her charcoaled remains in this very seat....

"So, what is your current grade?" she asked briskly, trying to pretend she knew what the heck she was doing.

"Twenty-eight."

She made a noise which she hoped sounded like a small chuckle. "No, not the date. Your grade."

He shrugged and rat-a-tat-tapped a pencil on his thigh.

She stared at him. Closed her jaw. "I see."

He tossed the pencil on the table and pushed his chair back, a loud scrape on the hardwood floor. "If you don't want to do this..."

2

She grabbed his arm. "No! No. It's okay. I like a challenge."

He turned and raised one dark eyebrow. He had the shadow of what would one day be stubble across his upper lip. The shadow of impending manhood coupled with the arch of that brow made him look… unpredictable. Dangerous. Like the bad boy you're not supposed to want, but do. Oh, yes, by all that's holy, you most. definitely. do.

The leather of his jacket was smooth and warm under her palm, and she didn't let go, even though she probably should have, until he settled back in his seat.

"A challenge," he repeated. "I don't think you know what you're getting into."

"Are you stupid?" she asked, the question blurting out of her.

His eyebrows slashed down and his jaw hardened. "No."

"Neither am I. I know perfectly well what I'm getting into. Chapter two. Rational numbers."

He didn't move, so she opened the thick text and lay it in front of him. Her hand shook slightly as if a current of electricity was coursing through her. "Don't underestimate me, and I won't underestimate you. Deal?"

Her heart beat like a wild thing in her chest as she waited for his response. Had she pushed him too far? *He's out of your league, Beacon!* the rational part of her screamed. *What do you think you're doing?* And even though she'd never felt more vulnerable in her life, she did the unthinkable.

She smiled at him.

He watched her a moment, his dark green eyes inscrutable. Then he reached into his backpack, pulled out another Twizzler, and held it toward her like a dare. "Deal."

Prep for making love with Grant:

1) Moisturizing body treatment ✓
2) Leg, bikini and eyebrow wax✓
3) Haircut ✓
4) Mani/Pedi—natural buff ✓
5) New underwear—matching bra/panty? ✓
6) Make-up—light blusher, mascara, lip ~~tint~~ gloss ✓
7) Candles, candleholders, lighter✓
8) CD of romantic music ✓
9) Buy:

      Dark Chocolate ✓

      Grant's favorite wine ✓

      Strawberries ~~(whipped cream?)~~ ✓

CHAPTER TWO

LIZ BEACON'S TOES DUG into Grant's bedroom carpet as she watched the single drop of water slither down his baby-smooth chest.

Huh.

Why had she always pictured his chest with more, well, *hair?* Did he shave it? Wax it? Did men just not have chest hair anymore? And how is it that after more than four months of dating, she'd never actually seen his naked torso?

She stood, staring at Grant's chest, puzzling over whether he man-sculpted or simply had naturally non-hairy genes, when he dropped the towel he'd been holding around his waist and reached for her.

She inhaled. *Oh my.*

Swallowing quickly, she sucked in her stomach, arched her back and tried *not* to tug at the fancy, new, "special-occasion" underwear that seemed designed to cut off the blood supply to her femoral arteries. *Not now,* she told herself. *Do not ruin this beautiful moment!*

She hadn't put in all those long hours working on the merger, fit in extra workouts to tone and smooth, and nursed Grant through that nasty bout of bronchitis for nothing! *No!* This night would be nothing less than perfect. So perfect, in fact, that in years to come, she and Grant would share a cup of Earl Grey in the Limoges china they'd gotten for their wedding, stare warmly into each other's eyes and reminisce over the utter romantic perfection of this very night.

And, she deserved this night, didn't she?

For all the chocolate binges she'd denied herself and youthful indiscretions she'd avoided… For all the nice-enough-but-go-nowhere-in-life guys she'd dated and, let's be honest, ditched over the years… well, let's just say it was no *accident* that she was standing here in pale pink, lace hipsters and matching push-up bra.

Liz Beacon knew where she was headed. She'd known, in fact, since that sweltering August afternoon when she'd stood in her parents' backyard in an unflattering sea foam green dress and watched her sister parade her pregnancy-enhanced breasts in an ironically white gown found at a local thrift shop. Liz had vowed then and there never to let this kind of careless disaster happen to *her*.

No. Liz had *plans*. She'd walked away from Sugar Falls, NH, ten years ago and never looked back. She'd shed her awkward teenage pounds, dysfunctional family and hokey lawn-ornaments roots for a fab career, killer abs and a man every woman would envy.

Yes, she still talked to her mother daily and had a hidden stash of Easter peeps in her underwear drawer. Okay, and maybe they weren't exactly killer abs, more toned. Okay, smooth. *Ish*. But none of that mattered now, because she was *this close* to consummating her relationship with Grant—the man who represented the cherry on top of everything she'd worked to become. Nothing could derail her now.

Not even ill-fitting underwear.

Resolutely ignoring her personal discomfort, Liz smiled at Grant. *Dear Grant!* From his polished, yet carelessly tousled hairstyle to that elegant, lean physique, it was as if he'd stepped right out of a Ralph Lauren ad and into her life. He was the ideal combination of style, ambition and athleticism. The man played racquetball twice a week and ran daily. Daily!

Swoon! Their children would be gorgeous.

She licked her lips, Grant's favorite Pinot Grigio still tart on her tongue, and threw herself into the moment. A soft adagio swept the room with romantic violins. True, she would have preferred Norah Jones or even a little Phillip Phillips, but this night was about Grant.

Grant ran his hand up her arm, and Liz closed her eyes. "Your skin is so soft," he said into her ear. Mmm. It had better be for all she'd shelled out for that seaweed/aloe/vitamin E wrap in anticipation of this night.

Liz marveled over the sliver of picture-perfect Chicago skyline just visible through Grant's bedroom window. They sank to his bed, kissing, Grant's hands sliding over her shoulders, her back.

She fingered the sheet behind his head as she debated whether the volume of the stereo was too loud. "Your sheets feel like butter," she said.

"They're bamboo."

"Really? Wow." She should have known he'd choose eco-friendly bedding material. What an incredible man.

"So," Grant said, rolling her onto her back, "where were we? I don't think it was discussing my sheets." He nuzzled behind her ear again.

"The light's still on," she said over his shoulder. She squiggled free and leapt from the bed. "I'll be right back." She flicked off the switch by the door and remembered the scented candles she'd brought over just for tonight.

"I'm getting chilly here all alone," Grant cooed from the bed.

"I'm just lighting the candles," she cooed back.

"I don't need candles."

"It'll put us in the mood," Liz said, blowing lightly on the last candle until a neatly flickering flame appeared. There. *Perfect.* She let out a smooth exhale and turned.

Grant lay on his back, his face in shadow. "I'm already in the mood," he said, reaching for her hand.

Liz smiled down at him and gave his hand a squeeze. "I just want our first time together to be absolutely perfect."

"I know." Her heart gave a delighted lurch as he pressed a kiss to her knuckles. *So sweet!* "But you don't have to try so hard, Liz. It's just sex." He gave her arm a tug, pulling her on top of him, then he growled—*growled?*—and rolled her beneath him.

"It's more than just sex," she insisted, catching her breath.

"You know what I mean," he said against her lips.

She kissed him, once, then pressed her palms to his chest, thinking. "Actually, I don't. What *do* you mean?"

"I mean, just enjoy it. It doesn't have to be this Big Event."

"It's our first time!"

"Not unless we actually do it."

She gave him a little shove, annoyed at the silky feel of his chest under her palms. "Meaning?"

Grant rolled to his side. "Meaning, I've been ready since you walked in the door, but you insisted you needed time to make things perfect. So I took a shower. Now we have to do the whole music and candles thing? Will we have to jump through these hoops *every* time we have sex?"

Liz scooted to a sitting position. "I was making an effort to make things romantic."

He ran a hand through his hair. "I know. It's just... I'm a sure thing, Liz. I appreciate the effort, but you don't have to work this hard."

"You've said that already."

"Listen, I know this night is important to you. You don't have to be nervous."

"I'm not nervous."

"I understand if you are. I know you don't have a lot of experience."

Liz bit her lip as his fingertips stroked her hair from her face. Okay. So maybe she'd misrepresented that aspect of her personal history a teensy bit when he'd first asked, but who wants to leap into bed with a coworker on the third date? Everyone knows it's corporate suicide to have a disastrous office affair. She wanted to be sure he was a keeper before getting that, um, involved. But now… "I trust you," she said, stroking his hair in return.

"I don't want to fight," he said.

"Neither do I."

Yes. Back on track. Liz smiled and closed her eyes as Grant leaned in for a kiss. Could life be more perfect? The merger was nearly complete, she was within spitting distance of her goal weight and she had Grant in her arms. She sighed as his hand slid over her breast and…

Dum. Dum. De-dum. Dum-de-dum-de-dum-de-DUM…

Liz's eyes burst open as her cell phone vibrated atop Grant's dresser, the funereal tune like a black fog seeping under the door in a B-movie.

Oh. Dear. God. In. Heaven. Could she have worse *timing?*

"I'm so sorry," Liz said, mentally kicking herself from here to Tuesday for forgetting to mute her cell phone. How could she have been so careless?! "Ignore it. I'll call her later." Liz pressed Grant back against the sheets again and kissed him with gusto. She would not let *anything* distract her from…

Dum. Dum. De-dum…

Grant's hands stilled. "You can take it," he said against her lips, trying to sit up despite her better efforts to keep him right where he was.

Liz slid her hands down his chest, reveling in the feel of his rock-hard abs. My God, you could actually *see* the man's six-pack. "I'm sure it's not important," she said.

He grabbed her hand before it slid further south. She reluctantly met his eyes. "You know she'll keep calling unless you answer."

"I'll turn off the ringer," Liz said a little desperately. *Not now! No more interruptions!* Grant arched an eyebrow. "We'll turn off your ringer, too!" she added.

Grant disentangled himself, no small feat, and stood up. "Answer it, Liz. I'll wait."

Liz let out a long frustrated exhale—four months!—and hurried to the dresser. "I promise I'll make it quick."

Grant stooped to pick up his towel.

Liz picked up her phone. "Hi, Mom."

"Elizabeth!" her mother yelled. Liz winced, having forgotten to hold the phone a safe distance from her ear. Her mother harbored a deep distrust of modern technology and was convinced any phone not connected by a physical wire must have poor reception. "Honey! I'm so glad I caught you!"

"Mom, now isn't the time—"

"I'll make it quick then! Is there any chance you could take some time off work to help out your dad and I?"

"Time off? I suppose I have some days accrued. What do—?"

"Wonderful! We need you to take care of installing our new patio. Well, not actually installing it, more overseeing it!"

"A patio? Mom, I can't come to Florida to—"

"Not in Florida! In Sugar Falls! We want to replace the old deck and put in a nice patio and walkway. Your father wants it done before we come home, so the grass has time to grow back before the heat of the summer. You know how he is about a lush lawn! We've got someone in mind, so it shouldn't be too much trouble. I spoke with your sister last week, and she thinks the job should only take a few days—tops! "

Liz's heart sank with disappointment as Grant pulled on a pair of sweats and T-shirt. He handed her her glass of wine. She took a slug for fortification. He nibbled her ear.

"If Trish is on top of it, why can't she supervise?" Liz closed her eyes as Grant's tongue caused little tingles to run down her spine. She didn't enjoy sounding petulant, but Trish's geographical proximity to the deck in question, plus her devotion to HGTV, would seem to make her a much better candidate for supervising a patio install than Liz. Also, Liz was busy.

Her mother sighed. Loudly. "You know I can't ask Patricia! With Russ's travel schedule and her hands full with the new baby, where would she find the time?"

Liz shrugged away from Grant's tongue. Talk of babies made her nervous when she was so close to a bed. "New baby? Clara was 'new' in December, Mom." Oh God, what was she *doing*? She could not get sucked into this conversation!

Her mother made a sound of disgust. Either that, or she'd accidentally swallowed the phone. "Well! If you'd ever settle down and give me a grandchild, you'd know that *new* lasts a whole lot longer than a few days where a baby's concerned!"

"You've had grandchildren since you were forty-eight years old, and you didn't seem so thrilled at the time."

"Nonsense! They are blessings each and every one of them! Anyway, you know we'd ask your brother, but I haven't heard from *him* since Thanksgiving. Your father has been up in arms over it. We thought maybe he was planning to surprise us down here for Christmas! Of course it *was* unseasonably hot this year, enough to keep anyone away. Airfares are all over the place, too!" Her mother *tsk tsked*. Grant made impatient throat-slicing motions with his finger. Liz mouthed, *I'm trying*! and shrugged apologetically. "It's all your father can do to stay comfortable. You know, it's really not the heat, it's the humidity. He should be thankful, I tell him! At least you don't have to shovel the heat…"

Grant rolled his eyes and left the room. Crap! Liz watched his retreating backside and grimaced, tugging at the leg-band of her underwear. Then, wandering into the living room herself, she sank onto Grant's dove-gray designer ottoman while her mother prattled on about hurricane warnings and prickly heat.

She'd been so right about the color. Liz ran an idle hand over the smooth, velvety fabric of the ottoman. It was the perfect complement to Grant's black leather sofa and chrome and glass end-tables. Plus, the deep ocean blue accent wall she'd painted in alternating stripes of flat and gloss paint gave the room a subtle 'pop.' Liz was quite proud of the effect. Clean and sophisticated. Like Grant. It was so sweet of him to let her play with his decor this way.

"Lawn or not," Liz cut in as her mother took a breath, "I don't see why this can't wait."

"Normally it could, but with your father's surgery—"

Liz leapt to her feet. "Dad's having surgery? For what?"

"He's getting that hip replacement the doctor recommended last fall!"

"Mom, it's *April!* He's been needing a hip replacement since last fall?" Liz paced back to the bedroom. How could Mom carry on about airfares and humidity when Dad was about to go under the knife? And, how could a woman who talked so incessantly communicate so little?

"You know how busy these orthopedists are down here. We'll be staying a couple extra months and coming home in July. Anyway, you always say you never take all your vacation time, and April in New Hampshire is beautiful."

"Right. Mud season followed by black fly season. Maybe I had plans for my vacation time this year." Liz blew out a candle. The vanilla-scented smoke was beginning to make her eyes water.

"Did you?" her mother bellowed.

"Um, no. But I might have." Fine. She was definitely sounding petulant now, but she didn't care. This was supposed to be *the* night. Liz didn't want to be stuck on the phone discussing grandchildren and hip surgeries and prickly heat. She wanted to be making sweet love to her boyfriend/future fiancé!

There was another audible sigh on the other end of the line. "Your father said I shouldn't burden you like this. And don't get me wrong, we're happy you're so successful, and you know we've tried not to hold you back or take advantage of you. You've earned it! But, I told your father if anyone can get this done right, it's our Elizabeth!"

As the guilt-producing silence stretched out, Liz sighed. She uncorked the bottle of Pinot Grigio and poured another glass, wishing it were a lusty Bordeaux instead. "Fine. I'll talk to Trish. I'll see what I can do."

"There's a good girl! Your father will be so relieved to have this taken care of."

"When is his surgery?"

"Friday morning."

"Fri—?" Liz took a fortifying sip of wine. It would serve no purpose to point out it was already Wednesday. "Let me know how it goes, okay?"

"I'll have Patricia call you. I've got to run. The real estate agent is expecting my call."

"What real estate agent?"

"The one that's listing the house! Really, honey, if you can't pay better attention..."

Liz felt a little sick, the wine roiling in her gut. "You're selling the house? *That's* what this is about?"

"Why did you think we were sprucing it up like this? We've decided we just can't keep up with it like we used to. Patricia suggested we get it listed as soon as possible—to take advantage of the summer buying season. Your father doesn't want to talk about it, but ever since the markets crashed, well, our retirement savings aren't what they used to be..."

For once her mother's voice had grown soft, and Liz felt an odd ache of unease in her chest.

"Anyway, Patricia will fill you in. Call her! I've got to run!"

Liz held the phone to her ear for a full five seconds before she realized her mom was no longer there. She set her glass on the edge of the dresser with a shaking hand. Sell the house? *They were selling the house?*

"Is everything all right?"

Liz sucked in a steadying breath and let Grant's sympathetic words wash over her. It wasn't a big deal. Really. Chicago was her home now. It was just the suddenness of it all that was throwing her off. Who wouldn't feel blind-sided? Wasn't it only natural to picture your childhood home—however imperfect it may have been—to still be there to go back to someday? That is, if you wanted.

Not that she had. Or did. It was silly to get worked up over it.

She thought about her own hefty savings and 401(k) contributions a little guiltily. It never occurred to her that the house in New Hampshire was all the 'investment' her parents had left. She'd always felt she'd made college happen through her own hard work, and yet... when she'd needed a security deposit for an apartment near campus her junior year her dad had mailed her a check, no questions asked.

Liz closed her eyes and licked her lips and tried to pull herself together. Good grief. She hadn't put all this effort into choosing special wine, scented candles and frilly underwear to stand here worrying about her father's hip or Florida's weather or an old farmhouse in rural New Hampshire she hadn't seen in years!

She was *here*, in Grant's bedroom, preparing to make love with the first man she'd dated in the past DECADE she could actually see herself—dare she say it?—maybe not yet, okay, at least *engaged* to, and it wasn't going to happen if she stood here and didn't even pucker her lips and make an effort to—

Crack! Crunch. Crunch. Crunch.

Liz's lips froze mid-pucker. "What *is* that?" she asked.

"A carrot. I got hungry. You want some?"

Liz stared at the orange stub Grant had thrust toward her. "No. I'm... no."

"You okay?"

She blinked, trying to focus. "No. I mean, yes. Yes. Everything's fine."

Crack! Crunch. Crunch. Grant stepped closer and reached out to smooth the hair behind her shoulder. He popped the remaining carrot into his mouth and stroked his hand down her arm, his fingertips cool on her skin.

"The music stopped," she said inanely, hating that she was near tears and not even knowing why.

"Don't worry about the music," he said. "I don't need music."

Liz closed her eyes, defeated. "I'm sorry, Grant. I know it's bad timing, but... I need to go home."

"Now? Did you forget something?"

She stepped back. "No, not that home... I mean... to New Hampshire. My parents need my help with something. I have to take a couple weeks. Time off. I'm sorry. I know we're wrapping up the merger and starting the new project next week, but.... I'll bring Janice up to speed, and I promise to e-mail and call every day. No, *twice* a day. You'll hardly know I'm gone..." She began to gather her things.

Grant stared at her for one long moment as he chewed. Swallowed.

"We're not having sex tonight, are we?" he finally said.

Before I leave for NH:

Book flight—print boarding pass

Get health cert from vet for Eddie

Call P.O. to hold mail

Reschedule dentist

Water plants —put in sink

Backup laptop: pack chargers for laptop/phone

Buy legal pads

Repay security deposit

CHAPTER THREE

TRISH WAS LATE.

Liz sat on a bench outside the Manchester-Boston Regional Airport and forced down another spoonful of beef barley soup as she waited for her sister to pick her up.

The flight to New Hampshire had been hell. Sandwiched in a middle seat between an overweight man with no concept of personal space and a homesick grad student who offered way too many details of his dermatologic history, she'd been forced to feign interest in the *Sky Mall* magazine for a solid hour and a half. Outside of *Don Quixote* from AP Lit Class in high school, it was probably the most boring publication known to man.

Maybe she should have taken Grant's advice and rented a car. Liz set the soup down on the pet crate at her feet. Eddie didn't take well to being boarded, and driving fourteen hours with a cranky, motion-sick cat as her only companion held less appeal than sitting outside the airport, slurping congealing, overpriced soup. Liz watched the sun sink toward the horizon and breathed a sigh of relief as her sister's minivan swerved to a stop in front of her.

"I know. I'm late!" Trish leapt from the van and flung open the rear door. "Be back in a minute. I need to change Clara's diaper. I think we have a major blow-out." Trish's hair appeared a little wilder than usual, and it looked suspiciously like she had her T-shirt on inside out.

"Oh. Sure." Liz wasn't precisely sure what 'blow-out' meant, but it didn't sound good from the looks of Trish's expression.

Trish tossed Liz her keys, waving vaguely with her free hand. "Just drive around a few times if they complain, but I'm gonna need running water for this." With that, she disappeared inside the terminal, blithely parading by the security guy who was trying to get her attention.

Liz opened the rear slider and came face to face with Max, Trish's black Lab.

She body-blocked Max, dumping soup down her sleeve, and reassured the security guy she was not taking the dog out of the car. Max lapped her wrist helpfully, slobbering all over her dry-clean-only Anne

Klein jacket as she tried to close the door again. "In! Get in, Max! I know. I sympathize. But you can't get out here. That security guy is *not* happy with us." Max's dark eyes pleaded with Liz through the window, and he gave a plaintive woof. Relenting, she cracked the door open a little. His nose wriggled giddily at the opening.

"Good doggie," she said, patting his snout. His nose was wet and clammy, but the fur on his head was soft and silky, and Liz decided even though he was a tad pushy, Max wasn't so bad. He'd actually mellowed with age.

They'd never had pets growing up. Mom didn't like animals in general—too much work—so she and Trish had always talked about how when they were grown-ups they'd have a menagerie: dogs, cats, birds, ferrets. They'd said 'menagerie' after Liz had read the word in *Doctor Doolittle* and decided it sounded both wonderful and exotic all at the same time.

Then Trish had gotten pregnant at eighteen, married Russ, adopted Max before Ben was even born and pronounced herself an idiot for getting a dog and having a baby in the same year. Liz looked down at Eddie's crate, his golden fur jutting out the air vents of his crate as he snoozed. A big, dumb dog and a one-eyed tomcat between them. So much for menageries.

Liz loaded her suitcase and the pet carrier in the back of the van and found a box of wet-wipes to blot at her sleeve.

Trish returned, the baby carrier knocking the terminal's doors even as they tried to whoosh themselves out of the way. "It's good you've eaten," Trish said, lurching forward. "Just so you know, I went by the house and left some cereal and turned on the fridge. Take-out menus are on the counter." Trish slammed the rear hatch closed and clicked baby Clara's bucket seat into its base before Liz could blink. "I'll swing by and take you grocery shopping Wednesday morning, but I've got back-to-back crazy until then."

"Wednesday?"

"Yeah, I know. But, after I drop the twins at preschool, I've got to swing back down here tomorrow to drop Russ off for an early flight. Ben has an eye appointment in the afternoon, then track practice. Tuesday is preschool for the twins again, then I've got a meeting with Ben's teachers, then karate, and if I drive after sunset, Clara screams the *whole time*. It's enough to drive you insane."

The way Trish's eyes looked slightly manic over the hood of the car convinced Liz this was not an overstatement. Of course, keeping track of four children, three of which were under five could do that to a person. "Wednesday is fine. It'll give me time to work up a list of things I'll need for the house."

Liz opened the passenger door, surreptitiously swept a few crumbs to the floor with her palm, and sank into her seat. It didn't matter if she had food. She'd be happy to be in her own space. After that awful flight, it felt good to breathe fresh air and stretch her legs again.

Trish flumped into the driver's seat and threw her oversized tote on Liz's feet. "Oh, and I got some food and cat litter for Eddie back there for when he comes round again."

"Thanks."

Trish pulled away from the curb. "Before I forget, I brought over a few potted plants to dress up the front porch, and I left a can of mis-tint paint I picked up cheap on the kitchen counter. I thought it'd be good to recoat the front door. It's flaking like my elbows in winter."

"I'm painting the front door, too?"

"God, yes. And trim the bushes. Seriously, they look like Audrey from Little Shop of Horrors. Though Dad's tulips are starting to bloom, so there's some nice color, at least."

"Right." Liz held the dash as Trish blithely cut off a surly looking guy in a pickup.

"Did you know they were planning to sell?" Liz asked, scootching her sister's bag aside before her feet started to fall asleep.

Trish took a giant gulp out of a travel mug and shrugged, ignoring the rude gesture from the pickup's driver. "Mom and Dad? They've been talking about it for ages. It only makes sense. With them living in Florida most of the year, it's crazy to keep up two places. And they're not getting any younger. Dad's already onto replacement body parts."

"I can't believe it."

"What's not to believe? He's been popping Advil like candy for two years, and the kids keep asking why Grandpa is doing an Igor imitation when it's not even Halloween."

"Not that. I meant the house. I can't believe they're planning to sell. They've lived there thirty years."

"And it shows. As if a new patio will sell the place. Seriously, it has zero curb appeal, and that kitchen is disgusting."

"I suppose some new appliances—"

"It needs gutting, if you ask me, but Dad nearly had a coronary when I suggested it. That's probably why they called you. They figured a number-crunching computer geek would stick to their tightwad tendencies."

"Technically, I'm a business analyst. And, frugality isn't a character flaw."

"If you say so. Personally, I'd rather have pots of money and not have to worry about pinching pennies ever again. Russ' company just laid off another eight— SCREW YOU, A-hole! I don't give a crap!"

Liz tried to smile appeasingly at the pickup's driver even as Trish leaned across her to flip him the bird. Trish gunned the minivan, losing the pickup in traffic. "Was that really nec—?"

"That guy has *no* idea what I'm up against," Trish muttered. She suddenly braked hard at the sight of a police cruiser with a radar gun.

Liz thanked heaven for a police presence and momentarily considered motioning to him for help. Surely a police escort would be safer than riding with her frazzled, half-demented sister. "I'm sorry, I hadn't heard about Russ. So, um, where's John? Can he help me with the house?"

"John?" Trish's snort over their wayward brother wasn't encouraging. "Who knows if he's even in the state? I haven't heard from him since he bagged out on us at Christmas."

Lovely. "So, how long do you think this house redo is going to take?"

"One. Maybe two—"

"Weeks?"

"Months," Trish corrected, chugging again from her travel mug. "You do have personal time coming, don't you?"

Liz blanched. "*Months? Seriously?* I don't have—"

Trish snorted on her coffee. "I'm kidding! *Geesh.* Lighten up. I don't have a crystal ball. Who knows how long it'll take? You'll have to figure it out when you get there. Anything's better than nothing."

Liz rubbed her temple. This house thing could *not* take that long. She had to get back by the end of the week. Next week at the very latest. The Meds2u-Super Scripts merger was complete, but they were starting a whole new project, and if she weren't there... Oh God. Then there was Grant. She had to get back and make it up to him. After the disaster the other night...

"Look, I'd help if I could," Trish was saying, "but Ben's acting up at school again, and they're hauling me in Tuesday for another parent-teacher conference so they can tell me what a lousy mother I am." She stepped on the gas to make it through a yellow light and the van lurched toward the on-ramp. "Speaking of which, you think you'd mind watching Clara for an hour or two?"

"Me?" Liz turned to look at the five-month old slumped in her car-seat behind them, her round little baby face angelic and serene in the baby-view mirror. It was a little frightening.

"It won't be long," Trish was saying, "Pete and Jess have preschool until three. But they've got the school psychologist and everyone coming for Ben, and asked if it could be 'adults only.' I seriously don't want to go."

"I... sure. I'd be happy to help." Liz's mouth said the words despite the low-level panic taking residence in her gut. Truly, though, she should think of it as an opportunity. She'd be smart to get a little hands-on experience for when she and Grant had children of their own—starting one year after the wedding and every other year—until she turned 35, of course, when the risks to mother and child statistically increased. Lord knew she had no plans to pop out babies willy-nilly like a Pez dispenser. "It'll be fun," she asserted.

Trish gave her a look. "You've never spent much time around babies. Are you sure? I could ask Mrs. Vanderpoel."

"Mrs. Vanderpoel? Isn't she like ninety-seven years old? She must be in a rest home by now."

"Ninety-three, and I think they allow visitors."

"Oh, for crying out loud. I'm perfectly capable. Clara looks… sweet. We'll be fine."

Trish looked dubious but let it go.

How much trouble could one little baby be? Liz settled in for the ride, determined to ignore her sister's reservations. True, she didn't have much experience with infants, but it was a tad insulting taking flak from a woman who couldn't even get her shirt on right side out.

A while later, as they neared the outskirts of Sugar Falls, Liz began to fidget in her seat. Seeing the familiar, rolling hills and occasional cow-studded field, the quarry where the in-crowd used to go drinking… It made her skin feel tight—like fat, old Beth was trying to squeeze back in.

Maybe it was because everything looked more or less the same. There was the Connecticut River, wide and tranquil, an endless dark green mirror reflecting the budding trees on either side. They'd see the falls soon. Then Main Street.

Sugar Falls would look like it had for generations: picturesque, in a forgotten, hard-working New England way with blocky brick woolen mill buildings along the river and grand Federal and charming Victorian homes around the common. Everything would be just as she—

"Hey! When did you get a Walmart?" Liz sat up in her seat.

Trish gave her a sidelong look. "Five years ago."

The van swerved suddenly into the passing lane, and Liz grabbed at a baby rattle and half-eaten granola bar as they skittered across the dash. "Um, Trish? The speed limit's only forty here."

Her sister threw a wary glance at her daughter in the back seat... and floored it. "Screw the speed limit. The sun is setting. There's no time to lose…"

18

LIZ STOOD ON THE UNEVEN cement walk outside her parents' house, the cool, moist, evening air seeping through her clothes. Ten minutes earlier, Trish had handed her a key to the front door, unloaded Eddie's crate and Liz's luggage on the drive and roared away in a cloud of gravel dust.

Liz had been standing there ever since.

She tugged her blazer closed and stared at the old, rambling farmhouse she used to call home. The passing years had not been friendly. Paint cracked and peeled. Shingles curled. The holly bushes, once compact and orderly, now jutted awkwardly toward their neighbors as if fighting for space. A broken branch on a large rhododendron lay brittle and brown against a window sill.

Liz tried not to remember the crisp fall Saturday she and her father had planted the glossy-leaved holly bushes along the drive, or the way each Mother's Day the rhododendrons by the house would hum like hives from all the bees attracted to their abundant flowers.

Dad had always prided himself on a neat landscape. But now, last year's golden rod tilted in unruly brown clumps by the side of the garage. And his collection of garden ornaments still sat in the lawn, having never been tucked away for the winter.

When had the place become so... tired? It was like a weary, middle-aged woman who'd given up on herself and taken to wearing elastic-waist pants and sloppy ponytails.

Liz smoothed a hand over her own, sleek, low ponytail, picked up Eddie's crate and mentally itemized the obvious punch-list items. Trim shrubs. Clean bird bath. Weed walk. Repaint front door.

Rent a bulldozer and raze the place.

She sighed, pulled her cell phone out of her pocket and dialed the one person who never failed to make her feel good about having left Sugar Falls when she had the chance.

"Bailey!"

House Cleaning To-Do:

Scrape/paint front door.

Trim bushes/weed front walk

Clean bird bath

Rake planting beds—Edging?

Pick up branches in back yard.

Re-attach hinge shed door—lock.

Rehang/replace? hose reel.

Wash windows.

Patch screen back bedroom

Clean track/lubricate sliding door

Fill nail holes in stairwell and dining room. Paint.

Stop looking for things to fix!

CHAPTER FOUR

BY THE NEXT AFTERNOON, thanks to Trish, Liz had eaten more Peanut Butter Captain Crunch than her diet allowed in a lifetime, cleaned out all the front gutters and stripped most of the paint off the front door. Which is why, when Bailey pulled into the drive to say hello and drop off a quart of yogurt and a bag of apples late that afternoon, Liz welcomed the diversion like a starving model welcomes an all-you-can-eat buffet.

Bailey flipped the tab on her take-out coffee cup and sipped, her short, blonde pony-tails jutting out to the sides. "Sucks being you," she finally said, balancing the to-go cup on the birdbath and peeling open a Snickers bar.

Liz's mouth watered. It was the one thing about Bailey she had always envied—her ability to eat anything and not gain an ounce on her pixie-framed figure. The deadbeat father, the crazy mix-up of half-siblings, the trailer-park upbringing—all that made Liz feel gratefully superior, of course, but the super-charged metabolism? *That*, she envied.

Liz stepped backward down the front walk toward Bailey and squinted to soften the harsher realities the afternoon sun seemed determined to highlight. "I know it's in tough shape. But, it has good lines. You've got to give it that. And old farmhouse charm."

"Sure. If you can see beyond the peeling paint, ugly aluminum storm windows and shingles that are rolling up like burnt hair."

Liz looked askance at her friend. "Nice visual."

Bailey shrugged and toed a clump of grass that was heaving up a chunk of cement on the front walk. She sipped her mocha latte, a drink she'd been addicted to since discovering it in high school. "Just trying to help."

Liz turned back to the house with a sigh. She had been home all of one day, and already her 'to do' list was three pages long. The home she'd always thought of as quaint and picturesque now just looked shabby.

And the town, well, even though most of it felt disturbingly unchanged, there were other parts she didn't even recognize. For instance, when had they redone the intersection of Route 6 and Miller Brook? If Trish hadn't been driving, she'd have been half way across Vermont before she figured out her mistake.

All in all, Liz felt like a stranger in her own hometown which only made her feel childish knowing she'd half-expected the world to stand still in her absence.

"Snarky comments aren't helpful," she finally said aloud. "I'm shooting for curb appeal. A little fresh paint on the front door, a little pruning out front, maybe a pot or two of flowers and a welcoming chair by the door. Who knows, maybe buyers won't notice the rest."

"If you're looking for distractions, there's a crazy cat lady in my neighborhood who has an even larger collection of lawn ornaments than your dad. Want me to see if she'll lend you some more? This yard is just calling out for flamingos. The gnomes look lonely. I think they need pets."

"No pets," Liz said. But she grinned, nonetheless. Of all the things she missed about Sugar Falls, it was Bailey. They'd been BFFs since before it was even an acronym. Thank God for cell phones and e-mail.

"You're no fun. How about a puppy?"

"Be serious."

"Okay, I'll be serious. How is Lover Boy taking the disappointment of not scoring Wednesday night?"

Liz picked at a fleck of paint sticking to her shirt and wished she hadn't shot down the flamingo idea. "Pretty well."

"I can't believe he's okay with waiting to do the deed with you. Is something wrong with him? A man that can wait this long..." Bailey trailed off and stared meaningfully at Liz as she took a long sip of latte.

Liz frowned. "Nothing's wrong with him. He's very respectful of my need to take things slow, that's all."

Bailey rolled her eyes. "I can't believe he bought that load of bull."

"It's not bull. It's a statistically sound strategy. Ninety percent of couples that have sex in the first thirty days are broken up within a year. That's only a ten percent success rate. *But*, by waiting ninety days, we increase our likelihood of remaining a couple to *one in four*."

"*Mmm*. How romantic."

"Besides, do you know how disastrous an office affair can be? If we get caught, one of us needs to leave the firm. It's company policy. If my career is at stake, I'm not starting something unless I'm pretty darn sure it's leading somewhere serious."

"Is it? Serious, I mean?"

"Actually, yes. Just the other day he said he thought we should take things to the next level."

"Exact words?"

"Exact words."

"God, I wish I were you." Liz gave her a sidelong look. "I do! I have fantasies that I wake up living your life. Then *I'm* the one who's smart. Successful. Makes enough money to live on her own. I think I was more disappointed than you after the other night. I had such high hopes."

"Stop. You do not fantasize about my life."

"Hello? I live in a trailer with my mother, am currently cleaning people's toilets for a living and haven't had sex with a partner other than myself since I got toasted New Year's Eve. I'd be crazy if I *weren't* fantasizing about living someone else's life."

"It's not a trailer. It's a double-wide. And besides, you know you have a lot going for you. Your time will come. You'll see."

"Right. Like I'm going to meet my soul mate over a toilet bowl."

"It could happen."

"Only in your world, honey. Hence the fantasies."

"There must be somebody in Sugar Falls worth dating."

Bailey shoved the rest of the Snickers bar into her mouth and chewed. She stared over Liz's shoulder. "Define 'dating,'" she said.

Liz turned at a sound in the driveway. An unfamiliar pickup coasted to a stop, the driver's door creaked open, and a weathered boot hit the ground. Two sneaker-clad feet followed. Liz got a brief glimpse of a masculine, jean-clad backside as the man picked up the empty boot and threw it back into the pickup, then slammed the door shut. He turned.

Liz froze.

Oh. My. God.

Carter McIntyre?

Liz smacked Bailey on the back. "What the hell is *he* doing here?" she whispered. "His uncle was supposed to be coming!"

Bailey just shrugged, swallowed, and chugged her latte.

Carter's sneakers scrunched on the gravel drive as he loped toward them, head bent, fishing in his jeans pockets for something and clearly not finding it. Liz was grateful, as it gave her a few precious moments to collect herself. She swiped at the flecks of paint still clinging to her arms and old college T-shirt as she peered at him through her lashes.

Wow, he'd changed. So had she, of course, but knowing that only made her feel foolish for expecting him to look like the teenager he'd been ten years ago. His hair was thick and dark and slightly unruly as ever, but gone was the almost too-lanky frame of youth. His shoulders had broadened, and his face was fuller somehow, yet still lean and expressive. His pecs jumped under his tee as he finally looked up and extended one solid, muscular, man-sized arm toward her.

"Wow," he said. "Beth 'the Brain' Beacon in the flesh! Long time no see."

"It's 'Liz' now."

She reflexively extended her hand, resenting him acutely even as her fingers reached for his palm like a drowning victim reaches for a life preserver. For one thing, he was two hours late, clearly no more driven or reliable than he was ten years ago. Two, he was as smart-mouthed as ever. And three—her eyes skittered from the tips of his dust-covered sneakers to his tanned, smiling face—he was even more sinfully gorgeous than she remembered.

Liz swallowed before she drooled and made a complete fool of herself. Why couldn't he have turned out all pot-bellied and prematurely bald for crying out loud?

The next thing she knew, his hand closed over hers.

She pumped his hand twice—just to be polite—then yanked hers away again before the firm calluses on his fingers had a chance to register in the part of her brain that was checking him out in a way she didn't intend to acknowledge.

What the hell was wrong with her? Had she no self-respect? No shame?

Granted, any woman's heart would skip a beat when faced with that testosterone-ridden, mega-watt smile he was flashing. She was only human after all. But still.

Liz tugged the hem of her T-shirt down over her belly button.

"Hey, Bailey. How's it going? Still over at Willard's Auto?" Carter's eyes passed over Liz's chest as he spoke.

Bailey shook her head. "No. Willard and I had a parting of ways after I kneed him in the balls for pinching my ass. I'm cleaning houses now until I can afford my own shop."

Carter's eyes made a second pass over Liz's front even as he raised one dark brow at Bailey. "I'll consider myself forewarned."

"Oh, honey," Bailey laughed, her blonde ponytails bobbing, "You don't need to worry. I only knee smarmy guys."

They chuckled at each other, Carter grinning charmingly, Bailey's baby blues twinkling over the lid of her mocha latte.

"Well," Liz interrupted, stepping between them. "I hate to rush you, but we should probably get started." She pointed to her watch. "You *are* late."

She couldn't say why she felt the need to point that out, but it was disconcerting having him standing there all relaxed and sexy and confident and flirting with her best friend when her stomach was doing odd little flip-flops in her gut right under her belly button. It annoyed her, especially, that he could waltz up to her after ten years, flash that trademark smile and make her feel like time had stood still.

But, of course, it hadn't.

His eyes registered a moment of irritation, but he quickly covered it with a wider smile and something he did with his eyebrows that looked slightly naughty and made her woman bits stand up and take notice in a way they had no right to in old sweats being almost-engaged and everything.

"So. Liz, huh?" he asked.

Liz hid a smile. You'd never hear Grant saying the word 'huh.' If it even *was* a word.

"Yes," she articulated in her most business-like tone. "In my first job, my boss' wife was also named Beth." She wasn't about to admit she'd harbored a three year crush on said boss and had daydreamed of his choosing her over his 'other favorite Beth' until a reorganization in the firm had saved her from sure lifelong humiliation. "I decided I preferred Liz."

"Fair enough." He stared at her chest again. *Hello! I'm up here!* she wanted to yell.

They stood a few feet apart, Bailey uncharacteristically silent, Liz staring at a point beyond Carter's left ear, Carter staring at her boobs— the sexist jerk. He was probably wondering if they were real. Would it be such a shock that she'd actually grown into a B-cup in the last decade?

Okay. *Fine.* Maybe he was just looking because she could not stop swiping at the damned paint flecks. Liz forced herself to drop her hand and look him in the eye. Chickadees tweeted inappropriately in the trees nearby.

"So," he said again looking at her face for a change, "Bates? I thought you went to someplace in California."

Liz stared down at her own chest. Oh, good God, he was looking at the *logo*? She felt her already flushed face creep up the heat scale a notch. "Bates was undergrad. I got my master's at Stanford."

"Right. Hard to get farther from home than that."

"It wasn't like that."

His eyes told her she was lying through her teeth. Which she was, of course. The pervert mind reader. "So. What's the job you want quoted?"

Bailey cleared her throat, causing Liz a momentary pang of guilt for having forgotten she was even there. "Well, love to stay and chat with you two, but I'm late picking up my mom. I'll call you later, Liz. 'Kay?"

"Sure." Liz watched Bailey start her old Toyota and drive away before turning her attention back to Carter.

He raised that eyebrow again. Curse it.

Smoothing her hands over her sweats and telling her woman bits to calm the heck down already, Liz motioned for him to follow. Despite going through the charade for appearance's sake, she had no intention of hiring him—even if he was her great-aunt's best friend's grandson.

After all, when you've spent the better part of your youth harboring a one-sided crush on the high school bad boy, you don't generally want him to see you single, unkempt, and scraping your parents' trim boards ten years later.

Unless you were single. Which she most definitely was not.

"Patio," she said succinctly as she pointed around the back corner of the house.

"Patio?"

"My parents want a patio instead of the deck. It's old and in disrepair and needs replacing."

"So you want a similar footprint?" He leaned against the back split-rail fence, afternoon sunlight accenting the dark highlights in his hair.

"I guess." Liz was only half-listening. The other half of her brain was wondering if his hair was as silky as it appeared. Her woman bits perked up at the word silky.

"Should I include cost of demolition and disposal for the deck?"

"I suppose. I mean, how much will that run? On second thought—no. I'm here. I'll take care of it." She licked suddenly dry lips, her fingers flexing at her side, wondering why they were bothering to discuss a job she had no intention of giving him. Except she hadn't told him that. Yet. She made a mental note to add 'deck demolition' to her to-do list.

"I'll quote it just in case. So what are we using? Concrete pavers? Bluestone? Was there a particular look or color you've seen that you like?"

"Ah, no. Just, you know, a patio. Whatever's cheapest and quickest. My parents didn't say."

He paused, his pencil poised over a grungy notepad he'd finally found in his chest pocket, and Liz fought not to squirm under his gaze. His eyes were a deep green, like an old Coca-Cola bottle. But rather than wholesome familiarity, the color gave an air of reckless changeability to his expression.

That and his lips. He had firm, beautiful lips. *Kissable lips*, she thought. How often had she daydreamed about this man's lips? But who wouldn't? He could smile broadly, the quintessential class clown; tilt them cockily, the smug rebel; or spin some sort of magic spell that transformed his face such than no woman—young or old—could resist his dazzling charm.

"Can I ask you a personal question?"

26

The lips moved, and it took Liz a moment to realize words had passed over them. Her eyes slid up to his. "Uh, sure," she said, wishing she could stop thinking about this man's lips long enough to gracefully send him on his way. Oh Lord, had she just said *uh*?

"Are you free for dinner?"

"Dinner?"

"Yeah, you know, where they serve food. I'm starved, and I'm thinking if I give you a few minutes you'll know what you want me to quote out here, and I won't pass out from hunger."

"Oh. I don't think dinner's a good idea. I'm not staying. In Sugar Falls, that is. This is just a vacation. Sort of."

Plus I have an almost-fiancé, she wanted to add, realizing she was starting to babble for some unknown reason, perhaps because *The Lips* were now softly curving in a manner that could only be described as sinfully sensual. Although why she was thinking about 'sin' and 'sex' in the same sentence at that particular moment was something she didn't intend to think about.

One dark brow shot to the sky. "You don't plan on eating while you're here? You'll get even skinnier than you are now."

Did he just call me skinny? the unhelpful part of her brain squeaked delightedly. "Of course I plan to eat," she scoffed. "Besides, I'm a mess. I'd need to clean up. Change..."

"No problem. I can wait." He flipped his notepad closed and crammed it in his back pocket. Liz couldn't help but notice how his jeans pulled taut across his hips as he did so.

"I... fine. All right," she said. She told herself she was agreeing because Trish had yet to take her shopping. It had nothing to do with the shivers of awareness that tickled her spine every time those mesmerizing green eyes slid her way.

Carter smiled again, nodded, and strode away before she could reconsider. Moments later her cell phone rang from her pocket. Liz pulled it out with a shaking hand, glanced at the screen then stuffed it back in. She'd call Grant later.

Just as soon as she figured out why on earth she'd agreed to go on a sort-of dinner date with her high school crush.

CHAPTER FIVE

LIZ GUZZLED A GLASS OF WATER, stripped like a mad woman and showered in under five minutes. She was downstairs again in fifteen.

She glanced at her knee-length khaki skirt and pale blue tee, satisfied she'd chosen something no-nonsense and sensible, something that said "this is not a date" without going so far as to imply she had no self-esteem or desire to be acknowledged as a woman. It was a lot to expect from an outfit yanked hastily from one's suitcase, but Liz wasn't one to leave these things to chance.

Her heart beat high in her chest as she stopped briefly at the hallway mirror on the way by, feeling for all the world as if she were sixteen again and ducking into her locker to check her teeth and hastily chew a stick of Juicy Fruit before study hall.

"This is exactly why I didn't want to come home," she muttered, cinching her ponytail tight. Coming home made her feel disoriented. And flushed.

Like the flu.

She blew out an impatient breath.

She hadn't chewed Juicy Fruit in years, but one look at Carter's disarmingly crooked grin and lazy, loping stride and she was fat old Beth "the Brain" Beacon again, nervously re-sharpening her pencils as she waited in the back room of the library for their weekly tutoring session.

God. She could still remember the giant, slab oak tables. The heavy chairs. How, if she leaned close enough over his trig text and inhaled long and slow she could just catch the intoxicating scent of fresh air and leather and something else she didn't recognize but knew, instinctively, was way, way better than chocolate.

"Except everyone knows chocolate is bad for you," she said aloud to her reflection.

Her reflection did not appear to be buying it.

Liz rummaged in her purse for her Altoids and popped one into her mouth, the mint sharp on her tongue, then marched out the door.

Thank goodness she was no longer the ridiculous, naïve girl she'd been in high school.

A ridiculous, naïve girl, for instance, would get all fluttery at the sight of Carter as he stood at the end of the driveway, leaning against his truck, all swagger and sex appeal in faded, torn jeans, navy tee and tattered Converse sneakers.

Liz felt nothing. Nothing but minty fresh pragmatism.

Carter pushed away from his truck as she approached, his cell phone to his ear. "Sorry, I can't make it tonight," he said into the phone. "My last job is running late... No. I'll grab something.... I know you don't want me to miss it... I'll do my best... Yeah... All right. See you then." He hunched away a little. "Love you, too," he murmured, then he slipped the phone into his pocket and turned to Liz. "Ready?"

Och! Liz tried not to stare at the pocket of his jeans where she could just make out the outline of his phone. His poor girlfriend! She was probably nice, too. Carter always dated nice girls you wished you could hate except they volunteered at the food pantry or humane society and had alcoholic fathers or siblings with Down Syndrome so you felt sorry for them and envious all at the same time. No doubt his girlfriend du jour thought she could reform the reckless, bad boy in him and would only blame herself when she failed miserably.

Thank goodness *she* had solid, dependable Grant waiting for her at home.

"Ready." She stepped toward the truck and tugged the door handle. She tugged again.

Carter stepped forward and gripped the handle over her hand, pulling hard, his fingers warm and firm atop hers. The door lurched open. "Sorry," he said. "Sticks sometimes." He gestured toward the seat. "Just, ah, shove that out of your way."

Liz stared, aghast at the mess on the seat and the floor, but Carter was already halfway around the truck. Lovely. The man clearly lived on caffeine and sugar. Using the side of her purse to shovel loose papers, candy wrappers and what-not toward the center console, she tried not to touch anything with her bare hands. She brushed the seat lightly with a paper napkin she'd found, decided it would be rude to lay it out on the seat as a protective liner, and hoisted herself into the cab. A Mountain Dew can burbled its last dregs onto her shoe.

Carter threw the dirty note pad from his back pocket onto the seat next to a half dozen others and stuck the key in the ignition. He followed her gaze as she stared down at the empty soda cans, coffee cups and—was that a beer bottle?—on the floor. "Sorry. Keep meaning to clear that out."

"*Mmm*," she said non-committally, praying her skirt would come clean after sitting on his seats. Lord only knew what was on them. She set her purse on her lap and gripped it primly. His girlfriend must have tiny feet. Or, if she were smart, her own car.

Liz threaded the strap of her purse through her fingers as they pulled out of the driveway. She swallowed and glanced as his profile. "So. I didn't realize you were working for your uncle now."

"Yeah. Have been for a while."

"That must be... nice." She nudged a coffee cup that kept falling on her foot, the silence stretching out between them. If he couldn't even keep his own car clean, did she want this guy working on the house? She'd eat first *then* tell him she wouldn't be needing his help.

She should probably pay for her own meal, though. After all, she wasn't rude.

Carter slowed at a traffic light. "You in Sugar Falls for long?"

"Only a week or two. My parents are moving to Florida full time. They asked me to take care of some improvements to get the house here ready to put on the market."

"Selling, huh? How much do they want for it?"

"I'm not sure. I haven't spoken with the realtor yet."

"Much land?"

"Six and a half acres."

"It's a nice spot out here."

"I've always thought so."

The conversation petered out and he looked at her, his green eyes dark, like deep, secret pools you could happily dive into and not care if you ever resurfaced for air.

Not that she was thinking that or anything.

Liz shifted in her seat. She should ask him to stop at the store. Then she could pick up a few basics. Mixed greens. Boneless chicken. Some brown rice.

Cat food. She couldn't forget cat food. The stuff Trish left was mostly fillers. Eddie had a very sensitive tummy. Cat food and *then* she'd tell him he wasn't hired.

"Is that why you've never been back?" Carter asked.

"What? I've been back."

"Not much. After high school, you pretty much disappeared."

"California's a long way from home, and I interned most summers. Anyway, I'm sure nobody missed me around here."

He winked. "Maybe I missed you."

"Please," she scoffed, though his words and the flash of a dimple in his cheek had her heart slamming in her breast and her woman bits perking to attention. She made a pretense of restacking the papers on his center console.

Broccoli. She should *definitely* pick up broccoli...

"I did! I missed those roast beef sandwiches you made that time we studied for trig at your house. Remember that?"

Remember? She'd made a shrine to that day in her journal. *Carter McIntyre ate in my kitchen!!*

"God, they were amazing! Beef, bacon, onion, swiss cheese and that sauce you whipped up..."

"Horseradish mayo," she said.

"It had a kick to it," he grinned again.

"I can't believe you remember that."

"Yeah, well, food is important to guys. We never forget a good meal." Liz grabbed the dash as Carter turned a hard left. "You know what? Forget going out. We'll do one better. We'll make your famous roast beef sandwiches. Now that I've mentioned them, I've got a real craving for them." He turned into the grocery store parking lot and swung into a space. "What do you think?"

The air in Liz's lungs seized as she momentarily wondered whether Carter could read minds as well as make women spontaneously ignite with a single eyebrow twitch. The grocery store? Good Lord. And, cooking for him? Cooking would be far more intimate than grabbing a bite at a local sandwich shop. No. Going home was a bad idea. It was dangerous. And spending time with Carter McIntyre had always been dangerous.

As dangerous as seven minutes, blindfolded, in the darkened pantry at Jenny Whitmeyer's sixteenth birthday party and only ever knowing the first boy she'd ever kissed had silky hair, tasted like Twizzlers... and smelled like fresh air and sweet rebellion.

"Sounds like a great idea," she said.

CHAPTER SIX

"I'M NOT AN AXE MURDERER."

Liz stared at Carter in shock, the memory of that long ago kiss still on her lips. She clutched her purse a little tighter. "What?"

"Just in case you were worried. I haven't turned into an axe murderer or anything over the last ten years."

"Why would I—?"

"Because, usually women worry about that sort of thing when a guy invites himself to their house. I just wanted to reassure you. I'm not a murderer. I'm just hungry."

"I hadn't..." She flushed, the idea of Carter being violent the *last* thing on her mind.

"You just got all quiet there for a minute, and I thought you might be having second thoughts. We can pick up a sub or something if you want."

"No. No. It's fine. It's good. I actually need a few things. I was just, ah, planning my list in my head."

"Great."

"Great."

Liz hopped out and hurried toward the entrance, visions of Carter doing unscrupulous things dancing through her head.

The automatic doors whooshed aside, and Liz reached for a basket. She was overreacting. What harm could come from getting a few things at the store and sharing a casual meal with an old friend? That's all this was. For all the axe murderer talk, she didn't believe Carter McIntyre had a mean bone in his body. The man was dangerous, sure, but not in *that* way.

Besides, it's not like anyone was going to dare her to sit in a dark pantry tonight waiting for some anonymous boy to give her a kiss. Those days were long behind her.

She decided who kissed her now. And when.

"Forget the basket," Carter said, skidding to a halt beside her with an empty cart. "I've been working all day, and I'm starved. I'll push. You lead."

"Oh. All right. Let's start with produce." Liz pulled her purse up on her shoulder and shook her head as Carter zipped ahead down the aisle, one foot on the back of the cart like a scooter. So much for leading.

She set some lettuce into the cart and silently marveled at how surreal life was sometimes. She was grocery shopping with Carter McIntyre. How many times had she dreamed about this very thing? The minivan? The adorable toddlers? The blissfully domestic existence as if they were a modern-day version of the *Leave it to Beaver* re-runs she used to watch every Saturday with her dad?

To think she'd actually imagined Carter growing up and becoming half of an adult couple. The man couldn't even push a simple grocery cart without treating it like a riding toy. If she didn't get this over with, her inner June would probably start humming liltingly and reaching for imaginary aprons. Liz rolled her eyes and tossed a red onion into the cart.

Dum. Dum. De-dum. Dum-de-dum-de-dum-de-DUM...

"Oh, crap," she said.

Carter turned to look at her. "Is that your cell phone?" Liz nodded. "Unusual ring tone."

"I prefer to think of it as an early warning system." Carter's eyebrow did that wingy thing at her in question. "It's my mother."

Her purse strap jingled again.

"Aren't you going to answer it?"

"I can call her back." Liz picked up a bulb of garlic and sniffed it. She looked at Carter. "What?"

"Your mother is calling."

"I—" Oh, crap. That's right. Carter didn't *have* a mother. She'd died when he was little. Some terrible accident. Liz fought not to squirm under his gaze. She pulled out her phone. "Hi, Mom!"

She gave Carter a cheery smile and braced herself for the volume. He'd think she were a cad if she held the phone at a safe distance from her ear like she usually did.

"Elizabeth! I'm glad I caught you! How's the weather? I hear you might be in for some rain this week! You can never trust the Weather Channel, though. They are so often wrong! Elizabeth?"

"Yes?"

"Oh, I thought I'd lost you! You're so quiet!"

"I'm in the grocery store, Mom."

"Where?"

"The— nevermind. What do you need?" She glanced guiltily at Carter. "I mean, why are you calling?"

"It's your dad! He's worried about the patio. He doesn't want the pavers to have grass growing out of them. You know how awful that

33

looks! Can you make sure they use that special sand that keeps the grass from growing?"

"Special sand that keeps grass from growing? I've never heard—"

"Polymeric," said Carter as he threw a watermelon into the cart.

A watermelon?

Liz put her hand over the phone. "What?"

"Polymeric sand. It keeps grass from growing between the pavers. Tell her it's standard now for all our jobs unless the customer wants wider, greenscaped joints."

"I have no idea what you're talking about," she said to him.

"Here." He reached out. "Let me talk to her."

"I don't think—" But he'd already grabbed the phone.

"Mrs. Beacon? Hey! It's Carter McIntyre. Yeah... I know, quite the coincidence that we're both here." He winked at Liz. "Listen, just so you know, I use polymeric sand all the time now... Yes. It is a little more, but I know you and Mr. Beacon will be happy with the results... Absolutely... Any time... Sure... You take good care, too."

Carter handed back her phone, and Liz stared at him, shocked he'd managed to have a meaningful exchange of information with her mother in less than twenty seconds.

"Mom?"

"She hung up. She had to go. By the way, she says you need to eat more red meat. You're looking pale."

"She did not."

"Okay. She didn't, but I think we've spent enough time in the produce section. I need protein."

"Protein?"

"Something other than bunny food."

Liz rolled her eyes. "Right."

She continued on, trying to focus on selecting whole grain bread and carrot sticks and 100-calorie, low-sodium pretzel packs, but Carter kept throwing in things like chips and sour cream dip. Bricks of cheese.

Before long, Liz found herself reaching for manly things without even thinking. Big red slabs of meat. Potatoes. *Bacon.* Which didn't even make sense, because hadn't she and Grant sworn off nitrates? But there it was, lying in the cart with everything else. And, truly, the roast beef sandwiches weren't anything without the bacon.

Forty minutes later, they stood in line at the check-out, Carter throwing in Twizzlers from the candy rack and Liz pretending not to notice how ruggedly sexy he was as she casually flicked the end of her ponytail over her shoulder. More than once.

She caught herself mid-flick and made herself reach for the jug of milk without any more flirtatious body movements.

"Carter McIntyre? Is that you? I swear, you are the hardest person to get ahold of!"

Liz stilled, the milk jug sweating in her palm. She'd know that sicky-sweet, never set a pinky-toe below the Mason Dixon Line, fake Southern Belle voice anywhere. *Valerie Stinson. Bleh.* Liz could almost feel her ankles swell and her breasts deflate with every saccharine syllable gushing from Valerie's annoyingly bow-shaped lips. She watched out of the corner of her eye as Val tucked a wisp of blonde hair behind one ear and smiled dazzlingly—at Carter, of course.

"Wait. Is that... *Brainy Beacon?*"

Liz squinted at the label on the milk jug—as if deeply in need of determining its nutritional value before placing it on the conveyor belt.

She didn't think it was a stretch, acting as if she didn't recognize Valerie, seeing as Valerie hadn't been this particular shade of blonde in high school nor this buxom-y, either, to Liz's memory. The cashier was waiting for the milk, though, so Liz handed it over.

"What? Valerie? Valerie Stinson? Wow. It's been... ages, hasn't it? Actually, Carter and I—"

"—were just heading home for dinner. Liz, you forgot the wine."

"Wine?" Liz fumbled the bacon, and it shot out of her hand at the cashier. The cashier gave her an annoyed look.

"Yeah. Get whatever you like."

"But, we shouldn't hold up the line—"

Valerie batted her baby blues at Carter before her smile faltered. "Wait. Are you two... *together?*"

Now why would that be such a shocker? Liz wondered. She slapped a chuck roast onto the conveyer with slightly more force than necessary.

Valerie had never liked her. Liz had no idea why. Val had always been skinny and popular and super tanned. But, ever since that birthday party at Jenny Whitmeyer's, Val hadn't just ignored Liz like she once had, she'd taken every opportunity to give her the evil eye. Aside from the fact that Liz had thrown off the grading curve in World History class, she couldn't fathom what she'd ever done to earn Valerie's ill will.

"They're still bagging. You've got time." Carter said, giving her a pleading look.

Liz mumbled an excuse and scurried off to the wine aisle.

She stared blindly at the display—red or white?—grabbed one of each color and hurried back toward the check-out. On impulse, she picked up a six-pack of ale as well.

When she arrived, Valerie was still hovering, and, not unexpectedly, giving her the evil eye.

"I thought this might go better with the sandwiches," Liz explained, passing over the ale.

Carter beamed and set it on the belt. "Perfect. Have I told you today how much I love you?"

Liz might have stuttered if she'd had the breath to reply. Running to the wine and beer sections reminded her she'd skimped on her morning workouts two days straight. Loved her? She pinched her lips together. Was that the same way he loved his poor girlfriend? Val could have this guy.

"Well." Valerie's bow-lips looked like she'd just swallowed a lemon. She glanced back and forth between them. Carter turned to swipe his credit card. "Like I was saying, I'd love to see you at the Dinner Dance. Friday after next. Seven o'clock until... whenever," she drew the last word out meaningfully, speaking as if she and Carter were the only ones there.

"We'll be there," he beamed, then he yanked Liz tight against his side, knocking the remaining breath out of her. He grinned and plucked his receipt from the cashier's fingers.

"What—?" Liz struggled to regain her balance, but Carter already had their bags in the cart and was headed toward the exit. She caught up with him in the parking lot. "What just happened in there? And what dinner dance?"

"The Alumni Dinner Dance. And you just saved me. Remind me to kiss your feet later."

Kate's toes wiggled excitedly in her flats. Faithless piggies. "Saved you? Is she an ex-girlfriend or something?"

"Are you kidding? Vampire Val?" He visibly shuddered. "You didn't know that's what they called her back in high school?" He was quickly gathering their bags while simultaneously glancing over his shoulder as if afraid Valerie would actually chase them down in the parking lot.

"No. We called her other things."

"Yeah, well I'm just glad I was never a victim." He made little nipping motions at his neck with his fingertips as if Liz hadn't already gotten the point. "She's been leaving messages on my voice mail for two weeks. I figured if I pretended we were together, it'd nip any stalking tendencies in the bud."

"I live in Chicago. How could we possibly be together?"

"Long distance relationship. I could totally make her believe it. You don't mind, do you?"

Liz stared at him with a look that must have conveyed her complete and utter disbelief at his gall, because Carter grinned. "So, you do mind?"

She shook her head and opened the truck door with a hard yank. "If I were you, I'd be more worried about whether my girlfriend would mind."

Carter stopped, half a dozen bags dangling from his fists. "What girlfriend?"

"Exactly."

"No. Seriously. What girlfriend?"

"Don't pretend you don't know what I'm talking about."

He chuckled and then stopped laughing when he saw her expression. "I'm pretty sure I'd know if I had a girlfriend. What makes you think I do?"

She rolled her eyes. "You know. The one you were talking to on your phone? Back at the house? The one you supposedly love? *Jeez.* I feel so sorry for her."

"You feel sorry—" Carter repeated as he stared at her strangely, then his chin went up as he set the bags in the truck on top of the empty bottles where her feet should go. "Oh. *That* girlfriend."

"So you do remember her! Nice. I'd say Valerie's lucky you haven't returned her calls."

"You know, I think I'm seeing a whole new side of you I never knew in high school."

"You mean the side that isn't conned by charming smiles and witty banter?"

"You think my smiles are charming?"

She climbed onto the seat. "Off topic."

"*And,* you think I'm witty, but I'll let that go. No, I was actually thinking I was seeing a whole, new, less pleasant side of you."

"If you mean I'm not as gullible as I once was, I'm okay with that."

He shut the door and spoke through the window. "I was thinking, downright cynical."

Liz settled her purse on her lap as Carter slid into the driver's seat, but instead of starting the engine, he fished his wallet out of his back pocket. "You know what? I'd like you to see my so-called girlfriend."

He shoved a worn photo under her nose. Liz pushed it away then pulled it closer again.

"She's—"

"My grandmother."

"*You're dating your grandmother?*"

"No!" Carter yanked the photo out of Liz's hand and stuffed it back in his wallet. "Oh, I get it. You're laughing at me. Well, that's not funny. That's just creepy."

Liz stopped laughing, although his horrified expression was still pretty entertaining. "No, creepy is a grown man who keeps a photo of his grandmother in his wallet."

"That's not creepy. It's sweet."

"No. It's kind of creepy."

"See? You're more judgmental than you used to be, too. I happen to have a good reason for carrying this picture around. I promised Grams that if I ever do a job for one of the rich widowers around the lake, I'll put in a good word for her."

"Okay. Now *that's* creepy."

"That's not—" He sat back in his seat. "Shit. You're right. I'm pimping for my own grandmother! I was just trying to keep her from signing up for one of those internet dating services she keeps threatening to join. You've no idea how many weirdos are out there..."

"I'm getting an idea."

"But, this is so much creepier."

"Yes. But, in a good, well-intentioned sort of way, I'll give you that."

"No, pretty much in a 'I think I need to gouge my eyes out' sort of way." He put a hand to his gut. "I feel nauseous."

"So, you don't have a girlfriend?"

"No."

"Just a randy grandmother looking for hook-ups."

"It's not like that." He looked askance at her. "Okay. It's a little like that."

"And people wonder why I wanted to get out of Sugar Falls."

Carter chuckled, a self-deprecating, charming rumble as he started the engine, and for the first time since seeing him again Liz felt... relaxed.

She grinned back and began rummaging through the bags at her feet. "Do you remember where they packed my pretzels? I'm starved."

"Forget pretzels. Where are the swiss cake rolls?"

Liz sat up. "You can't be serious. Those are pure sugar! You'll feel sick eating those on an empty stomach."

"What are you, my mother? Have you ever even had a swiss cake roll?"

"No. But—"

"Then how would you even know? They happen to be the perfect balance of light, chocolaty cake and whipped confection." He leaned over the shifter, the back of his hand grazing her calf as he fished around for the box. "Ah! Here they are! I'm doing the happy dance now." He tore the box open and offered her a plastic-wrapped treat.

"No thanks."

He shrugged, peeled back the cellophane and ate half a cake roll in one bite as he threw the truck into reverse. He closed his eyes decadently as he chewed. Liz would have preferred he look where he was going.

"Speaking of dancing," she said, doing her best to ignore his little moans of pleasure as she simultaneously wrestled with a teeny package of pretzels and checked for obstacles in the truck's path, "what's this dinner dance thing you and Valerie were talking about?"

"The Tenth Reunion Alumni Dinner Dance," Carter said around a mouthful of chocolate as he drove toward the exit. "Val's chair of the organizing committee. She's been sending e-mails and calling people for months. I'm surprised you haven't heard of it."

Liz's mouth began to water as Carter finally swallowed and bit into the second half of his swiss cake roll. For all their empty nutritional value, they did smell awfully good. "I didn't see any reason to provide a forwarding address when I moved to Chicago, seeing as I didn't expect to be back."

"You're here now," he said, holding the second treat toward her mouth.

She shook her head, but he didn't move his hand and was coasting awfully close to the car in front of them, so she took a tiny bite. "Reunions aren't my thing," she said around the chocolate.

"What? Afraid everyone will be staring at you?"

"I just don't see any reason to reconnect with people who weren't important enough to keep in touch with in the first place."

"Don't you even want to see who has gotten fat?"

Liz gave him a look as the remaining cake roll disappeared between his lips.

"Jenny Whitmeyer. Now Jenny Otterman."

"No."

"Yes. Big as a tank, sad to say."

"But she was so tiny in school! What happened?"

"I think the sixth kid is what really tipped the scales."

Liz's jaw dropped. *"Sixth?"*

Carter nodded. "They've been busy. So you sure you don't want to come? See who has hair plugs? Who's on probation? Who's already divorced twice?"

"Someone's gotten divorced twice? Who? It's only been ten years!"

"You'll have to come to find out."

"I don't know..."

"Come on. I'll be the envy of everyone to have you walking in on my arm."

"I don't think that's—"

"Unless you've already been asked, which, seeing as you've just found out, seems unlikely."

"I'll probably be back in Chicago by then."

"Look, if you don't want to go, just say so. No hard feelings. I'll just ask my girlfriend."

She gave him a look. "You're right. It's not funny," she said.

"Told you."

Liz fought not to smile as she looked out the side window, the familiar old brick facades of downtown passing by. Well. It wasn't like it would be a *date*-date, she silently rationalized. More like a friend-date. Like tonight. "If I'm still here, I don't suppose there's any reason not to."

"Gee. Don't get too excited."

"It's not that. It's just—"

"Hey, don't sweat it." He stopped at a red light and laughed. "You always took things way too seriously. I'm just poking at you."

The light turned green, but before he started moving, he grabbed another pack of swiss cake rolls from the box and tossed it in her lap.

"For you," he said. "Even though you'll never admit it... I know you want it."

CHAPTER SEVEN

Twelve years earlier…

"BAILEY, COME *ON!* I need your help! Blue, green or pink?"

"Black."

Beth made a sound of disgust as she lowered the headbands she'd been holding up. "Would you stop sulking? I've got ten minutes before I've got to be at Jenny's. You were invited, too, you know."

Bailey rolled her eyes which looked kind of freaky behind the heavy layers of goth make-up she had taken to wearing ever since she found out Jim Croce was dead and not just retired. Like Tinker Bell gone to the Dark Side. "Can't. I'm getting my nose pierced."

"You're not! Are you, really?"

Bailey flumped to her back on Beth's bed, her black combat boots dangling off the side. "No. I've got to work. Turns out when you're the lowest man on the totem pole you don't get time off for parties. Not that I'd go even if I could."

"Well, I'm going." Beth put the green headband in her hair then switched it for the blue. "You know who's going to be there."

"Everyone who's anybody, yes, I've heard." Bailey inspected the fake rose tattoo she'd drawn on her forearm with a Sharpie. "You do know why you were invited."

"I don't care."

"—because your tutoring kept Chip Otterman from failing Algebra and getting kicked off the varsity basketball team. Jenny would have been devastated if she couldn't do her goofy 'Chip, Chip, Hooray!' cheer for him anymore. God, what a bunch of dorks."

Beth pulled the blue headband out and sucked in a nervous breath. "Wish me luck?"

TWENTY MINUTES LATER—because her brother, John, was taking his own sweet time—Beth was finally on her way. She sank down in the

41

seat of John's beat-up Chevette and gripped her little purse in her lap, having decided against stuffing her lip gloss, compact, folding comb/brush combo and Juicy Fruit gum in the pockets of her jacket in case they gave her unsightly bulges. "Just drop me off at the corner. I'll walk," she said a little breathlessly.

"Beth, it's raining." John stopped at a 4-way intersection and turned to look at her. They were only a couple blocks from Jenny Whitmeyer's house. How wet would she get?

Water sheeted across the windshield.

"It's okay," Beth said, trying to adjust the padding in her bra without her brother noticing. "I don't want you to waste gas."

He gave her another look and turned the corner before Beth could make a grab for the door handle.

Before long they were pulling up to the Whitmeyers' big colonial. A handful of cars were parked in the driveway and street, groups of teens loitering under the eaves of the garage and on the front porch. Beth's heart skipped a beat as she surreptitiously cupped her hand over her mouth to check her breath. She could smell nothing but mint, though, having brushed her teeth like an OCD dentist twenty times before leaving the house.

John's door creaked. Beth rounded on him in horror. *"You're not getting out, are you?"*

"I left a case of soda in the trunk."

"Can't you get it later?" she hissed. There were people huddling under umbrellas not far from the car. *Important* people.

"I thought I'd share," he said, pulling his hoodie over his head and ducking out of the car.

Beth creaked her door ajar and popped open her umbrella. Lovely. John had parked her smack dab over a river. If she leveraged herself, though, she could maybe make it to the curb without stepping in it up to her ankles. Her velvet flats would be toast if she got them wet.

She scooched to the edge of her seat, rain zotting dark dots on her shoe as she reached awkwardly to the curb with her foot. She pushed against the door and lurched onto the wet grass in front of Jenny's house. There. She pushed the door hard and it slammed with a clunk behind her. Beth looked around to see if anyone had noticed her ungraceful arrival.

John was at the back of his car, his head ducked under the open lid of the trunk with a couple of the senior guys standing around. Wow. They must really like soda.

Beth licked her lips and sucked in her stomach, her bra feeling unusually tight for all the nylons she'd stuffed in there. She'd chosen nylons, because they were flesh-toned. Just in case.

In case of what, she had no idea.

She forced a nervous smile as she saw Valerie Stinson start over. Valerie and a couple other popular girls were huddled under a large golf umbrella and they giggled and twittered as they moved as one toward some of the guys standing around John. Beth wished he would leave already; although, having him there made her feel less alone.

"There's chips and dip in the house," Valerie called to her. The other girls giggled. Beth pretended to laugh with them even though she had no idea what was funny.

"Thanks," she said.

They giggled some more.

Valerie brushed her blonde hair behind her ear, effectively showing off the white tan line where her watch should have been. Beth had never actually *seen* Val wearing a watch, but the little white circle and band line were like a permanent tattoo on the girl's wrist. "Not a problem," she said.

But, Valerie wasn't looking at Beth anymore. She was turning to make a circuit by the boys on the way back into the house. "Hi, John," she said as she passed by. The girls twittered.

Beth watched as her brother ducked his head, a strange look on his face. "Hey, Val."

CHAPTER EIGHT

LIZ SWALLOWED.

Oh. My. God. She just ate a swiss cake roll. Correction. *Two* swiss cake rolls.

Grant would be appalled. Hadn't he only last week asked her to start adding flax seed meal to her entrees so he could up his Omega-3's without worrying about mercury? He'd never understand the decadent sweets she'd just inhaled!

Cripes. Forget about what Grant would think. *She* was appalled! Where was her self-control? Her good judgment? Here she was eating junk food and agreeing to maybe go to some reunion thing, and, God help her, hiring Carter for the patio job, because it would be way too complicated to explain to her mom why it was a bad idea *now*. Och. Not in town 24 hours and already things were railroading downhill on her.

Back at the house, Liz surreptitiously wiped chocolate cake crumbs off her skirt as Carter carried in the bags. She unpacked the food onto the table and began carrying perishables to the fridge. "If you give me the receipt, I'll get you a check before you leave."

Carter handed her the watermelon. Who bought watermelon in April? "You're cooking, aren't you? Why should you pay for the food?"

"Even so, I was stocking up. If you leave the receipt—"

"Forget it. You can make us dinner another night if it makes you feel better."

Liz held the refrigerator door between them like a shield. Her breath stuck in her windpipe. "Another night?"

He handed her a dozen eggs and she stared at the carton pensively before sliding it into its protective bin. She squelched her inner June who was already giddily planning the next meal's menu. "Or not. Sorry. Thinking with my stomach again. No, don't put the dip away."

Liz handed over the dip and picked up the chuck roast. What the heck was she doing with a chuck roast? Feeding her teenage fantasies, that's what. "No. You're right. Dinner's a great idea. I'll invite Bailey, too. It'll be fun."

"Absolutely."

Liz nodded and handed him the bag of chips. "You surprised me, you know. My Aunt Claire said your uncle would be stopping by today."

"He threw his back out, so you got me." Carter glanced at her as he popped the lids off two bottles of ale and handed one to her.

"I'm sorry to hear—oh." She paused. "That's why you were late today, isn't it?"

"Yup." He took a long slug of ale.

Her face flushed. "I'm sorry. I don't know why I even mentioned it. I think I'm just stressed over everything that needs to be done around here." She let her voice trail off. It sounded like a lame excuse even to her own ears.

Carter handed her the bacon.

Liz blew out a little breath. "I've offended you."

"Not offended," he said, his lips tilting a little at the corner. "More annoyed."

She frowned. "If I annoyed you, why did you invite me out? I mean, why did you ask me for dinner, er, to get food?"

"You were indecisive. I was hungry." His eyebrow did that wingy thing again as his lips twitched. "You didn't think it was a date, did you?"

"No! Of course not! How could it be?" She gave an awkward laugh. "That's the *last* thing I'd want—"

"Right, then."

"Right."

Liz gripped the bacon, mortification coursing through her veins. Of course it wasn't a date! Hadn't she been telling herself that very thing? "Well, at least we've cleared that up." She forced another chuckle, taking her own sip of ale, the taste smooth and foreign on her tongue. She hadn't had a beer in ages. Grant was more of a wine guy. "I really am sorry about your uncle. I hope it's not serious."

"No more than usual." Carter shrugged. "It's what you get from making a living off your back."

"Maybe, but he's awfully young to be disabled by—"

"He's *not* disabled."

"I didn't mean to—"

"I know what you meant." Carter cut her off again then seemed to realize how abrupt he sounded. "He's fine, that's all. It's not like he needs to retire or anything. He's fine."

Liz nodded wordlessly and decided she had better get dinner started. Soon the bacon was sizzling in a pan. She took another sip of ale and wondered if the text Grant had sent was important.

Carter fiddled with the bottle opener. "So, what's John up to these days?"

"Who knows? I haven't heard from him in months."

Carter grimaced. "Sorry. I'd hoped he'd settled down some."

"You're not the only one." She swiped at grease spattering up at her arm and adjusted the burner a little. "I suppose you hoped it was John helping my parents out. So you could catch up with him, I mean."

"I'm glad it's you."

"You are?" Liz fumbled the fork she was using to flip the bacon and wiped hot grease dots from the back of her hand. "Why would you...?"

Carter leaned against the counter, studying her. He took a sip of ale. "You always seemed to have big plans. I guess I was curious how you'd turned out."

Liz's heart caught in her throat as she absently flipped a slice of bacon. "And how did I turn out?"

It shouldn't matter, whatever he had to say shouldn't matter one whit.

But it did.

Suddenly, Carter's face turned serious, focused in a way that made Liz's pulse race erratically and her nerves sizzle like the bacon in the pan. He licked his lips. Her tongue darted out in answer. He met her gaze. *Oh my.* That look could only mean one thing!

"Don't panic," he said, breaking into her thoughts, "but your bacon's on fire."

"My—*what?!*" Liz jumped from the stove as flames slicked across the skillet and shot into the air. *"Ohmigod!"*

"It's okay. Not a problem." Carter stepped in front of her, turned off the burner then grabbed a lid from the pot rack and dropped it over the flames. "It'll burn itself out."

Liz stared, frozen, as smoke poured from under the ill-fitting lid and rose to the ceiling. Carter flipped open cupboard doors until he found a box of baking soda. He lifted the lid and poured the baking soda over the skillet.

"There." He yanked open the back slider. "It's out. You can stop panicking now."

"I wasn't— *the cat!*" she shrieked as Eddie darted through the open slider. "He's not supposed to go out!"

Liz raced out the slider, as a blur of orange tabby zipped behind a rhododendron. "Eddie, honey? Come on. Don't be scared." She flipped on the rear spotlight, hoping to shed some light into the shadows by the house, and pointed to the bush. Carter caught her eye and rounded the other side. "Eddie. Come out. Please?"

"Your parents have a cat?" Carter asked as he inched toward the far side of the bush.

"He's mine. He doesn't like to be boarded, so I brought him with me from Chicago. He's not used to being outside," she whispered so as not to alarm Eddie. "I think the commotion scared him."

"Is that why he's growling?" Carter whispered from somewhere in the shrubbery.

"That's not growling. It's a fear moan. I think. He's generally quite friendly to people who like cats." Liz wrung her hands then noticed the action and dropped them to her sides in self-disgust. "Can you reach him?"

Carter was on his belly now, half hidden beneath the branches. "I think so— Christ! This is your cat? He looks like Tony Soprano. Are you *sure* he's friendly?"

"He's a pussycat. Unless he's scared, then he can be a little... unpredictable."

"Uh-huh. Here goes nothin'." Eddie gave a short yowl of protest, and then Carter was backing out from under the bush. He stood up, clutching Eddie tightly in his arms. Neither looked particularly happy.

"Did he scratch you?"

"Are you kidding? I'm a professional."

"A professional cat-nabber?"

"Just get the door. Your cat's giving me the evil eye. I don't think he likes me."

"He always looks like that," she said a little breathlessly as she followed Carter into the house. "If he hasn't bitten you yet, you're way ahead of the cur..." But the rest of her words died on her tongue as she turned toward the kitchen.

Smoke clouded the room. Black soot coated the ceiling. She coughed, adrenaline pumping sickly through her veins. "Oh God. And here I'm supposed to be making the house fit for sale?"

Carter shooed Eddie into the dining room, closed the door and turned on the stove exhaust. Liz opened the window above the sink. Carter waved a dinner plate toward it. "Come on. I think your folks will be amazed with what you've done so far." She watched as his dead-pan expression tilted into an easy, infectious grin. "I'm thinking we set off a few small explosives and our work here is done."

"It's that bad, isn't it?"

"It's not great. I won't lie. But I've seen worse. Why don't you put together those sandwiches and point me toward a fan so we can keep this smoke from drifting through the rest of the house?"

"You don't have to—"

"I'm hungry, Liz. Make some sandwiches, and I'll start cleaning." He gave her a look. "If you don't, I might be forced to eat the rest of the swiss cake rolls." His lips twitched charmingly. "You know you like them."

"They're full of sugar and preservatives."

"That's what makes them so good."

She shook her head, the scent of burnt bacon overwhelming. Classical music filled the air.

"Liz?" Carter said.

"Yeah?" she said, trying to ignore the obvious.

"You're pocket's ringing."

"I know." She pulled her cell phone out of her skirt pocket. Grant again. "I'm sorry, but I'd better take this. There's probably a fan in the front hall closet." As Carter left in search of the fan, she turned toward the back yard. "Hello?"

"Liz? *Finally!* I thought you were going to make yourself available."

"Sorry. Some things came up."

"Yeah, well things came up here, too, and I could use your help. Now's not the time to go AWOL on me. Did you get my text? My e-mail?"

"Not yet. I was out. What's going on?"

Something wrong? Carter mouthed, box fan in hand.

Liz shook her head. *Work,* she mouthed back.

"...Janice is having a fit about the disaster recovery meeting Friday. I thought you worked that out with her," Grant said.

"I did. I—"

"And, I need you to send me the schedule again. I can't find the copy you left me, and Ethan's getting annoyed we don't have it posted on the board already."

"No problem. I—"

"No problem? You're not having to deal with all the fires that keep creeping up! The Scrips2U people are complaining that some of their CSRs can't access the ordering system, and to top it off, the software vendor isn't returning my calls."

"Okay. I'll call Andy. I'm sure it's—"

"It's a pain in the ass is what it is! Where have you been? I sent you a text about this over two hours ago!"

Had it been that long?

Liz gritted her teeth as Carter set the box fan in the window and plugged it in. "I doubt it's a software problem. If it's only some of the CSRs, they're probably forgetting to enter their new ID codes. The system will lock them out after three attempts as a security measure. Just have a shift manager enter his/her override numbers for now, and I'll have Andy sort it out in the morning."

"The job is done, Liz. We shouldn't have to hold their hands like this."

"It's our job to hold their hands. If these transitions were easy, they wouldn't need us."

Grant heaved an audible sigh. "The wrap-up is complete. We did what we were contracted to do. Sometimes you need to cut the cord and move on. Andy needs to take care of this now. Not you."

"You know Andy is getting married next week. He's preoccupied."

"It's a civil ceremony, Liz. At the town hall. It's not a big deal."

"It is to them," she said, coughing a little. The lingering smoke was beginning to irritate her throat. "Listen. I'm sorry, but I'm in the middle of something. I'll follow up with Andy, and I'll e-mail the schedule as soon as we hang up. Anything else?"

"No. That's it. For the moment."

"Great," she said.

"Great."

Liz pocketed her phone and hurried to open the back slider as Carter waited to take the still-smoking skillet outside. She avoided his eyes as he walked past, her gaze drawn to a large, sooty handprint on the hip of his jeans, the dark outline of fingertips just brushing his back pocket.

She swallowed in alarm.

Grant wasn't the only one with fires to put out.

CHAPTER NINE

Twelve years earlier…

BETH STOOD ALONE at the far end of Jenny's living room and carefully sipped her cup of punch. Her stomach growled. The Whitmeyer's owned The Old Mill Bar & Grill across town and were notoriously cool. They were probably watching horror movies in the master suite upstairs, while their famous hot wings and potato skins sat in chafing dishes for the masses.

Beth eyed the cookies, salsa and tortilla chips on a nearby table, but there was no way she'd risk dribbling salsa down her shirt or getting cookie crumbs in her teeth. Besides, she couldn't eat in front of boys. No way.

They came in periodically, the boys that is, raiding the chips bowl, jostling and joking and dropping crumbs on the floor in testosterone–fueled orgies before they elbowed each other and laughed their enticing, low laughs and wandered away again. Beth sucked in her stomach and pretended to be engrossed in her manicure like she'd seen the other girls do. She let out a nervous exhale. She'd thought the pale mauve looked quietly elegant and understated but now it just looked like she'd borrowed nail polish from somebody's grandmother.

Wishing she were more the type that could get away with metallic blue, she set her paper cup down on a window sill. Bailey was right. It was stupid to come.

She was just about to walk down the hall in search of a restroom when Valerie and her gang stepped out of the kitchen. They flipped their hair at the boys who were lingering around the cupcakes. "Hey, guys."

Chip Otterman, Dan O'Connell and a few other popular guys stood around, periodically dipping their fingers into the cupcake frosting and licking it off. Dan winked at Valerie. "Hey, gorgeous."

Valerie preened and flicked her hair again, her giant silver hoop earrings glinting as she did so. "You're not going to stand here all night and eat cupcakes, are you?" she teased.

He eyed her as only a horny teenaged boy can, a mixture of hope and confidence warring on his features. "Got any better ideas?" he asked.

"Oh, I've always got ideas," Valerie cooed. My God, she was good. Beth watched as Valerie pulled an empty wine bottle she must have retrieved from the recycle bin from behind her back. "How about we all have a little fun? Who's up for Seven Minutes of Heaven?"

Dan frowned. Chip looked hopefully at Jenny. The other boys chuckled nervously.

"Oh, come on," Valerie urged. "Where's your sense of adventure?"

Chip nudged Dan. "Why not?"

"Shut up. You just want to kiss my girlfriend."

"Worried?" Valerie asked, sauntering toward the door. You could tell she already knew she'd won. "Afraid he's a better kisser than you?"

"Heck, no," Dan said, grabbing Valerie's waist. He licked her ear. Beth could see his tongue snake out. "I'll make sure you only reach heaven with me, baby," he said.

Gag!

Beth did her best to blend in with the upholstery, horrified at the turn of events. This was *so* not where she belonged. A make-out game? *Ack!* No amount of reading Trish's *Cosmo*s on the sly could make her good at *that*.

She could hear voices outside the front door. Great. More people to ignore her.

She took a step back into the curtains, waiting for everyone to leave so she could go find a restroom. Hide. But, just as they were about to disappear into the kitchen, Valerie turned and looked Beth straight in the eye.

"Coming?" she said.

51

CHAPTER TEN

CARTER KNOCKED LIGHTLY before entering his grandmother's living room. It was one of three small rooms on the ground floor in Ma and Pop's house Grams had been given to use after her knee replacements. He scootched by the TV and Grams' recliner and pulled a slip of paper from the pocket of his sweats.

"Here's your ticket and receipt. The lottery commission thanks you again for your donation."

Grams snatched the scratch tickets out of his hand. "We'll see who's laughing when I hit the jackpot. Ooh! *Shh!* They're starting again!"

She set the lottery tickets on a side table by her chair and waved impatiently for him to sit.

"Sorry I missed dinner. I—"

"Never mind that." Grams waved away his apology. "Leftovers are in the fridge if you want to take them home. Okay. You've already missed the recap of last week's episode, so I'll bring you up to speed. They've done the little vignette on each of the three finalists. Now he's gone into seclusion to decide which two he wants to take on the final adventure." She leaned forward in her recliner to see around him as he toed off his sneakers.

Carter plopped onto the loveseat. "As if he can actually find 'true love' after ten episodes. This show is completely rigged."

"Is not," Grams retorted, riveted to the screen. "I read about him in *People*. He's a lonely widower and would love to find love again, but it hasn't happened. Let's face it, he's thirty-five now. Time's a tickin'. As he pointed out in the article, this show isn't any different than having a friend set you up on a blind date."

"Except my friends don't follow me around with a camera crew."

"*Pfft*. Marcia says the couples forget the cameras are even there."

'Marcia' was the host of the popular reality show and the supposed "matchmaking guru" who used her own proprietary romantic screening process (probably a Magic-8 ball) to "handpick" candidates to date the lead. Unlike other dating shows, Marcia believed real-life challenges were what made or broke relationships, so dates were less about wine and cheese picnics and more about changing a tire in the rain, hosting a birthday party for a pack of preschoolers or getting lost (i.e. dropped) in the woods and having to find your way back to civilization with only a roll of aluminum foil, a rope, a chocolate bar and a towel between you. (That was a fun episode.)

"Go ahead and poke fun. I love this show. It's the classic tale of finding true love."

"As observed by twenty million Americans in their living rooms." Carter helped himself to popcorn and settled in for the season finale. They had the same conversation every Monday night. He wouldn't have missed it for the world. Grams lit up when she talked about true love. Who was he to deprive her of that?

He just needed to keep creepy old men from capitalizing on her naiveté.

"Don't make that face, young man. It's not becoming. True love is true love regardless of whether it's on national TV. And if you keep this up, I may write Marcia and sign you up to be the next bachelor. *Hmm.* Or maybe Ian…" She tapped her lips thoughtfully with her index finger.

"Oh, no!" She sat up straight. "Did you see his eyes in that shot? I don't think he's going to pick her! Can you believe it? *Tsk.* That'll be a mistake."

"You think that's a mistake? What about last week when he ditched the masseuse? *That* was a mistake. And, *no,* you may not sign me up for this show."

Grams slid him a derisive look. "The one with the purple hair streak? She was trampy. And don't push me. I have e-mail, and I know how to use it."

"Trampy in a good way. Remember the slumber party episode? Maybe you *should* sign me up. That pillow fight looked entertaining…"

Grams snorted indelicately and reclaimed the popcorn bowl. "Fine. Ian would make a better bachelor anyway. He's got that whole successful, lonely bachelor persona. It would serve you right if he got his own slumber party episode."

Carter flattened his hand to his chest. "So now I'm not good enough for the show? I'm crushed." He grinned and tossed a handful of popcorn into his mouth.

Grams ignored him. They sat through a couple of commercials in silence. "So, have you submitted your bid for the fountain job?"

Carter chewed a little more slowly. "They haven't released the work specs yet."

"Well don't forget to follow through. I hear they not only want to replace the fountain but add a garden trellis and a little stone half-wall for seating. Doesn't that sound lovely?"

He swallowed. "It sounds like you told the committee that's what they should have."

Grams pursed her lips. "It was only a suggestion. Anyway, make sure you bid. A job like that would get you noticed... get you started on the right foot for when you take over the business."

"Don't get ahead of yourself. Nothing's been decided yet."

"What's to decide? Your uncle spends more time at the chiropractor now than I do. He's up in bed right now, stiff as a board. It's time for him to retire. Time for *you* to take over."

"He can work in the office. I'll take the heavy work. Nothing needs to change."

Grams rolled her eyes. "He hates paperwork as much as you do and you know it. You need to step up to the plate and take on responsibility for—"

Carter swiped a piece of popcorn off his lap. "Maybe I'm not ready to be responsible."

Grams followed the bit of popcorn with her eyes and raised an eyebrow. "You never will be if you don't try."

"Trying isn't always the problem."

Grams huffed. "Well, I'm not going to talk about it if you're going to give me attitude."

Carter heaved a sigh and bent over to pick up the popcorn. Grams meant well, but she could be a royal pain in the backside sometimes. "I'm not giving you attitude, Grams, just facts. The *fact* is I do the best I can, but it's not always good enough. I'd love to do the fountain job, but it's right in the damn center of town, and you and I both know that if something goes wrong people will notice. I'm better off sticking to less high profile jobs."

"So you're not even going to bid?"

"I didn't say that."

"Fine. We'll talk about it later."

"I'd rather not."

Sappy mood music bellowed from the TV, signaling the return of the show and saving Carter from further discussion. They watched in silence for a few minutes.

"Did you stop by the Beacon's today?" Grams whispered, as if Carter cared a hoot whether he missed anything. It wasn't as if he disliked the show, he actually found it pretty entertaining. Just unrealistic.

"Yup."

"And?"

"They want a patio."

"Don't be obtuse. Did you see Claire's grandniece? Elizabeth Beacon?"

"Yup." He pulled the bowl of popcorn back toward him as the show broke for yet more commercials.

"I hear she's done very well for herself—though not married. Be sure to say hello from me."

"Okay."

"*Carter*," Grams said in frustration.

"What?"

"Are you even listening?"

"Maybe."

She harrumphed and nearly fell out of her recliner to poke him with a bony index finger. "Why are you being difficult?"

He laughed at her look of consternation and helped her back up before she fell to the floor. "Grams, why are you trying to set me up again? This is the third time in a month."

"Who's setting you up?" she evaded, pretending an intense interest in acid reflux medication.

"Grams, come on. I don't have any problems meeting women. I'm doing just fine in that— *Ho! You've got to be kidding!*" Carter gestured abruptly toward the TV where they were showing a preview of the dramatic moments to come. "He's going to get rid of the professional chef? What's *with* this guy?"

Grams waved dismissively at the TV. "You're not meeting the right kind of women, Carter. I think I can help."

"How do you know they're not the right kind?"

"For one thing, you almost never bring them around to meet the rest of the family."

"Maybe I don't want to scare them off."

"Stop it. Tell me what you thought of Elizabeth."

Carter winced as the professional chef criticized the bachelor for being inept, unimaginative and prematurely deflating her soufflé, as it were. *Ouch.* "She was... fine."

"Fine as in a fine wine?" Grams prompted.

"Fine as in neutral-fine. As in either hamburgers or hotdogs for dinner are fine." He tossed another piece of popcorn into his mouth.

Grams pursed her lips. "Now you're toying with me. When are you going to stop playing the field and settle down?"

"I don't know. Maybe I like the game too much."

He watched as the camera zoomed in on the chef, her mascara streaking down her cheeks as she sobbed out her disappointment on national TV. *Never leave them angry,* he cautioned the bachelor silently.

"Don't be afraid of love, Carter. It can't hurt you."

"Yeah, right. I'll bet my mom would have something to say about that." At Grams' soft but unmistakable intake of breath he turned—and instantly regretted the flip comment. "Grams. I'm sorry. I—"

"No. You're right." Grams let out a long sigh and turned down the TV. "You're right." She shook her head, emotion clouding her eyes. Carter gave himself a mental kick. This was their night for enjoying the ridiculousness of reality TV, not a time to bring up an old family tragedy.

Grams' slim, arthritic fingers toyed with the tassels on the afghan she had draped over her lap. "You're right, of course. I'm sure your mother wasn't thinking of the danger to herself when she went back for your father. But I don't blame her. I've never blamed her. How could she have lived with herself if she hadn't tried?"

Carter swallowed, a piece of popcorn lodging uncomfortably in his throat. They rarely spoke of the fire that had killed his parents. He'd been all of six when it happened. Ancient history. But, as much as his aunt and uncle had stepped in and become the parents he'd lost, he sometimes wondered about an emotion that would consume so much of your good sense you'd risk your own life for it. "She wasn't thinking about me or Grace or Ian either, was she?"

"Maybe. Maybe," Grams nodded, the grief etched into her features. "But I hope someday, for your sake, you'll understand just what kind of love they had." She sighed deeply. "Now that... *that* was true love."

"Like this show?" he said, trying desperately to lighten the moment.

Grams laughed and took back the popcorn bowl, wiping away a tear as she turned the volume on the TV up again. "No, this isn't true love. It's just silly drivel. But I still enjoy it." She patted his hand and settled back in her recliner, a slight smile determinedly erasing the sadness from her features.

Carter stared at the TV screen. He didn't like the idea of loving so deeply nothing else mattered. Unlike his grandmother, he didn't watch this show hoping the couples would find true love so much as come to their senses.

"So," Grams interrupted, "do you think those are real or implants on the travel agent? I've been trying to figure it out for three weeks now."

Carter shook himself out of his daydream and grabbed another handful of popcorn, grateful he wasn't in danger of falling in love. "Those? *Definitely* implants..."

CHAPTER ELEVEN

"HOLY CRAP. This place is a mess!" Trish exclaimed the next day with what appeared to be no small amount of wicked glee. She'd dropped by with baby Clara before her meeting with the school psychologist and, despite Liz's attempts to keep her at the front door, had insisted on putting her expressed breast milk in the fridge *personally*.

"If you think it's bad now, you should have seen it before we cleaned." Liz stumbled a bit as Trish handed her Clara in her bucket seat. Jeez. Were all babies this heavy?

Trish swung toward her like a lock-on, gossip-seeking missile. "*We?*"

"Eddie and I," Liz said, carefully setting the baby down. "So, anything special I should know before you head out?"

Trish looked vaguely disappointed at the change of subject, but a quick check of her watch had her looking harried again. She swung an enormous diaper bag to the floor. "Okay. Quick run-down. She just pooped, but that doesn't mean anything. Extra diapers, onesies and fresh outfits are in the big compartment. She's got a little diaper rash going, so use the ointment that's in the side pocket, but don't let her get her fingers in it, because she'll eat it. I'd take off my necklace if I were you, because she's starting to get grabby, and you'll probably want to keep your hair in that ponytail.

"I fed her twenty minutes ago, so if you're lucky, she'll sleep till I get back. But, she's growing again, so if she's cranky, she probably wants to eat. Just bring the bottle to room/body temperature. If she's still cranky, it's probably teething. The Orajel is with the diaper cream, but you can let her suck on something cold, too. Back-up formula is in this compartment over here if she drinks all the milk," Trish indicated vaguely to the far side of the diaper bag, "but I should definitely be back before you'll need either. Any questions?"

Liz blinked at her sister and mentally reviewed the rudiments of infant CPR she'd Googled that morning. Okay. Now to ask a pertinent question to make it clear to Trish she had everything under control. "Do you have emergency numbers for me, just in case?"

Trish waved a dismissive hand. "In case of what? She's a baby. What kind of emergencies can she have?"

"Won't she be upset when she wakes and you're not here? I haven't seen her much, and I've read that babies this age—"

"If you have milk, she won't care if you're Freddy Krueger." Trish planted a quick kiss on her daughter's hair. "I have my cell phone. I'll be back in a couple hours." And, then she left Liz. Alone. With the baby.

Liz stared at her niece, her fluffy blonde hair glowing in a beam of sunlight.

Hmm. Would it be too hot in the sun? Liz eased the bucket seat a few inches to the left, her gut clenching as the baby stirred then settled. Liz let out a long, slow breath and marveled at the scary, sweet scent of infant that wafted through the air.

Okay. Now what? Should she continue to clean? Probably not. The noise could disturb the baby. She could put a primer coat on the front door! *Hmm.* But then she wouldn't hear if the baby woke up. Liz slumped into a kitchen chair. How in the world did mothers ever get anything done?

After removing her necklace and snugging her ponytail, she decided she should use this forced quietude to formulate a revised list of all the things that needed tending. Yes, then she could rank them according to urgency and whether they were weather dependent. But typing might disturb the baby. She'd better do it longhand.

A half an hour later, and six months worth of tasks enumerated on a legal sized yellow pad, Liz jumped at the sound of the doorbell. She rushed through the house before whomever it was struck again. She swung the door wide.

The moderately friendly greeting she was about to deliver died on her tongue. "What are *you* doing here?"

Valerie Stinson brushed a lock of platinum blonde hair off her forehead and pursed her bow-shaped lips. Her perfectly manicured nails glinted in the sun. "Nobody mentioned I was stopping by today?"

"Um, no. My parents are in Florida. In fact, my dad just had surgery..."

"I know. How did it go?"

Liz blinked through the screen door. Valerie Stinson knew about her dad's surgery? *Too?* "Good. Well. I mean... I think so. My mother didn't say otherwise..."

At least she hadn't mentioned that he'd died or anything the half dozen times they'd spoken since Friday despite Liz's pointed inquiries about her father's health. Liz assumed if he *had* actually expired on the operating table, her mom would have thought to tell her. On the plus side, she was fully up-to-speed on the happy news about Mrs. Wells' cat being back from the vet and no longer suffering from diarrhea.

"He's resting," she finally said, assuming that were true.

Valerie opened her mouth to speak when a strange noise interrupted from inside the house.

Liz's heart lurched in her chest. "Oh, no. She's awake! You'll have to excuse me—"

She shut the door again and rushed back to the kitchen just in time to see baby Clara's face scrunch up and emit another long, plaintive wail. "Oh, honey! It's okay! It's okay. Auntie Liz is here. Hold on." Liz swore under her breath, then pleaded forgiveness for corrupting the tender ears of a minor as she fumbled with what seemed an inordinately complex buckle system. My God, astronauts were probably buckled less securely.

Clara thrashed her little baby fists in Liz's face, her outrage clearly evident. Finally, the latch freed itself. Liz pulled the buckle and straps over her niece's reddened cheeks, lay a burpie cloth on her shoulder as she'd watched her sister do, then picked up the wailing infant.

She attempted a nonchalant, confident posture as she tucked her niece down into the crook of her arm. Babies cried, right? It was no big deal. She'd get rid of Valerie and see to her niece like the competent Auntie she was.

Clara continued to scream and began to thrash her head as Liz tried to give her her binkie while opening the front door again. "I'm sorry. I'm babysitting, as you can see, and I need to calm her down. I think she's teething. Perhaps there's a better time for you to—"

"Oh, for crying out loud. She's not teething! She's shaking her fist, not chewing on it. You're just holding her wrong." Before Liz knew what was happening, Valerie had swung open the screen door, plopped her purse on the floor and plucked Clara from her arms.

"You have to hold her upright so she can see what's going on. Babies this age hate to stare at the ceiling. It's boring." Valerie sat Clara on her hip and bounced lightly, oblivious to the smears of baby tears and saliva that Clara deposited on her blouse.

Liz watched, the binkie sticky in her palm, as Clara quieted in Valerie's arms then marveled traitorously over Valerie's shiny fingernails and thick turquoise pendant necklace. The baby hiccupped loudly, one tiny, angry tear glistening on her cheek, and gripped Valerie's index finger like it was the lone port in a storm.

"There, there now. You're all right," Valerie crooned. "Just settle down. We'll work this out."

Liz's forehead felt clammy. "How—?"

"I had five younger siblings. I was babysitting kids her age when I was nine."

"That's so young!"

"You do what you have to do. So, this is it, huh?" Valerie began walking around the living room, Clara shockingly content, as Liz trailed behind. "I like the crown molding. That's a nice detail. Is it throughout the house?"

"I'm sorry?"

"The crown molding? Oh, never mind. I'll see for myself." Valerie pushed open the door to the dining room. "*Hmm.* A little cut off from the living room, but this wall could always be opened up. Nice view of the side yard. I assume the kitchen's through here?"

"Yes, but... I'm sorry. Why are you here?"

"I'm your parent's listing agent. Nobody told you I was doing the walk-through today?"

Liz swallowed the lump in her throat. Valerie was her parents' listing agent? Could it get any worse? "No. No, they didn't."

Valerie turned away, but not before Liz caught her rolling her eyes. Great. A real estate agent with attitude.

"What can you tell me about the well and septic?" Valerie asked as she pushed through the door to the kitchen.

"You might want to—"

"Holy shit!—pardon my French—what happened in here?"

"A little grease fire. It's not a problem. I was painting the ceiling anyway."

Valerie looked around disdainfully. "And the cabinets, too, I hope."

Liz nodded. She was *now*.

Valerie continued to wander around, opening doors, peering out windows, asking questions and generally making Liz uncomfortable. Baby Clara cooed in Valerie's arms, happily swinging the forbidden pendant as they marched toward the second floor.

Liz followed behind. "Do you want me to take her now?" she asked, feeling acutely unnecessary. Valerie stopped on the upper stair landing to look at her. "So you can take notes or something?" Liz added.

Valerie turned away. "I think I can do my job," she said.

"I never said you couldn't," Liz muttered under her breath.

"Well." Twenty minutes later, they stood outside the front door, Clara face-planted against Valerie's generous cleavage and snoring contentedly. The traitor. "Once you get the new patio in and finish the painting, let me know and I'll come take pictures for the listing." Valerie arched an eyebrow at the gnome peering up at them from the edge of the stoop and heaved a resigned sigh.

"Look. I know your parents have made an effort to clear the house of personal photos and knick-knacks and things like that, but I'll be honest with you. In today's market, unless a home dazzles, well, your folks won't get out of it what I know they're hoping to."

Liz was a little taken aback. Straight, honest, helpful talk from Valerie Stinson? The apocalypse must be near.

After decades working a factory job, though, Liz knew the house was all the nest-egg her dad had. If Valerie had any advice, Liz needed to swallow her pride and listen. "Is there anything I can do?"

"For starters, you can get rid of that." Valerie pointed toward a black, fat-bottomed silhouette of kissing children Dad had perched at the edge of the yard.

Liz sighed. "For once, we agree on something."

Valerie almost cracked a smile. Almost. "Just see if you can freshen the place up a little. Think light and airy." She handed Clara back to Liz. "You were always smart. I'm sure you'll figure it out."

"THEY WANT ME to drug him," Trish declared miserably later that afternoon. Clara was making happy nursing noises under Trish's shirt, the twins were running around the yard trying to tag each other and Ben, the nephew under discussion, was poking a stick repeatedly at the trunk of the lone apple tree.

Liz wordlessly handed Trish a cup of coffee. She wasn't sure whether coffee was okay for a nursing mother, but Trish seemed to need *something*.

They stared out the slider as Ben's stick broke. He kicked the tree instead.

"I'm sure that's not what they said," Liz placated.

"You weren't there." Trish took a long gulp of coffee and set the mug on the counter. "They said he's got attention deficit, hyperactivity, doesn't read social cues, is impulsive, disorganized, shows poor judgment, suffers from anxiety and that, considering everything, I would be 'well advised' to consider medication." Trish pulled Clara out from under her shirt and flumped her over her shoulder. "Isn't he just being a boy? Seriously, look at him! Don't all boys do stupid, loud, impulsive stuff?"

Liz watched as her nephew body-slammed his younger brother, did a backwards somersault and then raced away. "Maybe it might help him moderate himself," she offered.

"He's not always like this. Being in school all day makes him antsy."

"Has your pediatrician ever talked to you about Ben's, er, impulsivity?"

"Sure, but I never seem to have the time to follow up on it." She sighed. "Or maybe I'm afraid of what they might say when they start looking more closely. He's a good kid, smart even, but his grades…" her voice trailed off and her eyes filled.

Liz patted her on the shoulder. "Hey, it's not the end of the world. I saw lots of kids like Ben when I was in college. Can it hurt to go to a specialist to find out what you're dealing with? Who knows if the school is right? He might have some underlying learning or memory issues that make everything else worse, and if you can just address those…"

Trish swiped at her eyes. "How do you know all this?"

"I worked as a peer tutor in college. They put us all through a training program on how to help students with various learning styles and disabilities. You may not believe this, but I helped a kid with ADHD, short-term memory and long-term recall issues go from an F to a B+ in Accounting."

"No kidding?"

"No kidding. I'll look up some info for you. Trust me. Ben's not hopeless."

Ben slammed into the other side of the slider from them and laughed, a giant, goofy smile lighting his facing at having startled them. "Mom! I'm hungry! Can we stop for chicken nuggets on the way home? Please? Please?"

Trish nodded and Ben whooped delightedly before charging off again. "But what if they do what to medicate him? What if it changes his personality? I don't want him to be a zombie."

"I don't think that's likely."

CARTER THREW THE discarded beer can he'd collected by the road and tossed it into the bed of his truck with a few others. If there was one thing he hated it was trash on the roadside. It didn't look much better in his pickup, but he figured it was one step closer to being recycled.

"Whoa! No unauthorized cargo!" Carter caught the boy by the shoulders a moment before the kid hurled himself head-first into the back of his pickup. The boy laughed up at him, breathing heavily and looking over his shoulder.

"Thanks! My brother is after me. I didn't see your truck."

"Didn't see it? You might need to get your eyes checked then, buddy."

But instead of laughing, the boy's smile disappeared. "There's nothing wrong with me," he said.

Carter picked up a paver from a stack near the tailgate. "I was kidding." But the boy looked like a puppy that'd been kicked. He turned to leave, his slim shoulders sagging under his Star Wars T-shirt. Carter tapped him on the shoulder. "Hey, what's your name?"

"Ben."

Carter extended a hand. "Carter McIntyre. Owner of the truck you almost creamed." The boy shook hands awkwardly. "Sorry. I guess I'm not as funny as I like to think. No hard feelings?"

Ben shrugged, his gaze glancing off Carter's. "Guess not."

"Great. Say, I'm mocking up a couple edging patterns. Would you mind helping me carry these out back?"

"Sure." Carter handed the boy a couple pavers. "I can take more," said Ben. "I'm stronger than I look. I take karate."

"Impressive. I can see your muscles. *I* can move two tons of stone in a single day."

"Wow!"

"I know. We landscapers are amazing that way. Here, I think you can take one more, I'll take a couple, then we'll see what the lady of the house has to say."

"The lady of the house?" Ben asked as they rounded the corner to the backyard. Carter pointed through the glass slider. "That's not a lady. That's my mother!"

"I heard that." Liz's sister, Trish, stepped onto the back deck and cupped a hand to her mouth. "Peter! Jess! Front and center! Five minute warning!" A baby snored over her shoulder as she turned back to Ben. "Just for your information, mothers can be ladies, too. It's not mutually-exclusive."

Ben rolled his eyes, but grinned under his mom's teasing. "Where do you want these?" he asked Carter.

"Just set them on the edge of the deck. I'll get the rest in a minute."

"I can do it!" Ben said, dropping his load of pavers and charging away again.

Carter watched the boy round the corner of the house. "Sorry. If you have to leave—"

Trish waved a hand. "Let him go. He's had a hard day. It'll do him good to keep busy while I corral the twins."

Ben roared around the corner of the house again and dropped his pavers on the others. A corner chipped off one and sailed through the air.

"Ben!" Trish gasped. "Be careful!"

"I'm so sorry!" Ben stared at the chipped corner, and then at Carter, his eyes welling up as if shocked by his own powers of destruction.

Carter knew all too well how that felt.

Impulsively, Carter grabbed another paver and dropped it on the pile. A corner chipped off a second paver. "Look," he said. "No big deal. Happens all the time." He picked up the damaged paver and flipped it over in his palm, held it out. "Luckily, they have two sides."

When he saw the still-useable face, Ben grinned gratefully and looked at his mom as if to say, "See?" before running off again.

"Thanks," she said. "He doesn't mean to be careless. He just has a lot of energy, you know?"

Carter nodded as he watched Ben disappear from view. "Yeah, I know."

CHAPTER TWELVE

"I'VE GOT IT, POP." Carter snaked in front of his uncle and grabbed the handles of the wheelbarrow before the older man could try to lift it. He cocked his head toward the house. "I think I smelled Grams cooking up a batch of those pocket pastry thingies for her friends. Better get 'em while they're hot."

His uncle gave him a long, quiet stare before he finally let go of the handles and stood, a slight grimace the only indication his back was still giving him trouble. "You're not fooling anyone, you know."

"The bacon and herbed cheese are the best. I highly recommend them."

His uncle shook his head and bent to pick up a trowel from the grass nearby. He looked at it a moment then stuck it point first into the mortar in the wheelbarrow. "You were a lot cuter when you were little," he said as he walked away around the side of the house.

"Love you, too, Pop!"

Carter watched his uncle walk away, his chest tight, then backed the load of mortar through the kitchen door.

"Don't mind me, ladies. Just carry on. You'll hardly know I'm here." Carter wheeled by the dining room where Grams and her friends were getting ready to play cards. Whenever they played at Grams he made a point of stopping by, because Grams was a firm believer that wherever two or more are gathered, there should be food.

Grams stepped into his path and smacked his chest with a potholder. "Stop! You can't roll that thing through my house as if it were some construction zone! You'll track dirt all over. It's bad enough the whole yard is torn up fixing the septic system." She ended on a near whisper, presumably because septic systems were a subject polite ladies didn't speak about.

Claire Walker, Liz Beacon's great-aunt, sat at the table sipping a mixed drink from a tumbler and picked up her poker hand one card at a time. With her deadpan expression, chin-length gray hair and hideous bowling shirt, Carter was tempted to hand Claire a cigar to complete the picture. "That reminds me," Claire announced, "Lydia wants to know if she should withhold fluids. I told her you had plenty of bushes outside if she was desperate to go." She winked at him.

"Oh, for Pete's sake, Ruth said we can still use the bathrooms." June Hastings, another of Grams' friends, gave Claire a reproving look. "Why do you say things like that? You know how gullible Lydia is."

Claire's lips twitched. "That's what makes it fun."

Carter lifted the wheelbarrow handles again, but hesitated, torn between making his escape before his mortar set up and trying to wheedle one of the hot hors d'oeuvre thingies Grams had just set on the table.

"Lydia? Are you coming?" Grams called. "Claire's dealt already! Now, about you," she said, turning toward Carter again, "I want you to do a nice job for the Beacons. They're old friends."

"But, not too nice," Claire said, fanning out her cards. "Keep your pants on."

"What?" Carter said.

Claire took a sip from her tumbler. "Don't think I don't know what you're about, young man. You've got that same look as your father. Liz used to be a little plump but she's slimmed down now and filled out rather nicely, if you know what I mean. Boys like you always have one thing on their minds when they see an attractive girl. Just sayin'."

Carter met his grandmother's eyes pleadingly. She wasn't helping.

"Why am I getting a lecture here? What have I even *done?*"

"You've eaten dinner there. You put out a grease fire and you *saved her cat,* and we all know what *that* means." Claire enumerated her points as if they were charges against the accused instead of acts of friendly goodwill.

"You saved her cat?" June asked.

"He got loose. I caught him. Who told you that, anyway?"

"Lydia and I let the cat out by accident when we went to visit Elizabeth yesterday. He's a sprinter, that one. Shot out like a rocket." Claire eyed him. "Anyway, we heard the whole story. If you're around enough to be putting out grease fires and saving cats, then you're around enough for other things, too, by my way of thinking."

"I'm just putting in a patio."

"See," said Grams, finally coming to his rescue. "No nefarious intent involved."

"Exactly," Carter said, breathing again. "She's a nice enough person and we knew each other in school, but she's not my type."

An eye-watering cloud of perfume entered the room moments before the visual assault of Lydia Sweet's Technicolor caftan. "I have a situation," Lydia pouted. She held up an empty maraschino jar. "I'm out of cherries. *Again!"*

Grams and June glared at Claire—who just rolled her eyes. "Fine. I had a couple. If she didn't take so long to get going, I wouldn't have been standing there nibbling. I could have blood sugar issues, you know. Maybe I *needed* to eat them."

"Grams, if you want these steps laid—" Carter began, but Grams held up a hand in his face and wagged a finger at Claire as if directing traffic. "The Lord's watching you, Claire Walker. And, everyone knows you're healthy as a horse."

"The Almighty's got better things to do than strike me down for eating a few cherries," Claire grumbled.

Carter made his escape while he had the chance. He'd snitch a pastry later.

He pushed the wheelbarrow to the breezeway entry, selected a stone, mixed the mortar he'd left to slake in the wheelbarrow and contemplated the job at hand. Grams' shadow appeared in the doorway above him.

"What makes her not your type?" she demanded as if the conversation wasn't over.

Carter let out a long-suffering sigh. No sense pretending he didn't know who she was talking about. "So, first you guys want me to like her, then you want me to stay away from her and now you want me to like her again? Make up my mind."

"I want to know why you won't consider her."

"I'm taking her to our class reunion. Clearly I've considered her."

"You know what I mean. I mean *seriously* consider."

Carter raised a dark brow and shook his head. "Seriously consider? She's in town for what? Two weeks? What's to seriously consider? Besides, she's a Vice President or something now. A big shot. Like I said, she's not my type." He got up to grab another stone, but his grandmother's hand stopped him.

"Don't you dare," she whispered fiercely. "You're a hard worker, Carter. You'll be taking over your uncle's business soon. Don't you dare think you're not good enough for the Elizabeth Beacons of this world. When are you going to give yourself the credit you deserve?"

He couldn't meet her eyes. He knew they'd be filled with love and compassion. It was the fierce mama-bear look she'd always given him when she thought he wasn't living up to his potential. And it made him feel eight years old again.

"What do I deserve, Grams? You know I don't do well with the straight and narrow. Never have. Heck, Liz Beacon *is* the straight and narrow. This is a pointless conversation. "

"Maybe you've misjudged her. How come you quit the fire department?" The sudden change in topic threw him off balance, which was probably intentional. Carter closed his eyes. He'd been a volunteer firefighter ever since dropping out of college.

Until last week, that is.

"It took too much time."

"Uh-huh," she nodded, although her expression told him she didn't buy it. "Well, maybe it'll fit your schedule again in the future."

"Maybe." He scraped the mortar in the wheelbarrow.

"Carter."

"Grams, some things just aren't meant to be."

"Are we talking about Liz or the department?"

"I don't know. Both."

"Then why are you taking her to the reunion?"

Carter shook his head in frustration wishing he were done so he could leave. "I can't believe we're having this conversation again. It's getting old. Doesn't it feel like it's getting old to you? *I* think it's getting old..."

"Fine! Take her. But remember, she's here to help her parents. She's not here to have her heart broken because you can't move beyond—"

"I'm not breaking any hearts, Grams—*sheesh!* —I'm putting in a patio! I promise not to do anything Liz doesn't want me to, okay?" Carter bent down to test the sizing of the stone he'd selected and set it aside.

"Don't lift like that! Use your knees or you'll end up like your uncle!"

He sat back on his heels with no small amount of exasperation. "Don't you have a game to get to?"

"In a minute," she waved a hand dismissively. "Lydia needed a bathroom break. For never having had children, that woman is amazingly poor at holding her fluids." She stood watch like a garden gnome in a calico apron as he laid the paving stone in its mortar bed with a few hard raps of the trowel's handle.

"So, I followed up on the fountain project. The specs will be out this week. It's a short timeline, though, because they want it finished by Founders' Day, so keep an eye out for it."

Carter slopped a trowel full of mortar down for the next stone with more force than he'd intended. My God, the woman was like a terrier with a bone. Or a calico-printed battering ram. "Follow up on the fountain project, consider Liz, stay away from Liz, don't break anyone's heart and bend with the knees. Did I miss anything?"

"Don't be snarky," Grams sniffed, sitting down on the bench beside him despite the fact that he'd heard the downstairs toilet flush like two minutes ago. "And, yes, I know what that means. I'm just trying to be helpful. We all saw your last girlfriend. She had so many tattoos I wasn't sure if she was a person or a billboard."

"Marlena was colorful, I'll grant you that," Carter murmured. "But, she was also—"

"I don't want to know!" Grams held up a palm in alarm. "But I do want to see you happy. Oh, honey, you're not happy dating the women you've been dating. A grandmother can tell."

"Is that so? I feel happy…"

"Well, you're not. Those women are far too superficial for you."

"Maybe I'm attracted to superficial."

"No, you're not. You only *choose* superficial because it seems safe, but these women don't see the real you. And they won't make you happy."

An image of flexible, colorful Marlena flashed in his mind's eye. "Actually—"

"You know," Grams cut in, clearly not in listening mode, "I can't believe I didn't see it before. You're *exactly* like that Brian on *Happily Ever After!*" Carter choked on his surprise at being compared to the current bachelor on the matchmaking show. "Don't you agree, girls?"

Unanimous sounds of agreement floated in from the next room as Carter dropped a glob of mortar on his boot. Good grief. He should have known they were all listening. "The stamp collector? Gee, thanks. The man was stupid enough to get rid of a chef *and* a masseuse."

"He was a respected antiquities dealer, but that's beside the point. Don't you see? He was originally attracted to Amber and that Ellen girl, you know the ones with the big—? Anyway, but then that Julie Anne snuck under his radar and made him see himself differently. See?"

"Uh-huh." He didn't see at all.

"What you need is an under-the-radar girl!" Grams announced.

"So I can see myself differently?"

"Exactly."

"And who, pray tell, is radar girl?"

Grams wiggled her eyebrows.

"*Liz Beacon?* You think Liz is Radar Girl?" he whispered in disbelief.

"*Under-the-radar* girl," she whispered back.

CHAPTER THIRTEEN

"WHAT DO YOU THINK you're doing?"

Liz swiped at the sweat beading on her brow from the unusually warm spring sun and thanked the Fates the black flies had yet to make an appearance. She turned to her sister. "What does it look like I'm doing? I'm tearing out the old deck."

"You should be wearing a mask. Old pressure-treated lumber is full of arsenic."

"It's not asbestos, Trish. Arsenic leaches into the soil; it doesn't float in the air. Besides, there's not much left of it. I'm not even sure it was pressure-treated. Oh, yuck!" Liz jumped back from a rotten board as a handful of black ants scurried away.

"Are those carpenter ants? You'd better have the house sprayed while you're here. Just last week I saw a show where this guy's house was eaten right out from under him by termites. Literally, his La-Z-Boy fell right through to the basement *with him in it*."

"Termites don't live this far north." Liz kicked the board aside with the others and grabbed her hammer and crowbar. It was Thursday morning. She'd been hard at work for two days, cleaning, scraping, weeding and raking and had no intention of adding a single item to her 'to do' list. "Once I get rid of this rotten wood," she huffed, "the ants will leave."

"I know a good exterminator."

"Fine. Leave the number on the counter."

"By the way," Trish popped the baby over her shoulder and began patting her energetically. "I think I can convince Dad to gut the kitchen now that you've torched it. Just say the word. He's still pretty loopy on painkillers. He'd agree to anything."

"Mom and Dad can't afford a remodel. And I don't have time for one. I'll just get some paint, cover it up, and get it on the market."

Trish sat at the picnic table and stared back at the house. "I don't know how you can be so detached about this," she accused. "This is our childhood home they're selling out from under us."

"Selling out from—? What are you talking about? You couldn't wait to move out!"

"And you hung around any longer than you had to?"

"That was different. I had plans for my life."

"And I didn't?"

Liz closed her eyes. "That's not what I meant."

"I know what you meant," Trish said, tucking the baby back under her shirt.

Liz flumped onto the bench next to Trish and reached for her bottled water. "I didn't hate living here," she said. "I actually like the house. It always seemed so Waltons, you know? I just..." She sighed and took a sip of water, looking out over the back fields. "I knew I wanted more out of life. The ways things had become, everything going on with John... I was afraid if I stayed in Sugar Falls I'd end up unhappy like everyone else. I didn't *hate* it here, I just couldn't wait to move on, you know?"

Trish harrumphed. "Who could? I got so sick of Dad's disappointed looks and Mom's making excuses, I took my first ticket out of here. Getting knocked up by Russ was easier than getting into college, anyway. Or so I thought." Trish pulled her shirt down again as baby Clara flapped it around in her fist.

"You're not unhappy, are you?" Liz asked.

"No. I got lucky. I may make Russ get snipped after this one, but I'm not unhappy. Not like *some* people." Trish gave Liz a look.

"I'm not unhappy!"

"Sure. You're single, attractive and rake in more dough than you know what to do with, and yet you live with an ugly cat in an apartment you hate. Why? I'll tell you why. You're waiting for Prince Charming to sweep you off your feet, marry you, and carry you off to your little Walton-esque, white picket-fenced house."

"I am not."

"Why are you here, then? Why are you not off using your vacation time like a normal single person—traveling to hot, sandy islands where the men don't remember how fat you used to be?"

"Okay. You know what?" Liz said, standing up. "I'm getting back to work. And for the record, I was only a little plump."

Trish grabbed her elbow and yanked her back down. "You know I'm just kidding. It's the postpartum hormones talking. They make me bitchy. I'm just jealous because you don't have any baby fat to work off. I ate like a horse with this one, and I'll be lucky to get the weight off by the time she graduates high school. I'm just saying, ripping out rotten decks on your vacation doesn't seem right. Even for you."

"Maybe I wanted to come home. My tenth reunion is next week, you know."

"*Ugh*. Reunions are hell. Everyone secretly hates them."

"It might be fun. Besides, I've committed to go."

"This wouldn't have anything to do with a certain guy whose initials are carved into the inside doorframe of your closet, would it?"

"I have no idea what you're talking about."

"You know, the C.M. carved above E.B. with a plus sign between them?"

"You're imagining things. Postpartum hormones can do that to a person."

Trish nodded sympathetically and pushed off the picnic table as if still pregnant, the baby asleep across her chest. "Right. Well, I've gotta go. Preschool lets out in ten minutes. Call me?"

"Sure."

Liz watched her sister drive away then scurried to find a piece of sandpaper before the house revealed any more embarrassing secrets. Who ever said coming home made you feel *good*?

"GRANT!" LIZ PICKED UP the call on her cell phone as she pulled sandwich makings from the fridge. The deck demolition was harder work than she'd expected, and she was starved. "Hi! I was just making myself some dinner."

"It's only four-thirty."

"I skipped lunch."

"You know that's bad for your blood sugar levels." Liz was silent as she grabbed a bottle of Russian Dressing. To hell with calories, she'd worked hard all day. "Listen," he said, "I'm glad I caught you. We need to talk."

"Talk? Is something wrong? I sent the revised timeline you asked me to work up hours ago." She kicked the fridge door shut and tucked the phone under her chin so she could wash her hands.

"No. Things are good..." Grant paused, and Liz frowned. She got the sense this call wasn't his usual nightly check-in. For one thing, it was about four hours early.

"Listen," he said again. "Ethan asked me to join him tonight for this... function. It's a business thing."

"He didn't mention anything in his e-mail earlier. Are you meeting a client?"

"Uh, yeah."

Uh?

"Who? Do you need help preparing something?"

"No. No. I'm all set." He paused again, and Liz wiped her hands dry, waiting for him to continue. She folded the towel. Grant exhaled. "I wanted you to know... I've been thinking. About us."

"Us?"

"About how out of sync we've been lately. Let's face it. We've been so wrapped up in this merger the last few months, we've hardly had time for us. You've been distracted... irritable—"

"Irritable? I haven't—!"

"I'm not pointing fingers, Liz, and I'm not trying to pick a fight. I'm only saying... I know we've been talking about taking things to the next level. But, I think it's good you're home and... away for a bit. It'll give you a chance to see things from a fresh perspective. It'll give you some space. Some breathing room."

"I don't need..."

"It'll give us *both* some space."

Liz caught her breath. She swallowed. "You need space?"

"I'm only saying I think a little siesta will do us both some good. Then, when you come back—"

"What do you mean 'siesta'?" she asked.

"Don't be difficult, Liz. I'm trying to be understanding here. I'm trying to be patient. But, it's clear you're having trouble commit—"

"Trouble committing?" She interrupted. "But..."

"I don't want to get into this over the phone. It'll get us nowhere. Look, I'm sorry. I am. But, I've got to go. I've got that—thing, and I've got to get ready. I just wanted you to know I'll be gone for a couple, few days, okay? I'll call you early next week."

"*Next week?* Why—?"

"Liz," he sighed, "I've got to go. Enjoy the weekend, all right? All right?"

"Sure. I— You, too."

Liz pressed *end* and set her phone on the counter.

A siesta? Did he mean he wanted to take a break? And what did he mean she was having trouble committing? She wasn't having trouble committing! She was ready to commit! *Had* been ready to commit.

Unless it was Grant who needed the siesta.

Liz swallowed again and looked out the slider at where the deck used to be. Was he trying to tell her he was tired of waiting? But, *she* wasn't the one holding things up. He'd had bronchitis, and then they were busy with the merger. And, that night at his apartment... he couldn't blame her for *that!*

Liz frowned at the deli meat. True, she hadn't relented as Grant had pressed—ever more frequently—to consummate their relationship, but she wasn't the one reluctant to bring their romance into the open. In the nearly five months they'd been dating, not once had he dared ask her out even to the corner deli in case they were seen. As if Ames & Reed had spies lurking around every street corner ready to nab randy employees.

A siesta? Liz peeled a slice of swiss cheese from the package. It didn't sound like a restorative break. It sounded more like a stalemate in a buy-out negotiation, each side needing a leap of faith from the other before they would proceed.

You're waiting for Prince Charming to sweep you off your feet, marry you, and carry you off to your little white picket-fenced house, Trish had accused.

Liz shook her head as she laid the cheese on the bread, feeling like all her plans were like so many sheets of paper caught in a sudden gust of wind. Why was it up to her to stop everything from flying to pieces? Why was it up to *her* to think and plan and organize and *commit*? And what was Grant doing all weekend that he couldn't pick up a three-ounce cell phone and call until next week?

She didn't want a break or a siesta or whatever the hell he'd called it.

She didn't want time to *think*.

Why was it always her job to be the one who planned ahead? Followed through? Took responsibility?

Liz shook her head and slapped roast beef onto the cheese, even though it was entirely the wrong order in which to make a sandwich.

Whatever.

Trish had it wrong.

Liz wasn't waiting for Prince Charming to carry her away. She was just waiting to be carried away. Period.

There was a world of difference—and a pair of laughing, sexy green eyes—between the two.

HOMEWORK

History
- Chapters 10 + 11
- Review: Democracies vs. Republics

Lit: 2K Essay – Hamlet: Hero or Coward?

Math practice probs 1-32

Biology: Diagram mitosis

FOR PARTY:

Iron shirt

Shave legs

Pore cleaning strips

Polish Nails

Brush Velvet Flats

CHAPTER FOURTEEN

Twelve years earlier…

OH GOD! Oh God! Oh God! How did she get into these things?

Beth trailed after Valerie, her velvet flats scuffing on the hardwood floors of Jenny's house, the nylons in her bra growing sweaty and itchy against her skin. She dared not scratch, could barely breathe, as she tried to blend into the white-on-white color scheme of the Whitmeyer's newly-renovated kitchen.

The room smelled of cinnamon and apples like a Yankee Candle store, wholesome and welcoming except for the cold sweat dripping down between Beth's shoulder-blades as she waited for the others to do whatever it was they were going to do. She hung back by the door, while Valerie playfully positioned the participants—boy, girl, boy, girl—in a circle on the floor.

Beth grew a little light-headed from holding the air in her lungs and then it came out in a surprised whoosh as she noticed the lone figure standing in the far side of the room.

Ohmigod. Carter McIntyre.

He rested one shoulder against the refrigerator, a slight smirk on his features as he took a sip of soda from a can. At least, Beth thought it was soda. It was hard to tell now that Valerie had dimmed the overhead lights. Rain pounded outside, a steady drumbeat matching the pounding of blood in Beth's ears as she watched Carter. He had on that vintage motorcycle jacket he always wore, the one that creaked a little as he moved. He took another drink from the can, raised his head and caught her staring.

Beth felt a warm flush heat her cheeks, but she didn't look away. Couldn't have even if she tried. She smiled tentatively.

He winked at her.

Her smile froze on her face as she tried to figure out whether he was teasing her or flirting. It was so hard to tell. When he smiled and joked during their tutoring sessions, did it mean he liked her, or was he just taking pity on her?

She was sure her emotions were plastered over her face—the fawning attraction, the nervous self-doubt—and she wished she were bold and sexy and confident like the girls leaning into the guys on the floor, running their fingertips over the boys' arms in casual flirtation, laughing gaily, throats lifted up in invitation for who knew what.

Beth glanced across the room again. Carter's lips hitched up a little on one side and he took another drink. He looked away.

She swallowed, her cautious smile fading altogether as Valerie spied Carter loitering outside their little group. "Carter! No voyeurs! You have to play."

He took another sip. "I'm an odd man out." He gestured to the group on the floor. "I'd throw off your numbers."

"Oh, I'm sure we can find—Beth! Stop hiding in the corner!"

Beth pushed away from the wall. "I wasn't hiding," she lied. "And if Carter doesn't want to—"

"Nonsense!" Valerie popped up to grab Carter's arm playfully. "Carter's always up for a good time. Aren't you?"

Beth swallowed, her gut twisting as she knelt on the floor. The couple next to her shuffled aside to make room. She bit her lip, her gaze bouncing off of Carter's, Chip's, Jenny's.

Dan O'Connell, varsity everything, most popular boy in the junior class, stared at her chest for a long moment and then slowly met her eyes.

Beth flushed and looked away.

"Okay. We all know the rules." Valerie said as she spun the wine bottle on the floor with her index finger, expertly twirling it in a slow hypnotic circle. "Ladies first. Once the bottle has chosen, the lucky lady waits in the pantry for her seven minutes of heaven. Boys, no excessive licking or groping."

"Define 'excessive,'" Dan drawled as he ran a finger down Valerie's arm.

Valerie swatted his hand, and he let it fall to her thigh. Squeezed. "Oh," she said, "and most important—*no kissing and telling*. Half the fun is guessing who you're with." She batted her eyes at Dan and licked her hot pink lips until they glistened. "Shall we begin?"

Beth watched the bottle spin round and round, the rhythmic sound of it scraping against the floor causing her to clench her fingernails into her palms. She dared not look at anyone, particularly anyone *male* for fear they'd know she was thinking about being in the pantry with them. Which she was, of course.

The bottle slowed, growing uneven and wobbly. Then it stopped.

It pointed to her.

CHAPTER FIFTEEN

LIZ SWIPED THE LAST STROKE of mis-tint paint onto the front door and sighed. Much as she tried to make herself like it, it looked about as pleasant as old, dried-up mustard. Oh, well. She'd call it a base coat and buy something more attractive later if she had time.

She cleaned up her painting supplies and decided she'd better return her mom's calls. All four of them. After Grant's bombshell the day before, Liz hadn't felt like talking to anyone, but if she put it off too long her mom would probably send out carrier pigeons.

"How is Dad today?" Liz asked.

"Oh, as good as can be expected," her mom replied. "The man sharing his room, though, is in *terrible* shape. All these tubes and what-not! He was giving the nurses such a hard time about the lunch today, too. It's hospital food, I said to your father! Nobody expects it to taste *good*. But, no, the mashed potatoes were pasty, he said. What other texture would they be? Wait... are you on a landline?"

"Yes," Liz lied.

"Call the phone company, then, and have them check it. It's sounding staticky."

"Maybe a storm is brewing. That can do that sometimes."

"I didn't see anything on the Weather Channel."

"We might be in a radar blind-spot. Those exist. Anyway, *about Dad...*"

"Oh, he's doing as well as expected."

Liz waited for her mom to elaborate. She didn't. At least they'd established he was alive.

"So," Liz said, "Valerie Stinson stopped by yesterday."

"Oh, good! She said she'd list the house ASAP, you know. Such a nice girl. Married that Dan O'Connell, I think, right out of high school. Remember him? His mother had that dead tooth from that skateboarding accident? If you ask me, she should have known better at her age. Or maybe they've divorced. Makes no difference, because she's a hard worker, isn't she? She's really made something of herself. You've got to admire that."

Liz stared at the phone for a moment before putting it back to her ear. Were they still talking about Valerie? What about Liz? Hadn't she paid her way through college? Scraped by on ramen noodles and financial aid and strung-together work-study jobs? Where was *her* pat on the back?

"Yeah, Valerie's something all right," she said.

"I'll say so. Her mother had bunions, you know. Horrible. They stuck out like nobody's business. No surprise there. Comes from all that standing. But, she had those kids to support, so there was no getting around it." Her mom *tsk tsked* and Liz frowned, completely confused. She'd never heard a word about Valerie's upbringing except about how her dad was some big venture capitalist in New York or San Francisco or something, and every Christmas he used to send a giant FedEx box with video games and designer jeans for everyone.

It had sounded better then than it did now.

"You know, your dad will be so glad to finally have that patio done. What with his hip bothering him last fall—and the rain we had!—he wasn't able to get to any of the painting or odd jobs he'd wanted to get done before we left."

"I know," Liz said. "I'll do what I can." She sank into a chair at the kitchen table and looked around, her conversation with Valerie from the day before replaying in her mind. The run-down, weary state of affairs around the place made her think of how her father used to look at the end of a long shift, sitting in his recliner and watching the news.

Maybe the house had been weighing them down more than Liz ever realized. It was probably good for them to let go of all the maintenance and worry and cash-out while they could still enjoy life.

Life hadn't always seemed hard, but maybe she'd been too young to recognize the undercurrent of financial worry that seemed to dog her parents in later years. By her early teens, it was a constant refrain. "You have to apply yourself, John, or you'll end up in some dead-end job with nowhere to go but the grave!" Or, "If you're going to knock yourself up, Patricia, you'd better hope the father intends to support you, because they're cutting back your father's shifts again, and *we* won't be able to help."

"...it had a layer of mildew so thick you could *peel* it off," her mother was saying. Liz had no idea what her mom was talking about, because she'd stopped listening after her mom's neighbor pulled a rat out of her sink drain. Or maybe it had been a hair clog as *big* as a rat.

Liz sighed. She knew her parents were right to sell the house, but it depressed her to see it emptied of memories. Everything looked care worn and sad, as if the façade of their lives had been stripped away leaving them standing around in nothing but old, dingy underwear for all to see.

The cookie jar that had graced the counter for decades? Gone. The photo display of their childhoods that had lined the stairwell? Nothing but countless nail holes to fill and repaint.

"Why didn't you tell me you were planning to sell?" Liz cut in.

Her mother stopped. "It never came up."

"Never came up? That's the kind of thing, Mom, that doesn't come up in everyday conversation. Things like 'we're planning to sell the house' and 'your dad's having surgery' are the headlines you have to bring up to *have* a conversation about them."

"We're talking about it now."

"That's not the point." Liz stared morosely out the back slider and tried to remember what her point had been. Ever since she could remember her family had been horrible at communication. Like the time she'd been at college and nobody had thought to call and tell her Grandpa had died—for a full week. She'd only found out when Trish called to ask if she could borrow a black dress from Liz's closet because, *I've still got that baby fat and can't fit in any of my own.*

"Maybe my point is I might have wanted to be informed that the house I grew up in, the one Dad gutted and re-built with his own hands, was being put up for sale. Maybe I might have wanted the chance to see it one last time before you handed the keys over to some stranger."

"You're upset."

"I'm not upset! I'm just... stunned." *Okay, maybe a little upset.* "Why now? Why all of a sudden?"

"We've been talking of selling for years. You just haven't been around to hear."

Liz didn't reply. Was it true? In escaping all that had been less than comfortable during her teenage years—the unfulfilled crushes, the awkward social maneuverings, the time they had to send her brother away to juvie after he blew up the Dickenson's boathouse with an illegal stash of fireworks—had she turned her back on the good memories, too? Maybe she *had* walked away without a backwards glance. Still.

"I can't believe you got rid of Cookie Rooster," she sulked.

"Oh, stop. He's in the corner cupboard. I was going to give him to you last Christmas, but with all the hubbub with the new baby and those storms that kept you in Chicago, I forgot."

Truthfully, she'd been glad of the storms. It meant she didn't have to come up with a less credible excuse. Work had been busy, and she and Grant had been spending more and more time together.

"Listen," her mother said, cutting into her thoughts. "I've got to run. The orthopedist just came in."

Liz mumbled a goodbye, hung up and looked around at the counters with their faded, worn laminate and metal trim and dull, brown cabinets, functional and well-built, but no more attractive than when they'd been installed decades ago.

The funny thing was, ever since all those "Leave It To Beaver" reruns she used to watch with her dad, she'd always envisioned herself as an adult in this very kitchen—a modern-day June Cleaver wearing a cheery apron in her bright, retro-inspired domain, the scent of cookies filling the air.

Of course, her fantasy self had a husband with dark hair and green eyes. She would coolly handle running the kitchen, their household, and their two point two children—one boy, one girl plus a twinkle in her eye—as she juggled a satisfying professional career, respected and admired for her keen intellect.

Liz sighed and went to rinse her glass. That was a girl's fantasy of what adulthood would bring. Yes, she'd matured and grown more self-confidant, working hard to achieve financial security and a weight she wasn't embarrassed to fudge on her driver's license. But what did she have to show for it other than a healthy nest-egg for which she had no specific plans whatsoever?

Maybe Trish had been right after all.

Liz pushed aside the tired, faded café curtain over the sink and stared at the old orchard just beginning to brighten with small green leaves. The blossoms were mostly gone by now, their pale pink and white petals carpeting the ground.

She let the curtain drop back into place.

It wasn't that she actually thought she'd grow up to live the June Cleaver fantasy. It wasn't even that she believed the husband or the house or even the cookies would make her magically happy. The hard part about coming home, she realized, was that if it were so easy to up and take time off, if she were that quick to say 'yes, I'll come home,' then maybe the career, the relationships, the life she'd built elsewhere over the past decade weren't making her blissfully happy either.

She sighed again. Wonderful. She wasn't even thirty yet and she was having a mid-life crisis.

Liz swallowed and turned toward the room. It looked empty and dully sterile without the odds and ends of life to populate it. While she sent up a silent cheer that the hideous, harvest gold bicentennial canister set was nowhere in sight, it seemed like the home she'd thought she'd see one last time was already gone.

Bending low, Liz pulled Cookie Rooster out of the corner cupboard and placed him on the counter. His bright red and yellow plumage and portly belly never failed to cheer her.

Maybe because she'd spent so many days as a teenager baking chocolate chip cookies. She'd often hid in the kitchen, come to think of it. Cooking and imaging a rosy, idyllic future.

Liz ran her hand over Cookie Rooster. She hardly recognized herself since coming home. She'd gone from a Liz who ate quinoa and had an almost-fiancé to a Liz who ate swiss cake rolls and accepted dates with men who she'd fantasized about way more than she'd ever admit to.

It was enough to give anyone an identity crisis.

She repositioned Cookie Rooster to best advantage and made a mental note to add chocolate chips to her grocery list. And quinoa. Just in case.

CHAPTER SIXTEEN

THE OCCASIONAL SOFT GRUNTS drew his attention first. That and the denim cut-offs hugging Liz's hips as she attempted to clean the ceiling above the stove from the top of a stepladder. Carter tapped on the slider window with his knuckle and waved. Liz bobbled her sponge and stepped down to retrieve it, giving him a pleasant, albeit brief, view of her backside. She slid the door open.

"Carter! What are you doing here?" She smoothed her hair behind her ear, the faded Bates T-shirt she'd worn that first day pulling snug over her curves as she stepped back for him to enter.

"I ordered the wrong retaining wall blocks for another job, so I have some unplanned free time. Anyway, I know you said you'd take care of it, but it was such a nice afternoon, I thought I'd come help rip out the deck. I see someone beat me to it." He stepped into the kitchen from a cement block someone had set as a temporary step outside the door.

"I tore it out yesterday. You said you wanted to get started Monday, and I only have a couple of weeks before I've got to get back myself."

"*You* tore it out?"

"And I've got the muscle aches to prove it. It felt good to get rid of it though. It never suited the house."

Liz's tongue flicked over her bottom lip, and Carter's focus zeroed in on that one glistening spot. Her mouth looked soft, wide and full. He thought about how it'd feel under his.

"I could give you a back rub," he offered.

"A back rub?" She gave a short, nervous laugh. "That sounds like some bad pickup line from college."

She fiddled with the sponge, her breasts rising and falling beneath the thin fabric of her shirt. Carter wasn't entirely sure she was wearing a bra. The uncertainty spiked his pulse a notch. To hell with Grams and her admonitions. Maybe he just enjoyed women. Did everything in life have to be serious?

"That would presume I was trying to pick you up." He smiled.

"Of course you weren't." She turned abruptly to her bucket, dipping the sponge again. "*Idiot,*" she mumbled.

"Did you just call me an idiot?"

"*No!*" She whirled, water splattering the floor. "No. I was... talking to myself." Pink tinged her cheeks.

"You do that often?" He stepped over and took the sponge from her fingers, set it on the stove. He was so close now he could see the light freckles on the bridge of her nose. Somehow they were both endearing and strangely erotic. Liz was always girl next door appealing, but now... ten years later... she was a knock-out. Why had he never asked her out?

Probably because the girl he remembered hadn't glanced up from her college applications long enough to notice he'd had more interest in her than just passing trig.

"Not usually. No," she said.

"I get the feeling you don't think I'd be serious about giving you a pickup line."

"You wouldn't." He watched her swallow. "Would you?"

"Why wouldn't I?"

"I'm leaving in two weeks," she said, her eyes staring at his mouth.

"So, that just means I'd need to make it a really good pickup line. So we don't waste time. Right?"

Her eyes met his, wide, luminous, the soft hazel turning a shade of something that reminded him of skittish woodland creatures. "You're teasing me," she whispered, a mixture of wariness and anticipation warring on her features.

His tongue darted out to stroke over his lips. Was he? "Only if you want me to be," he replied, suddenly feeling quite serious. The blood thrummed in his veins, and if she stared at his lips like that one more second, he'd be forced to show her exactly how they tasted.

Her eyes darted away and she grabbed the sponge, sliding out from between him and the stove. "Well, as you can see, I've got work to do, and I'm sure you do, too, so I won't keep you." She was wringing the sponge out at the sink to within an inch of its life. "Thanks for stopping by. See you tomorrow? We still on for dinner?"

Carter nodded. If he hadn't made that promise to Grams, he would have pressed the advantage. It was obvious he had an effect on Liz Beacon, and the fact that she'd only grown into a body to match the appeal of her intellect did nothing to curb his desire for her.

But he couldn't treat Liz like other woman. For one thing, Liz had always treated him differently. She treated him as if he were smart. She'd taught him how to play chess and graph a parabola, and if he'd noticed somewhere along the line that she was pretty in a quiet sort of way, he hadn't wanted to mess up a good thing.

So why was he tempted to do so now?

"Just for the record, I'm told I give great back rubs. Should you ever need one," he said.

He had to tamp down the streak of lust that shot to his midsection as her gaze found his lips across the room.

"I'll keep that in mind," she murmured.

THE FOLLOWING EVENING, Carter stood at Liz's door, his hands behind his back as he elbowed the doorbell.

"I hope you like pot roast," Liz said as she swung the door wide.

Carter smiled. Her face was lightly flushed, and a few strands of hair had escaped her ponytail, curling sweetly at her temples.

"Love it. Here." He thrust his right hand forward. "I brought some wine for dinner. And, something for you." He held out his left hand.

"Oh, you didn't need—swiss cake rolls?" she laughed, taking the box from his outstretched hand.

"I think we pretty well decimated your supply the other night. I know not to get between a woman and her chocolate fix."

"A wise man." Her smile was cautious. "By the way, Bailey called. She had to cancel. Something's up with her father, so it's just us."

"Just us, eh?" He liked Bailey well enough, but he couldn't say he was upset by the news.

Liz licked her lips again and stepped back. "You should probably come in. Before Eddie makes a break for it."

"Oh. Right. How is he?"

"He mostly hides in the bedroom unless he's in the mood to escape."

"He's probably still getting used to being here."

"Could be. I keep wondering if I should have boarded him like Grant suggested."

"Grant?"

"A friend. In Chicago. Coworker, actually." Liz smoothed the wayward tendrils from her face and reached for the bottle of wine, avoiding Carter's gaze. "I'll go, ah, check on dinner."

Carter trailed her into the kitchen and inhaled the robust scent of roasting meat and vegetables. Tossed salad sat in bowls atop the counter, and there were some baked goods under a dish towel that looked suspiciously like cookies. "Smells like heaven. You didn't have to go all out like this, though. You're here to work on the house, not cook fancy meals. I know I suggested it, but I'm feeling a bit like a freeloader."

"You're not freeloading. I offered. I enjoy visiting with... old friends. Besides, I wouldn't call it fancy. Pot roast isn't hard to make, and I plan to eat the leftovers for days, so it's somewhat self-serving."

"Self-serving," he murmured as he settled at the kitchen table to watch. She lifted the lid and fragrant steam billowed out. His stomach growled. He jiggled his knee impatiently. "Want me to set the table?"

"Sure. That'd be great. The silverware—"

"I remember where it is." He jumped up, glad for something to do. Her gaze met his then skittered away. "Of course you do."

"So, this Grant guy... coworker you said?"

"Mm-hmm?"

"You wouldn't by chance be sleeping with him?"

The spoon she'd been testing the broth with clattered to the floor, little dots of pale gravy spattering the linoleum. "No! Of course not. Why would you even ask?"

He shrugged, pleased this Grant guy wasn't getting any. "Just wondering."

Liz swiped at the floor with a sponge, her slim khaki pants molding tight over her rear as she pounced on each little dot. "I fail to see how it would be any of your business even if we *were*—which we're not." She swept the sponge up a dribble on the table leg. "You know, maybe this wasn't a good idea. I'm sorry if I gave the wrong impression, but I—"

She stopped mid-sentence as his hand covered hers. "I can take it from here," he offered.

Her fingers flexed, then she slid her hand from under his, avoiding his gaze. "I don't know what I'm doing here."

"I believe you were cleaning the table leg."

She stood abruptly and tugged the hem of her shirt into place as she returned the sponge to the sink. "I'm being serious."

"So am I."

"You're making fun of me," she accused, turning to meet his gaze. "And I'm not the one who asked the inappropriate question."

"Inappropriate? I wasn't the one that got all flustered and red-faced when his name came up. An office romance, Liz? *Tsk. Tsk.* I thought you were smarter than that."

"I—" The stove timer dinged and she turned to pull a tray of biscuits from the oven. "I'm sorry to say this, but I think having you here is a mistake."

"Because I ask awkward questions or because you don't want to answer them?"

She pursed her lips and refused to reply.

"Aw, come on," he coaxed, grabbing the bottle of wine and inserting the corkscrew. "We're just old friends catching up, right? I'll behave and won't ask any more questions about your little interoffice flirtation, and we'll enjoy a nice, relaxing dinner together. What do you say?" The cork popped temptingly and he poured a splash of wine into two tumblers he'd found in the cupboard and held one out to her.

HOT GUYS I'D LIKE TO BE STRANDED WITH ON A TROPICAL ISLAND...

Bailey had no part in this. She wants that on the permanent record. She said she'd rather be stranded with a Swiss Army Knife.

So, if we all get stranded on an island together, I get first dibs.

Johnathan Taylor Thomas

Luke Perry

Leonard DiCaprio

(Titanic Leo, <u>Not</u> Man with an Iron Mask Leo)

NSYNC – But especially Justin Timberlake

George Clooney – I don't care if he's old!

Mr. BIG

CHAPTER SEVENTEEN

Twelve years earlier…

"I DON'T NEED TO GO FIRST."

Beth stared down the neck of the wine bottle like it was the barrel of a gun.

Valerie's annoyingly perfect, bow-shaped lips smirked. "Nervous?"

"No," Beth lied. "I just don't want to, ah, take the fun away from you guys."

"I'd kiss her," Rudy West piped up.

Beth's heart thudded hard in her chest. Rudy had thick, red hair and beefy lips and was on the wrestling team. Beth dared not meet his eyes, looking instead at his sausage-like fingers. She imagined them groping her up in the Whitmeyers' pantry. She swallowed over the lump in her throat and prayed no one would discover her nylon-enhanced boobs.

"Maybe it's her first time," Cindy Townsend murmured from across the circle. Beth turned toward Cindy and wondered what she'd ever done to have her say something so evil. Except Cindy didn't look like she was paying attention to torturing Beth seeing as Evan Rollins had his hand up the back of her shirt. As if no one could see!

Valerie rolled her eyes. "Come on, Beth. We're waiting. If you're not going to play the game…"

"I am," Beth said, standing up hurriedly. "Sure. Why not? Of course, I am." She laughed in what she hoped was a carefree, adventurous way so no one would suspect the icy dread slicking through her veins.

"This way," Valerie said, leading her out of the kitchen into a little back hall and an even smaller, dark room off of that.

The room was lined with shelves. Fancy pasta. Soup. A large stand mixer in the corner. Beth turned as Valerie unwound a long silk scarf from around her neck, revealing a giant purple hickey beneath. Beth stared at the hickey and then Valerie tied the scarf around Beth's eyes. It was still warm from Valerie's neck.

"Can you see anything?"

"No," Beth answered. And she wasn't lying. She'd hoped the gauzy scarf would have given her a little sense of the world beyond, even just the outline of a profile. But she saw nothing. Sensed nothing. Nothing but the faint scent of Valerie's perfume as she adjusted the scarf at the back of Beth's head. The idea that a boy would come in and touch her, kiss her, made Beth feel intensely vulnerable.

"No peeking," Valerie warned, her voice growing fainter as she moved away. "Have fun."

And then Beth was alone. At least, she assumed she was.

She swallowed, the fruit punch in her stomach making her slightly queasy as she stood there, waiting, wondering. She licked her lips and strained to listen outside the confines of the pantry, but Valerie had closed the door on the way out, so all Beth could hear were distant, muffled voices and the steady beat of pounding rain.

She had no sense of time. It had probably only been a couple of minutes since Valerie left, but it seemed like hours already.

A dog barked somewhere in the neighborhood. Beth wiped her mouth with her hand, then wiped her hand on her jean skirt. She stuck her hands in her pockets and then took them out again. What was she supposed to do with them anyway? Was she allowed to touch him? Would she want to?

The idea of kissing a pair of lips without touching anything else struck her as slightly ludicrous and a bubble of nervous laughter rose to her lips before she tamped it down again. God forbid he find her in the closet laughing to herself. He'd think she was unstable.

Maybe they all did.

Beth bit her lip.

Who was to say they weren't planning to leave her in here? Maybe they were all in the kitchen right now laughing their butts off because they'd tricked dorky Beth Beacon into standing in the pantry… waiting for her first kiss.

Beth fought back tears behind the blindfold.

What a fool she was.

There was a thump outside in the hall and she jumped, wringing her hands together. She let out a long, shaky sigh.

Oh God! She was an idiot for thinking she could do this! A fool for imagining she could fit in with these people and play a game where she didn't know the rules and couldn't imagine the stakes. All she knew about *that stuff* came from watching *Sex in the City* on the sly with the sound turned off, so she only knew half the story even then.

She let out another uneven breath.

She should start walking home *right now*. Forget about waiting for John. Forget about trying to preserve her dignity. She didn't belong here. Never would.

But just as she decided to reach up and remove her blindfold... the latch of the door snicked open.

CHAPTER EIGHTEEN

"TELL ME ABOUT your business. What's your specialty? How do you market yourselves? Are you into using eco-friendly materials? Where do you see yourself in five years?"

Liz and Carter had retreated to the corner of the living room after dinner to play a game of chess. Carter glanced up, his hand hovering over one of his pawns. "*Sheesh.* I haven't felt grilled like this since I got caught with Beth Peabody behind Old Man Richard's barn." He held her gaze. "Nothing happened."

"Yes, well, she's a lesbian. I could have told you that wasn't going to happen." Liz felt her face flush. "Anyway. I'm sorry. I didn't mean to come on so strong. It's just... stream-lining and improving business operations is what I do."

Carter shrugged and picked up his pawn. "We do a lot of hardscapes. I like building stone walls. Word of mouth, I guess." He paused. "What was that last one? Oh, yeah. Five years?" He blew out a breath. "Damned if I know." He set the pawn down again.

"You can only jump two spaces the first time you move your pawn."

Liz reached out to move his pawn back into position, inadvertently touching his hand as she did so. A warm tingle, not so much electricity as a sweet heat, infused her fingertips. She rubbed her fingers down her thigh under the table and picked up her tumbler of wine before she got the urge to touch him again.

He's too close.

Technically, he was a respectable distance away. Across the table, in fact, but the table was small, and if she wasn't careful, his knee would occasionally knock against hers, making her acutely aware of the earthy, richly masculine scent of him as he bent his head over the chess board.

He tapped his fingers on the side of his can of soda as he contemplated his move.

"Really, you don't have to over-think it," she said. "I haven't played in years. Probably you were the last person I played."

"How come?"

"Gr—That is, I really haven't had a lot of opportunities."

"Doesn't like chess, huh?"

"Who?" she evaded, knowing exactly who he meant.

"Your interoffice guy."

"He's not—Move your knight or I'll get him with my bishop."

"Thanks. You're blowing my concentration is all," he said amiably.

"Maybe you should concentrate on the game instead of trying to stir up gossip."

"You're not playing fair. You plied me with good food, liquored me up and now you're distracting me while I'm planning my next move."

"The wine is technically your fault, and I'm just sitting here."

He glanced up, his eyes sliding warmly over her face, pausing a moment at the base of her neck, leaving a trail of awareness wherever they lingered. "Like I said. Distracting."

Liz bit her lip and studied the board. No man should be blessed with lashes that thick and dark. She captured his other knight. Smiled. "I really do enjoy chess, though. Thanks for suggesting it."

"Of course you enjoy it. You're winning."

"As I recall, we used to be pretty evenly matched. That is, when you were paying attention."

"I'm paying attention." He took one of her pawns and picked up her wine tumbler. Took a sip.

"I thought you were done for the night," she commented, oddly excited by the small intimacy of having him drink from her glass.

"Not even close," he smiled.

She took his second rook.

"Ouch," he winced. "You're ruthless tonight."

"Not ruthless. Focused."

"I've always had a hard time with that." He leaned forward and captured her queen. "But sometimes I can pull it together. *Checkmate*, by the way."

"What?" Liz studied the board a moment then threw her hands up in defeat. "I can't believe it! You've got me!"

"*Ah*," he sighed. "Could you say that again? I so love hearing those words."

She threw him a glance as she cleared the board. "Please. Don't tell me you're still a gloater."

"A gloater? Would you deny me the pleasure of my victory? *Tsk. Tsk.* Don't tell me you're still a poor sport."

"I was never a poor sport. I just enjoy winning more than losing."

He grinned and finished her wine. "So do I."

The air in the room sparked with awareness as Carter held her gaze. She didn't think they were talking about chess anymore, but it was hard to tell. He had a perpetual air of casual indifference which made it nearly impossible to tell whether he was serious.

She set the chess set on the shelf and smoothed her shirt.

"Well. It's getting late. I should probably go," he said, rising from the table. "Thanks for dinner. It was terrific."

"You're welcome. Did you want any cookies? For the road, I mean?"

"You have to ask?"

"I'll be back in a minute." Liz hurried to the kitchen, pulled a plastic bag from the drawer and filled it with cookies.

"You spoil me."

Liz jumped as Carter reached from behind her to take the bag of cookies. Good heavens, the man moved like a cat.

She smoothed her hair and darted a glance at the kitchen clock. *9:53?* How did it get so late? "When will I see you again? I mean, when do you expect to start on the patio?"

Carter swallowed a bite of cookie he'd snitched from the bag. "Weather allowing, tomorrow work for you?"

"To—" The ring of her cell phone interrupted. Liz jumped and pulled her phone from her pocket. She set it face down on the table. "I'm sorry."

"Do you need to get that?"

"No. It'll go to voicemail. I can call back. So, tom—?" Again, the phone rang.

"Go ahead and pick up. I know my way out."

Liz nodded and picked up the phone. She followed Carter to the living room. The front door clicked shut as she answered the call. "Grant! You're back! Hi… Sorry. I was just... away from the phone for a moment."

"I thought I might have had the wrong number. So, did you get the e-mail I sent you on N.S. Utilities?"

"Not yet. I haven't checked e-mail since this morning. I thought you—"

"Liz?" Liz spun around to find the front door open again, Carter poking his head around the jamb. "Thought you might want to know your brother's here."

"My—?" She turned back to the phone. "I'm going to have to call you back. John's just arrived."

"Is that who I heard in the background?" Grant asked.

"No. That was... *yes!* Right. My brother. I really should go. I'll call you later?"

"Check your e-mail, Liz. I need your input before the meeting tomorrow."

"I'll check it before I go to bed. Promise."

Liz hung up and walked to the door.

"Your folks?" Carter asked.

"Business call."

Carter's eyes met hers. "Kind of late for business."

Liz ignored the comment as she watched her brother negotiate the steps at the end of the walk. She paled. John was clearly intoxicated or... something.

"Thanks for coming," she said too brightly, hoping Carter would take the hint and leave. Like *now.*

Instead, he leaned closer, the warm brush of his body making her jump. "Do you need help?" he asked.

"Why would I need help?"

"For one, I think your brother's pissing on the mailbox."

Liz sucked in a mortified breath and clenched her eyes shut. "He's not," she gasped.

"Nope. Sorry. My mistake. It's the bird bath."

She turned from the driveway as tears of humiliation burned the back of her eyes. *"Please go,"* she said.

"I would, but I've been meaning to talk with your brother for a couple weeks now. Seems as good a time as any to catch up.

"And besides, his car is blocking mine."

HIGH AS A KITE.

Carter watched Liz's brother more or less re-zip his fly. Who knew what John had ingested, smoked, or shot himself up with this time? Better to stick around a bit to make sure Liz didn't need the help she'd already declined.

Carter pasted a benign grin on his face and waved. "Hey, John! Long time no see!"

John spun around slowly, a bewildered expression crossing his face as he squinted toward the front stoop.

"It's Carter. Carter McIntyre."

John stumbled up the path and stopped. He frowned at them. "Carter? Beth? Whaddr you doin' here?"

Liz gaped at her brother, her nose wrinkling as he approached, then seemed to recover her composure. "I'm on vacation. Helping mom and dad clean up the house. What are *you* doing here?"

"Need to crash," John mumbled, his face turning slightly green in the pale porch light. "Feeling a little... off."

Liz's eyes shot to Carter. "He can't drive in this condition," she murmured in alarm.

"He got here," Carter muttered back. "But you're right. Do you want me to take him home?"

John swore and they looked toward him. "Can't go home," he mumbled. "No more. No more..."

Liz let out a short breath. "He'll have to stay I guess."

Carter helped John negotiate the threshold, grateful he wouldn't be risking his truck's upholstery. "Where do you want him?"

"The couch? I don't think stairs are a good idea. I'll get some old sheets to put on it, though. Just in case."

Carter nodded and helped John sit so he could take off his shoes. John was so far gone, he only mumbled incoherently from time to time. It was a miracle the guy had made it there in the condition he was in.

Liz returned with an armload of bedding and began to spread sheets over the sofa. She wrinkled her nose again as Carter helped John collapse onto the makeshift bed. "He positively reeks. Do you think we should take him to the hospital?"

"No. I think he'll sleep it off."

She nodded and allowed Carter to lead her away. She looked pale, worried. And deeply embarrassed.

"I'm so sorry." The apologies started pouring out of her as soon as she stepped into the kitchen. "You shouldn't have to see this. Or deal with this—"

"Neither should you," he interrupted.

She nodded then, an abrupt movement, her lips a taut line.

"You know this doesn't reflect on you, Liz. You don't have to explain it away."

"I know." She said the words, but he could see she felt she were somehow responsible for her brother's actions. Her eyes met his. Grateful. Weary. "Thanks for helping."

"No problem." He shuffled from foot to foot, unwilling to leave. Unwilling to leave her looking so... lost. "Will you be all right? I can stay if you want."

"I'll be fine."

He doubted she'd sleep a wink, but there wasn't much he could do about that. "Does eight o'clock work for you? I usually start earlier, but considering—"

"Eight o'clock is fine."

He walked to the slider, not wanting to remind either of them of the unpleasant reality lying on the living room couch and wished he could recapture the easy camaraderie they'd shared earlier. "Thanks again for dinner."

She nodded and her fingers brushed his arm. It warmed him in ways he couldn't explain. "Carter?"

"Mmm?"

"I'm glad you came. I had a good time tonight. Before—"

"Me, too." He flashed her a smile and inclined his head fractionally. He wanted to kiss her. To be honest, he wanted to do much more than kiss her. And, for a moment, he almost gave in to the impulse to take that half step forward and lose himself in her full, soft mouth. Instinct told him she wouldn't push him away.

Common sense told him they'd both regret the timing.

Swallowing his disappointment, Carter reached up to brush a strand of hair from her temple. His thumb lingered on her cheek, drawing an idle circle. He wouldn't draw her to him, he told himself. He wouldn't take advantage.

He gave her a half smile and dropped his hand. "Goodnight."

"Goodnight," she replied. Her eyes filled with some emotion he couldn't name as she took a step back, but then her hand snaked out at the last minute to grab his arm. "Wait! You can't leave!"

He stopped, relieved. He didn't have to feel guilty after all. If Liz wanted it, too...

"You need to move John's car, remember? I'll get his keys."

Carter bit his lip. "Right. Thanks for reminding me."

"SHIT."

Liz winced as her brother's hoarse curse colored the morning air. There were a couple thumps and grunts in the living room, a few more curses, then the kitchen door opened abruptly. John stood, wavering and bleary-eyed, blinking at her. "Beth? What are you doing here?"

"Making breakfast."

He made a grunt of acknowledgement as he wandered in and slumped into a chair, eyes bloodshot, skin ashen. "I guess I'll have whatever you're having."

Liz pursed her lips and slid the over-easy eggs she'd been cooking onto a plate next to toast then turned to hand it to her brother.

He paled. "On second thought..."

Served him right. She set the plate at her own setting and sat in front of it then took a sip of coffee and watched John scan the counters with hooded eyes.

He hoisted himself from his seat, helped himself to a couple of cookies then pulled a carton of milk from the fridge. He didn't bother with a glass.

He sat down again, and his head sank to the table.

"So what are you doing here?" she asked after a bit, unsure whether he was still conscious.

He lifted his head and wiped a hand over his eyes. "Visiting," he said. "Long time no see."

"You're not here to see me. You had no idea I was here."

"Can't a brother be glad to see his kid sister?" He took a bite of cookie, but at her look, he sighed. "Okay. I came to crash. Had a rough night...." He let his words trail off as he half-heartedly swiped cookie crumbs off his shirt onto the floor and stared at the floor as if it had severely disappointed him.

"Real rough. I should have called the cops on you. Drinking and driving? You're thirty years old, John!"

"Stop yelling. It's giving me a headache."

"Stop yelling? You could have killed someone! You could have killed yourself!"

"Relax. I haven't had a drink in months. And I didn't drive drunk." He frowned, concentrating. "I remember stopping at that store... and then driving here. I was listening to that song, you know? The one about the Pina Coladas? I hate that song. So I opened a beer... Next thing I know I'm waking up on the couch with some cat from The Walking Dead staring down at me."

"You got soused sitting in your car in the driveway? Don't you have a place of your own?"

He grimaced and took a swig of milk. "I'm between places right now. Been staying with a... friend off and on." He sighed and wiped his face again. "But, that's not working out anymore."

Liz made a mental note to get fresh milk. "Well, just so you know, you'll have to find another place to crash going forward. Mom and Dad are selling the house."

"Huh," he grunted by way of reply. He took another half-hearted sip of milk and stuffed another cookie in his mouth. "Got anything else? Other than," he waved at her plate, "those?"

"Just some leftover pot roast."

"Surprisingly, that sounds really good right now. Do you mind?" Liz shrugged, and John rummaged in the fridge, taking out containers and sniffing the contents as if they'd been in there long enough to go bad. "Is my memory playing tricks on me, or was Carter McIntyre here last night?"

"He was here."

"Wasn't interrupting anything was I?"

Liz shoved the eggs to the side of her plate. Somehow, they'd lost their appeal. "No, you weren't interrupting anything. He came for dinner. He's putting in a patio for Mom and Dad. We were just catching up."

"*Hmm.*" John loaded a plate with pot roast and shoved it in the microwave.

Liz gathered her dishes and set them in the sink. "When you're done eating all my food, you know your way out."

"Oh, come on, Beth. I could really use—"

"Your car keys are in the vase on the mantle." At John's perplexed expression, she continued. "For some reason that escapes me now, I thought it best you not drive last night."

"Beth?"

"What?"

He heaved a sigh, his eyes inexplicably watery. "Don't you want to stick around a bit? Catch up?"

Liz paused in the doorway, resentment rising in her throat as the pot roast spattered the inside of the microwave. She swallowed. "I think we've done all the catching up I'm in the mood for."

He nodded, grimaced again. "Sure. But... before you go..." He glanced guiltily up and away. "...could you loan me a little cash?"

With a sound of disgust, she left the room.

She needed air.

What was *wrong* with him? Didn't he even care that Mom and Dad were selling their childhood home? And how could he sit there and make innuendos, eat all her food, and try to bum money off her when he still reeked of his binge from the night before?

Impulsively grabbing her coat, Liz shoved her feet into sneakers and stalked out the front door. She closed it firmly behind her and stopped for a moment on the front steps to let the morning sun wash over her.

She swallowed, unclenched her jaw and reminded herself to breathe. Her brother and his life choices weren't her problem anymore.

Liz took another deep breath and glanced at her watch. *8:42. Hmm.* So much for Carter arriving by eight. She wouldn't give him a hard time about being late today. With any luck, it'd give John a chance to clear out before he made any more comments that would only embarrass her and taint the enjoyment of an innocent evening with an old friend.

She started down the driveway when classical music sang out from her coat pocket. Liz popped open her phone.

"Hello?"

"Liz, it's Grant! Where the hell have you been? I texted you a question an hour ago and the stakeholder meeting is in *ten minutes!*"

"Sorry. Something... came up."

"Are you avoiding me? Is this about that personal matter we talked about a few days ago? If so…"

"No! Of, course not. That's— we'll talk. Like you said."

"Okay. Good. Sorry. I'm just stressed. Ethan asked me to justify the timetable you set out for implementing the new CSR software and you didn't put that info anywhere in the presentation, I didn't—"

"It's in the appendix."

"It is? Oh, thank God. Okay. Great. I just need to know one other thing then…"

A familiar pickup rounded the corner at the end of the drive.

Liz listened to Grant with half an ear. She replied on autopilot, then ended the call, more grateful than she should have been to see a particular dark-haired contractor bearing nothing but a coffee tray and a smile.

Lord, she needed a break.

"Good morning." Carter's voice cut into her thoughts as he grabbed a bag in his other hand and kicked the truck door closed.

Liz's heart skipped a beat. "Good morning."

"I see John's still here."

"He's leaving soon."

"I brought doughnuts." Carter waved a bakery bag temptingly.

"Don't bring them inside unless you plan to share. The freeloader masquerading as my brother is still emptying the fridge."

Carter winced and waved her over to his pickup. "I've got just the picnic spot then." He pulled down his tailgate and spread his jacket over the end. "Hop up."

With a tentative nod of agreement, Liz scrambled onto the tailgate and accepted one of the coffees he handed her. "I have coffee inside," she said, even though she took the cup. Hot, fragrant steam tickled her nose.

"Yes, but your coffee is inside... and we're here. This is much better."

"How?"

"Coffee consumed in the sunshine always tastes better." A smile teased the corners of his mouth.

"Is that so?"

"Try it. You'll see."

She took a tentative sip, her heart fluttering in her chest as he watched her. "You may be onto something here."

"Either that or it's the company." He winked.

Her heart did another flip-flop. The man was far too free with his flirtatious expressions, not that she was complaining. "Definitely the sunshine," she said, grinning into her cup. "So what's in the bag?"

Carter hopped onto the tailgate beside her. "Not telling until you pay the toll."

His thigh brushed hers casually, sparking an answering heat. She didn't move away. "The toll?"

"I get a chess rematch after lunch."

"Why would you want a rematch? You won."

"I'm just trying to be fair. You were all tipsy on wine and on the verge of a chocolate chip cookie coma when we played last night. I was virtually taking advantage of you." A smile played around his lips as he eyed her over his coffee.

"Taking advantage, huh?" Liz tugged the bag from his fingers. Dear heavens, what would it be like for this man to actually take advantage of her? She peered into the bag to hide the blush coloring her cheeks. "Tipsy, you say? Okay, buster, you're on. Though, I warn you now. Lunch may be take-out given the way my brother was inhaling the leftovers."

"Even the pot roast?"

At Liz's nod, Carter scowled. "I hope you don't take this the wrong way, but I won't be sorry to see him leave."

"You're not the only one," she said, sinking her teeth into a chocolate-covered doughnut. "You're not the only one."

CARTER RESTED HIS ELBOW on his shovel as he watched John walk down the front walk. The guy was barely over thirty, but his gaunt features and weary bearing made him look a decade older.

Maybe now was a good time to get a bottle of water... and some information. Carter headed toward his pickup. "You heading out?"

"Yeah." John paused. What was probably meant as a grin twisted his features.

Carter eyed John's car. Rust holes dotted the bottom of the door. "How are things going these days? Working?"

John eyed him warily as he pulled a cigarette from his shirt pocket and lit it. "Getting by."

"I hear you." Carter leaned amiably against the side of John's car. "Didn't know you were still in the area. Haven't seen you around much."

"Oh, you know." John blew some smoke toward the trees and shrugged. "I've been... away. Sort of a vacation. Seeing some friends. You know how it is."

"Sure." Carter smiled and reached into his pocket for a mint. Popped it into his mouth. According to the local rumor mill, the last vacation John had taken had been a stint in the county jail, but Carter wasn't anyone to point fingers. He'd made his share of bad choices over the years.

There was a time they'd hung out together. Cruising around town. Sharing a few beers at the old quarry. It seemed a lifetime ago now.

"So, you, ah, doing okay?" Carter asked after a bit. "You were in rough shape last night."

John took a long drag and toed the ground in front of him. "I've been better."

"Surprised the crap out of your sister."

John grimaced. "Sorry about that. I got some bad news is all. Shook me up."

He took a long drag and exhaled slowly through his teeth.

Carter rolled the mint around on his tongue. "Say, you wouldn't happen to know a guy named Rick Mercer, would you?"

John frowned and took another drag. "Why?"

"Just thought you might have run into him. He hangs out at Lucky's sometimes, heard he had quite the party a week or so ago." He hadn't heard a thing, but he had a sense it was true.

"What kind of party?"

"You know. Just like old times." Carter bit into his mint with a crack and flashed a grin.

John frowned, crushing his cigarette under his heel. "Kind of got the impression you weren't into that anymore."

Carter shrugged and swallowed the mint. It tasted sharp on his tongue. "I enjoy a good time now and again."

It was eerie how easily it came back, the friendly banter, the unspoken exchanges. It shocked him how quickly he fell into the rhythm of it, how natural it still felt after so many years. He could be seventeen again, standing in the rain behind a beat up Chevette and bumming a cigarette and a beer off Beth's older brother.

By the time John was on his way, Carter had all he'd hoped for right in his back pocket. There was someone he needed to talk to. Someone who needed to realize he was being given a second chance before it was too late for him, too.

CHAPTER NINETEEN

"YOU ARE AWARE THERE is a grocery store in town, right?" Carter's cousin, Jim, frowned as Carter pulled a container of cole slaw out of the refrigerator and set it next to the sandwich makings already there. Yes, Carter knew there was a grocery store, but, truth be told, it was boring sitting at home eating by himself. And Jim's wife, Kate, had fallen into the habit of inviting him over for dinner on the days she did admin tasks for the landscaping business at Carter's home office.

"I'm helping Kate with dinner. Plus she invited me."

"You do realize she only asks you over out of pity. She sees how you live."

"And you only allow it because it gives you an ego boost to show off your beautiful wife and family. Admit it. You think you're hot shit."

Jim reached over Carter for a soda, popped it open and relaxed into a chair at the kitchen table. "There is that. Where is my lovely bride anyway?"

"Upstairs giving Lily a bath. I think Liam is helping."

Jim eyed the ceiling warily. "She hasn't called for reinforcements?"

Carter tore open a bag of sub rolls. "Not yet."

Jim sipped from the can and set it down, lord o' the manor style, on the table. "So, what about you? Got the itch to get yourself a wife and family of your own?" He swept his arm to encompass the dishes in the sink, the toy cars on the floor and the burpie cloths stacked on the placemat in front of him. "Just think, all this grandeur could be yours."

A loud *thump!* rattled the ceiling above them, and Liam, the three year-old squealed something about Noah and floods.

Carter nodded toward the doorway. "You want to check that out?"

Jim bit his lip. "No. I'm good. I have every confidence in my wife. Plus, that upstairs bath is too small for all of us at once. I can't believe we're a family of four sharing a single bathroom."

"Ah, way to sell the grandeur of it all."

Jim laughed, an easy chuckle, and Carter felt a momentary stab of… something. It seemed like everyone was getting married, starting families, growing up. Jim's sister, Rachel, had her first baby just after the new year, and Lily had been born barely a month ago.

The grandmothers, of course, were ecstatic.

Carter was close enough to Jim and Kate to know the road hadn't always been easy for them, and day-to-day life wasn't necessarily smooth or flood-free, but he knew they were happy in a way few people were.

Maybe that kind of happy was only for some people. Jim was different. He was the responsible guy everyone turned to when they needed to get out of trouble. Carter was the guy they called when they wanted to have fun.

Or he *had* been that guy.

He thought about Liz and her brother and realized it had been quite some time since he'd been *that* guy, either. And yet, when the crap hit the fan down at the fire department, he'd been the first one Ted had turned to when he started pointing fingers. It didn't matter what Carter was now. It only mattered he had the reputation of being *that* guy...

Another *thump!* followed by a door slamming, the sound of running feet and more doors slamming came from upstairs.

"There's no room for the towels in the bath," Jim explained. "That was probably Liam getting one from our closet."

Carter shook his head. "I know you love this place, but you should build a bigger house."

"I've been talking to your brother about that very thing. He's been talking again about buying the lot up on Blackberry Hill."

"Not for Ian. For *you*. What does Ian need a house for? All he needs is a laptop and an internet connection. He doesn't even have a cat."

"His accountant said he should own rather than rent for the tax deduction. And who knows, maybe he's thinking about settling down. Grams seems to think you both should."

"Grams is a hopeless romantic. Thanks to you and Rachel, she has babies on the brain."

"She told Kate she thought there was a possibility of you connecting with Beth Beacon when she's in town." Jim waggled his eyebrows. "Who knows? Maybe Beth is *The One*."

"Are you kidding? I've been to her house all of three times since she's been back. How would I know?"

Jim shrugged. "Is the sex good?"

Carter raised an eyebrow. "Funny you should ask, because even though I've known her over ten years, not once have we slept together."

"Astounding."

"I know. How long was it before you and Kate slept together?"

Jim cleared his throat, then stood and began to load dirty dishes into the dishwasher. "I think that's irrelevant."

"Oh, that's right. You knocked her up within like a week of meeting her, didn't you?"

Jim paused. "In my own defense, my wife is smokin' hot."

Carter rolled his eyes as Jim nodded in sudden understanding. "Oh. Beth must have a terrific personality."

Carter laughed as he stuffed pastrami into the sandwich rolls. They both knew 'terrific personality' was code for 'unattractive.' "Actually, she's a knock-out."

"I'm confused. I thought Grams said she was single. And she hasn't fallen into bed with you? You're losing your touch."

"Single. Attractive. In town. I know. Who would have guessed you could put this," Carter gestured to himself, "in the same room with a hot woman and in ten years we *still* haven't had sex?"

"Mind boggling. But you're planning to, I take it."

"Hoping is more the word I'd use," Carter corrected as he reached for the chips as an image of Liz's full, soft lips popped helpfully to mind. "Definitely hoping."

"You're really superficial, you know that?"

"That's not superficial. It's honest. And you're one to talk. At least I'm not walking around chasing widows with kids."

"I didn't single Kate out like that. It was... chemistry," Jim tidied the kitchen counter around Carter and stuffed the chips bag back in the cupboard.

Carter chuckled. "Like cold fusion chemistry. The next thing you know you'll be telling me you knew when you first locked eyes with Kate that she was *The One*."

"It's not like that."

"No?"

"It's more like a fog that creeps in and before you know it, you're socked in."

"Nice metaphor."

"Thanks."

"So, Kate is a menacing weather front now and not the love your life?"

"I don't even know why I talk to you."

"I keep you on your toes. Besides, we're family. It's like super glue. Once stuck, nearly impossible to shake off.'

"Nice metaphor."

"Thanks. So, about Kate, and I'm genuinely curious here, why Kate? Aside from the fact that she's—"

"What am I?" Kate asked as she padded into the kitchen with the baby splayed over her shoulder. Her T-shirt was soaked, she was missing one sock, and water dripped from the right side of her hair.

"Gorgeous," both men said at once.

"You guys are such suck-ups. I love you." She leaned in toward her husband for a quick kiss. "And I'd love *you* if you'd watch Liam for some male-bonding time while I mop up the bathroom floor and change."

"What am I? Chopped liver?" asked Jim.

"No. You're holding Lily." She handed over the baby.

"Are we still calling her 'Oops'?" Carter asked as he brought plates and cole slaw to the table.

"Not to her face," Kate murmured. "And by the way, I think I feel a chill in the air." She turned a raised brow toward her husband. "You might want to check the forecast."

Jim winced. "You heard that, huh?"

"I heard you stuff your foot in your mouth, yes. I haven't heard you pull it out yet."

He stepped closer to her. "You truly want to know the first time I knew you were different from all those other women I've never dated?"

"Yes. Tell me."

Jim smiled at his wife. "Chicken raft."

"Really?"

"Really."

"Get a room, you guys," Carter said, but Jim just laughed and hugged his wife over their baby, swept his arm behind her back and silently mouthed, *this could all be yours.*

Symptoms of ADHD:

- Impulsivity
- Distractibility
- Excitability and/or Excessive Anxiety
- Dreaminess/Inattention/Lack of Focus
- Fidgeting/Restlessness/Can't sit still
- Self-medicating: smoking, sugar, caffeine
- Bored easily
- Makes careless mistakes
- Quick tempered/defiant
- Loses or misplaces things/loses track of time
- Difficulty remembering things
- Difficulty following instructions
- Interrupts/Blurts things out/Acts without thinking
- Difficulty maintaining control of strong emotions

CHAPTER TWENTY

———————————

LIZ MOANED, rolled over and tried to ignore Eddie as he insistently poked his paw at her cheek, hoping she'd get up and serve him breakfast. No doubt the rustling noises and occasional clang of metal outside were the sweet sounds of progress. A quick peek at the clock told Liz it was barely seven a.m.

She groaned. Despite falling into bed some time after midnight, she had work to do. Sliding out of bed, she did a few stretches to get the kinks out of her lower back then padded to the window.

She slid the curtain aside. Carter was in the driveway lifting supplies off the tailgate of his pickup, the muscles in his lightly tanned forearms flexing with the effort. Her skin tingled, as a warm flood of purely feminine appreciation washed over her.

She frowned.

She shouldn't be noticing his forearms. Or tan. Or musculature of any kind.

She let the curtain drop back into place and headed toward the bathroom. She should be showering and getting on with the business at hand. Like checking her e-mail for the morning. And making sure Grant didn't need any clarification on the spreadsheet she'd sent before falling into bed the night before.

She had no business checking out Carter like he was the pool boy. It was unseemly. Unprofessional. Un—

A loud *thunk* from outside had her rushing back to the window. A heavy looking machine was on the ground beside a trailer. Carter was frowning and swearing at the machine, or so it appeared, and rubbing his shin. She must have made some noise of alarm, because he glanced up and caught her eye.

He waved hello.

Liz waved back automatically then leapt from the window with a groan. *Perfect.* She'd just waved good morning to the guy she wasn't supposed to be having inappropriate thoughts about—wearing nothing but a T-shirt and panties!

She let out a quick breath and told herself she was being ridiculous. He probably hadn't even noticed she wasn't wearing pants. She would just put on some sweats, finger-comb her hair and go get her coffee like every other morning. No need to worry about her appearance. Carter was here to work, not socialize.

Liz had her hand on the bedroom doorknob then turned toward the bathroom.

It couldn't hurt to brush teeth. Brushing teeth was simply good hygiene.

It had nothing to do with the last dream she had before waking up— a dream of kissing a sexy, dark-haired man in the rain.

"HELL-O," CARTER MURMURED under his breath as he straightened again, the bruise on his shin forgotten. "And good morning to you, too."

An appreciative smile creased his face as he maneuvered the compactor to the side of the driveway and began loading hand tools into his wheelbarrow. A sight like that could bring more cheer to a man's morning than a cup of coffee and a sunny day combined.

Carter pushed the wheelbarrow to the backyard and plugged an old radio into the outdoor socket. He waved to Liz through the slider as she got her morning coffee and counted himself a lucky man. He'd be doing this job alone.

Normally, he'd bemoan the lack of a second pair of hands. Certainly having help would have prevented the bruise to his shin from the compactor as it slid off the side of the trailer's ramp, but a bruise was a small price to pay to spend an extra day or so on the job. Not that Pops would have been much help unloading the compactor anyway.

Carter turned as Liz opened the patio door.

"Did you want some coffee before you get started? You can drink it in the sunshine."

Carter held up the travel mug he'd filled at home.

Her smile faded. "I guess you're all set."

"Can I take a rain check?"

"Of course. There's water in the fridge. You know where the coffee pot is. Help yourself. Whenever. Just don't let Eddie out."

"I'll be careful."

"Well, if you need anything, let me know."

He felt a gut punch of desire as her teeth worried her lower lip. His mind worked in overdrive to think of a reason to keep her there. She looked sexy as hell, like she'd just rolled out of bed. "Actually, if you don't mind, I could use a hand with screeding later. Pops is at the chiropractor's again."

She gave a half smile. "That presumes I know what 'screeding' means."

"Leveling the sand with a straight edge before I start laying the pavers."

"Oh. Sure. I'd be happy to help. Sorry about your uncle. Is it serious?"

He shrugged. "An old back injury, it's just been acting up lately. He had it operated on back when I was in college, but it got infected. Pretty nasty."

"My God, that's awful! And, when you're self-employed, there's no workman's comp to fall back on."

He nodded, impressed she understood. "I did what I could to keep things going until he was back on his feet."

"But you were in college. How did you—?"

"I quit. Heck, probably wouldn't have made it through anyway, right?" He flashed a grin and took a long slug of coffee, ignoring the sympathetic, curious expression on her face. "Well, back to work. I'll let you know when I need that extra hand." Unfortunately, she wasn't done.

"Why didn't you go back to college? When your uncle was better?"

"What was the point?"

"But, I thought you were getting your business degree. Certainly it made sense—"

He laughed without humor. "No need when I'm working off my back."

"Don't sell yourself short. You've got so much potential. Your business, I mean."

"I've got plenty of work. No degree needed." He walked over to retrieve a roll of mason's line that had rolled under his wheelbarrow.

"Yes, I'm sure you do," she said, trailing after him. After a moment, she said, "But after our conversation the other night, I had some ideas on how to strategically grow the business, really make a brand for yourself. I'd love to share them with you. Not that you're not doing fine as you are, but I was thinking there's such an opportunity here for you to capitalize on the eco-building materials/hardscape niche.

A denial sprang reflexively to the tip of his tongue, but she pressed on. "Think of the clients who have the money to do those sort of projects; they're the same clients who can afford to go green, right? Some selective advertising in local home and building publications… a carefully prepared photo portfolio of past projects…"

A carefully prepared portfolio? Where did she come up with this stuff? He looked at her, and she paused. "Anyway," she said, giving a small, self-conscious laugh, "only if you're interested."

He straightened, ready to tell her 'thanks, but no thanks,' but then her tongue darted out to wet her lips, and he felt something in him soften. "I'm interested. Potentially." He felt himself smile. "Can't hurt to talk."

She grinned. "Great. I look forward to it. Well." She bit her lip. "I should let you get back to work."

But she didn't go.

He glanced up. She looked uncertain for a moment. "I wanted to mention," she said, "what you did the other day for Ben... that was really nice." Carter frowned. "You know. When you made him feel okay about chipping the paver? I just wanted you to know, I thought it was sweet of you."

"We all chip things now and again. I've chipped enough pavers for ten people combined over the years."

"I suppose you're bound to in this business." She chuckled, but then paused, a considering look on her face.

Carter shrugged. "Or maybe I'm just careless." He took a sip of coffee.

"I didn't mean—"

"It's all right. We're not in tenth grade anymore. It's not like I won't graduate if I chip a few pavers, so we don't have to dance around the obvious. Precision isn't my strong suit."

"*Mmm,*" she said, although he got the sense she wasn't listening.

"Mmm?"

She blinked and looked at him. "Wh—? Oh." She chuckled, a short awkward sound. "I was just thinking."

A notepad fell out of Carter's pocket and he bent to pick it up. "About?"

"About your carelessness and... *hmm*... how you lose track of time."

Carter rose. "How I what?"

"...how much sugar and caffeine you ingest...." They both stared at the travel mug in his hand.

Liz continued, obviously on a roll. "Are you aware you have a dozen of those little notepads, but you never seem to remember where you've left them? That you have a tendency to act impulsively? And you fidget more than the average person? Back in high school it was all you could do to stay focused sometimes when I tutored you." She exhaled and made a helpless gesture with her hands. "Look, Carter, what I'm trying to say is..."

He blinked, still reeling from the list she'd just rattled off.

She put her hands on her hips and looked at him matter-of-factly. "What I *am* saying is: You might have ADHD."

"I might have *what?*"

She swallowed. Flushed. "Look, I was up until after midnight gathering information for my sister. I've read the web sites. I don't know why I didn't see it sooner. You have ten out of ten symptoms." She frowned. "Except oppositional defiance. You don't score high there."

He stared at her.

"I'm sorry to be blunt. I thought you knew. Sort of like being bald. At some level you can't *not* know, right?"

"Are you saying I'm bald?"

"No. No, you have excellent hair."

He raised an eyebrow at her. "Good to know."

She stared at him.

He stared back.

"It doesn't make you unintelligent," she blurted. "That's the thing. A lot of people with ADHD are very smart. In fact, I read that their inability to filter ideas makes them unusually creative." She bit her lower lip again. "I should stop talking now, shouldn't I?"

"Probably." He set his travel mug down and turned to get ready for work. The coffee had suddenly lost its appeal. She trailed after him again.

He blew out a silent breath. He forgot she had a tendency not to let things go.

"Have I upset you?"

"Only by implying I was bald," he said over his shoulder.

"Carter, I didn't mean to make you uncomfortable, but I actually know a lot about this condition. There's nothing to be ashamed of. In fact—"

He stopped abruptly. Turned. "I get it, Liz. You've got me figured out. Good for you. But it doesn't do much for me, does it? It's like telling me I'll die someday. True, but what am I supposed to *do* about it?"

"But, that's just it. There are treatments available. Counseling. Medications!"

"So now I need a shrink?"

"No, a counselor is someone who can help with executive functioning skills like prioritization of tasks and time management. The research says—"

He held up a hand. "Liz, I'm fine."

She bit her lip. "Of course you are."

He blew out another breath. There was probably some truth to what she was saying, but knowing that didn't make him happy to be analyzed like a lab specimen.

He shook his head then abruptly turned, leaning forward and peering at a point near her left ear.

She stepped back. "What are you looking at?"

"There's something…" He squinted and leaned closer.

She flicked at the area with her hand. "What? Is there something in my hair?"

"No. It's… *hmm. Wow.* You might want to get that checked out."

"*What is it?*"

He stepped back. "I'm no expert, but it appears to be a pretty advanced case of over-zealousness. I wouldn't leave it untreated if I were you."

She pursed her lips. "Ha. Ha."

"No, seriously, I wouldn't fool around with that. I'm sure there are treatments available. Counseling. Medications…"

She had the grace to look chagrined. "Let me know when you need help with that screaming later."

"Will do." He watched her walk away, her ponytail bouncing.

Screeding, he corrected. But only to himself.

CHAPTER TWENTY-ONE

"TELL ME AGAIN WHY you're going to this thing tonight?" Trish asked for the third time since she'd stopped by. She sat on Liz's bed and half-bounced, half-patted Clara in her lap.

It was Friday afternoon, and Liz had taken a break from working on the house to figure out what she planned to wear to the reunion dinner that evening.

She made a face at herself in the mirror. "I thought it would be fun?"

"Fun like a root canal. And, please, tell me you aren't wearing *that*." Liz looked down at herself. "I'm wearing this."

"You won't even look like a wallflower in that, you'll just blend in with the wall!"

"Black is slimming," Liz retorted, albeit feebly. "Besides, I packed for remodeling and cleaning, not dinner dances. This is the best I could do."

"You look like a post. You owe it to all the overweight, unpopular girls out there to go shopping. You've come so far."

"I beg your pardon?"

"Come on, I've only got an hour before preschool lets out."

"I'm not buying a new—"

"Shut-up. I've got credit cards, too. We're going."

Twenty minutes later, Liz was pushing the baby in her stroller while Trish rapidly sifted through dresses on the racks of the town's only boutique dress shop. Trish held up a navy shift, shook her head, and popped it back on the rack. "If we don't like anything here, we still have time to try *Second Chances*. But consignment shops are so hit or miss, and we don't have time to get anything cleaned…"

"Dress slacks and a tailored blouse are considered classic," Liz said as Trish rifled through the hangers.

"Don't make me vomit. You look like a waiter. We'll find something. It's got to be sophisticated, but funky. Not too long, a little sexy… *A-ha!*" Trish whipped her selection off the rack and thrust it at Liz. "It's perfect! But it's the only one, so make it fit."

Liz frowned at the dress. Okay, so it *was* rather nice, with a fitted, sleeveless bodice, v-neck and full, just-above-the-knee skirt. It had a retro flavor, but the rich plum silk gave it a modern feel. Still, maybe she should keep things casual. After suggesting Carter get counseling yesterday, it might be better to not get too worked up about tonight.

A few moments later, Liz stepped out of the dressing room.

"It's perfect!" Trish nearly squealed, yanking the zipper up.

Liz struggled to take a breath. "The bodice is a little snug."

"Then skip the bra." Trish fluffed the crinoline underskirt. "I tell you, it's perfect. And I have just the necklace to go with it. Did you bring heels? Never mind. I saw some fabulous shoes in the window next door." She yanked the zipper down again and pushed Liz toward the changing room. "We'll take it," she announced to the salesgirl across the shop.

"Thank you. You're being awfully nice," Liz said a short while later as she loaded her new purchases into Trish's minivan. She had refused to let Trish pay after Trish had revealed they were hinting at more lay-offs in Russ' company.

Trish shrugged and snapped the baby seat into the car. "I kind of jumped ship when we were teenagers. I didn't get to help you primp for your prom or any of that sisterly stuff." She eyed Liz's somber outfit. "And I think it's high time the world stopped seeing you as just a brain."

"Thanks." Liz glanced out the window at passing traffic. She'd missed this, she realized. They'd been closer once—she and Trish. They'd shared a room, secrets. But that was before the awkward, difficult teenage years and life events had pushed them apart.

"So, you're saying you want the world to see me as a liver and pancreas, too?"

"You always did have a questionable sense of humor." Trish rolled her eyes and sipped from the travel mug of coffee that followed her everywhere. "You know what I mean. You always shied away from letting people see how pretty you were. Especially men. And, don't deny it. It's true. You used your smarts as a shield. Probably still do, but I'm here to put a stop to that."

"Oh, really?"

"Yes, really," Trish said, warming to her topic. "You don't realize it, but you still dress as if you weighed twenty pounds more."

"I don't wear baggy clothes!"

"You don't wear clothes that draw attention to you, either. Are you afraid you might get noticed? Heaven forbid some guy should take an interest in you. When's the last time you went out on a date?"

Liz was about to tell Trish she didn't need help attracting the opposite sex but decided to keep her mouth shut. She didn't think bringing up Grant would be helpful. And, she certainly couldn't boast about going out a lot.

"I see it as my sisterly duty to make up for not being there for your prom," Trish continued.

"I didn't go."

"Why not? I did, and I was preggers at the time."

"No one asked me." It wasn't the full story, but it was more than ten years ago now. No doubt, she was the only one who remembered it. Thankfully, she was no longer starry-eyed Beth Beacon anymore.

Trish gave her a stunned look. "That's—seriously, Liz—that's *so* sad!"

Trish pulled out her cell phone and starting tapping the screen. "Well, I guess we're making up for lost time. I'm calling my hairdresser. She's fantastic." She started the car.

"Why do I need—?"

Trish covered the mouthpiece and rolled her eyes. "Honey, stop thinking like a post and start thinking like the life of the party, will you? Meg!" Trish hurriedly uncovered the phone as she pulled blithely back into traffic. "It's Trish. Clear your schedule. I've got an emergency, and I'm heading over..."

CHAPTER TWENTY-TWO

RUTH PEARSON PULLED the plastic wrap off her tray of hors d'oeurves and set them on Lydia's sideboard. She fought not to roll her eyes. Lydia had been a friend for decades, but the woman had the decorating tastes of a five year-old: the brighter, the sparklier the better. What she saw in those majolica eyesores she collected was beyond Ruth's comprehension. Her dining room hutch looked like a Mardi Gras float.

"Ooh!" Lydia cried. "What did you make today? These look adorable!"

On the other hand, Lydia *did* have fine taste in food. "Mini cranberry goat cheese balls and blue cheese pops rolled in toasted almonds with pretzel skewers. My grandson, Ian, found me this website with thousands of recipes. I'm trying a new one every day."

Lydia plucked a cranberry goat cheese ball off the plate and popped it in her mouth.

"Are we eating or playing cards?" Claire wanted to know. Claire was such a sourpuss sometimes.

June shook a box of crackers into a napkin-lined basket and set it on the table. "Both," she said.

Claire sniffed and rearranged her cards. "I dealt ages ago. *Mmm.* Hand me one of those nutty ball things. They look good."

Ruth held out the hors d'oeurves tray as Lydia and June picked up their cards.

"So," Lydia said, eyeing the box in front of Ruth, "have you finally gotten yours hands on the wedding photos?"

Ruth patted the box in front of her. "You'll see."

"Only if you win the hand. You don't get bragging rights unless you win." June reminded them all of their unique twist on poker—the prize being the right to repeat any story heard by one's dearest friends dozens of times without threat of groans or interruption. After all, only the very best of friends would get together faithfully each week to hear the same old stories.

"I can't wait to see them," Lydia enthused. 'I hope you win."

"Rules are rules," said Claire. "We stretch them now, all hell will break loose. Who but a bunch of old ladies will want to see every last one of them? But only if Ruth wins."

"Who are you calling old?" June wanted to know.

Ruth glanced down at her cards and smiled serenely. "Ante up, ladies. We'll start by playing a round of mystery photo per Lydia's request."

"I just love surprises, don't you?" Lydia said around another cranberry goat cheese ball.

All the women slid a photo face down toward the center of the table. As bidding commenced, more photos—these face up—littered the table top. "I see your record snowfall with a picture of my flooded basement..." said June.

"I'm out," Lydia announced on the next round.

Claire turned on her. "Don't you dare fold just because you want to see the wedding pictures! That's like cheating!"

"If she's out, so am I," June said. "Truly, I've got a lousy hand."

"Fine. I call. What have you got, Ruth?"

An appreciative murmur rounded the table as Ruth laid down a full house.

"That's nothing," Claire boasted, fanning her own cards on the table. "Read 'em and weep, ladies. A royal flush. In *hearts.*"

"*It's happening again!*" Lydia squealed. "Quick! Look! Who's in the pot?" Her silver bangles tinkled madly as she sifted through the pile of photos on the table. "Oh! The mystery photos! I'll bet the happy couple is hiding in the mystery photos! This is so exciting!"

Claire sniffed. "I can't believe you still believe that hoo-ha about a royal flush in hearts meaning somebody in the pot will get married."

"It has happened *twice!*" Lydia nearly shouted. "That's more than a trend! What are the odds of a royal flush to begin with? Now *three* times—?"

"And you think the 'happy couple' is in the mystery photos?"

Lydia's palms hovered over the face-down pictures like a seer at her crystal ball. "I can *feel* it. They're in there!"

Claire popped another cheese ball in her mouth. "Let's see them then."

Lydia flipped over a photo of a man smiling into the camera, a bottle of wine tipping toward his glass. "I saw it in a travel brochure for a vineyard in California. Doesn't it look romantic? I've always wanted to visit wine country. I wonder if he's single."

Claire rolled her eyes. "You and your male models. If they weren't so easy on the eyes, I'd call you on it. June?"

June flipped over a picture of newborn Lily in a bouncy seat. "Isn't she gorgeous? I just can't get over how precious she is! Although, she's unlikely to be married anytime soon."

Ruth leaned forward at their shared granddaughter. "I hadn't seen that one. I gave her that nightgown, you know..." She flipped a picture of her grandson, laughing—and soaked—in a black tux after he and the rest of the wedding party had jumped into the lake. "Carter made such a handsome groomsman, don't you think? It's one of my favorites from the wedding. I don't know why. He has his mother's smile, I suppose."

"And he's single!" Lydia nearly swooned.

Claire looked at each of her friends, then with great fanfare flipped over her picture of...

"A *cat?*" Lydia cried, clearly crestfallen. "Why would you make your mystery photo a *cat?* This won't do at all!"

"I thought he was cute in a rough and tumble sort of way. He has character. Liz found him eating out of her garbage can—"

"What's wrong with its eye?" Ruth cut in, peering at the photo.

"Battle scar," Claire said. She looked down at the tuxedoed groomsman and her grandniece's cat, both appearing to smile mischievously at the camera. "You know, I think you're right, Ruth. She'd probably be good for Carter, now that I think about it."

"The pirate cat?" June asked, aghast.

"No, Elizabeth. The cat's owner. If we believe the cards..." She snorted again—a most unladylike habit—and grabbed another cheese ball. "Although I do have it on good authority from Ellen who's friends with Sandi who works at Meg's Super Styles that Liz and Carter are attending a school dance tonight, so you never know. Maybe the cards know something after all."

Ruth was still puzzling out the trail of gossip when Lydia squealed again. "Ooh! It *is* happening again! I don't care now that you won the pot, Claire. I'm so excited! Another wedding! I could *kiss* these cards! Or do you think it's *us?* Do you think we have the power to predict? My great-great-great grandmother on my father's side was said to have been a matchmaker..." She stared at her coral-tipped fingers in wonder.

Claire washed down her cheese ball with a healthy swallow of gin and tonic. "All right, Ruth. I know I won, but I don't have anything to talk about, and Lydia here will have a conniption if we put it off any longer, so let's see those photos. If this grandkid of yours is going to marry my grandniece I want a good look at him..."

CHAPTER TWENTY-THREE

SKIMMING HER FINGERS over her skirt, Liz glanced at her watch. *7:02.* Carter should be here any minute. She bit her lip and tried to decide if she needed more lip tint or mascara.

Truthfully, she hardly recognized herself. Meg was as good as Trish had said, adding soft highlights and lowlights that brightened and added depth to her hair without making it look fake. And, the new, long layers and soft, side-swept bangs made the most of her natural waves.

Liz resisted the urge to tug the hem of her skirt down and practiced smiling casually at herself in the mirror. After feeding Eddie and refilling his water for the second time, then reorganizing the items in the small black clutch Trish had lent her, Liz checked her watch. *7:26.* She put her palm over her belly. It fluttered and flipped like the night of Jenny Whitmeyer's party all over again.

Except this time, it wasn't raining.

Liz pursed her lips and checked her watch a third time. *7:26.* Still. That was okay, right? If they weren't there right at the dot of seven, wasn't that considered fashionable? It wasn't a tax deadline or anything.

She wouldn't call him. Calling him would seem desperate, and really, Carter wasn't even thirty minutes late yet. There was bound to be some explanation.

As if on cue, a deep rumble sounded from the driveway. Liz peered through the front window. And froze.

Dear God in heaven.

"Sorry about the wheels," Carter apologized as he strolled toward her up the front walk. "The bracket holding the exhaust pipe on my truck rusted through. It was too hot to wire it up right away, so it's a good thing it's warm tonight. You ready?"

Liz stared, mouth agape at the motorcycle that stood in the driveway. "You expect me to ride *that?*"

"I know it's not ideal, but consider it an adventure. If you'd driven here instead of flying, we could've taken your car."

"If you'd called me, I would have borrowed my sister's, but it's too late for that now."

"It is? Don't tell me..." Carter peered at her watch and winced. "Ooh. That late, huh? I've smashed so many watches by accident over the years I just don't wear them anymore. Well, I guess we'd better head out."

"I'm in a dress, Carter!"

He whistled appreciatively. "And a very nice one, too. Thank goodness it's short enough to get on the bike."

"I don't even have a helmet!"

"You can wear mine. I hope it doesn't mess up your hair, which, by the way, looks fantastic."

"Thank you." Liz stared at the bike nervously. Carter waited. She let out a short breath. "I'll get my purse."

He followed her into the living room and lingered while Liz collected her purse and the thin black cardigan she'd decided she might need despite the unseasonably warm evening.

"Ah! Looking at the old yearbook were you?"

Liz blanched and tried to snatch the book before Carter could get to it.

Damn, the man was fast.

"Let me guess," he teased, pinning her with his eyes. "You were mooning over this page because you had a crush on a certain someone in high school?"

"Give me the book." *Oh God, was she that easy to read?*

"I'm right, aren't I?"

"Just give me the book, Carter."

"Who was it? Can't be Bill Nelson. I can't see you going for the whole Goth look. And Chip Otterman was into Jenny even then. *Hmm...*" He grinned devilishly, his finger scanning over the photos, but then he stopped and pressed his lips together. "Of course."

Liz paled and tried to snatch the book again, but Carter pulled it away. *Ack!* Would the humiliation of high school never end?

"It was Dan O'Connell wasn't it? Mr. All-Star everything? Heir to the inglorious O'Connell auto dealerships?" Carter tossed the yearbook onto the coffee table and shook his head. "Why wouldn't you have a crush on him?"

Liz grasped the book from the table and held it to her chest. "I think every girl in school had a crush on Dan at one point or another."

"Including you," he said. He cleared his throat and walked to the door as if impatient to leave now that he realized how late they were. "Ready?"

Liz looked down at the open book in her hands. She hadn't been looking at Dan O'Connell at all. She'd been staring at the unusually sober-faced photograph of Carter McIntyre and the scrawled inscription beside it.

To Beth 'Beautiful Brain' Beacon, Shine on! Carter

Beth closed the book and set it on the table again. She really was an idiot.

HE WAS AN IDIOT.

Carter strode toward his bike, scowling at the ground as he walked. To think he'd actually been looking forward to taking Beth, no Liz, to the dance tonight—and here she was hoping to catch up with Dan-the-Jerk-Jock-O'Connell? And in the outfit she had on, who would blame Dan for taking a second look?

If the gods were smiling on him, Dan would be suffering from some horribly ironic fate, like bankruptcy or irritable bowel syndrome. But, Carter knew better. He'd run into Dan just last week at the gas station. Dan had been driving a brand new BMW and bragging about the unbelievable returns on his investment portfolio.

Carter flung his leg over the seat of his old bike and slid forward, handing Liz the helmet. If she had her eye on Dan, there wasn't a lot he could do about it. Carter McIntyre wasn't anyone's first choice unless you were looking to rebel against your parents. And they were long past that phase.

"You know I once dated a trauma surgeon that called these nothing more than brain buckets," Liz said, sliding the helmet carefully over her hair.

"Fun guy."

Carter closed his eyes as Liz slid behind him and adjusted her skirt, tucking the folds of it under her thighs. Lord, why did he have visions about those legs wrapping around him?

"Where do you want my feet?"

Her words skittered across his cheek, and he licked his lips as he caught a whiff of something sexy and exotic float by him on the warm spring air. He glanced down at her feet, clad in sleek, strappy high-heeled sandals. "Right on those," he pointed and nodded as her feet found their perches. The legs fantasy would *not* go away.

"What do I do?" she wanted to know as he started the engine.

"Just hang on."

He felt her nod again and set the bike it motion, rolling toward the end of the drive.

"Ack!"

Carter braked hard and reached behind him to catch Liz before she headed to the pavement. "I said hang on!"

"To what?" she cried. "There isn't anything to hang on *to!*"

Taking her clutch and stuffing it into his shirtfront, Carter grabbed first one of her hands, then the other and positioned them on his waist. "To *me.*"

"I'm sliding into you," she complained, pushing away with her hips and sliding forward again. Repeatedly. "This skirt is too slippery."

Carter all but groaned. "Liz, if you keep doing that, I might begin to think you were trying to get my attention."

Abruptly, she went still.

"Not that I was complaining."

More silence.

"You holding on?" he finally asked.

"Yes," came the muffled reply. She had her face pressed to his shoulder, not that he was complaining about that either.

"Here we go." He tried to go easy as he entered the main road, as much to reassure her as to prevent her helmet from smacking him unconscious when he went over a bump. Her fingers clutched his ribs through his sport jacket, the warmth of her body intimately merging with his own. He blew out a breath and decided he'd better make it to this alumni thing sooner than later.

They rode in silence, Liz's grip easing somewhat as she became familiar with the feel of the bike. Carter slowed to take the turn around the town common. He felt as much as heard Liz's sharp intake of breath.

"What happened?" she cried over the sound of the motor.

Carter pulled up near the curb and braked. "What?"

"The fountain!" she pointed.

He nodded as they turned toward the local landmark. It had always been a favorite backdrop for prom and wedding pictures and, despite the signs prohibiting it, cooling toes on a hot summer's day. The ornate center pedestal of the fountain was missing and one low wall caved in like an ancient ruin. Yellow tape flagged the area.

"What happened?" she repeated.

"Jack Adams. Choked on a chicken nugget while driving last year and passed out. Creamed it with his pickup."

"That's awful!"

"It's all right. His steering wheel performed the Heimlich. He's fine."

"But the fountain! I can't believe I didn't notice before!"

"Don't worry. It'll be fixed by Founders' Day. The Beautification League raised enough to fix it, re-lay the stonework around it and everything."

"Oh? Are you and your uncle doing the work?"

Carter shook his head in answer.

"But the stonework around the base and all, I just thought—"

Carter gunned the engine and pulled back into traffic. "Too busy!" he hollered.

It was a lie, of course. In addition to Grams' nagging, Pops had also told him to bid on the job, but Carter had balked—because Pops made it clear Carter's name would be the only one on the bid.

He wasn't ready. He knew Pops wanted him to take more of a leadership role in the business, take on more of the responsibilities. But, he preferred the physical labor. Once you moved into the contracts and paperwork, well, things always got complicated and disorganized.

And screwing up a prominent public project wasn't something Carter wanted any part of. He might have ADHD, but he was at least smart enough to know that.

CHAPTER TWENTY-FOUR

Twelve years earlier…

"CARTER, SIT DOWN," Valerie ordered. "I'm not done."

Carter crouched down again in the Whitmeyers' kitchen, not quite sitting this time, his old leather jacket creaking a little at the shoulder seams as he propped his elbows on his knees. It had belonged to his father—the jacket, that is—back when his father was young, vital… alive. It was the only thing of his father's that he owned that had survived the fire. Grams had found it in the back of a closet when cleaning out for a church yard sale and given it to him, because it was too small for Ian.

It barely fit Carter, but he wouldn't admit it.

He wore it everywhere.

Carter bit his lip and waited for the ridiculous game to end. He needed a smoke and that beer he'd guzzled at the back of John Beacon's Chevette was making him feel a little fuzzy. And not in a good way.

Valerie gave him another one of her flirty looks and Carter half-smiled, his eyes feeling a little glazed, just so she wouldn't get mad at him for not noticing. He felt sorry for her, always trying to get attention. She was pretty enough she didn't need to sell herself short, but she didn't seem to trust it. She flirted with every male body that crossed her path.

He didn't feel like pissing off the jocks in their hoodies and varsity jackets, though. Although it happened often enough. Was it his fault girls gravitated toward him like moths to a flame? And, he was a teenaged boy. It wasn't like he didn't enjoy looking back. And more.

Sure, he was big enough these days nobody much bothered with him, but he was smart enough to know he was outnumbered here and shouldn't piss anybody off by flirting with their girlfriends right in front of them.

He bit his lip again and waited for the bottle to stop spinning. It was making him dizzy watching it go round and round. He half wondered whether Beth was still in the pantry or had high-tailed it out of there already. She was so painfully shy she'd probably self-destruct if a guy kissed her.

The thought made him smirk a little at his own joke.

The bottle stopped.

Carter stopped gnawing his lip. He looked up, surprised he cared who the stupid bottle had chosen. But, somehow, he did.

It pointed to Dan.

CHAPTER TWENTY-FIVE

"CARTER!"

Carter turned toward the shrill greeting. The way Valerie was charging through the crowd of alumni, you'd think she used to play offense for the varsity team instead of being the head cheerleader. "You're late," she chided.

"Car trouble."

Valerie's gaze slid over Liz before settling on him again. "You always were trouble," she murmured. "Bad boys are always bad boys, aren't they?"

"Sometimes they're just misunderstood," Liz replied. Somehow her hand had found his elbow. He wrapped his fingers over hers gratefully.

Valerie raised her over-plucked eyebrows. "Really? I didn't think misunderstandings required bail. Not that I'm one to point fingers," she chuckled and leaned close, and Carter wondered if she'd been making use of the cash bar. She'd never been one to shy away from liquid courage. "God, you look good in a suit," she purred. "Come with me. The photographer from the local paper is here taking candids. I know the perfect spot for us."

"If it's posed," Liz cut in, "it's hardly a candid."

"We just got here," Carter soothed, noting Valerie's flash of irritation. "I think Liz and I will just mingle for a while. Catch you later?"

"Sure," Valerie smiled, her lips taut, then pulled him close to murmur in his ear. "But if Miss Goody-Two-Shoes can't keep up with you, you know where the fun crowd will be." With that she waved at another late arrival and slipped away.

"I think I'm going to be sick," Liz mumbled.

"That makes two of us," Carter concurred.

"No, I mean I don't feel well. This dress is so tight, I can hardly breathe. I feel lightheaded."

Carter peered at Liz's chest as she swayed ominously. He reached out to hold her up, then frowned, his fingers pressing into her sides. "Good God. What have you got on under there?"

Liz's cheeks bloomed with color as she batted his hands away. "My bra." He raised one of those blasted eyebrows. "It's lightly padded," she murmured.

"Lightly? There's got to be a good quarter inch of stuffing working against you. Just go take it off and you'll have room to breathe."

"You sound like my sister. This silk is so thin, I'm afraid—"

"Someone might notice you have breasts? Too late. I see them."

"This is mortifying."

"More so than fainting into the cheese buffet? Take it off, Liz. You'll feel better."

"I don't—"

"Do it or I'll do it for you," he warned as he propelled her down a nearby hall.

"You wouldn't."

He grinned, enjoying the way her white teeth nibbled her lip nervously. "Is that a dare?"

"No! Anyway, I can't do it. If you must know, my sister zipped me into this thing. I can't reach the zipper myself."

"How did you plan to get it off when you got home?"

"I hadn't thought that far ahead. I just bought it six hours ago."

"No pre-planning? That's not like you. Sure you don't have a touch of ADHD yourself? Well, worry yourself no more. Turn around."

"Why?"

"I'll unzip you," he said magnanimously. Far be it for him to stand around while a woman suffocated in her own undergarments.

"Here?"

"We're behind the potted plant, nobody's looking. Now's your chance."

"I think I'd better go in the ladies room."

"I can't go in there."

"Afraid it'll impinge on your masculinity?"

"No. They banned me from it eight years ago. Long story," he added at her raised brow.

"I'm sure."

"Turn around. We can do this." He gently grasped her shoulders and maneuvered her around.

"Oh, all right. Just make it quick."

"Now those aren't words I usually hear from a woman when I'm unzipping her dress..."

"Carter."

"Okay. The coast is clear." He gripped the zipper pull and leaned toward her ear. "Do you want me to unclasp you while I'm at it?"

"What?"

"Do you want me to unclasp you, you know, while I'm back here?"

Her cheeks went crimson as she turned away from him. "It's a front closure. Could we please hurry?"

Carter slid down the zipper and pushed at the shoulder straps of her dress—just to be helpful—as Liz practically snapped her bra off into his face. She was just shrugging the shoulders of her dress back up when footsteps approached down the hallway.

"Carter McIntyre? Is that you? Ho! How's it been! And Brainy Beacon?"

Carter stuffed Liz's bra into his pants pocket as Liz shot upright beside him, the back of her dress flapping wide. She brushed her hair behind her ear, in part, he surmised, to keep her straps from slipping down her arms.

"Dan O'Connell!" she gasped, a strained smile plastered to her features as she positioned one hand high on her hip and the other in a casual posture on the wall behind Carter. "What a surprise!"

"What are you two doing back here?" he asked. "Not already into the hard stuff, are we?"

"What? Oh! No!" Liz stuttered. "No. I, um, lost something. It rolled back here, behind the, ah, plant. I think. Carter was helping me find it."

"What did you lose?"

"An earring..."

"My ring..." Their words stumbled over each other.

"I misunderstood you, Liz. I guess it's a *ring* we're looking for, Dan," Carter said. Liz nodded earnestly.

"What did it look like?"

As Dan crouched down to peer behind the plant, Carter grabbed Liz's zipper pull and yanked it up. She gasped and craned her neck, pulling at the hair he'd inadvertently caught in it. Dan stood up again. Liz's neck was held tilted at a slight angle toward Carter, so he put his arm around her shoulder.

"Well, we don't mean to keep you," Carter offered.

"It really wasn't a very special ring. I may have even left it at home now that I think about it," Liz added.

Dan nodded and his eyes fell to Liz's chest. "It's good to see you again, Beth."

"I go by Liz now, actually."

"Liz." He nodded at Carter, his eyes never leaving Liz. "Carter."

"See you later, Dan." Liz waved. She leaned toward Carter. "Can you please uncatch my hair?" she hissed.

"What? No 'thank you?'" he teased.

She gave him a baleful look, so he slid the zipper down again. She yanked her hair free then held it out of the way as he slid the zipper up, the back of his fingers gliding over the smooth nape of her neck as he did so. Her skin was incredibly soft.

Liz shivered and turned, her face flushed. "Well, that went well. I can't believe I'm saying this, but where's my bra?"

Carter pulled the strap from his pocket. He was somewhat disappointed when she snatched it from his hand and shoved it into her clutch. "Thanks. I think."

"Better?" he asked.

"Actually, yes."

"You don't need that bra, you know."

"You don't have to tell me I'm built like a board, and nobody notices my chest anyway."

"No, I was actually going to say you didn't need any augmentation. Why do you wear that battle gear anyway?"

"Battle—? Oh. It covers... *things*."

"Well, speaking from a man's point of view, there are some *things* that don't need covers."

She stared at him then, that 'I can't believe you just said that' look in her eyes. "I can't believe you just said that!" she gasped. "That is so incredibly sexist!"

"Maybe," he grinned without remorse. "But you like going commando, don't you? I'm just saying you shouldn't feel guilty about it. At least yours move. I think Valerie's have been Botoxed. Have you noticed they don't shift—at all? I'm tempted to knock on them to see if they're hollow."

Liz snorted indelicately and gave him a look. "Botoxed?

"Makes you feel a whole lot better about what they'll be saying about your chest now, doesn't it?"

"Who's going to be talking about my chest?" she wanted to know, dragging her feet.

"Come on. Let's get a drink. I think we're just in time for the main course."

"You're drinking? But I can't drive that motorcycle if—"

"Relax. I meant I want a soda. But you can have all you want, so long as you can still hang on at the end of the night."

"A soda sounds perfect," she replied as she walked toward the bar.

CHAPTER TWENTY-SIX

Twelve years earlier…

VALERIE PURSED HER HOT PINK lips and stared at the bottle on the Whitmeyers' kitchen floor as if willing it to keep rotating.

Nobody spoke.

Carter stood up. "I need a smoke. Can I bum a cigarette off anyone?"

Dan stood and pulled a pack out of his pocket and held it toward Carter. Virginia Slims? Carter fought not to roll his eyes. Jesus. Dan was such a girl. "Thanks," he said.

He eyed the cigarette and folded it into his palm and headed to the door. Dan followed behind him.

Valerie jumped up from the floor. "You're not actually going, are you?" she said. "I mean, come on, it's *Beth Beacon*."

Dan shrugged. "You wanted to play. I'm playing."

Val looked around, flicked her bangs off her forehead. "Fine. Just don't go catching any herpes cold sores or anything."

Carter frowned. As if Valerie with her mongo hickey should be questioning where Beth had ever been. He looked to Dan.

In typical jock fashion, Dan was puffing up his chest. "Don't you worry. I'll make sure she enjoys herself."

The other guys snickered and hooted.

Carter turned back to the door. Morons.

Dan laughed and caught up with him in the hallway. "Hey, Carter! Which door is it?"

They were alone. The door to the kitchen had shut again. The Whitmeyers' back hallway looked like the set of Alice in Wonderland with black and white tile floors and doors up the wazoo. Carter looked toward the back door where the rain fell in sheets off the eaves. He gestured with the tip of the cigarette to the pantry and decided he didn't feel like standing in the rain. He pulled out a lighter, lit up and took a few deep drags.

Dan chuckled and flexed his fingers as if preparing to play the piano or something. He wiggled his eyebrow at Carter and grinned. "Wanna watch?"

Carter coughed, cleared his throat. "Excuse me?"

Dan nudged him with his elbow. "Is that why you're standing out here? Hoping to watch? Learn a few things from the master?"

"I just came for a smoke, man. That's all."

Dan laughed and pulled a Chapstick out of his pocket. He smeared it over his lips.

The beer from earlier churned in Carter's gut. Maybe he'd go outside after all.

Dan shrugged. "I'm game if you want to." He gestured toward the pantry and leaned closer. "I'll bet little Beth in there will like it, too. She's all into learning, that one. What do you say we give her an education she won't forget?"

Carter blew out a long, measured breath, the menthol of the cigarette cool in his throat.

"I don't think so," he said.

Dan shrugged again. Smacked his lips. "I would have thought you were more adventurous than that what with your Rebel-Without-a-Clue jacket and all." He laughed again, a low chuckle. "My mistake."

Carter dropped his cigarette and wordlessly ground it out with his heel as Dan reached for the pantry door.

CHAPTER TWENTY-SEVEN

"THANK YOU ALL for coming tonight!" Valerie beamed from the podium. She wasn't exactly behind the podium, Liz noted somewhat cattily, more lounging against it, no doubt to allow the audience a fuller appreciation of the designer knock-off column dress she wore. Liz watched as Valerie slid one leg out the side slit of her dress in a feat that seemed to defy gravity considering how far she had to lean the opposite way to maintain verticality. "It was getting a little warm in here with all these hot bodies, so I had the management crank up the A/C," she cooed, fanning herself with a wine menu she'd snatched off a table and smiling silkily at the men in the audience.

Truthfully, Liz was stunned at the turn-out. Nearly half their class was probably in attendance, which just proved that either her class hadn't made it far in life and were still milling about Sugar Falls, NH, or there were more of them scared of Valerie than just her and Carter.

"It just so happens we have none other than our valedictorian—Beth Beacon—here tonight, so let's give her a hand and invite her up to tell us what she's been up to these past ten years!"

Liz blanched and swallowed her bite of dinner roll as half-hearted applause filled the room. "I don't think anyone's that—"

"Oh, Beth, don't be shy!" Valerie crooned, eyeing her like the wicked witch she was. "We're all old friends here, aren't we? And if our valedictorian doesn't have anything to crow about, we're in sorry shape, aren't we? Come on!"

Liz pushed back her chair and nodded to her classmates as she stepped up to the microphone.

"Hello, everyone," she smiled, her eyes skidding over the crowd. Carter caught her eye and thrust his chest out, presumably to remind her not to slouch. Liz pushed her shoulders back slightly and nodded as he gave a thumbs-up.

"So, you want to know what I've been up to," Liz said, hating Valerie for putting her on the spot like this. No doubt it was the vile woman's way of trying to make Liz look like a fool.

Valerie wanted a few words? Fine. Liz could handle this. She turned a warm smile toward her former classmates. "Well, I think you'll find the life of a valedictorian isn't so different from anyone else's.

"Like many of you, I went to college, earned my degree and found a job. Or two. The first one doesn't really count, I don't think, because the interns were making almost as much as I was, if you know what I mean." Some small chuckles from the audience encouraged her.

"I'm sure many of you have married and started families. I, on the other hand, have had eight cats, which isn't the same, I know. Except one cheated on me with the family next door who lured it away with luncheon meats, so maybe some of you *can* relate to that. I hope not!"

"Oh!" Valerie interrupted. "Even her cat left her! Oh, Beth, that's so sad!"

"It was a terrible shock," she said dryly, "but I've recovered. Anyway, it's good to see you all again. I know the alumni committee has worked hard to put together a great evening for us, so I won't keep you from it. Have a terrific night, everyone." She waved and stepped from the podium.

"Hold on," Carter strode toward her.

"For those of you who might not recognize him, may I welcome the man voted Mostly Likely to Smuggle a Keg to Graduation, Carter McIntyre!" Valerie cooed into the microphone as Carter body-blocked Liz in the aisle.

"Where are you going?" he demanded under his breath.

"Back to my table," Liz said.

But Carter grabbed her elbow and pulled her toward the podium again. He leaned toward the microphone. "Liz glossed over a few things, so I'll take the liberty of filling in the blanks."

"Carter? What are you—?"

"First of all, did you know she graduated from Stanford with high honors? That's where she earned her master's. Now she's Assistant Vice President of Ames & Reed Consulting, one of the most respected business consulting firms in the Midwest."

"Carter, please," Liz murmured uneasily.

"Not only has she volunteered at the local animal shelter for years—which explains all the cats she's rescued, rehabbed and found homes for—she also organized a collaboration between area businesses and the local *Homes for All* chapter, which earned her a key to the city."

Liz stared at Carter. She'd only been making small talk the other night. Catching up. But now that he repeated it, it sounded so boastful. "It wasn't actually a key to the city," she corrected, leaning toward the microphone herself. "Just a letter of appreciation from the mayor's office. Really, not a big deal."

"Well," Valerie choked into the silence. "Maybe we need to nominate Beth to sainthood."

"She goes—" Carter began.

"—by Liz now," finished Liz. "And technically, you can't be sainted until your dead."

Valerie's wilting look said that could be arranged. "Well," she said, "enough reminiscing. We have a short video presentation by Kat Dailey and Rich Emerson, our former yearbook editors, giving us a trip down memory lane, and after that, our cover band, *My Generation*, will be playing until midnight. They're taking requests, so stick around! Ready, Kat?"

Liz pulled away from Carter's grip and strode right past their table toward the bar. She intended to order something tall, fruity and alcoholic. Carter appeared at her side. She refused to look at him. "How could you?" she hissed.

"How could I what? You were painting yourself like some drop-out with a weird cat thing going on instead of what and who you really are."

She gave her order to the bartender and then half-turned to him. "Weird cat thing? I'd rather that than have everyone think I'm some uppity saint wannabe. I've fought all my life to be something *other* than Brainy Beth Beacon, and just when I get people seeing me as a regular, *normal* person you have to go and screw it up!"

"Screw it...? Now wait a minute... You're *mad?*"

"Damn straight, I'm mad!" she yelled under her breath. "You couldn't have made me—"

"Hey, Liz? I'd love to talk to you about that *Homes for All* collaboration you set up. How long are you in town?"

Liz turned and smiled tautly at Dan O'Connell—easier done now that her dress wasn't flapping in the breeze. "A couple weeks maybe."

"Think you could fill in as a guest speaker at our next Rotary meeting? We'd love to have you."

"Oh! That's... that's very flattering." She tucked her hair behind her ear and ignored Carter's glower. "I suppose I could put something together. Give me a call." She scribbled her number on a napkin and handed it to Dan. "We'll see if our schedules mesh out."

"I'll let Kat Emerson know. She books our speakers." Dan smiled as he pocketed the napkin, and Liz felt the full force of his all-American good looks as if she were ten years younger. "Maybe we could get together first, you know, to talk it over, just the two of us? There's a great new Indian place on South Main."

"Oh. I'd enjoy that. I love Indian food."

"I'll call you."

"I look forward to it." Liz paid for her drink as Dan sauntered away.

"Christ, Liz, you think you could at least wait until I was out of the room?"

"What?" Liz spun around to find Carter glaring at her, his green eyes like a stormy sea.

"You just agreed to a date with Dan right in front of me!"

"That wasn't a date. He just wanted to talk about the thing—"

"Just the two of you? It was a date. Something I thought *we* were on. My mistake."

"You thought we—? Carter, wait!" Liz found herself scrambling after him as he strode toward the exit. "He caught me by surprise!"

"So your first response was 'yes'? Funny, every time *I* catch you by surprise you say 'no.' Or recommend therapy. I guess I know why now. I'm no Dan O'Connell. Never was. How ironic. Well, enjoy, Liz. I'm out of here."

"You can't leave! You're my ride!"

Carter's eyes raked her body. "I'm sure you'll find someone to give you a lift."

Liz stared at his retreating back and fought against angry tears. She'd tried not to believe tonight was anything other than a fun trip down memory lane, but who was she kidding? She hadn't bothered worrying about her zipper earlier, because a part of her had imagined the new Liz would be brave enough to ask Carter to do the unzipping. And now he was walking out the door?

"You guys hoping to liven the party up?"

"What?" Liz turned to Dan. It wasn't fair to blame him, but he *had* caused all this to happen.

"Carter. I saw him leave…"

"We had a disagreement." Liz blew out a breath and walked back to the bar. Her drink was sitting there with its frilly umbrella like a girl dressed up for a date and left behind. She knew just how it felt.

"Sorry to hear that." Dan was so close now she could smell his cologne, feel the heat of his body. But rather than appealing, he just felt... hot... next to her.

"What were you arguing about, if you don't mind my asking?"

"Ironically, you," she muttered against her straw.

"Me?"

"He seemed to think you asked me out on a date."

"I did ask you out on a date." Dan's lips tilted with confident sensuality.

"*Oh.*" Liz could only stare. Daniel J. O'Connell, the heartthrob of Sugar Falls High had asked her out? Why did that not excite her the way she'd always imagined it would?

"For the valedictorian of our class, you're a bit slow on the uptake aren't you?" he chuckled.

"I'm only in town a couple of weeks. Why would you want to go on a date?"

"Maybe I like what I see." Dan's eyes slid to her chest, and Liz fought the urge to hunch her shoulders. He looked up again. "So tell me, is your brother in town?"

Liz shook her head. "I don't know. We're not that close. Why?"

"Just curious. He always enjoyed a good party." Dan swiped on his cell phone, stared at it a moment then shoved it in his pocket. "Never mind. Say, I'm gonna go mingle. You hanging around here for a while?"

"Seems so."

"Great. Keep my seat warm."

Liz gagged on her straw and wondered how the night could get worse.

Just then her phone rang in her clutch. She pulled it out. *Perfect.*

"Grant!" She knew her voice was falsely bright, but she wasn't feeling herself. She took a long draw on her straw and let the ice-cold rum-soaked fruit juices numb her tongue.

"Liz, I..." There was a pause and Liz smiled tautly to some classmates hurrying by on the way to the video presentation. "Where are you?"

"Oh. Right. Funny that. Believe it or not, I'm at my class reunion." She took another long sip and stopped because she was on the verge of brain freeze. "Long story."

"I thought you hated high school."

"Very true. Very true. Yet here I am." She bobbed her straw in her drink. "I got cornered at the local grocery store by Valerie Stinson, chair of the organizing committee. Couldn't say 'no.'"

"Stinson? Isn't she the snotty bimbo you said hated you for no reason?"

Liz caught sight of the bimbo in question and nodded. "Yup. One and the same."

"Why didn't you just blow her off?"

"It's a small town. People talk. Besides, I didn't hate everyone." *Until now,* she thought irritably, remembering her non-ride home.

"What do you care what people think? You're only there for a few days."

Good point.

"Anyway," Grant continued, "I sent you a few more files to run some numbers on. You think you could handle it for me?"

"Sure," Liz agreed absently, wishing, yet again, she were smart like Bailey who routinely blew these events off. Oh, well. A shame Mandy hadn't come back. It would have been fun to catch up with her. Or Eileen.

Liz sighed and realized belatedly Grant was still talking. "The end of the week is fine. I sent everything I have so far..."

"I'm sorry," Liz interrupted, "poor connection. Are you passing off this project entirely?"

"It shouldn't take more than a day or two—"

"But, Grant, I have work to do *here*! What's the rush? I didn't think they needed this until June."

"Ethan wants it done before... before the end of the month."

Liz stared into the distance and shook her head. Was no one reasonable anymore?

"You know what?" Grant said. "Never mind. It's clear you're busy. I'm sorry I asked. I had hoped you'd be willing to help—"

Liz rubbed her temples. "I am. I am. I..." She let out a cleansing breath. "When I get home, I'll look it over and see what I can do, okay? I've just had a less than fun evening so far. I shouldn't take it out on you."

"Sure. We'll talk later." There was a pause. "Thanks."

"No problem."

"I hope your evening improves."

"Yeah. Me, too."

Liz tucked her phone back in her clutch and sucked on her straw as she watched the video presentation from the bar. It was the predictable collage of "candid" snapshots from senior year set to an unpleasant medley of all the songs she associated with awkward high school dances.

Shoving her half-finished cocktail aside, she stood up. Even if she had to walk the whole way, she promised herself sulkily, she was going home.

Five self-sorry steps from the bar, Dan reappeared at her side.

"Leaving? How about I give you a ride?"

"Oh, I couldn't trouble—"

"Really. No trouble. Turns out I need to head out myself."

Liz let out a breath. "Thank you. I could use a ride." She started toward the rear door.

"Oh, I'm not out back." Dan took her elbow and propelled her toward the side exit. Only then did she notice he looked somewhat peculiar.

"Dan?" She paused, lightly touching the sleeve of his jacket. "Are you feeling okay? You look a bit flushed."

"Me? I'm fine. Just a little hot in there. I could use some air is all. But I am in a bit of a hurry."

"Sure. Of course." Liz pushed open the door.

140

"*Stop! Police!* Put your hands in the air where we can see them!"

"*Ohmigod!*" Liz squeaked as an officer rushed forward. "What's going—*Dan?*" She gaped as an officer pulled at the corner of what appeared to be a plastic baggy of confectioner's sugar hanging out of Dan's coat pocket. "What—?"

"Your purse, Miss?" A second officer held a hand out for Liz's clutch.

"My purse?"

"May I see your purse, please?" Liz stared wide-eyed as the other officer handcuffed Dan and began to read him his Miranda Rights.

"Oh, really, there's nothing..."

Liz noticed a small crowd gathering behind two flashing squad cars as the officer took her clutch from her fingers. He looked familiar and she tried to recall where she'd seen him before, but then she remembered what was inside her clutch.

"No!" she cried, lunging for the bag. "*Please don't!*"

And, with sickening awareness, as if it all had become slow motion, Liz watched her bra slide from her purse and hang merrily from the officer's fingertips as the flash of a camera burst before her eyes.

Trish was right. Reunions *were* hell.

CHAPTER TWENTY-EIGHT

"WHAT'S GOING ON HERE?"

Carter cut through the sea of murmuring, gawking bystanders as they took pictures of the commotion with their cell phones. He strode toward Liz, his sole thought that he was to blame for this. He shouldn't have left her. He should have at least gotten her home. Now she was standing there like a deer caught in the headlights, and it was all because he'd impulsively stalked out and gotten half-way home before he was calm enough to recognize he'd overreacted.

"Sir, I'm going to have to ask you to stay where you—"

"*Jeff!*" Carter bellowed over the shoulder of the young officer holding him at bay. "Jeff! What the hell's going on?"

Jeff Dayton closed the rear door of the squad car and strode over. "Later, Carter. We're in the middle of an arrest."

"You're arresting Liz? For what?"

"I didn't do anything! I swear!" Liz asserted to the nearest officer. She was shaking, he noted, and her face was unusually pale with two high spots of color on her cheeks. "Dan was walking me out. I don't even know what was in that baggy. It wasn't drugs was it? Was it drugs?"

"Liz, stop talking," Carter advised as calmly as he could over the excited chatter of the crowd.

"*Sir,*" the kid cop warned him.

"What?" Liz asked, craning her neck to see Carter.

More people had crowded out of the hall to see what was going on, including an agitated blonde in a red dress.

"*Dan!*" Valerie yelled, screeching over the crowd and practically body-slamming Jeff Dayton in her attempt to scream at her ex-husband. "Dan!" she yelled, pounding on the squad car window. "How could you? How could you be so *stupid?!*"

"Ma'am!" Jeff barked. "Hands off the squad car!"

Valerie glared at Jeff and returned to bellowing through the window.

"Stop talking until we get this all straightened out," Carter repeated over the din.

Liz blinked. "Am I in trouble?" she asked, her voice uneven. "I didn't do—"

"Ma'am, in the car, please," the young officer said.

Carter's fists clenched at his sides as he watched Liz slide into the second squad car. Her eyes sought his helplessly.

"We'll work it out there. I'll meet you at the station," he promised as the officer closed the door.

"Do you know who that woman is?" someone asked at his elbow.

Carter watched the cruiser with Liz pull away. "Yeah. Liz Beacon."

"Is that short for Elizabeth?"

Carter turned, only dimly aware of the man beside him, notepad in hand. "Screw yourself, Flanders. She didn't do anything."

The newspaperman smiled. "Just looking for a caption for my photo," he grinned. "Thanks."

Carter strode toward his motorcycle and threw his leg over. So much for showing Liz how much fun she'd have tonight. He gunned the engine and squealed out of the parking lot.

Minutes later, he was throwing the door to the police station wide. "I need to speak to Jeff Dayton," he informed the deputy on duty as calmly as he could manage.

"I'm sorry, sir. Officer Dayton is not available right now."

"I need to speak with him before he speaks to Elizabeth Beacon."

"Are you her lawyer?"

Carter shoved a hand through his hair. Banging this kid's head into the wall, as much as it was tempting, would probably not help the situation. "No. But if you could please tell him Carter McIntyre is here and that I have information he might find useful, I'd appreciate that."

The young officer nodded and left him alone. Moments later, Jeff appeared. "Carter, this had better be good. I've got—"

"Oh, cut the crap! You know Liz isn't involved in any of this."

"*Sir*," Jeff interrupted, "this is an active investigation. If you have any information you'd like to share, I'm happy to hear it, otherwise—"

"In private," Carter agreed.

Jeff wordlessly opened the security door and let Carter through. "I'll just be a minute," he said to the other officer before leading to an empty room down the hall. He shut the door behind them, turned on Carter. "Christ, Carter! I don't care if I did date your sister back in high school, you can't just waltz in and—"

"Liz didn't do anything wrong," Carter interrupted, "you and I both know that. She's as squeaky clean as they come. Plus, she's only just gotten back to Sugar Falls. She's been gone for years. She's not a user and she's certainly not a dealer."

"John Beacon is her brother."

Carter blew out an impatient breath. "That's not her fault."

"And you were once friends with John. Are you still?"

Carter narrowed his eyes. "Are you asking that as Jeff Dayton or Officer Dayton?"

"I'm on duty."

"The answer is no—*Jeff*. I have nothing to hide. I hadn't seen John for ages until he showed up at Liz's parent's house this week."

"Where's he living now?"

"No clue."

"Then it looks like we're done here." Jeff turned toward the door.

"Wait! Is that who you think supplied Dan? If that's true, Liz doesn't have a clue, either. I guarantee it."

"I can't comment—"

"Enough! Stop being a cop for a second, will you? Liz was caught in the middle here. I guarantee she knows nothing."

"Do *you* know something?"

"Other than that Dan O'Connell is a dipshit?" He let out a frustrated breath.

Jeff let out a frustrated breath of his own. "Then you have nothing that can help me."

"Okay, maybe. Don't ask me how I know, but I think I may have an idea who's dealing in town. Or at least someone who'd likely know. Just leave Liz alone."

Jeff rolled his eyes. "*Don't ask me how I know*? Did you really *just* say that to me? A uniformed officer? Christ, I cannot believe small towns." He raised a hand. "No! For the love of God, stop talking. Before I have to arrest you, too. I'm busy enough tonight."

Jeff ran a hand through his short-cropped hair. "If what you say is true, if Liz Beacon has nothing to hide, then she'll be free to go. We'll just want to ask her a few questions. In the mean time... go get a cup of coffee or something before I change my mind and tell the newbie out front to strip search you."

Carter nodded. "Thanks, man."

Carter stepped back into the hall a few minutes later—at the same time Dan O'Connell was being escorted to a nearby room. Their eyes locked.

Dan looked pale, old beyond his years. And scared.

And, in that moment, after years of hating the guy, Carter only felt sorry for him.

It could have just as easily been him.

Not that he was into any of that now, he reminded himself, but he hadn't always been a saint. It took dropping out of college, partying too hard and totaling his car to figure out he was on a fast road to nowhere.

That and Gramps' little pep talk. The old guy always did have a way with words. And, after his stint working as a guard at the state penitentiary back in the day, he'd painted a picture of life in prison Carter hadn't had any interest in experiencing first-hand.

Carter returned to the waiting area and pumped some coins into the coffee vending machine. His gut told him John was certainly capable of dealing. But if Liz's brother wanted to hang himself, Carter didn't intend to be the one to supply the noose.

CHAPTER TWENTY-NINE

"'*FORMER VALEDICTORIAN Lunges for Lingerie During All-Star Alum's Drug Bust?*'" Liz lowered the morning paper. "Your local news guy has a sick sense of humor."

Trish had the gall to laugh as she picked up the paper. "I think it's kind of witty. Besides, what are you complaining about? The dress looks fabulous in that photo. Glad you took my advice about the bra."

Liz snatched the paper back. "*Ack!* You can tell I'm not wearing a bra?"

"Other than the fact that it's dangling from that cop's fingertips? Look at his face! I swear he was laughing. Did they arrest you?"

"For being naïve? No. I answered some questions, but I wasn't the one with the heroin, so they let me go."

"Valerie Stinson was feeling quite the Chatty Cathy last night wasn't she? They've got no less than three quotes from her about the drug ring they were trying to crack and how you might be involved. She's quite shocked by the way. And you the head of your class! *Tsk. Tsk.*"

"Sure she was." Liz rolled her eyes. "Though I shouldn't laugh. I find it just as shocking Dan was arrested. I mean, this is Sugar Falls. This stuff doesn't happen here."

"Some things you can't escape." Trish took back the newspaper. "Ugh. Now you're making me depressed, and I was feeling so happy earlier."

"You're happy I nearly got thrown in jail?"

"There was never any danger of that."

"Of course not. I'm Miss Goody-Two-Shoes. That's what Valerie called me last night. Can you believe that?"

Trish laughed. "You sound disappointed."

Liz pondered her coffee. "Maybe I'm just disappointed—"

"You leave town for ten years, and *this* is the homecoming you plan?"

"Hi, Aunt Claire. Welcome." Trish got up to pour another cup of coffee. "We were just celebrating Liz's front-page splash."

"Is that decaf?" Claire peered through her bifocals at the carafe.

"High test," Trish assured her.

"Good. Never understood the point of decaf."

Liz made room for her great-aunt at the table. "Is there anyone that doesn't know about last night?"

"I doubt it," said Bailey, walking in with a to-go cup in her hand. "I tweeted about it as soon as I bought the paper this morning. Plus about nine of our classmates updated their statuses last night with your picture. Stuff this juicy doesn't happen every day in Sugar Falls."

"Lovely." Liz looked at Bailey. "Who let you in?"

"Me? John. He's out front fiddling with that lamp post at the end of the driveway that never worked."

"Why would he—? Forget it. Forget it! I don't care. I've got enough to worry about."

"So where's Carter this morning?" Aunt Claire asked, peering out the slider. "He's not hiding just because I'm here, is he?"

Liz narrowed her eyes. "What makes you think he'd be here?"

"I thought you might be on good terms considering all he did last night."

"What do you mean, 'all he did?'"

Aunt Claire's eyes widened like an owl's. "Didn't he tell you? Bev from the post office says he stormed over there after they dragged you off in the squad car to be sure they let you go—offered to swear to your upstanding moral character or something and wouldn't leave until you were cleared."

"*My* upstanding moral character?"

Bailey chugged her latte. "Oh, don't get your panties in a bunch. They didn't have anything on you, from what I hear, so you weren't in any actual danger. Although, if they didn't like the looks of you, they might have held you overnight."

Liz closed her eyes. Being held overnight—in jail—didn't bear thinking about. "I saw Carter when I came out, but Officer Dayton had already offered me a ride home. I was so embarrassed; I left out the back door. I didn't even talk to Carter."

"Sounds like you owe him a thank you," Aunt Claire said.

"A thank you? If he hadn't ditched me, I wouldn't have been walking out with Dan to begin with!"

"Speaking of which, I don't approve of you riding around with drug addicts," Claire sniffed.

"I didn't know he was into drugs!"

"I'm guessing this isn't a good time to see how you are." Carter stood in the doorway, looking sheepish and gorgeous all at the same time. The cad. "I knocked, but you were obviously too busy yelling about me to hear."

"I should install a revolving door…" muttered Liz.

"Good morning, young man!" Aunt Claire greeted him. "Thank you for bailing out my ungrateful niece."

"He did *not* bail me out," Liz corrected. "I was never charged."

"But I did leave you stranded, and for that, I'm sorry." Carter swept a giant bouquet of gerbera daisies from behind his back. "I didn't mean to get you arrested."

Liz tucked her hair behind her ear and stared at the flowers. "I was never arrested, just brought in for questioning…"

"Still, you must have been frightened."

She glanced up, expecting to see his green eyes mocking her, but instead he seemed as somber as his senior photo. He handed her the flowers. "A little," she admitted, not wanting to admit she'd been scared out of her wits.

His fingers brushed hers, but rather than pull away, his palms wrapped around her hands, held them, all warm, rough and delicious. Liz tried not to soften, although she was doing a poor job of it. How did he know she was a sucker for daisies?

"I'd love to stay and chat, but I have a job to get to." Bailey said.

"I'd better get going, too," Trish said, dumping her coffee in the sink. "Russ isn't used to caring for the baby on his own. Aunt Claire?"

"Oh, for heaven's sake, I'm leaving. No one needs to beat me over the head to take a hint." She stood and shuffled around Carter. "Better get those flowers in some water, you two, before they wilt."

Liz nodded. "Yes. Of course. Right away. Thanks for coming."

No sooner had the door closed behind her relatives than Carter stepped closer, his fingers still holding hers. "I'm really sorry."

"For ditching me or the drug bust?"

He winced as she regained her senses and yanked her fingers away. She starting opening cupboards in search of a vase.

"I suppose you have a right to be miffed," he said.

"I'm not miffed, I'm mortified! They have a picture of my *bra* on the front page of the paper!"

"That's actually partly your fault. I would have been happy to keep it in my pocket."

She stared, bug-eyed, at him for a moment then shook her head at the absurdity of it all. "Touché."

"Come on. You have to admit. It is kind of funny."

"You're not the one with your underwear on the front page."

"Would it make you feel better if I were?"

Liz found a vase and began to fill it with water. Her lips twitched. "Maybe."

"Think of it as the education you never got in school."

"I think I've done just fine without knowing what it feels like to be almost arrested."

He stepped closer. "Who cares if people saw your underwear? You were complaining last night that everyone still thinks of you as Brainy Beacon. This is your chance to redefine yourself. You don't always want to be on the outside of life looking in, do you?"

She frowned, stuffing the flowers into the vase. "Who says I'm on the outside of life?"

"Come on. You've never been almost arrested. You've never ridden a motorcycle. Never gone without a bra in public. How many other things are on the Liz Beacon 'never' list?"

"Are you saying I'm boring?"

"No, but why do you shy away from... living? Even when you were a teenager, you played it straight and narrow. I never saw you cruising around town, drinking at the quarry or skinny dipping at Miller Brook. How come?"

"Maybe I saw what unhappiness saying 'yes' to those kinds of things could bring to a person—a family—and I didn't want any part of it. You're right. I never did do drugs or drink or any of that other stuff most teenagers do. I went to college. I made something of myself. I wasn't about to be some loser who—"

"Is that what you think I am?" His words cut through her rant, and suddenly she realized how she'd sounded.

"No. Of course not. I was only saying—"

"Don't bother. I think I know what you were saying." Liz's chest grew tight with regret as his playful expression faded. He stepped away as if to leave.

"Carter, wait!" Liz threw her back against the kitchen door, blocking his chest with her palms. "I wasn't talking about *you*, I was talking about other people... people like my brother."

His eyes pierced hers, dark, haunted. Hurt. "And how am I different than him? You know my past isn't squeaky clean. I never finished college, Liz. Never 'made something of myself.' I think you've made it perfectly clear what you think of me."

"I don't think you have any idea at all."

"Name one thing that differentiates me from someone like your brother," he demanded.

She stared at his mouth, at the firm, set line as serious and defiant as his senior picture. "For one thing, I never wanted to kiss *him*."

Her eyes flew up as she uttered the words, as the shock of her own frankness drew an answering look of surprise—and awareness—on Carter's face.

For a moment, she couldn't breathe, the air trapped in her lungs, her mind a riot of thoughts, feelings. But then she realized she felt more than the urge to kiss him. How could she tell him she'd always admired his dogged optimism and carefree attitude—despite his tragic childhood? He'd lost his parents at a young age, gone into business with his uncle when college hadn't been the right fit. He was self-assured, sexy and unrepentantly stubborn—everything Liz had always wished she were and wasn't. Plus, she'd had a killer crush on him since before she had braces.

"I should hope not," he finally said.

"I've never thought of you as a loser," she whispered.

His mouth tilted at one corner. "I've never thought of you as boring."

Her tongue darted out to moisten her lips as the air sparked between him. "Thanks for the flowers."

"You're welcome."

She stared at his mouth. It was softening now, the corners lightly curving. "I imagine you have to get to work," she said to his lips.

"It's Saturday. It's raining. I don't have to be anywhere."

She nodded, afraid to look him in the eye. Afraid of what she might see there. If he didn't kiss her, if he walked away, she'd know he didn't return her interest. That was fine. She could live with that. She had thus far, hadn't she?

But what if he *did* kiss her? What would she do? Would he stop at one kiss? Should she stop him? Did she want to? Would he sweep her away? She didn't need romance, per se, she—

"Liz."

She swallowed and continued to stare at his mouth. *"Mmm?"*

"Liz."

Taking a shallow breath, she dared to tilt her chin up to meet his eyes. "Yes?"

He didn't reply. Instead, he held her gaze, leaned closer and brushed his lips against hers. Soft. Warm.

Heavenly.

Her eyes fluttered closed and she clamped down on the impulse to drag him toward her and grind her mouth against his the way her body craved, fearing what might happen if she took even one tentative step down that slippery slope.

Instead, she let herself glory in the moment. Finally! Here! Today was the day Carter McIntyre kissed her again! Had she imagined it like this? His lips so incredibly warm? His breath melding with hers as his mouth parted ever so slightly? *Journey* playing 'Open Arms' in the background?

Okay, maybe there wasn't a rock ballad playing on cue, but she made up for it by humming a soft moan of pleasure somewhere in the back of her throat as she let herself sink into the pleasure of this one, perfect kiss.

Just like the first time.

After a few heady moments, Carter pulled back, an easy, sensual smile lingering on his lips. "I guess you can cross 'Counted Carter's Fillings" off that 'Liz Never' list," he said. "Anything else I can help you with today?"

Liz gasped. Here she was, winded, overwhelmed, needy in ways she'd not remembered feeling for a *long* time—if *ever*—and he was making light of it? "Is this just a joke to you?"

"Come on, Liz. Have a sense of humor."

She squiggled out of his arms. "Pardon me if I don't have the sense of humor of a thirteen year-old." She brushed the hair from her temple with a shaky hand. How could he make light of something that felt so monumental? She'd spent the better part of her youth mooning after this guy and dreaming about one stupid kiss shared in a dark closet and when she finally gets the nerve to relive that moment after ten, *long* years, he makes a crack like that?

"It was just a joke," he said.

"It wasn't funny."

Carter sighed and shrugged and stepped away. "You need to lighten up, Beacon."

"You need to think before you speak."

His eyes flashed, but he didn't say anything else except. "I'll see you Monday."

She nodded curtly, not trusting herself to be polite in return and wordlessly walked him to the door. She closed it softly behind him.

Carter McIntyre wasn't worth a slam.

CHAPTER THIRTY

BAILEY WAS BACK at Liz's door, knocking, within ten seconds of Carter leaving.

Liz opened the door. *"What?"*

Bailey raised an eyebrow. "Somebody's in a pissy mood."

"Yes, somebody is. I also have no sense of humor, so watch out."

Bailey walked in without being invited. "I forgot my bag. Got halfway to my job and realized I don't have keys to get in."

"Sorry, go ahead. I'm sure it's around somewhere."

Bailey started walking toward the kitchen. "I was afraid I might have to sit in my car for a while. Didn't want to disturb you two if Carter was still apologizing."

"Yes, well you're lucky he quickly made an ass of himself."

"It's only been ten minutes."

"He works fast."

"What happened?"

"Remember that kiss back in high school?"

"The one you wrote sonnets about?"

"Mmm. Well, we kissed and you know what he says? He makes some crack about my counting his fillings. Can you believe it?"

"Did you?"

"Of course not! It was a beautiful... moment."

"Until he didn't recognize the magnitude of the occasion."

Liz refilled her coffee. "When you put it like that..."

"It makes it sound like he was getting that scary chick vibe and wanted to redirect away from all the heavy emotional stuff?"

Liz looked at Bailey over the rim of her mug. "You think I'm a scary chick?"

"Serious. Just serious. You need to lighten up sometimes, that's all."

Liz closed her eyes. "U*nless* he already told you to lighten up... in which case you need to kick his unfeeling ass right on out of here! Ah, here's my bag!"

Liz sighed and flumped into a chair. "You're right. I blew it. I finally get the courage to kiss the guy after all this time and it's—honest to God—as incredible as I remember, and I go and spaz out on him. Lovely."

"The good news is this isn't *Fatal Attraction* spazzing. You can recover from this."

"How?"

"Getting naked usually helps." Bailey fished in her bag without looking up.

"It was hard enough kissing him. I don't think getting naked is in the cards."

Bailey popped a peanut butter cup into her mouth. "My experience is, where there's unfinished business, getting naked is always in the cards.

"By the way, I think you should look outside."

TO-DO:

1.)

CHAPTER THIRTY-ONE

LIZ STOOD IN THE DINING ROOM and stared out the window at the string of smiley-face lights Carter had hung along the roofline of the shed. She had no idea when he'd done it. Probably yesterday before he came inside with the flowers. They hung there, glowing and smiling goofily, even though it was pouring rain over their little faces.

She hated them and loved them all at the same time.

Liz sighed, watching the rain drip off the shed roof and puddle on the ground. Because of the rain, she'd spent her Saturday afternoon tackling indoor punch-list items before spending the night second-guessing every action of her adult life.

Did she take everything too seriously?

By the time Sunday morning rolled around—still damp and cold— she hadn't come to any epiphanies. She rose and dressed early with every intention of getting started on a fresh to-do list for the day but, instead, found herself staring at her yellow legal pad on the kitchen table, sipping her third cup of coffee and wallowing in self-doubt. It was nine o'clock, and she'd only gotten as far as writing 'to do' at the top in bold, purposeful letters.

Was she boring? *Had* she shied away from living? Did she really have no sense of humor? Those questions and more had plagued her fitful night, in part, because she knew they held a grain of truth in them.

True, she hadn't sought opportunities to rebel against her parents. Hadn't she seen firsthand how hurt they were by John's reckless behavior? How frightened they were when he'd stagger in the door at three in the morning? How Mom would cry when John argued with Dad? Liz could still hear the slam of the door as he'd storm from the house. Again. Then Mom would quietly, resignedly call the police to pick him up, because she knew he wasn't fit to drive.

Liz had vowed never to cause such pain. Then, when Trish had gotten pregnant and moved out, Liz had made a second vow to be the perfect child. To never cause her parents a moment's worry.

But, where had that gotten her? Here she was, in her parents' home, the only one *not* doing whatever she darn well pleased with her life because she was still busy being the dutiful child.

Still busy being everything everyone expected of Brainy Beth Beacon.

But what if I wasn't? she wondered. *Who would I be? What would I do then?*

"Go skinny dipping—at noon," she murmured as she penned the words on the notepad. She stared at them and laughed a bit self-consciously at herself. It wasn't as if she actually planned to follow through on it. It felt freeing, though, if even in fantasy, she could escape from the boring box she'd painted herself into.

Grinning, Liz added another item to her list. Then another. Before long, she was at number ten. She tapped her pen on the pad and pondered.

Then, laughing out loud, she added one final item to the list and headed up to shower.

"LIZ? YOU HOME?"

Carter knocked on the slider door and waited, the weather wet and overcast again this morning. The heavy rains they'd had overnight would make it difficult to continue the patio until things dried out or he'd make a mess of their yard.

He'd made up an excuse to come over anyway, intending to talk to her about the design for the side walkway. In truth, he was still a little peeved about how things had gone the last time he'd been over. Peeved and a little turned on.

It was not a pleasant combination.

He couldn't say why he'd cracked the joke when he did. Maybe it was because Liz was looking at him in that intent, vulnerable way she had, and he'd wanted to put her at ease.

Now, he wanted to shake the superior out of her. Figuratively speaking, of course. *He* needed to think before he spoke? Pot calling the kettle black.

Probably just as well she wasn't home given his mood.

He tucked the brochures he'd brought in the casing by the door, but as he pushed away, the slider moved, and he realized it was unlocked.

He cracked the slider open an inch. "Liz?" No answer.

Spying a pad of paper on the table, he walked over to jot down a brief note then stopped short when he read what was there. He hurried back to the door. Maybe it would be better to leave a message on her cell.

"What are you doing here?"

Before he had time to register her question, Liz snatched the legal pad from the table. Carter stood at the slider, speechless. She'd been showering. Her hair hung in wet locks, her robe snugged tight around her waist, damp patches making the fabric almost translucent in places where her hair had lain against it. Her face was scrubbed clean and pink. All he could think about was number one on her list.

He found his voice with difficulty. "I came to check on the job and tell you I'll finish when the weather clears and the yard dries out, but I, ah, wanted to know if you've decided to extend the pavers around to the driveway. I had some ideas for—"

"How did you get in?"

"The door was unlocked."

She frowned and strode toward the slider, heedless of the state of his libido. "It was?" She fiddled with the lock/unlock knob, her thin robe molding to her curves.

"You should be more careful with that. Eddie might get out again. But, I'm glad you're here, because you saved me the trouble of writing a note." As he said the words, her eyes flew to his. He smiled guilelessly. "No need now. I didn't want to drip across your kitchen, anyway, so you've saved me the trouble of cleaning up after myself."

She forced a smile, he could tell, because her fingers clenched the legal pad tightly despite her bright expression. "Glad I caught you, then," she said.

He watched her throat move as she swallowed.

"I'm glad you stopped by," she said. "I want to thank you for the lights. The smiley-faces?" She gestured with the notepad in the general direction of the shed and then sucked it back to her chest again when she saw the words she'd written there waving around for all to see. "They're charming. The lights. Very sweet." Her tongue darted out to her lips. "And, I want to apologize for over-reacting yesterday."

Carter looked at her. He stuffed his hands in his pockets. It was hard to be peeved when she was extending the olive branch like that. Especially dressed the way she was. "Two," he finally said.

"What?"

"I have two fillings."

She stared at him a moment, a nonplussed expression on her face. "I have five."

"Five?"

Her lips tilted guiltily. "I liked sweets as a kid."

157

He smiled, genuinely now, inordinately pleased that perfect Liz had her faults, too. "So, I stopped by because I wanted to talk about the design for the side walkway. I was thinking a more fluid curve instead of hard angles. I could sketch a couple op— *Wait*. I brought some brochures…" He leaned out the door a moment to retrieve the flyers he'd placed there. He heard paper tearing behind him. He turned back around. Paused.

Liz waited, her breath coming in light bursts, the legal pad at her side.

He squinted at her. Frowned. "*Hmm.*" he said.

"What?"

"Nothing. It's just…" He gestured vaguely toward her chest where she'd clearly stuffed the paper. "Are you a little, um, lopsided?"

"What?" She clutched the legal pad to her chest again. "*NO!* Why would you even ask?"

He met her eyes. "Because I could have sworn things were, um, even five seconds ago."

Liz's face turned crimson. "Don't be ridiculous."

My God, she was cute when she blushed. He decided to take pity on her. "My mistake. So, are we doing the side walkway or not?"

Liz pushed her wet hair aside like she was still trying to figure out whether she could trust him. Short answer? No.

"I'm still running the numbers." Her gaze skittered away from his.

She chewed her bottom lip.

He stifled a groan.

"Pavers would certainly dress the place up," she said. "But I'd want to do the front walkway, too, so it would all match."

"The front, too? You're snowballing on me."

"Snowballing?"

"Otherwise known as while-we're-at-it-itis."

She closed her eyes for a moment, holding the notepad like a shield. "I just always had this vision of what the place should look like, you know? What I would do if it were mine. I even had a scrapbook I made of it, if you can believe that. It's kind of hard to let it go.

"It was my grandparent's house before my parents bought it and rehabbed it. I always thought it would stay in the family." She shook her head as if to rid it of ridiculous notions and backed toward the swinging door. "I'd better get to town if I'm going to finish priming the kitchen today. And, I need new paint for the front door…"

"Want a ride?"

She stopped, the door at her back. "I can call Trish."

"I'm happy to do it. Nothing better to do. It's still raining."

"I have to dry my hair… Get dressed…"

His smile grew wider. "I can wait."

IT WAS NOT A BIG DEAL. If he saw the list, he saw the list, right? What was on it anyway? Liz unfolded the wad of paper she'd stuffed in her bra and winced.

Skinny dipping at noon.

Okay, in the scheme of things, that wasn't such a big deal. How many people have gone skinny dipping? He'd probably think it was out of character for her, borderline exhibitionist given the timeframe, but he wouldn't be put off by it.

She groaned as she looked at numbers two and three. Obviously she'd had naked skin on the brain, because 'Try a thong' and 'Play strip poker' came next, followed by 'Learn to play piano', 'Visit the Grand Canyon' and 'Ride Space Mountain.' 'See Niagara Falls', 'Explore a real castle' and 'Learn to shoot an arrow' were all innocuous enough.

But what made her worry her lip as she pulled on a pair of jeans and T-shirt was number ten. Dear heavens, why had she put pen to paper on *that* one? Crumbling the list into a little ball, she went into the bathroom—and promptly flushed it down the toilet. *There.* That was where silly thoughts like that belonged.

Carter was waiting for her when she descended the stairs ten minutes later with the shreds of her dignity as taped together as she could manage. "Sorry to keep you waiting."

"Waiting? That was the fastest I've ever known a female to get ready in my life. I'm impressed. Nice hair, by the way. The new style suits you."

Liz felt the heat of his compliment warm her cheeks as she gathered her purse and coat.

The ride to town was companionable despite the fact that she'd been caught stuffing her bra with paper products.

"I can get you a contractor's discount," Carter offered as they walked through the entrance of the local building supply store.

"Oh, that's not—"

"A problem? You're right. What do you need?"

"Just a few supplies. A quart of paint for the front door. A bucket of primer for the kitchen."

"No paint for the kitchen?"

"I'm still deciding. White is probably the best choice. Those old kitchen cabinets are in tough shape, but I'm waffling. White is so sterile."

"How about off-white?"

She stared at him then, one of those looks women give men when they haven't a clue.

"Okay, if you don't like off-white, what would you paint the cabinets if the house were yours?" Carter asked.

"Celery green," she said immediately, forgetting to mock him as she pulled a sample card from the rack in front of them. "With white subway tiles on the backsplash and cherry-red ceramic knobs." She glanced up and slid the card back into place. "But, white is the sensible choice, and I might as well get the paint while I've got your truck to haul it." She pulled another card from the rack. "This shade looks fine. Bright. Clean. I'll get enough for the ceiling and walls, too. Then I'll only have to mask off the floor."

He grinned a little at that.

See? She had a sense of humor.

"And seeing as I'm here, I'll get this for the dining room," she pulled a paint chip out of the rack. "And this for the living room. Then I'll be done."

"Nicely decisive," he said. "Okay, I'll get the paint while you collect the other stuff on your list."

"I'll take a look at light fixtures. I'd like to replace the front coach lanterns. They're badly rusted."

"You might have trouble getting an electrician on short notice."

"I think I can figure it out."

But just to be sure, she scribbled 'Home Electrical Guide' on her shopping list.

CARTER JIGGLED HIS KEYS impatiently as he stood in line and hoped the cashier wouldn't recognize him. They'd never actually dated, more hung out a few times at Lucky's. He'd driven her home once. And while she'd clearly been hinting for more than casual barstool conversation, he'd exercised enough self-control to heed the warning bells in his head that had told him she was sweet but a little wacky.

For one thing, she liked to pretend she was twins.

The cashier caught his eye, and Carter fought a groan as she smiled. He nodded in return and searched the aisles for signs of Liz.

It wasn't that he was a hopeless flirt—or an absolute Don Juan—but in a small town, it was hard being young and single and not run out of options after a while.

The line moved forward and the cashier—what was her name again? Jill? Marina? One of those—maybe both—was batting her mascara-laden lashes at him. He grimaced and she seemed to take it as a positive overture, because she waved coyly and tucked her hair behind the half-dozen earrings in her right ear. He remembered her hinting about having other piercings she was willing to show him.

Marina was the wild twin. He remembered now.

"What do you think of these?" Liz tapped him on the shoulder, and he turned, relief and inexplicable joy flooding his body. She pointed to a pair of light fixtures in her cart. "I know they're more Craftsman style, but I really liked them, and they're on clearance, so the price is right."

"Nice. Very classic," he said.

"That's what I thought." Liz absently tucked her hair behind her ear. Carter smiled at the small gold hoop. It was small, elegant and very *Liz*. "Is the paint ready?"

Carter pulled his mind off Liz's earlobe to concentrate on her question. "Already in the truck. The cashier should have the slip."

Liz set her purchases on the counter, oblivious to the dark looks Jill/Marina was now flashing her as she recognized that he and Liz were together.

"I'm sorry to have kept you waiting. I won't be but a moment checking out." Liz reached into her purse and frowned. "Oh, no."

"What is it?" Carter peered over her shoulder.

"My wallet must have dumped." She scrounged quickly amid the jumble on the bottom of her purse to find her credit card and handed it to the cashier. "No big deal. I'll reorganize it later."

Carter accepted the receipt from the cashier with an apologetic smile as Liz bundled her purchases into the cart.

It wasn't as if the cashier wasn't attractive or even friendly. But, as Liz fought to make it through the double-doors—the painting poles falling askew and one of the cart's wheels wedging into a crack in the concrete—Carter couldn't help but admire the fact that Liz wasn't immediately turning around to find some man to bat her eyes at to save her from her plight, or worse, someone to blame. Instead, she laughed—a low, self-deprecating chuckle. Then she gave the cart a solid shove and grabbed the poles moments before they attempted to skewer an incoming customer.

Carter was used to women looking to him for something. Whether it was a good time, help opening a jar lid, or an attractive date to hang off their arm for the infamous family wedding. Women had turned to him again and again. Except Liz. A person had to admire a woman who wanted to do things for herself.

Especially when her jeans fit her so damn nicely.

Carter bounded after Liz. She was already unloading her purchases into the truck when he grabbed what remained in the cart and stowed it away. He held her door for her—a gesture he took for granted but which brought a fresh blush to her cheeks—and smiled to himself.

The air was clean and fresh, the rain clouds beginning to clear, and all Carter could think was how much he enjoyed watching Liz blush and how much he envied her an afternoon of industrious activity.

He pulled up to the traffic light, and tapped his toe as he waited for it to turn green. "So, would you mind if I stuck around to help paint?"

Liz blinked at him like he'd just offered to scrub the soap scum off her shower stall. "Oh, no. You don't have to spend your Sunday—"

"Helping an old friend? Not a problem."

She looked as if she wanted to protest further, but he flashed her a bright grin and asked how her father was doing. That distracted her long enough and soon they pulled into her drive.

She slipped from the cab and hurried to the front door. Carter followed more slowly, the paint cans a solid weight in his hands.

He balanced one on his knee as he waited for Liz to open the lock, enjoying the flex of muscle in his arm, the tension in his thigh. If anyone asked, he would have readily admitted he liked manual labor. The exertion, even the sweat. It felt good to put his mind and body toward one purpose. It helped him feel centered, calm almost.

As Grams always said, the right kind of activity kept him out of trouble.

"You really don't have to—" Liz began again as he followed her through the door.

"I'm not charging you for it, Liz. I just want something to do with my hands." Her eyes flashed to his, and suddenly he heard his words in a different light and wondered if he were keeping out of trouble or stepping into it. "I like to keep busy," he said somewhat hoarsely, wishing he hadn't been picturing something entirely different he might be doing with his hands.

"Of course," she murmured, scurrying toward the kitchen. "Let's get started then."

He blew out a ragged breath and told his hands to behave themselves.

Trig   chpt 12 prob 1-32!

DON'T FORGET

milk
bbq sauce-big jar
HAM-boneless kind

red label?

CHAPTER THIRTY-TWO

Twelve years earlier…

IT HAPPENED IN A BLUR. One minute Carter was grinding the half-smoked cigarette under his heel, the next minute he'd pinned Dan-the-Jerk-Jock-O'Connell against the wall in the Whitmeyers' hallway, his fist at Dan's throat.

"I don't think so," was all he'd said.

"What the f—?" Dan sputtered. "Lay off! What the hell's wrong with you?"

"Nothing." Carter said, the adrenaline pumping through his veins like an electric current. "There's *nothing* wrong with *me.*"

He leaned closer, perversely enjoying the sheen of sweat beading on Dan's brow. "Now, listen up," he ground out, his voice lower and more gravelly than it had been in all of his seventeen years. "You're *not* going in there. You're *not* giving *anyone* an education. And you're *not ever* going to breathe a word of this to anyone. Got it?"

Dan shook Carter off, but that's only because Carter chose to let him go. "Christ," Dan swore. "Are you fucking high?" But, he backed away anyway, straightening his jacket and glancing over his shoulder to make sure no one had witnessed anything. "I don't need this shit," he said. "If you want her so bad, she's all yours."

Carter raised an eyebrow in reply.

"Asshole," Dan muttered as he retreated down the hall.

Carter waited until Dan was gone before he exhaled. His body was humming, still throbbing with whatever emotion had made him act on animal instinct, because it sure as heck hadn't been his brain. If he'd been using his brain, he wouldn't have pinned the most popular jock in class against the wall and gone psycho on him.

There'd be no repercussions, though. There'd been no witnesses. Dan wasn't stupid enough to admit he'd been bested by an outsider whose muscles didn't come from lifting weights in the gym but from shoveling manure and throwing rocks around for his uncle's landscaping business.

Carter glanced at the door in front of him.

She's all yours.

Shit. He couldn't just leave her there. How humiliating would that be? Beth wasn't so bad. A little nervous maybe. A lot serious. But she had a sweet smile and she'd sat in that library week after week drilling him on trig until he thought he'd dream in parabolas. No, he couldn't leave her there.

He swallowed. But, if he went in there now, he'd taste of beer and cigarettes for sure. She'd know it was him.

Rummaging through his coat pockets, he dug out a package of Twizzlers and crammed one into his mouth. It was better than nothing. He spotted a room deodorizer on the hallway table, rubbed it lightly on the outside of his coat to cover the smoke scent on his clothes and figured it was now or never.

Swallowing the last of the Twizzler, Carter took a breath... and snicked open the pantry door.

She stood in shadow, the light of an outdoor streetlight only half illuminating her. She had her hands clasped in front of her and her head held high, her lips in a faint smile as if amused by the situation.

Carter smiled, too, even though she couldn't see him, and closed the door.

He almost said hi, just to put her at ease and let her know he was there, but the sudden alertness in her posture told him she already knew. Her smile faded.

Now what?

He realized he was shaking, an aftershock from his run-in with Dan, no doubt, but it left him feeling oddly nervous, something he wasn't used to feeling around a girl. He took a step closer and reached out to touch her hand so she'd know where he was.

She jerked then gave a soft, nervous laugh. "Sorry," she whispered, although it sounded louder in the small room. "You surprised me."

Her lips formed a half smile under the blindfold and Carter found himself staring at them. They were a soft pink color. He'd never noticed before how sexy they were. How wide and full and tempting. He found himself looking forward to a taste.

He took another step closer, and her tongue darted out as his toe knocked against hers. She laughed a little and he took the opportunity to steady himself by resting his hands on her elbows.

He didn't let go.

He just needed to kiss her. It shouldn't be hard. Hell, he'd made out with girls for a hell of a lot longer than seven minutes, and at this point, he didn't think anyone was counting. But, if he didn't make an effort, didn't make it last a little while, Beth would be crushed thinking she'd somehow disappointed.

No. No matter how bad she was at this, he had to at least give her five minutes before he quit. He owed her that much.

Her chest rose and fell in shallow breaths, and he slid a hand up her shoulder, instinctively trying to soothe her, and cupped her nape. His fingers flexed, discovering the soft, silky skin there, and he ran his fingers lightly up and down her nape again, enjoying the feel of it.

She leaned into his hand, a soft gasp escaping her and he took that moment to lean forward and press his lips to hers.

She went rigid for one surprised second, and then softened underneath him, a faint smile forming against his mouth for a brief moment before she leaned more firmly into him, seeking. Trusting. Melting.

He lost himself in that kiss. Lost himself for long, drugging, blood-thrumming moments as Beth Beacon came alive in his arms, a warm, rich heat seeping into him as her hand found the back of his head, her fingers lightly resting there as they shared sweet, lazy kisses, one after another after another.

He eased closer, less of a premeditated move than a desire for more.

His tongue snaked out lightly at first, testing, teasing. She pulled away slightly, but then she began to explore on her own, tentatively then more boldly.

Dipping further.

He pulled her against him then, and her hand sank deeper into his hair, as the kiss grew hotter, intensified.

Her breathing was quick and light now, her kisses like heaven, and he didn't even know he was doing it as his hand slid down her back to cup her and hold her soft, feminine curves against him.

She went still, and he realized where his hand was.

What he'd been thinking.

He let out a shaky breath against her lips. He throbbed in ways he knew he couldn't satisfy, and if he didn't somehow find a way to pull himself back, he'd be giving Beth the very education he'd tried to spare her.

Still kissing her deeply, fully, earnestly, he reached up and grasped her hands in his and pulled them down to her sides. Then he cupped her face and slowly, slowly pulled away.

She moaned softly—a protest—and he bent to lay one last kiss on her still-parted, upturned lips.

Their breaths were shallow, the air thick with desire. Inexplicably, impossibly, Beth smiled.

"Thank you," she whispered.

He nodded, even though she couldn't see him, and rested his index finger against her well-kissed lips. They puckered briefly, full and moist, pressing a kiss to his skin, before she stepped away, folding her hands together again as they'd been when he'd first entered.

She didn't say another word, only stood there, her breath light, her lips forming a half, knowing smile as he stepped out and closed the door behind him.

CHAPTER THIRTY-THREE

LIZ SLUMPED INTO A tarp-draped kitchen chair, her arms already weary from working muscles seldom used. With the priming nearly complete, she could start the finish coat by dinnertime. She could be done with the kitchen and back on schedule by Monday night.

It felt good to make so much progress. And, it was fun.

Because of Carter.

Liz turned and smiled despite her fatigue. He had his back to her, his cargo shorts and T-shirt splattered with white primer, his muscles flexing in his arms as he stroked the roller over the ceiling in time to the rock music he'd insisted on blaring.

"I've decided to go for it!" he said over the din.

"What?" she yelled back.

"The fountain project," he said, pausing to turn down the radio. "I'm going to bid on it."

"I think you should."

He nodded as he set his roller in the tray next to her brush. "You know what this means, don't you?" He cocked a grin at her. "It means I'm finally growing up."

"You've been grown up for a while."

He helped himself to a soda. "My uncle wants me to take over the business."

"He— Carter, that's wonderful!"

He popped open the can, looking somewhat pensive. "This would be my first solo project."

"From what I've seen you've been working on your own for a while."

"I know. But, if Pops isn't working at all, I'll probably need an extra hand. That means hiring an employee or two, scheduling…" He ran a hand over his face and looked at her soberly. "As I said, growing up."

"Take heart. It happens to the best of us."

He sat down. "I just never expected it to happen to me."

She chuckled at the lost boy look on his face and got up to get a drink as well. "I have to say, I'm feeling as proud of you as the day you came home with a B+ on that trig test. I couldn't have been more pleased—"

"I cheated," he said.

She whirled around. *"You didn't!"*

"No," he laughed, standing up again. "But, your expression just now was priceless."

She *harrumphed* and went back to pouring her iced tea. "Worry not. You haven't grown up as much as you think."

"Aw, but that's what makes me so loveable," he said.

She turned, intending to tell him he wasn't all that loveable, either, but the words died on her tongue.

"Thanks," he murmured, eyes dark, sober, as his lips hitched up at the corner endearingly. "You always did make me reach higher than I ever thought I could."

The look on his face made her nerves hum like they had the night she'd waited for her first kiss in Jenny Whitmeyer's pantry.

"You always did have more potential than you gave yourself credit for," she murmured. And then he went and flashed her a bright smile, and her stomach hit the floor.

Holy. Smokes.

Liz struggled to take a breath, her blood roaring in her ears.

It couldn't happen that quickly, could it? It didn't even make sense! How could she be standing here, minding her own business (thank you very much) and have a feeling like *that* rush over her?

She was far too pragmatic for it to be true. Besides, it was totally inappropriate on so many levels. She didn't even live in Sugar Falls anymore! They had nothing in common. He was completely irreverent, and she was completely and utterly…

And yet, the wave of certainty that flooded her as his brilliant smile hit her in full force was just as unquestionable.

She didn't just have a crush on Carter McIntyre anymore. She'd gone and fallen head over heels in love with him.

"Should we call for a pizza?"

"What?" she asked, shaking her head as if *that* would bring her to her senses.

"Pizza. It's quick. It's easy. And I'm starved."

"You have paint on your cheek," she observed distantly.

Strangely, she didn't even care that he was talking about food in the midst of her making the most monumental emotional discovery of her life. Somehow it was fitting. Real.

Because, she suddenly realized, she no longer wanted a fantasy of love, she no longer wanted the possibility or promise of love sometime in the future. She wanted the imperfect reality that stood before her. Hungry. Smudged. Smiling, wondrous reality.

Lord help her, she wanted Carter McIntyre.

She told herself it had to be some other woman. It certainly wasn't *Liz* who stood, took a paper napkin from the table and calmly wiped the smudge of paint off Carter's cheek, licking her thumb and rubbing it over the light shadow of stubble as it tugged at her flesh, marveling at how good it felt to touch his face.

And it wasn't Liz who swallowed in anticipation as she became acutely aware of the scent of his body, the air in her own lungs as they filled deeply, involuntarily, then caught when his eyes turned almost imperceptibly darker. It couldn't be Liz who licked her lips and smiled, who forgot about being straight or narrow or responsible as she took a step closer.

Carter didn't speak. The man who always seemed so quick with a wise-cracking comment was completely silent as he reached a hand out to cup her cheek, his thumb rubbing ever so lightly over her skin. And when he pulled her forward and pressed his mouth to hers, it was she who made a primal sound of surrender deep in her throat as her lips parted.

So good, she thought, her hands sliding up to pull his head closer. He tasted, felt *so* good. Never before had she felt so blissfully whole, so *complete* simply from touching her lips to a man's.

Except once.

Carter melded their mouths, his lips soft yet firm, light touches following searing pressure. Liz sighed into his mouth and learned his brilliant smile all over again in a way she'd never dreamed possible but had dreamed about a thousand times.

She didn't want it to end. She wanted to be this woman who could kiss and be kissed with such deep passion her entire life.

Heaven help her, *she wanted.*

Another small moan of pleasure escaped her as his hands slid, hot and firm down her back to cup her rear. Then he pressed her against the kitchen table—the same kitchen table she'd eaten pancakes at as a girl—and she realized with a hint of excited alarm that she was picturing them *on* that same table.

She pulled him to her. Hard.

Carter grunted in surprise and tried to pull back, but Liz would have none of that. Not now. No, now that she'd decided to be this new woman, there was no turning back. Gripping his head with one hand and his right buttocks with the other, she held him tight, nipped his bottom lip with her teeth.

And grinned.

"You're right. Two," she said.

HE CHUCKLED AGAINST her lips. He knew she was smiling. He could feel the curve of her lips under his own, but the sensation of her wide, soft lips curving against his fought for supremacy in a riot of sensations from the rasp of her jeans against his thigh, to the surge of desire pulsing through his veins.

He had no idea how they'd gone from contemplating pizza to practically sprawling on the kitchen table, but it was beyond his capacity to think about anything other than that wicked gleam in her hazel eyes or the light nip she'd just given him.

He didn't know this Liz. The Liz he'd known was lovely, appealing. Predictable.

This Liz was sensual. Passionate. Focused in a way that was uniquely Liz but bowling him over with heat and intensity.

She was a fire in his hands, in his blood, and he struggled to keep up with the need that flashed hot and bright within him, seemed matched by her own breathless assault.

His lips hovered over hers. "What are we doing?" he gasped between kisses. "I'm covered in paint."

"Me, too." She giggled and squirmed and Carter lost the will to protest as she pulled off his battered, paint-spattered ball cap and tossed it in the corner.

He couldn't believe he was doing this. Somehow taking Liz Beacon on her kitchen table didn't seem right. Didn't seem real. He looked around for a slightly more padded surface. "We should stop. Or pause..."

"No."

He laughed then, relishing the give of her body as he pressed himself into her soft curves. Just *no.* She didn't ask why they should stop. She didn't agree with him. She'd simply stated in that firm, business-like, Liz Beacon way, 'no.' And, how could he argue with that?

"Take off your shirt," she ordered hoarsely, fumbling with his fly.

His eyebrow arched at her command, but he grinned, too. Picking her up despite her squeal of surprise, he sat her on the edge of the table, toed off his sneakers and pulled his T-shirt over his head. He was still half-dressed, but he felt more naked than he ever had in his life.

She was quiet, her lips full and pink and well-kissed as she stared at the bulge in his shorts. Then her eyes flashed up to his and he saw the moment of uncertainty there.

"We don't have to do this," he said.

Christ, could they? Suddenly he realized heavy petting was all they'd be doing if she wasn't prepared. And why would she be? It wasn't as if she'd been expecting him to jump her bones on the kitchen table while the paint dried on their brushes.

Great. Now, he was a half-naked horny guy with an obvious erection, and she was probably wondering how she got herself into this. He bent to rebutton his cargo shorts.

She reached out a hand to stop him. "Don't."

"I don't have anything on me," he said. Maybe the universe was trying to tell him something.

"Are you clean?"

"I beg your pardon?"

She blushed furiously, her cheeks brilliant as she repeated the question. "I know you tend to be fairly popular with women. I just..."

"I'm clean," he said. "And the rumors of my popularity are highly inflated." He gave her a look. "I'm careful," he said, when he saw she wasn't amused.

"I'm sorry, but these days you have to ask."

He tipped her chin until she'd meet his eyes again. "You?"

She laughed, a self-conscious burst. "Are you kidding? I'd have to have sex—" but she cut herself off before finishing the sentence. "I mean, it's not that I'm— I mean, I've *had* sex..."

Carter stroked her arm with his fingertips and chuckled. "I'm not thinking you're frigid if that's what you're worried about. I'm more thinking I'm standing here thinking thoughts I shouldn't be thinking because I've got no way to follow through on them."

"I have protection," she blurted. "In my purse." They looked at her purse on the window sill. "So we can. If you want to."

"You have to ask?"

But, she didn't laugh. Instead she let out a long breath and glanced out the slider, her arms across her chest. "I'm sorry. This is so awkward now."

Carter nodded. "You've changed your mind. That's cool." He reached for his shirt.

"No!" She protested. "It's just... the whole responsible conversation kind of takes the wind out of the sails of being irresponsible, doesn't it?" Her eyes pleaded with him to understand.

"You want to be irresponsible."

"Responsibly, yes."

He grinned. "Strangely, I think I understood that. Okay, how about we do something to put us back in the mood?"

"Like what?"

"I don't know. A game?"

"A game."

"Isn't that what horny teenagers do? Truth or Dare? Spin the Bottle?"

"We're not thirteen."

"Don't look so skeptical. It'll work. Truth or Dare. Have you ever played?"

"No."

"Then it's about time." He winked. "But I'll be nice. I'll let you go first."

"How does this work?" All business, she started to slide off the table. Carter stopped her with a kiss.

When he finally pulled back, she had that lightly flushed but wary look back in her eyes. *Progress.* "You ask whether I want a truth or dare and I pick one," he instructed.

"Okay. Truth or dare?"

"Truth. Now ask me a question."

She frowned slightly, little furrows forming on her brow as she thought. He nuzzled her neck, enjoying the clean, sweet scent of her. "Is today the first time you've thought about kissing me?"

"No. My turn."

"When was the first time?" she demanded, pulling back enough to make eye contact.

"Uh-uh. I already answered your question. Your turn now. Truth or dare?"

She pouted, but answered anyway. "Truth."

"Is today the first time you've thought of having sex with me?"

Her eyes flew to his. Maybe he'd pushed too far. It was hard to know where the boundaries were with a woman who was splayed on the kitchen table one moment and biting her lip nervously the next. "Let me rephrase that. Is today the first time you've thought of having sex with me on your kitchen table?"

She smiled shyly, the sexy heat now returning to her eyes. *Better.* "Yes. Truth or dare?"

"Dare."

"You'll do anything I want?"

"Or I have to answer a truth."

"Are you sure this is the way the game is supposed to be played?"

Her fingertips fiddled with the waistband of his shorts, the unconscious movement driving him crazy with desire. But he didn't draw her attention to it. He didn't want her to stop. He grinned instead. "Would I make up my own rules? Besides, it's not like there are 'truth or dare' police out there. We make our own rules. So tell me. What's my dare?"

"Okay. I dare you to do a striptease for me."

Carter glanced at himself wryly. "It'll be short-lived entertainment."

"Do you want a truth instead?"

"Do I get music?"

She smiled and pushed at his chest. "Stop stalling."

Carter started humming, a self-conscious, ridiculous base beat and gave it his all.

For her part, she was an appreciative audience and was blushing furiously even though he was the one standing completely naked in the middle of her kitchen.

"I'm feeling a little ridiculous," he confessed.

"You don't look ridiculous," she said.

"Maybe not, but you're definitely looking overdressed."

She licked her lips and toed off her sneakers. Smiled mischievously. His body answered the look in her eyes as he stepped toward her, his pulse thudding in his ears. "My turn. Another truth."

"I don't get to choose?"

"We make our own rules, remember?" He stood apart from her, not touching, the tension, awareness, as palpable as any contact with her bare skin. The air in his lungs grew thick.

Her eyes darkened.

"Okay. Truth," she said.

"Close your eyes," he commanded.

"That's not a question."

He stepped closer still, until he could feel as much as hear her quick intake of breath. "No, that's just the first part."

"A multi-part question? No fair. I think that's a different game." But she closed her eyes, nonetheless.

"It's not about playing fair," he whispered. "It's about playing to win."

She opened one eye. "There's a winner?"

He smoothed her eye closed with the pad of his thumb. "*Shh*. If we play it right, we both win. Now for part two. Ready?"

She nodded even though he noticed her nervous swallow. "Ready."

Carter leaned close, so close his lips grazed her ear. She smelled so good. Delicious. "Tell me your favorite candy."

"Twizzlers." She said, smiling softly.

"What a coincidence," he said, a rush of something sweet and innocent flooding his senses. "Mine, too. Now. Tell me about your first kiss."

"That's not a question, either," she said, her eyes popping open. "You're very bad at this."

174

He rubbed his thumb over her cheek again, enjoying the way her chest rose and fell in shallow, eager breaths. "Oh, but it is. You see, I want the truth. No holding back. All the details. Got it?"

She swallowed again. "And then what?"

He smiled to dazzle. "We both win."

She closed her eyes and for a moment he thought she wouldn't say a thing, but then her lips began to move and his entire body focused on the whispered words caressing his bare skin.

And he was a horny teenager all over again.

After she spoke, she went perfectly still, her eyes closed, as if she were afraid of his response.

And suddenly the game was over as her eyes met his, all flirtation gone, replaced with a raw hunger that matched his own. Another hot rush of fire to his groin made it impossible to speak even if he'd wanted to. His hands tangled with hers at the hem of her shirt, pulling it over her head, his fingers fumbling with the clasp of her bra as she pushed down her jeans. "Here. Let me," she murmured, pushing his hands away. Then her breasts were free, lovely and firm, as she bent to skim her panties to the floor.

When she stood again, the uncertainty was back in her eyes. He could see her thinking. Worrying. Wondering.

"Stop thinking so much," he chided her. "This is supposed to be fun."

"I've never done anything like this before."

"Sex?" he teased gently.

"No," she blushed. "*This.*"

"You mean sex on a kitchen table? It's easy, really, only a little harder."

"Don't you feel a bit silly? We're in broad daylight. Anyone could walk to the back slider and see us standing here in our altogether. What would they think?"

"That we were really hungry? Because I know I am." He pressed forward, flesh against flesh, heat against heat. Her hands came up to press against his chest and splayed there. His heart hammered against her palm. He'd never felt so relaxed and excited all at the same time.

"I've never had sex anywhere but in a bed," she confessed.

"Then we have some work ahead of us. There are floors, shower stalls, grassy meadows..."

"How do you know you'll want to do it again?"

"Good lord, Liz. I already want to do it again and we haven't done it once. Stop talking and touch me."

"I am touching you." She peered down at her fingers.

"I mean *really* touch me."

"Can I kiss you first?"

"God, yes."

Her lips brushed his, the softest most tantalizing caress that sent heat spiraling to his toes. He groaned and leaned into her.

"I just don't want to get it wrong," she murmured against his lips.

"Honey, the only way to get it wrong would be to tell me to stop." And with that he lifted her to the table again and kissed her like the first time.

"I DON'T WANT TO BREAK the mood, but can we get that pizza now? I'm hungry."

Carter's lips tilted in a lazy grin. "I thought you'd never ask." He rolled onto his side and slid his finger down her bare arm.

In the end they'd moved to the living room; although, now that she had rug burns in unmentionable places, Liz was only sorry the table hadn't seemed up to the task after all.

"Do you think we broke it?" she asked.

"I think I'm all right."

She swatted him playfully. "I meant the table."

He grinned and leaned forward to press a lazy kiss just north of her breast. "Nothing that can't be fixed. Just need to tighten a couple bolts, I think, and we'll be good to go."

She could feel her face warm. "I really am hungry."

"In a minute. You have gorgeous breasts, you know that? You should dress this way more often."

"You mean naked?" She laughed and felt the heat of a blush again, though she wouldn't have moved away from the warm brush of his lips for the world.

"*Mmm.* Suits you." He sighed and gave her breast one last peck before sliding up her torso and pinning her to the rug.

She looked into his gorgeous green eyes. Wow. She'd just made love to Carter MacIntyre. Correction. *She'd just fallen in love with him.*

The breath froze in her chest.

He frowned slightly. "You okay?"

"Yeah. Yes," she lied, forcing a smile. "Just, um, hungry."

Keep it light she counseled herself. She needed to get dressed. She needed to *think.* Oh God, she felt so *naked,* like every single emotion was laid bare for all to see.

"I'll get that pizza."

"Great idea," she said striving for a bright, relaxed, post-coital air. She scurried toward the kitchen for her clothes. Carter trailed her, naked, looking more glorious than any man had a right to.

She pulled on her jeans and shirt, needing to cover herself again as she tried to avoid staring at his body. If she looked at him again she'd probably blurt something out, like her undying love, and then embarrass them both. He'd signed up for sex not a china pattern.

Keep it casual, she told herself. *Feel him out.* "So, that was... something," she said.

His lips twitched as he pulled on his boxer briefs. "*Mmm.*" He said, stepping closer. He smiled. "Tell me why we never did that before? I'm feeling a little annoyed we've wasted all this time." He picked up his shorts and stood in front of her, bare-chested, the light smattering of dark hair there making her woman bits stand up and take notice most inconveniently.

Her heart fluttered happily in her chest. "We're here now," she said.

He pulled her into his arms and kissed her. "Not nearly enough time. When do you have to go back?"

Her heart skittered. "About a week."

His eyes went dark as he looked at her mouth. "Then we'll just have to make the most of the next seven days, won't we?"

She let him kiss her again as his words sank into her like a cold rain. *Seven days.* That's all he saw between them. And why would he see anything else? Oh Lord, and how could it *be* anything else?

She trembled as his lips pulled from hers.

He nudged her chin with his knuckle until she met his eyes. "No regrets?" he asked.

"No regrets," she said, forcing a smile.

"Good. I don't want to hurt you." His lips tilted. "I can do that sometimes without meaning to." He brushed the hair from her temple.

She sucked in a breath and forced herself to keep breathing. "I'm a big girl, Carter. You don't have to tiptoe around the fact that we're having a fling."

His hand stilled. "A fling?"

She waved her hand dismissively. "Hook-up. Friends with Benefits. Whatever you want to call it. I get it. You don't have to give me 'the talk.'" And she'd repeat that message over and over until her heart heard it loud and clear.

"A fling," he said again, pulling away to put on his shorts.

"Yes, well, what I mean is... nothing serious. Just casual sex."

"Nothing serious," he repeated, zipping his fly with a yank.

"Absolutely. I mean, we both know I'm only here a few more days, and then I'm headed back to Chicago. I have a job—a life—there."

"Right." He stared at her, and she swallowed, wishing he'd contradict her, praying he'd stop and tell her she was wrong, that it *wasn't* just sex.

But then his lips titled in a half smile. "I'm glad we're on the same page. Okay, I suppose I should get that pizza." And then he was tugging his T-shirt over his head, slipping on his sneakers and striding to the door as if her heart weren't breaking into a million, shattering pieces.

But at the last moment he stopped, turned and flashed a wide smile. "I suppose I should thank you. Because as cheap, casual, nothing-serious sex goes... I'll never forget it."

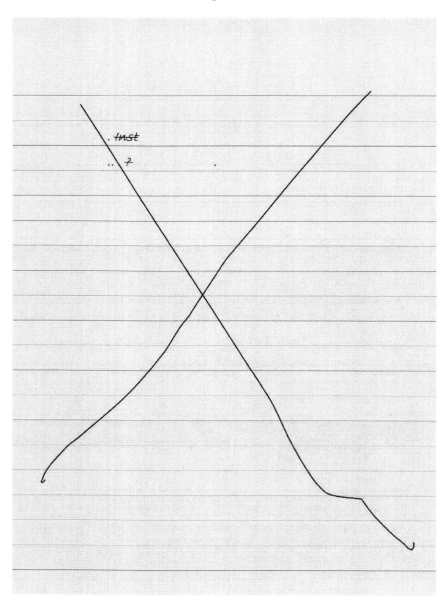

CHAPTER THIRTY-FOUR

ON THE SAME PAGE?!

Liz stopped, groaned, and turned to pace in the other direction.

She was *such* a fool! How could she be so *careless* as to fall in love with a heart-breaker like Carter?

It's not as if he meant to be hurtful, but she'd watched him roll through enough relationships to recognize the pattern. He'd start dating someone, they'd inevitably fall for him, and the next thing you knew, he'd given the old 'it's not you it's me' speech. What made Liz think she'd end up any differently? At least he was honest from the beginning about it.

But he was right. This *thing* between them couldn't be anything more than a fling. Practically speaking, they were too far apart. They lived in different states, for heaven's sake! They led different lives. Not to mention, they were *completely* ill-suited. She was punctual and orderly. He was habitually late and...

"I hope plain cheese works for you."

Carter's voice cut off any further thought. He hadn't knocked. Or maybe he had and she hadn't heard.

"You're back."

"I'm not going to let you starve," he said, setting the pizza on the table. He winked at her. "We need to keep our strength up."

For some reason she found it hard to look at the pizza sitting on the table. It seemed wrong to have something so ordinary and normal in the place where something extraordinary and carnal had just occurred. Something life-changing. Except what had really changed? She still harbored go-nowhere fantasies about a future with a guy who only saw her as a good lay.

Damn. This was becoming a pattern.

"Let me wipe that off before we eat," she blurted.

Carter stared at her, his eyes saying that her lips had already touched whatever had touched the table, and what did it matter? But she went to the sink anyway and squeezed the sponge under the water until it ran so hot she had to yank her fingers from the spray.

"Liz."

"It'll just take a moment. Plates are in the cupboard by the sink." She knew he knew where the plates were. The plates were in the same damn cupboard they'd been in forever.

"Liz."

"Do you want an apple with it?" she asked as she wiped the table in long, measured strokes. "A salad?"

"Liz."

She set the sponge by the sink and turned to face him. "I'm having iced tea. Can I pour you some?"

He was in front of her now, his cheekbones sharp angles over his taut mouth. "You mind telling me what's going on?" He stepped a little closer, and she could smell the scent of something earthy, forbidden lingering on his skin. His thumb stroked her cheek and she closed her eyes.

Gah! It was her own fault. She'd willingly participated—no, *invited*—what had happened between them. She'd opened herself up— again—to heartbreak at the hands of Carter McIntyre. But, continuing to be intimate with him when she knew the inevitable outcome would be like pouring salt in her own wound.

Her lips were suddenly dry and she darted her tongue out to moisten them. She took a quick breath and forced herself to look at him. "What happened earlier was... amazing," she said. *Amazing? How about earth-shattering? Soul-searing? A memory I'll take to my grave?* "And you are... incredible. But, I'm leaving in a week. I think it makes sense... to not let this happen again."

He stepped even closer and she could feel the heat of his body through her shirt. His eyes turned dark, and his gaze fell to her mouth. "To hell with what makes sense." Then he dipped his head for a kiss that left her clinging to him, breathless. He smiled as he pulled back. "I never gave a damn for what made sense before," he said as he abruptly let her go and turned toward the table. "And I don't intend to start now."

She stumbled to a chair and lowered herself in, her legs like noodles. "Carter, we shouldn't start something we can't—"

"Liz, I'm eating pizza now, because I *want* to. We had sex earlier because we wanted to. It isn't any more complicated than that."

"Sex is always complicated."

"It doesn't have to be." Carter pulled a slice of pizza from the box and took a bite. Liz's cell phone rang. They both looked at it where it sat on the middle of the table.

"I'll call him back," she said.

Carter's eyes narrowed as it rang a second time. He looked at her. "Him? Is this about your inter-office guy?"

Liz fought not to wince as she reached over to her phone and turned it off. She didn't want to think about Grant. Not now. Maybe not ever. "Of course not."

"Are you lovers?"

"What? No." She jumped up and opened the refrigerator door.

"Are you in love with him?"

Tea. She'd pour tea... "There's no point in talking about—"

"Are you?"

Liz sloshed tea into two tumblers, *this close* to throwing herself at Carter and taking what little he had to offer, dignity be damned.

"Why? What does that even matter?" She closed the refrigerator door. "It doesn't change the fact that I can't do this," she motioned vaguely with her hand between them, "with you. I shouldn't have the first time; but then you showed up, and you *kissed* me—"

"So now it's my fault we had sex?"

"*No!* No." She swiped a hand over her face. "It's not about fault. It's just... I don't *do* impulsive, Carter. I'm a planner. A list-maker. An I-know-what-my-credit-card-statement-will-say-before-I-get-it-in-the-mail type of person."

"So?"

"So, I need to think…"

"Christ, Liz, do I have to kiss you again? Because I will if I have to."

"Is that your answer to everything?"

"Do you have a better idea?"

"Yes," she said, half afraid he'd kiss her and half afraid he wouldn't. "Let's get back to painting." Her back and shoulders would ache like the devil in the morning, but if she didn't do something—*right now*—she'd no doubt blurt out something she'd regret.

He watched her in silence a few moments then finally picked up his drink. "You're more stubborn than I remember," he said, although his tone was slightly amused. He handed her her pizza. "Fine. I'll start the finish coat on the cabinets. You can go eat."

Liz glanced at the table. It was probably best if they were in separate rooms for a while. "Are you sure?"

His gaze lingered on the vee of her T-shirt a moment before he met her eyes again. "As sure as I am that if you don't leave, we won't get any painting done at all."

AFTER SHE ATE, she tried to return her plate, but Carter met her at the kitchen door and announced she was banned from entering until further notice. He told her he'd be too tempted if she tried to help and wouldn't it be nice for her to see the final unveiling? So, she settled in the living room and attempted to figure out the wiring instructions for the coach lights. But listening to Carter sing along to the radio and being alone with her thoughts did nothing to help her focus, and she soon tossed the manual aside in favor of painting over the hideous, mustard mis-tint on the front door with a couple of coats of refreshing periwinkle blue.

Around eight o'clock, Carter came out of the kitchen to announce he was between coats and was in the mood for Chinese. They got it to-go, and Liz pretended she was okay with casually eating take-out and casually touching one another and casual sex. Yet, every time he touched her, smiled at her, leaned in for one small kiss, her heart soaked it in like a drought-stricken land soaks in rain even though she knew that in seven days she'd be on a plane again... and it would all be over.

After dinner, Carter went back to the kitchen and Liz started a primer coat in the dining room. She could hear him through the door belting out the chorus to a rock ballad as he sang along to the radio, and even though she hated the song, it didn't stop her from wondering if things had been different... if they'd somehow gotten together in high school instead of now... would they have made it as a couple? Could it have worked then?

The hours passed, and sometime after midnight, Liz decided she'd had enough. She knocked on the door to the kitchen. "I'm going to bed."

She heard movement, and a moment later, Carter poked his head out. "*Mmm.* I'd love to join you, but I'm going to keep going. I won't be much longer." He kissed her quickly then smiled. "Keep my side warm, will you?"

She'd agreed, but he'd never come up. Liz was both relieved and disappointed.

She glanced at the clock on her nightstand and rolled to her back with a sigh.

It was nearly dawn, and replaying the events of the last twenty-four hours in her mind had done nothing to help her sleep.

She'd fallen in love.

She'd slept with Carter.

She'd forgotten about Grant.

God. How could she do that? How could she forget about a man she'd envisioned herself *marrying* not two short weeks ago? What did that say about her?

She groaned and threw an arm over her eyes. It wasn't the fact that she and Grant were on some sort of siesta. It was crystal clear now she wasn't in love with him and never had been. If she never saw him again, yes, she might be disappointed, but she wouldn't be heartbroken.

She swiped away a tear that had the nerve to escape down her cheek and threw back the covers.

She wouldn't go there. She'd cried those tears for Carter already, hadn't she? She wasn't a starry-eyed sixteen year-old anymore. She was a grown woman who had charted her course in life. Yes, they'd enjoyed something wonderful and memorable, but Carter didn't fit in her life and never would. Fantastic, mind-blowing sex didn't change that fact. Neither did a foolish, hopeful heart.

Liz swung her legs to the floor. She couldn't hide in her room forever. She needed to put on her big-girl panties and face things like a grown-up.

Tip-toeing down the stairs, she found Carter sprawled on the sofa. His shirt was off. No doubt it lay splattered with paint somewhere. She smiled, noting he'd at least taken the time to throw an old sheet over the sofa before falling asleep.

The faint light from the hallway illuminated his face. *He looks so vulnerable*, she thought. Awake, he was a dynamo. Always moving. Always using that never-ending charm and mega-watt smile to get what he wanted. Go where he wanted. But in sleep, it was as if all artifice melted away.

As if he, too, could be hurt by what they were doing.

Ridiculous. He was a grown man. He knew perfectly well what he was doing, and it wasn't falling in love.

Liz shook off the depressing thought and headed to the kitchen. She was thirsty, she rationalized, getting a drink. She wasn't peeking.

"Where do you think you're going?"

Liz froze, her hand on the kitchen door, as Carter's sleep-groggy voice touched her across the darkened room. "I'm thirsty."

"There's water in the upstairs bath."

"I need a cup."

"Liar."

She could hear the smile in his voice even as she pursed her lips and peered into the darkness.

"Go ahead and take a peek," he said. "If you can't wait. Go ahead."

"I just want a— *Oh.*"

He'd left the under-cabinet fixtures on, and even in the predawn light, the room was cool, serene. Breathtakingly lovely.

"Surprise," he whispered. She knew he was right behind her now, could feel the heat radiating from his sleep-warm body as they stood in the doorway.

"It's just as I pictured it," she murmured.

And it was. Soft, fresh, celery green nearly shimmered on the cabinet doors. Tomato-red ceramic knobs fought with brushed nickel hardware in her mind's eye before Liz could push the fanciful thoughts away.

Who was she kidding? Pretending she could keep this vision was as delusional as pretending she and Carter had a future together. She shook her head. "I know you meant well, but you shouldn't have. It's— You know I chose white."

"You chose this first."

She let out a sigh of regret. "But, then I decided on white." She squared her shoulders and turned toward him. "It's a neutral that will appeal to most buyers."

"But not to you."

"I'm irrelevant. I'm not a buyer."

"Maybe you could be." His hair was lightly mussed, bottle green eyes heavy-lidded with sleep, and seeing him barefoot and bare-chested in her home was as surreal as what he was suggesting.

She blinked. "Buy...? This? I've got a job, Carter, a... a ... *place* in Chicago. My life is there. We both know that."

But his words hung between them nonetheless. It was a ludicrous idea. It wouldn't bear the light of day, she told herself, even as the possibilities swirled like fairy sprites in her mind.

His lips formed a half smile that didn't quite reach his eyes as he wiped a weary hand over his face. "Right."

"It's beautiful," she rushed to assure him. "And I know you meant well. I just don't think—" But he cut her off with a single hard kiss that left her stunned, speechless, yearning for something she couldn't even name.

"Then don't," he ground out, the ferocity of his words catching her off guard. His lips hovered fiercely, temptingly, over hers. "For once in your life, Liz, *don't*."

Then he let her go, gathered his clothes, and said a curt goodbye before she could even ask what, exactly, she wasn't supposed to do.

CHAPTER THIRTY-FIVE

CARTER SAT AT THE DESK in his home office and closed his eyes, remembering Liz's whispered words from the day before.

The truth had hit him like a ton of bricks. It had been *him. He'd* been the one to give her her first kiss. He didn't know why it mattered or even if it did, but there was a sense of fate in knowing, a sense of relief that he'd intervened that night at the Whitmeyer's and it hadn't been Dan in there.

Not only for Liz's sake, but his own.

And yesterday, he'd relived the memory of that kiss right along with her—experienced its power all over again.

He'd always thought the fight with Dan had made the kiss more intense than it actually was. He couldn't believe a girl he'd overlooked so many times could blow him away with a single kiss.

And for the next few days, he'd looked at the world with new eyes. Everything had seemed brighter. Crisper. There was a promise in the air. A sense of possibility.

Carter ran a hand over his face as he waited for the printer. He glanced at the clock. It was almost eight a.m., and he felt like he'd ridden an emotional roller-coaster over the last twenty-four hours. He'd come home, exhausted and confused, and poured all that frustrated energy into working up the bid for the fountain project. Now, three and a half hours later, he was spent.

He pulled the completed bid from the printer and took a breath.

Well, this was it.

He laid it on the desk.

Ironic how a single project could hold such power. But, like that kiss, it felt like a turning point. Hell, he'd thought about his future more in the last couple of weeks than he had in the last ten years.

Liz did that to him. She got him thinking about the past and who they'd been and who they were now. And where they were headed.

He wouldn't pretend he didn't want the future he saw for himself when he was with her.

He reached for a pen and paused. He didn't blame Liz for balking when she saw the cabinets. He didn't blame her for looking at him like he'd lost his ever-lovin' mind when he'd suggested she buy the house.

Lord only knew what he'd been thinking, except he didn't want what he'd found with her to go away. He wanted to preserve the feeling that Liz always carried with her that the possibilities were endless, that any person could make him or herself exactly and whatever they wanted to be no matter what they'd been in the past. And, at four a.m., when he'd looked at her in the pre-dawn light, he'd not been able to stop himself from reaching across the divide between them just to test if it were as wide as she seemed to think it was.

A bittersweet feeling settled in his chest as he signed the bid, slid it into a manila envelope and wrote 'Beautification League of Sugar Falls' on the outside.

He blew out a careful breath. *Done.*

And just like ten years before, Liz would never know how close he'd come to believing they could magically become two people who had more in common than lust and a taste for Twizzlers.

He stared at the envelope. Weird that he wasn't more nervous. And yet, over the last couple of weeks, Liz had given him all sorts of ideas on how to improve cash flow, restructure pricing and create his own market niche in hardscapes. It was easy to see why she was successful. She had a knack for seeing how any business could work better.

Granted, a lot of it sounded like a bunch of marketing mumbo-jumbo, but even so, it sounded good.

She sounded good.

He leaned back in his chair with a sigh.

He got such a kick out of watching her mind work. Her eyes would light up, her pen would go a mile a minute on one of her yellow pads and it was as if she got as much of a thrill out of solving his problems as he got out of watching her do it.

He loved watching her. Loved...

Carter's chair snapped upright.

No. *No way.* He shook his head and leapt from his seat. *Shit!*

His chest felt tight, and he began to pace, alarm coursing through him.

As carefree as he was about so much in life, he was *never* this careless about his relationships. He always, *always* stopped himself before stepping over the line. Because, unlike casual sex, love was dangerous. And, yes, objectively, he knew love didn't always lead to a tragic end like it had for his parents, but he was absolutely sure of one thing.

Someday, somehow, *inevitably*... where love was concerned...
someone would get hurt.

what now???

CHAPTER THIRTY-SIX

AFTER CARTER LEFT, Liz threw herself into punch-list tasks. It made it easier to deny she'd been making one whopper of a mistake after another. Eddie joined her as if sensing she needed him. He sat on her extension cord.

What had happened to her since she'd come home? She'd gone from having everything clicking along like clockwork to spiraling out of control and falling in love with a man who was not even her boyfriend!

As if on cue, her cell phone rang. She contemplated letting it go to messages, but then decided she wasn't a coward. She could always pretend she'd lost cell service if things got dicey.

"Grant!"

"Hi," he said. "How are you?"

"I'm… okay." *Crazy. In love with another man. Horribly unfaithful.* "You?"

"Good. Good. Things are good. Really good, in fact."

"Good." She swiped her hand on her forehead and waited.

"You sound tired," he said.

She grimaced. "I am." *In so many ways.*

"That's probably my fault."

"Not entirely," she admitted. "But some."

He chuckled softly. It was strange to hear his laugh. It seemed a lifetime ago she'd been with him. "I deserve that," he said. "I know I've leaned on you more heavily than I'd planned to since you've been away. It's been crazy on this end. I've been pulling together a lot of loose ends, and I know I've been short with you, but things are coming together now. I'm sorry I made things stressful."

"Me, too. Crazy on this end, I mean. Too."

He paused. "Andy says thanks for the, ah, wedding gift."

She smiled. "I'm glad he liked it. I'm sorry you felt awkward about it."

Silence.

"Liz? I…" Grant lowered his voice. "I know I said we should take a siesta… to give you time to think about us, but I have to admit… I miss you."

"You do?"

"Yes," he chuckled again, warmer this time, "of course I do."

"But, I thought… I thought you were trying to tell me you needed a break. I thought that's what 'siesta' meant."

"A break? *No!* Is that why you've—?" He half-laughed then sighed. "No." She could hear him moving around, the click of a door. He was probably at work. He was nearly whispering now. "I didn't want a break, Liz, I thought *you* did! Even though we talked about it, planned for it, it seemed like you weren't really ready to move things forward, if you know what I mean." He sighed again. "And when we never talked about what happened that night… or *didn't* happen…"

"It's okay. You don't have to—"

He let out another sigh. "Maybe I'm just being a guy, but if you're not into me enough to want sex this far into a relationship, I've got to wonder if you're having second thoughts. Hell, maybe you were *never* into me…"

"Of course I was into you! I spent *days* planning for that night!"

Liz blew out a breath. That probably wasn't a tack she wanted to take right now, considering. "I'm sorry. I am. I know that night was a disaster. Sometimes… sometimes I work so hard to make things perfect, I forget to live in the moment.

"But, that's changing," she said. " '*m* changing. Coming home has forced me to lower my expectations." She thought of how that might sound. "Of myself! I meant of myself."

"It's okay. I got it." He paused. "So, where do we go from here?"

Liz couldn't answer. She thought about what she'd been doing over the last couple of weeks and how this man had been nothing but understanding, supportive and good to her. He truly was the man she should have chosen, and yet she'd gone and fallen for the heartbreaker who would only make her cry in the end.

Hadn't she known *that* twelve years ago?

"You deserve better than what I've given you," she finally said.

"I'll accept your best efforts at improving that in the future," he chuckled awkwardly. Paused. "That was a joke."

"I know." *God, did all men have dorky senses of humor?* "But, to be honest, I don't know what the future holds. Coming home has been very emotional for me. I don't think I can explain it over the phone. I still need to process it all." *Plus, there's the little matter of being in love with someone else.*

192

"Sure. I understand. I'm glad you're working through it. It seemed we hit a plateau a few weeks back, and it threw me off. I thought we were on a good course."

He blew out a breath and continued. "I know working together has made things complicated, but, I promise, that's going to change. I don't want to go into it over the phone, but I want you to know, I want to move forward with you, Liz. I think I've been patient enough. Don't you agree?"

Liz teared up at the hopeful tone in his voice. Now *this* was a good man. This was a man who understood that major life decisions require careful consideration, balancing of pros and cons. You can't just leap without looking. People have to make compromises and adjustments. This was a man who wanted to talk about their future!

"I'd love to—"

"*Great!*"

She'd been about to say, *but I don't know if I can,* but the relief in his voice stopped her.

"We'll talk when you get home?" he said.

"Yeah. We'll talk," the cowardly part of her agreed.

"Great. Take good care of yourself, Liz."

"You, too."

She hung up, her hand shaking.

Lovely. She couldn't wait to get back to Chicago to tell the man who'd waited months to make love to her that she'd jumped into bed with another guy after mere *days.* He probably wouldn't be so eager to take things to the next level with her then.

In the meantime, he still thought they were nearly engaged.

Which meant, until she talked to him and set him straight, she was, too.

CHAPTER THIRTY-SEVEN

"I HAVE SERIOUSLY underestimated you." Trish ran an admiring hand across a cabinet door as she pulled down a coffee mug. "These are gorgeous!"

Liz looked at the cabinets wistfully. They were bright, beautiful and brought a calming cheer to a cool, cloudy Tuesday afternoon. Exactly as she'd always pictured them. She bit her lip. "I'm having them repainted as soon as Carter's done with the walkway," she said, hoping he was well out of earshot.

Carter had been hard at work for nearly two days straight on the walkways. He and Liz had only shared casual pleasantries, dancing around one another, not talking about the monumental shift in their relationship, as if the elephant in the corner of the room were a natural part of the décor.

Trish whirled, coffee slurping from the pot. "Repainted? *Why?*"

"The color won't appeal to most buyers. It's better to keep things neutral. Isn't that the mantra of all those shows you watch?"

Trish waved a dismissive hand. "To hell with them. I like it. At some point you have to do what you damn well please. Besides, it looks a hundred times better than it did." She leaned forward. "But, if you're looking for an excuse to keep Carter hanging around, I certainly understand."

Liz stirred her coffee. "I'm not looking—"

"Please. It's obvious something is going on between you two."

"It is?"

"It is now," Trish grinned, dropping onto a seat at the table. "I was just fishing a moment ago. So, when? Tell me everything! This is so much better than TV."

Liz shook her head and sipped thoughtfully.

"What? Oh, *no*. No, no, no, no! Tell me you haven't."

"Haven't what?" Liz evaded as her mind provided a dozen things she shouldn't have done where Carter was concerned.

"You haven't gone and slid from lusting for the man straight to—? You have! Oh God, it's written all over your face!"

194

There was no use denying it as Trish stared at her pityingly. So she did. "Of course I'm not in love with him! That's ridiculous!"

"Not ridiculous. Understandable. I may have a husband, but I have eyes. But, seriously, this isn't good. He's never struck me as the settling-down type."

"Don't you think I know that?" Liz fired back. "He's already given me the 'this is just a casual thing' speech." She frowned. "Or maybe I did, but it doesn't matter, because he *agreed*. And it's just as well. I mean, I have a job and a *life* in Chicago..."

Trish nodded sympathetically. "True. Plus, he's... *you know.*"

What? Gay? Liz was pretty sure *that* wasn't true. Trish shrugged. "Not necessarily an upstanding citizen, if you know what I mean."

"What are you talking about?"

"You didn't hear?" Trish took a slug of coffee and leaned closer. "Word is he quit the fire department after they found empty beer bottles in his truck and a used joint in the break room at the end of his shift."

"He—? Was he arrested?"

"Not that I know of. Enough buddies at the station I guess. But I know he was asked to leave, and he didn't fight it, so people are saying they were his."

"Why didn't you say something to me before?"

"I didn't know you were, um, that involved before. I figured you were just having a little fun."

Fun like a funeral. Liz just looked at her.

"I'm sorry. I didn't mean to burst your bubble, but I'd hate to see you get hurt."

Liz nodded. "Me either." Her chest felt tight. "It's just, I've had a crush on Carter since forever," she whispered. "It's hard to let that go."

"Hey, no one said you have to give up your fantasies. But some things are better left that way, you know? I mean, do I seriously think Gerard Butler would be as good in bed as I imagine? Never mind. Don't answer that. Obviously a bad analogy. My point is..."

But Liz stopped listening. She knew Trish was trying to make her feel better, but the truth was reality was crashing in, and here she was, over ten years later, still hoping the future with Carter would somehow, miraculously, be different than the facts suggested they would be.

The fact was, as intoxicating as it was to finally hook up with Carter, that's all it was—all it *could* be—a hook up. She had a master's degree and a good job. Life experience. She was smart enough not to confuse the excitement of these last few days with real feelings that could last in the real world. What she and Carter had wasn't something lasting, something built purposefully over time on shared values and goals.

It was nothing like what she had with Grant.

And Grant still cared for her. He was good-looking and kind and stable. He *wanted* a future with her, and as much as it hurt, the pain she was feeling was no more than finally growing up and giving up the fantasies of a dreamy-eyed sixteen year-old.

She knew now what she had to do.

Carter wasn't the only one who needed to grow up.

CHAPTER THIRTY-EIGHT

CARTER ARRIVED EARLY the next morning to finish the walkways and saw Liz through the window. He hadn't stopped to chat much since Monday morning, not because he was too busy, but because he still felt a little ridiculous having suggested she buy the house. As if she'd move back to Sugar Falls just because she liked her kitchen cabinetry and they'd had sex a couple of times?

He approached the back slider and knocked. He held himself stiffly, nervously, unsure how to act around her now that his feelings had overflowed like an ocean of water poured into a pool. He ached to touch her again, hold her, anchor himself somehow. But he feared he might pull them both under if he did.

"Hi." He inclined his head as Liz let him in.

"Hi," she said.

He frowned as she turned away. He laid his hand on the back of her nape, a light touch. His fingers flexed, gently kneading, immediately aware of the tension beneath the surface. "Any coffee left?"

"Sure." She slipped away from his touch and poured him a cup, avoiding his gaze as she handed it over. She stared at the cabinet behind him.

Carter took a sip. It scalded. "I know what you're thinking."

"You do?" Her eyes flew to his.

"The cabinets. You still want them white, don't you?"

"You know I love the color." Her voice was firm, oddly resigned when she next spoke. "But, yes, I think it would be best to repaint them."

"It was a stupid impulse. I thought you'd change your mind once you saw them." He tried another sip. "But I'll fix it. As soon as I'm done with the walkway." He reached out to brush the hair from her face. She stepped away. His stomach clenched, and he let his hand drop.

"Don't worry about it. I'll take care of it," she said.

"I told you I'll fi—"

"*No.* Don't." She inhaled. "Carter, I need..." She took another breath. "There's something I need to say. Something I should have mentioned sooner. And, I'm not sure how to say it."

He gave her a lopsided smile despite the shot of unease coursing through him. "Just spit it out."

She grimaced and turned to straighten the salt and pepper shakers on the counter. "I want you to know, I've really enjoyed getting to know you again. I have."

"Me, too." He smiled, but it wasn't close to genuine this time. He could already see what was coming. He could read it in her eyes when she snuck a glance at him then looked away just as quickly. Good Lord. *She was dumping him?* It hadn't happened often, he had to admit, but he knew the signs well enough to recognize them.

"The thing is... you and I... we're very different. And..."

"And?"

She turned to face him. She blew out a breath. "I'm sort of engaged."

"*Engaged?*" Hell, he hadn't seen that coming. A flash of hurt, then anger, jolted through him. How could she be engaged and not tell him?

"Sort of. What I mean is—"

"*Sort* of?"

"We've talked about it. Grant and I."

"Oh, I see. You've *talked* about it."

"Well, yes. Given our shared values and profession and direction in life, it's a logical step—"

"That's the stupidest thing I've ever heard."

"I'm sorry?"

"Who talks like that? You make it sound like some spreadsheet analysis you've done to decide how to spend the rest of your life."

"It's not like that." She was getting annoyed, he could tell. He didn't give a crap.

"Are you in love with him?"

"It's complicated. We have a history," she said, "and… feelings for each other."

"Wow. You have *feelings* for each other. My best to both of you." He knew he sounded mocking. He also didn't give a flying shit.

Her hands rose pleadingly then dropped to her sides. "This isn't productive. I'm sorry you're hurt, but if you think about it, it's probably for the best that we—"

"Does he know about us?" He cut in. "Hell, does he know what we've *done?*" He gestured widely. They both looked at the table.

Her cheeks flamed. "I wish you wouldn't talk about that—"

"Why? Too messy for you? Too complicated? Oh, that's right, that's what you feel for him. What, dammit, do you feel for *me?*"

He began to pace now, the impotence of the situation nearly overwhelming him, forcing a need for movement. *Action.*

She looked at him in disbelief. Well, honey, that made two of them! Here he'd finally gone and fallen for a woman—*hard!*—and she was dumping him? Ha!

"Oh, please,' she said, "I'm not so naïve as to believe you don't have a string of women lined up ready to succumb to the fabled McIntyre charm."

He stopped in front of her, the irony of the situation forcing his fingers to flex in frustration. He wanted to grab her and shake her for acting so... so... *reasonable*... when he felt anything but. "Did it occur to you I'm not interested in a string of women? Did it occur to you I might be interested in *you?*"

She caught her lip between her teeth and for the first time he saw the glossy sheen of unshed tears in her eyes. "We're not right for each other," she whispered.

"Why? Shit, I'm not asking for a life-long commitment, Liz. I'm not trying to force things. I'm just trying to figure out why you're giving me the heave-ho. I thought we were—" He ran a frustrated hand through his hair. "I don't know—having fun."

God, that sounded lame. *Fun?* It had gone way beyond fun for him. For the first time in his life, he thought he understood the panic his mom must have felt knowing his dad was still in the house. Shit. If this is what love felt like, maybe he didn't want any part of it after all.

"I don't think we're looking for the same kind of fun," she said.

His mind spun as he tried to make sense of her words. "Seems to me it was a mutual thing."

"I'm nearly *engaged*," she repeated, as if that meant a damn thing to him.

"*Sort of.* What the hell is that anyway? You're not even wearing a ring." They both stared at her bare ring finger.

"It's not that clear cut."

"You either are or you aren't, Liz. No more complicated than that. Even I know that much."

"We've discussed it, okay? He wants to take our relationship to the next level, but we're coworkers, so one of us would need to leave the company."

"Next level? What is that? You make it sound like a video game."

"The next level," she ground out, "is getting engaged, getting married!"

"Did *he* say that?"

She blinked, then her forehead furrowed slightly. "Yes. I mean, not in so many words, but the intent was clearly—"

"Did it ever occur to you he might just want to get laid?"

"I beg your pardon?"

"*The next level.* He doesn't want to get married, for Christ's sake, the guy just wants to get laid! And here you're giving me a hard time just because I'm upfront about it? Fuck! The only thing complicated here is *you!*"

At her stunned intake of breath, he caught himself. "Sorry. I'm sorry." He raked his fingers through his hair again, anger and hurt and envy for this guy he'd never even met coursing through him. "I didn't mean—"

"*Don't.*" She held up a hand, let it drop to her side again. "Don't. You've said enough. Just... go."

"*Liz...*" But the look she gave him told him it was too late.

CHAPTER THIRTY-NINE

CARTER FROWNED at the orange juice his cousin Jim set in front of him and tried to ignore his sister's smirk as she draped herself over a neighboring chair. Clearly it had been a mistake to come here and expose himself to his family's scrutiny and opinions, but his sister-in-law, Kate, had invited him days ago. And he was out of milk.

He'd hoped for a private moment to talk to his cousin, man-to-man, given the fact that he'd clearly gone off the deep end. Hell, maybe there was a way to *undo* this mess he found himself in.

Just his luck, his sister was already sponging breakfast off Jim and Kate when he arrived. He'd been reduced to relating a highly edited version of the weekend's events.

"She shut me out," he said in conclusion, accepting a second helping of waffles from Jim. The guy ate like a king. "Why do women have to make everything so complicated?"

"Well, what did you expect?" Grace helped herself to the syrup and a generous spoonful of whipped cream. "Did you think just because she liked the cabinet color she'd up and decide she couldn't possibly leave them? Or Sugar Falls? Or *you?* Did you think," she laughed over a mouthful of waffle, "she'd fall in love with you over a paint chip?"

"It was a valid question. You don't have to make me sound ridiculous," he grumbled.

"I'm sorry. *I'm* making you sound ridiculous?"

"What I meant is... she's not *easy*. In my experience, women have always been easy." He turned to Jim for confirmation of this universal truth.

Grace snorted in disgust.

Carter frowned. "What I mean is, easy to please. Easy to figure out. You do nice things, say nice things to them, they do nice things and say nice things to you. *Easy.*" And nobody felt things they shouldn't feel.

"Easy to get into bed, you mean."

Carter scowled as he reached for the syrup. "I'm not talking about that."

"What? Carter McIntyre not bragging about his latest conquest?"

"She's not a—" He uttered a short curse and smacked his fist on the table in frustration. "Why do I even try?"

Shit. Is that what his exes felt like? Conquests? Is that how he appeared? He thought back over his dating history with new eyes. He'd never intentionally misled anyone, never talked about a future or kids or love. He'd thought it was kinder to quietly back away when things got too close. Easier. But, maybe it had only been easier for him… like pushing someone away to swim to safety alone.

"Don't be so hard on him, Grace." Kate set baby Lily in her bouncy seat and flashed him a reassuring smile.

He stabbed at his waffle knowing he was being set adrift and there was nothing he could do to stop it. He helped himself to the syrup. "Yeah. Shut up and pass the whipped cream. By the way, thanks for breakfast, Kate."

"My pleasure." She glanced toward Grace then back at Carter. "But I did have ulterior motives for inviting you two today."

Grace and Carter eyed each other warily.

"You did?"

Kate glanced uncertainly toward her husband then squared her shoulders. "The thing is, I don't think I can continue to help with the landscaping business. I simply don't have the time anymore." She gestured toward the sleeping baby meaningfully.

Carter's lips lifted in a half smile. "The first six weeks are the hardest. Rachel said so. After that, things settle out again. You're just talking temporarily, right?"

"Carter, the business is at a point where you need someone a minimum of part-time. Probably more. I thought with Grace between jobs, it was the right time to bow out gracefully. I've got my own business to tend to as well as the kids…"

Carter turned toward his sister doubtfully.

"Hey, I appreciate the breakfast and all," Grace began, "but I'm not the bookkeeping type."

"It's not just that," Kate said. "There is supplies ordering that needs to be done. It's actually very interesting. And you don't need to worry. I've got it all organized…"

Carter scraped his chair back and downed the last of his coffee. "You know, I appreciate your wanting to make things all neat and tidy, Kate, but I think I can work it out on my own if it's all the same to you."

"But with your uncle and his back issues, I know how much more work is falling on your—"

"It's okay. I know office work—it's not Grace's thing either. And you guys, you have your own stuff you need to focus on. Like you said. You've got everything organized now. I'll be fine."

"Are you sure?"
"I'll be fine."

CARTER RAN A HAND through his hair and frowned at the computer screen.

"I am *so* screwed."

He didn't do well with computers, particularly computers with accounts receivable programs that didn't function the way they were supposed to function. Or print when they were supposed to print.

Oh, the hell with it. He'd hand write the damn bill. Who cared that Mrs. Marston was notoriously anal about wanting every single paver itemized? She'd have to deal with it. He didn't have time to trouble-shoot the program; he needed to get paid.

As he shuffled through the desk drawer for an invoice pad, his hand bumped into the manila envelope addressed to the Beautification League. He stilled.

What a waste of time. There was no way, with Kate bailing on him that he'd take on anything like that now. He'd need a tender to help if he was going to do the fountain project, especially in the short timeframe they'd set out for it, and he wouldn't have time to hire anyone now that he'd be putting extra hours into admin tasks. Good thing he hadn't already submitted it.

He was stuffing the proposal back in the drawer and pulling out the invoice pad when the phone rang.

"Yeah?"

"Hey, Carter? It's John. John Beacon."

Carter wondered momentarily if he should pretend the connection was bad then regretted the thought. It was Liz's brother after all.

He stood and walked toward the kitchen for more coffee. "Hey, John. What's up?"

"Listen, I need a place to crash, and I was wondering..."

John paused and Carter glanced around his disordered condo. Newspapers littered the coffee table. Dishes sat in the sink. Yesterday's workout clothes hung over the back of the sofa. "Jeez. I wish I could help you. What about your folks place?"

"I don't want to get in Liz's way. All I need is a sofa. Just for a few days."

Carter picked up the dirty clothes in his fist. "All right. Sure. A few days."

"Thanks."

The obvious gratitude in John's voice made Carter feel like a jerk for having tried to beg off.

"Hey, I'm in Concord for the day, but I'll see you tonight. Will you be home around eight?"

"Yeah. I should be here," Carter said.

"Just a few days. It's all I need."

"You bet."

Carter hung up. There'd been a time he would have readily offered to have John stay. He must be getting old, because he didn't feel like drinking beer all night and waking exhausted and hung-over. He didn't want to deal with wondering if John would end up staying one night. Two. Or three weeks.

Good God, when *had* he grown up?

Reasons being single is good:

1.) Never have to wait to get into the shower

2.) Can do whatever I want to do

3.) Only have to share bed with Eddie

4.) All the coffee is mine. And the cookies.

5.) Don't have to lie about liking Happily Ever After

6-10.) Can stop shaving my legs.

CHAPTER FORTY

LIZ SCRUBBED THE SHOWER stall with a cloud of abrasive cleaner. It was time to go back to being an adult. An adult who'd made mistakes, for sure. But, especially, an adult who'd, in the interest of playing it safe, shied away from having the tough discussions that might cause conflict.

When had she become so afraid of making waves?

And, where had that reticence gotten her? *Almost* engaged? Carter was right to scoff! She felt like an idiot for not seeing it sooner. Did Grant even want a commitment from her? *Ever?* Had she been deluding herself into believing that, too?

Taking a deep breath, she decided to find out. She wiped her hands on her sweats, pick up her cell phone and dialed.

"Hi, sweetheart."

Liz froze, wondering if Grant thought she were someone else then forced herself to relax, realizing he must recognize her number from caller-ID. "Hi, Grant. I'm sorry to call you at work, but..." She paused and worried her lip. Maybe this wasn't a good idea. Maybe she should wait until they were face to face. Maybe...

"What's up? Did you have changes you wanted to make to the Eaton presentation?"

"No. No, the presentation is fine. It's just... there's something I wanted to ask you. Something I need to talk to you about."

"I'd love to talk, but I'm right about to pop into a—"

"Do you just want to have sex?" she blurted. "With me, that is?"

There was a moment's pause, a nervous burst of laughter. "Do I what?"

"Just want sex. Is that what we've been talking about? When we've talked about taking it to the next level?"

"What?" she braced herself as he paused. He chuckled awkwardly. "You've, ah, taken me by surprise here, sweetheart. I don't—"

"It's a simple question."

"It's not—" She could hear him exhale. "Of course, I want to have sex with you. I thought I'd made that clear." He lowered his voice. "I'm sorry, I can't... I can't talk now. Ethan's waiting or else I—"

"No!" she cut him off, glad he couldn't witness her humiliation in person. "No. It's okay. I understand."

"I'll call you later, all right? After I get out. I—"

"*No!* No. Please don't. Don't call. I have, um, things to finish here. I'm sorry I bothered you."

"You're not— I'm sorry you've been confused about us, Liz. I—"

"You know what? I'll call when I get back to Chicago. *Phew!*" she fake sighed. "I don't know when I'll have time to talk earlier. *Truly.* So busy here!"

"Liz—"

But she'd already hung up, the phone forgotten in her hand as she stared out the window, her body buzzing with humiliation.

How could she have been so *foolish?* Here she'd thought they'd been moving toward something, something meaningful, something *more*, and all he'd wanted was *sex?* She should probably feel flattered he'd care so much, would wait so long, just to get his hands in her pants, but she couldn't summon the enthusiasm for it.

She'd put her job on the line—the one she'd worked for for ten long, slogging years—and become romantically involved with a coworker all for the possibility of a quick shag?

It seemed she'd put her heart on the line doing the same with Carter, so she really couldn't point fingers at Grant.

Oh God, what a mess.

Liz buried her face in her hands and waited for the tears. They didn't come, damn it.

The phone rang on the bed beside her. Liz automatically flipped it open. *Trish.* "I know we're sisters," Liz said, "but now is not a good—"

"It's Aunt Claire," Trish cut in. "I just got a call from the hospital. She's in the E.R.... something about feeling dizzy and chest pains."

"Chest pains?" Liz stood numbly, a wave of dread washing over her. Aunt Claire was built like an ox, how could she be having chest pains?

"I have to pick up the kids from preschool... drop them off at the neighbor's. I can swing by to pick you up after that—"

"No! No. It's too far out of your way. I'll get there on my own. Just go. Make sure she's not alone."

Liz hung up, her fingers shaking, and dialed the only number that came to mind.

"Yeah?"

Even the distracted, impatient sound of his voice was calming, reassuring. "Carter, it's Liz. I need a favor."

"I know. Grab a coat on your way out. It's starting to rain again."

"My Aunt is—"

"At Sugar Falls General. I know. That's why I'm here."

"Here?"

"Out front."

Liz peeked out the window. Carter stood in her driveway, his shoulders hunched against the weather as he opened the passenger door of his pickup. Waiting. "I'll be right out."

A light drizzle chilled the air as she hurried down the front walk and slid into the truck. "How did you know?" she asked, still stunned and grateful he was there.

"Grams. Your aunt was complaining of palpitations and dizziness at their get-together Friday night. They finally convinced her to get it checked out."

"She's been having symptoms for four days?"

"On and off."

Liz pressed a hand to her eyes then straightened to look out the window. Time enough to worry about Aunt Claire when they knew more. "Listen, about earlier..." she began.

"Forget it."

Liz nodded and turned toward the window. She didn't want to talk either.

Seemed she was as bad at communicating as the rest of her family was. Must be genetic.

"Hey. It's probably nothing serious," Carter reassured her as he pulled onto the main road.

Liz nodded again and swallowed through the thickening dread in her throat. She hoped he was right. But she couldn't shake the feeling that life as she knew it was quickly unraveling.

CHAPTER FORTY-ONE

"IT'S NOTHING SERIOUS." Aunt Claire insisted, pursing her lips and pulling at the flap of her ill-fitting hospital gown. "I don't know why you rushed down here. They're just running some routine tests."

"If they're so routine, why are you in the E.R.?" Liz countered. "Besides, we didn't want you to be alone while you waited."

"We?" Aunt Claire asked as she peered at Carter behind Liz.

"Trish and me. She's coming as soon as she drops off the kids."

"And my grandmother will be here as soon as she's picked up June and Lydia," Carter added from the doorway.

"You'll all be bored. They've got me hooked up like a science experiment waiting for me to spit out data. But, it's your time…"

Liz sat in the chair by the bed, noting the worried crease on her great-aunt's forehead. "When did it start?"

"Friday. They come and go. Then they came again this afternoon. Scared me a little."

"You were smart to come and get checked out." Liz squeezed Claire's hand, knowing she must have been more than a little scared to check herself into the E.R.

Liz closed her eyes as Carter's hand brushed her shoulder. She wanted to lean into him, his quiet support, but steeled herself against it.

"I'll wait in the lobby," he whispered in her ear. "They don't want more than one visitor in here."

"You don't have to—"

"I'll wait," he said firmly, giving her shoulder a final squeeze before slipping out.

Liz caught Aunt Claire's speculative glance when she turned back around. "He's just a friend."

"Could've fooled me." Liz's face grew warm, but she didn't reply. "He's a good boy, Liz. It's nice to see you're smart enough to see beneath the surface."

"It's complicated."

Claire scowled as a phlebotomist came in the room. "Life's complicated," she insisted as he rolled up her sleeve. "That's what makes it interesting. Get used to it."

Liz slumped in the chair and sighed. "Then my life must be *very* interesting right now."

Claire shooed the phlebotomist on his way as soon as he was done. "Well don't hold back. What's interesting?"

"You don't want to hear. Besides, now is not the time."

"I've got nothing better to do."

"I come out of it looking pretty foolish in the end."

"I thought we were talking about Carter."

"Him, too."

"You'd better start from the beginning."

Minutes later, after editing out the steamier scenes in her little daytime drama, Liz sat back and spread her hands. "See? I've been wasting my time—and risking my job—dating a coworker for months who only wanted... a casual fling, and I've become... emotionally involved... with a man who has a reputation for using illegal drugs. I told you I'd come out looking foolish."

Claire shook her head and pinned Liz with steely eyes. "I thought you were smarter than this."

"I know. I know. Me, too."

Claire *tsked* impatiently. "Talk about thick-headed! If I weren't trussed up like a chicken I'd smack you 'side the head. I would have thought you—*of all people*—would be better about not judging others by their reputation! Haven't you railed against that your whole life? What did they used to call you? Smarty Pants? Beth the Brainiac?"

"Brainy Beacon," Liz mumbled.

"Ah, right. And here you are taking all the sordid gossip you've heard about Carter at face value? I'm shocked."

Liz eyed the heart monitor worriedly. "Please don't get yourself worked up right now..."

"*Pfft*. Then stop being a ninny!"

"I'm trying to be cautious. Being a ninny is what landed me on the front page of the newspaper with my underwear hanging out."

"Being a ninny is what has you sitting in this chair like a sad sack thinking you've run out of options."

"No, I've just run out of plans."

"Then smarten up and make a new plan."

CARTER STOPPED PACING the moment Liz entered the waiting

room. She'd been gone nearly two hours. He'd practically worn a path in the carpet. "How is she? Is she okay?"

"Yeah." Liz stepped toward him as if dazed, shaking her head, a small, relieved smile tilting the corners of her mouth. "She was just dehydrated. Can you believe it?"

"Dehydrated?"

"I guess too much alcohol and caffeinated coffee and not enough healthy fluids will do that. The doctor thinks the dehydration was triggering mild palpitations and dizzy spells and anxiety made them worse. Trish is taking her home as soon as she's discharged." Liz smiled. "I just ran into your grandmother in the hall. She's headed to the hardware store. It seems she's convinced a water filter will encourage Aunt Claire to drink more tap water."

Carter nodded, the relief rolling off his shoulders in waves. Despite their earlier confrontation, he'd hated to see Liz worried. Had felt her concern as if it were his own.

Liz fidgeted with her purse strap and glanced over his shoulder. "I'm sorry to take you away from your work for nothing. I suppose it's too late for you to get back to your job."

He didn't bother to tell her he hadn't been working. The intermittent rain had been a convenient excuse to spend the morning kicking himself for being so insensitive earlier. He'd acted like a jerk. "It's okay. I was happy to wait."

"Thanks." She glanced at her watch and Carter felt an overwhelming urge to keep her with him. To make it up to her.

"How about an early dinner?" he suggested.

She shook her head. "I don't feel up to cook—"

"We'll let someone else do the cooking. You look like you could use a break."

"I don't think—"

"Just friends," he insisted, though why he did he couldn't say. He didn't want to be friends with Liz. He wanted to be much more, in fact. "I know just the place."

Before she could protest again, he was tugging her with him.

LIZ ORDERED AN ICED TEA and slid into the booth as Elvis Presley crooned in the background. Aunt Claire was right. Liz had taken the gossip about town at face value, never giving Carter the benefit of the doubt. And here he'd been nothing but helpful, considerate and charming since she'd set foot back in Sugar Falls. Asking her out to dinner was just another example.

211

Meanwhile, she'd been no better than all those who'd never seen beyond the successful student to the Liz she was inside. Didn't she owe Carter more than that? She at least owed him her appreciation. She glanced gratefully across the table. "I want to thank—"

"Don't."

"Don't what?"

"Don't make me out to be some Good Samaritan. I didn't help today because I'm a good person, Liz. I did it because it was *you*."

Liz folded her hands on the table in front of her. "I don't believe that for a minute."

"You always gave me more credit than I deserved."

Perhaps compliments embarrassed him. Liz let the comment slide and tried to relax. The creak of the vinyl seat as she shifted position and the warm scents of coffee and fried food could almost lull a person into believing you could come home again. Almost. But she wasn't so naïve as to believe in happily-ever-afters even if she *did* believe Carter deserved the benefit of the doubt. Perhaps he wasn't as wild as everyone made him out to be, but that didn't really change anything.

She sucked in a bolstering breath and faced him.

"I fly back to Chicago in two days," she announced.

"To him?"

Liz straightened her napkin. "No."

"Good."

She glanced up in surprise. Carter's eyes were dark as he looked at her, that rare, serious intensity on his face, and she knew she couldn't pretend indifference anymore. Couldn't pretend they were just casual friends—or casual lovers even—enjoying a meal. They had shared more than a few nights of pleasant camaraderie. More than physical passion. He deserved to know the truth. And for some reason she couldn't explain, she *needed* him to know she was being completely honest with him. "You were right," she admitted. "About Grant. I called him after you left."

He didn't say a word, didn't ask what he was right about. They both knew what she meant. Liz mumbled a thanks to the waitress for their drinks then picked up her menu. She looked back at Carter. "What?" she prompted, embarrassment flooding her as he continued to stare. "No comment? No I-told-you-so's?"

"Is that what you want me to say?" he asked. "Would that make it easier to walk away? Go back to Chicago?"

"Walk away? Chicago is my home."

He grunted and picked up his coffee.

Liz sipped her iced tea and let out a sigh. Maybe agreeing to dinner had been a bad idea. Maybe she should have gone...

"*Godammit, Liz!*" The utensils chattered on the tabletop as Carter's fist slammed down on it suddenly. "It doesn't end here."

Liz's eyes skittered toward the other diners. "I don't know what you're—"

"Don't you? This. *Us.*" He gestured back and forth between them. "It doesn't end here. I won't let it."

"I don't think it's—"

"It's not about thinking!" he cut in, reaching across to grip her fingers in his. "You can't tell me what happened this weekend meant nothing! You can't sit there all quiet and calm and tell me you *felt* nothing!"

Her heart hammered in her chest as his fiercely whispered words pounded against her. "What do you want from me?"

"You're not 'sort of' engaged anymore, are you?" he demanded.

"No."

"Then there's nothing stopping you from giving us a chance."

"A chance? You make it sound like—"

"Like we have something good going here? We do. And it's something worth... exploring."

"I can't believe you're that hard up for sex," she scoffed.

His eyes glittered, and she felt his fingers flex over her own. "What makes you think this is about sex?"

"Isn't it?" she countered, slipping her hands out of his, her smile taut as the waitress returned to take their orders. She couldn't delude herself into believing it was more than that. Not again.

Carter sat back and all but tossed the menus at the waitress. "Two cheeseburgers. Medium. And a large onion rings."

Liz glared at him as the waitress retreated. "I was going to order a taco salad."

"Forget the damn food. Now what's this horse," he caught himself and lowered his voice, "crap about my wanting you only for sex? That's the stupidest thing I've ever heard."

"Stupid? I'm sorry. You haven't exactly been a monk all these years. I figured a zebra doesn't change his stripes."

"So you think I'm working this hard just to get laid? 'Cause let me tell you, I could get laid with a whole lot less hassle if I wanted to."

"That's flattering."

"It should be. I don't want some easy woman, Liz. I want *you.*" He shook his head and choked on a laugh as he shoved his hand through his hair. "For some reason I haven't figured out, I like your company more than other women. I like your lists. I even like your crazy, run-for-the-hills-every-chance-he-can-get cat. Sure, I like the sex, and I hope we can have a whole lot more of it, because I haven't begun to do to you all I've thought about doing to you, but—and I can't believe I'm saying this—even if we *didn't* have sex, I'd *still* want to spend time with you."

Liz stared at him, her heart thudding in her breast as she struggled to absorb his words. Fought against her own cynicism to believe them. "You would?"

He reached across and took her hands again. Warmed them. "*Yes.*"

She couldn't look away, couldn't tear her gaze from his as the energy—the need—coursing into her through their entwined fingers held her in its grasp. "So what do you want from me?" she breathed.

He shrugged. "Six weeks?"

Liz blinked, trying vainly to control her pulse and scattered thoughts. She pulled her hands back and folded them in her lap. "Six weeks?" she echoed.

Carter smiled, a brilliant, intoxicating light, as he leaned across the table again. "Yeah. Six weeks. If at the end you're done with me, that's it. We call it quits. If you're not—"

"If I'm not?"

"We renegotiate."

Liz twirled her straw in her tea, stalling for time. "I leave for Chicago in two days."

"Go back Sunday instead. Give us another weekend together."

"Even if I could get my flights changed..." She shook her head. "This is crazy. What do you expect to happen in six weeks? I'm not even going to be here most—"

"Just give me a chance is all I'm asking for. Let what's happening between us happen. Don't think about the distance or the logistics. No over-thinking. No excuses. Just... enjoy it. "

She bit her lip and studied him. "What about sex?"

"I'm for it. You?"

She shook her head even as a smile curved her lips, the warm suggestion in his eyes sending electric tingles to her toes—and other places. She doubted she'd ever find equilibrium again. "I can't believe I'm even considering this."

"Then say 'yes.'"

"I," she met his gaze and soaked in the promises unspoken there, forgot the humiliation, the rational arguments. Forgot to be jaded. "Fine. Six weeks," she said.

"Let's shake on it."

Liz reached toward him then yelped in surprise as Carter clasped her hand and all but pulled her over the table. "On second thought, let's seal it with a kiss."

"I—"

And that was the last rational thought she had as his lips slid over hers, teasing, tempting... until a polite cough intruded on Liz's consciousness and with her lips still planted on Carter's, she slid her eyes over to see the waitress who was waiting to deliver their appetizer.

CHAPTER FORTY-TWO

"I WONDER IF THEY'VE HAD SEX YET."

Ruth gave Lydia a quelling look. They'd arrived at Claire's house soon after Claire returned home from the hospital bearing food and non-alcoholic drinks to celebrate the fact that Claire wasn't, in fact, dying. At this age, it was always cause to celebrate when one left the hospital on one's own two feet.

"What? It's a perfectly reasonable question. I bet they have."

Ruth pulled the cover off her hastily prepared veggie platter and set to work making chicken salad sandwiches.

Claire sipped the lemonade they'd set in front of her and made a face. "They have. But it's too soon. Things aren't going well."

"Things are going perfectly well," June disagreed as she set a bakery box on the counter. The smell of chocolate wafted through the kitchen. "I've spoken to Kate myself. There's definitely something brewing there."

"They're barely talking," Ruth said. "Did you see how awkward things were when they left the E.R.? I'd say there's a definite problem."

"And I'm saying if he and Liz are having issues it means they mean something to each other. I think things are going swimmingly."

"I agree with June!" said Lydia as she gathered plates and utensils. "Kate even left town on Jim. Remember that? But that all turned out in the end. Give it time. If the sex is good, they'll be back together..."

"If the sex is good? Where'd you hear that?" asked Claire. "People have sex all the time without getting married."

"That's just everyday sex," said Lydia, popping a cherry tomato into her mouth. "Over the moon sex is entirely different."

"How do we know they're having over the moon sex?" Claire wanted to know.

"I suppose you could ask her," Ruth said.

"Yes!" said Lydia. "Ask her."

"Ask her. Right. I'll just walk up to my grandniece and ask if she's having over the moon sex with my best friend's grandson."

"Or, you could call her, I suppose."

Claire gave Lydia a look. "And I start this conversation how?" "Why don't you ask Trish?" said June. "She'd probably know." Claire shook her head. "Listen to us. It's not fortune telling cards that are bringing these two together, it's a bunch of meddling old women. I'm not asking anybody anything. Let's play cards."

"I didn't bring any pictures," Lydia said. "I want to talk about Liz and Carter."

"Me, too," said June.

"Me, too," said Ruth.

Claire sighed. "Fine. But if we're going to meddle, we need to do it right. We need to plan ahead. Lydia, bring me my calendar from the fridge. Now, if I invite them all to my birthday next month, that will bring them together again in a few weeks. And, Ruth, if you hold your annual Fourth of July barbecue, I can be sure to get Liz back from Chicago. I can always pretend they overlooked something with my heart and she needs to come home while she still can…"

All three of them looked at Claire, aghast.

"What? I could have been dying today! I'm not waiting around for things to work out on their own. Who's with me?"

Lydia picked up another cherry tomato. "I suppose I did see an adorable vintage teddy come into *Second Chances* yesterday. If you can get Liz to the shop, I'll point it out to her…"

"Now, we're talking," Claire said. She looked up at June and Ruth expectantly. "Any ideas?"

"Short of locking them in a room together, I've got nothing," said June. She set the cake in the middle of the table.

Lydia set the plates and utensils next to the cake and sighed. "I miss over the moon sex."

They were all silent a moment.

Claire picked up a knife. "I nearly died tonight. I'm eating dessert first…"

217

CHAPTER FORTY-THREE

THE NEXT MORNING, Liz watched from her bedroom window as Carter's truck pulled out of the driveway. She caught herself humming a chipper tune, turned and stared at her reflection in the mirror.

Her hair was softly tousled, her eyes bright, her skin luminescent. She looked thoroughly kissed, thoroughly pleased with herself—and thoroughly self-delusional.

Wasn't it pure and utter folly to become romantically involved with Carter McIntyre? Reality would come crashing into her idyllic dream-world sooner or later like it always did. Six weeks? What would that prove? That she was more infatuated with him than ever?

Liz let out a shaky breath and hugged her bathrobe around her more tightly. Infatuated, hell. She was solidly, undeniably in love with the man. She could try to rationalize it every which way but Sunday, but the truth was she was head over heels. And, worse than the puppy-love of her youth, the feelings she had for him now were far more intense—and far more dangerous to her heart.

Liz impatiently yanked on a T-shirt and sweats, shoved a brush through her tangled hair and stalked to the kitchen where she cracked the slider open a bit to get fresh, head-clearing morning air to her brain.

She was smarter than this. And yet, here she'd gone from being a sucker for Grant—and nearly ruining her career in the bargain—to falling into bed with a man notorious for being irresponsible.

What was she thinking?

Liz snapped the coffee filter into place and punched the 'on' button. She couldn't get side-tracked. Last night she'd been weak, distracted by all that had gone on with Aunt Claire. She'd been emotionally vulnerable, that's all. And Carter had been so...

Enough. That was yesterday. And, er, this morning. Today was different. Today she would get back on track.

Sure, he was gorgeous. There was no denying that. And attentive. Entertaining. Generous. But, he was flawed, too. Irreverent. Habitually tardy. Perhaps not enough to have him hanged, but surely enough to give her second thoughts.

She'd simply have some coffee, put her attention back on her to-do list and put fanciful notions of a long-term relationship with Carter McIntyre on the shelf where they belonged.

Liz stared down at the legal pad on her kitchen table and tried to concentrate.

It read: *Clean House.*

Exactly, she told herself, straightening purposefully in her chair. She needed to clean house. Sure, she needed to scrub walls and floors, the oven and sinks, but, more importantly, she needed to take stock of where she was and what she was doing. Like Aunt Claire said, she needed to make a new plan.

What, for instance, had made her so ridiculously susceptible to believing Grant wanted more than he did? Was she that short on prospects she needed to lunge for the first eligible bachelor to show an interest? Was she going to be forever haunted by the dreamy memory of a stolen kiss, forever measuring every man to that impossible yardstick?

Or, was something more at work?

"Work," she mumbled as she stared off into the distance, her to-do list forgotten. It surprised her to realize she missed being at work about as much as she missed Grant. Which was to say—not much at all. Both represented security, responsibility, a sense of what she was supposed to do with her life. Somehow though, at work and with Grant, she'd fallen into a routine that felt safe, sensible, predictable...

Perhaps that was what made Carter so unaccountably appealing. She never knew what to expect—like being blindfolded.

"But that doesn't make them wrong and him right," she murmured aloud.

"Who wrong and who right?" asked a voice from the patio.

Liz jumped, a hand plastered to her chest. "Valerie? You scared the heck out of me! What are you doing back there?"

Valerie lifted a camera into view. "I didn't see any cars in the drive, so I thought I'd stop and take some photos for the listing. I didn't realize you were home until I heard you talking to yourself."

"I wasn't talking to my—" Liz started to protest, except that's exactly what she'd been doing. She grabbed a mug from the cupboard. "Well, carry on. As you can see, I'm just getting coffee."

Valerie turned her back and snapped a couple more photos of the yard. "Seeing as you're here, mind if I come in and take some indoor shots? "

Liz shrugged. "Knock yourself out." She poured her own coffee and then felt guilty for being snippy. "Can I offer you a cup of coffee?"

"Sure."

Drat. Liz reached for a second mug.

"I've got a couple potential buyers I was worried about bringing over this afternoon, but I'll be honest, I'm shocked at how good the place looks now," Val stepped into the kitchen to take her coffee.

Hmm. Apparently vampires drank it black.

"Gee, thanks."

Valerie rolled her eyes. "I wouldn't have thought you'd need a pat on the back, but nice job."

"What's that supposed to mean?"

"It means I think it looks good. And, trust me, I see a lot of not good."

"No, not that. The first part. Why wouldn't I need a pat on the back? If you put your best efforts into something..."

Val rearranged a couple of things on the counter and shoed Liz aside to take a picture. She shook her head pityingly. "You never could get enough attention, could you? Valedictorian? Assistant V.P.? Queen of Charitable Causes? Should I be thanking you for trying to steal my boyfriend back in high school? You want a pat on the back for that, too?"

"Who? I never tried to—!"

Valerie lowered the camera. "Dan. And you *so* did." She took another sip of coffee. "*Hmm.* Good stuff. I never used to like it black. And, don't deny it. You always had a thing for Dan. But, you can have him now. He's all yours."

"Back up the train. I have *never* had a thing for Dan."

Valerie repositioned Cookie Rooster and snapped another photo. "Yeah, right."

"I didn't!"

"Oh, please. You've been after him ever since you sucked face with him at Jenny Whitmeyer's party junior year. And, don't deny it. Everybody knows."

Liz choked on her coffee. "*What?* I never—!"

"Tell me another one. He said you were so horny he had to physically pry you off him."

Liz felt the blood drain from her face before it roared back in a wave of humiliation. *Dan? It had been DAN in the pantry?* Oh, my God! And all these years she'd fantasized it had been Carter? No *wonder* Dan was so solicitous at the reunion dance!

Liz thought back. She remembered it all so vividly. The tentative kisses, the deeper explorations... the unmistakable feel of something surging toward her, warm and heavy and unknown... and then he reached up to take her hands from his shoulders and held them at her sides...

...he had to physically pry you off him...

Oh. God.

Her stomach roiled. How could she have been so *wrong?* Valerie took a swig of coffee and snapped another picture. "All these years, every time we had a fight all I'd hear was, 'Maybe I'll ask out Beth Beacon, she's really into me.' Well, have at it." Valerie turned and raised one over-plucked brow. "You okay? You look kind of peaked."

"I'm…"

"Whatever. Take him for all I care. You two deserve each other. He's a dick and you're desperate, so you make a good match."

"Excuse me?" Liz snapped back into focus. "I am *not* desperate. I've never been into Dan—*especially now*—and if I was horny it's because I mistook your boyfriend for my… my…" *My what?* "…Carter."

"*Your* Carter?"

"No, not *my* Carter, just Carter."

"Don't lie to yourself; he's never been *just* Carter." Liz turned as Bailey sauntered in, a to-go cup in her fist. She flumped onto a kitchen chair. "Hey, Val, how's the bat cave?"

"Piss off, Bailey. You were never funny."

"Bailey!" Liz said, grateful for reinforcements; although, she could use a little less in the way of expository comments. "How'd you get in?"

"Your brother. Do you guys not talk to one another? He's out front installing some new coach lights. They look good, by the way."

"He is?"

"*Your brother's here?"* Valerie gasped.

Liz shrugged. "Apparently."

Valerie looked like she was about to bolt. Or throw up. Hard to tell.

Bailey pulled a Snickers bar out of her pocket, the scents of chocolate and sweet mocha filling the air. "You appear to have swallowed a lemon, Valerie, if you don't mind my saying." Valerie's pink lips twisted in annoyance. "Do you have a problem with Liz's brother?"

"I don't know what you mean." Valerie set her mug on the counter and headed toward the slider. "I forgot to take photos of the garage. I'm going to go do that before I forget."

"It's shorter if you go out the front door," Bailey pointed out sweetly. Or, as sweetly as a mischievous fairy could be.

"Why don't you like my brother?" Liz demanded. "Or, do you have a thing against my whole family?"

Valerie's boobs inflated, straining the buttons of her satin blouse, as she took a deep breath then let it out again. "If you must know, and as painful as you will surely find this information, your brother and I have… a history."

"Oh my God!" Liz breathed. "You and *John?*"

Valerie's eyes flashed as she pointed a silencing finger at Bailey. *"Not. A. Word."*

"I can't…" Liz managed.

"Neither can I," Bailey said, around a mouthful of Snickers despite Valerie's laser finger directive. "You've been shagging Liz's brother?"

"We had a… relationship. Yes."

"Ew!" said Bailey and Liz in unison.

"But it's over now."

"Because she kicked me out." All eyes turned toward the swinging door to the dining room where John stood, moody and brooding and looking at Valerie like she was a chocolate fountain at a diabetes fundraiser.

"I didn't kick you out," she said. "We agreed we were moving our separate ways."

"We didn't agree on anything," John said, walking in and grabbing a coffee mug of his own.

Liz scowled. My God, was this a diner or something? At this rate, she'd have to make a second pot.

"I need to give my marriage another shot," Valerie said, albeit weakly.

"You're divorced, Val. You've been divorced four years. Dan had his shot."

"He wants me back," she said.

"Wait a minute," Liz interjected. "You just told me *I* could have Dan."

Valerie gave her the look of death.

Wow. No wonder vampires didn't want to look in mirrors. They'd scare themselves right out of immortality.

"It's complicated," Valerie said, turning back to John.

"He's a drug addict and a jerk," John spat.

"We all have our faults," Valerie murmured.

John just stared at her like Heathcliff brooding over Catherine.

Liz didn't want to tell either one of them that things ended badly in Bronte's world.

No one spoke for another long moment, and then John let out a sigh and turned toward the door again. "Thanks for the coffee, sis."

The door swung shut.

Bailey chewed her candy bar and turned to Val. "Aren't you just a little ray of sunshine?"

"Bite me," Val said, walking toward the swinging door as well. "I've got work to do."

Ms. Carter McIntyre
Mrs. Carter McIntyre
Mrs. Elizabeth McIntyre
Beth McIntyre
~~B.M.~~

CHAPTER FORTY-FOUR

Twelve years earlier…

BETH SAT IN THE HEAVY oak chair in the back of the library, her heart in her throat. It had been three days since Jenny Whitmeyer's party. Three days since she'd experienced the most magical, earth-shattering first kiss imaginable.

Three days since she'd first started thinking she might, possibly, perhaps, summon up the nerve to ask Carter McIntyre to the junior-senior prom.

It gave her goose bumps to even think about it—*her!* Who would ever have guessed that quiet Beth Beacon would have the guts to ask a boy out on a date, much less the tall, dark and charming Carter McIntyre?

She pulled a Twizzler from her backpack and bit into it on the sly—because food wasn't allowed in the library—and chewed, her eyes closing as she was instantly transported back to that wonderful, amazing, possibility-changing kiss. It was hands-down her new favorite candy.

She swallowed and took a deep breath, rubbing her damp hands on her skirt as she waited.

And waited.

"Sorry I'm late."

Carter came loping in, repeating the same three words he'd met her with every tutoring session since September and tossed his backpack onto the table. He shrugged out of his leather jacket, tossed it atop the backpack as well and pulled out a chair next to her.

Beth caught her breath as his thigh accidentally brushed hers. She didn't pull away. "It's okay," she said, reveling in the warm vitality of his leg touching hers. Did he feel it, too? "Why don't we get started?"

She watched him, her pulse thrumming through her veins, as he burrowed, head bent, inside his backpack for his trig text then thumped it on the table in front of them.

Oh, she ached to touch his hair.

They reached for his text at the same time, their hands colliding. Beth gasp-laughed and yanked her hand away and then berated herself for being so jumpy. How would she ask him out if she couldn't even touch his hand without panicking, for goodness sake?

He smiled at her, that winsome flash of a dimple that had her insides doing flip-flops, and opened the book to the next lesson.

Beth licked her lips. She could still taste Twizzler.

Carter raised one eyebrow questioningly. "Aren't we going to start?"

Beth coughed and fluttered to pull out a notebook for working out problems, her face growing warm. "Yes. Of course," she said, thankful she knew the drill by now. She glanced at the page he'd opened to. "Ah, yes. Oblique triangles and law of sines. Okay. Basically all this is doing is allowing you to find…"

Thirty minutes later Carter was jiggling his knee, frowning at the notebook and glancing at the clock on the wall as Beth's face flamed in embarrassment.

She bit her lip, frustrated with herself. No wonder Carter was confused! She'd started to describe the law of sines, gotten it mixed up with the law of cosines for a few minutes, caught herself, backtracked to the law of sines and thoroughly lost him along the way.

He ran a hand through his hair and looked at her. "Maybe we should try again next time."

"No! I mean, of course we can, but I know you'll get it. It's my fault for not explaining it right to begin with." Crap! Now look what she'd done! Why couldn't she have just paid attention and not let her mind wander off to places it had no business wandering? And here it was nearly time to go!

"It's okay, Beth."

But, it's not okay!

She felt her pulse racing as he started to shove his text into his backpack.

Ask him! Ask him now! The prom is in less than two weeks! If you don't ask now, it'll be too late!

Just suck it up and DO IT!

"So," she said, her hands visibly shaking as she closed her notebook. She tucked them in her lap under the table and swallowed, sure that Carter must be able to *hear* the pounding of her heart in her chest. "I hear a lot of people are getting excited about the prom."

Carter tugged at the zipper of his backpack. It caught a little and he had to lean in and yank it. "The food should be good," he said.

Beth nodded. Jenny's parents owned The Old Mill Bar & Grill in town and were catering for the prom. "The Whitmeyers sure threw a great party the other night, didn't they?"

Carter glanced at her, a funny twist to his mouth. "It had its moments."

She sucked in a deep breath as he stood to leave and stood, too. "So, Carter... I, um, was wondering... if ... like, as just friends... if you thought it might be fun to go, I mean, together. To the prom, I mean."

She couldn't breathe, couldn't even feel her heart any more, as she stood completely paralyzed, waiting for his reply. She felt as fragile as a piece of glass, wondering if those moments in Jenny Whitmeyer's pantry had meant as much to him as they had to her. His answer would surely tell her.

His lips tilted, in that wry, winsome way he had and he turned to grab his jacket. "I can't. Missy Green already asked. That's why I was late." He smiled wider and shrugged into his jacket. "But you don't have to have a date to go. There are plenty of guys going stag. Maybe I'll see you there?"

"Right," she said, straining to hold it together, straining to appear indifferent even though she felt completely and utterly shattered. "I'll think about it."

"Okay," he said. "See you next time."

"See ya."

And, then he left, and she broke into a thousand brittle pieces, vowing then and there that if she ever pulled together the shards of her broken heart, she would never, ever let it be in charge again.

Because, it was too easily led astray by charming rebels—and stolen kisses in the dark.

CHAPTER FORTY-FIVE

LIZ SPRITZED THE HALLWAY mirror with window cleaner and began to wipe it with a paper towel. The potential buyers Valerie had brought through the prior afternoon had certainly seemed interested. And why shouldn't they be? Liz had done a huge amount of work since coming home, and despite the fact that her personal life was quickly going down the crapper, she was stunned at how good the house looked.

She spritzed again.

She shouldn't think of it that way.

Getting dumped by Grant was a good thing. Okay, so he hadn't dumped her, just admitted he'd only wanted to get in her panties. But, the end result was the same: she now knew their relationship wasn't what she thought it was and, more importantly, wasn't what she wanted.

It all boiled down to the fact that she had a pattern of horribly misjudging men.

She'd spent more than a decade fantasizing about the kiss of the wrong man. And while Dan was a surprisingly good kisser for being such a schmuck, he wasn't *The One*. Grant, not as big a schmuck as Dan, clearly wasn't *The One* either. And Carter? She'd built him up to be something he never was, judged him on something he might not have done and pushed him away at the very moment he'd started to open up to her.

Pandora's Universe: 3

Liz Beacon: 0

Maybe Carter was the one for her and maybe he wasn't, but she'd promised him six weeks to figure it out.

Liz wiped the last streak from the mirror thoughtfully. Carter was taking her out for dinner later. Maybe she'd gain some personal insight then.

She jumped in surprise when the doorbell rang. Good grief. She'd have to buy that man a watch. He was nearly two hours early! Still, her heart was beating in happy anticipation as she opened the door.

"Hi, gorgeous!" she said.

Liz froze. Her breath stopped dead in her lungs.

"Wow. I didn't expect a welcome like that."

The man on her front stoop was tall, good looking—and *blonde.*

"*Grant!*" she gasped. "What are—? What a surprise!"

"Can I come in?"

"Of course!" She stepped back as he entered the living room.

A slight furrow creased his forehead as he turned to her. "I know this is unexpected."

Liz swallowed and shut the door before Eddie made a dash for it. "You could say that."

Grant bit his bottom lip, met her gaze for one brief moment and then stepped toward the living room. "So," he said, "I see you've been busy."

"Busy?"

"Painting." He looked back at her. "I see you've been painting."

"Oh. Yes. The front door, most of the downstairs, the kitchen… Yes. I've done a lot of… painting." *And crying and gnashing of teeth and second-guessing…*

"Looks nice," he said.

Liz nodded and set her cleaning rag on the window sill, determined to scrape together her dignity. "Can I offer you a drink?"

"Sure. That'd be great."

"Great." She stared at him, unmoving for a moment before she remembered she was supposed to be doing something and gestured toward the kitchen.

Liz led the way through the dining room and the swinging door to the kitchen, her mind running in circles. What was he doing here? Hadn't they broken up? Or, at least, hadn't she?

She poured him a glass of iced tea without asking what he wanted and handed it over.

"Thanks," he said. He gestured toward the cabinets. "The place looks terrific, Liz. But, I'm not surprised. You do have an eye for color." He sipped his drink and smiled over the rim. "A woman of many talents."

Liz gripped the edge of the counter she was leaning on and tried not to snap like a bow string. "Why are you here?" she blurted.

"After your call… When you didn't return my messages… I was worried. Ethan told me you planned to delay your flight back."

"Just through the weekend." She looked out the back window. "I need a little more time to wrap things up here."

"I had hoped you might need *me.*"

Liz frowned and looked back toward him. "Need *you?*"

"Is that so surprising? You're always there for me; I thought I'd return the favor."

"I don't understand." *Didn't we break up? Didn't you just want to do the wild thing? Am I genetically incapable of communicating with other people?*

"The last we talked you sounded... upset. Confused. Not yourself at all. I knew you were out here on your own, and when I heard you were extending your time off... I took the earliest flight I could manage. So, here I am."

"Yes. Yes, here you are." Liz let go of the counter and paced toward the back door. "The question is: *why?*"

Grant crossed the room and took her cold hands in his. "Why? You even have to ask?"

"Um, yes?"

"Because of what you asked me, Liz! As soon as you hung up, I realized we haven't been honest with each other. *I* haven't been honest with you. I needed to apologize... in person. I needed to make you understand."

She slipped her fingers from his. "You shouldn't have made the trip. I understand completely."

"No," he insisted, a confident smile tilting the corner of his lips as he brushed the hair from her temple. "I don't think you do."

Liz wished he'd stop sticking his fingers in her hair and get to the point. No such luck.

"Let's go for a walk. You can show me your new patio," he said.

Goodie. A nature walk. Liz opened the slider and stepped out, memories of Carter and the last few weeks slamming into her. She swallowed and made a half-hearted sweeping gesture with her hand. "Here it is."

"Nice." Grant was nodding appreciatively, totally ignorant of the magnitude of the patio in Liz's life—one of the few horizontal surfaces she and Carter had yet to, um, dedicate. "I see you redid the walkway, too," he said, following it around the side of the house.

Liz trailed after him.

"Grant..."

She nearly ran into him when he stopped abruptly.

"You told me your parents had eccentric taste," he laughed, motioning toward the storage shed, "you didn't do them justice. This looks like it belongs to the Griswold's from National Lampoon."

The string of smiley-face deck lights Carter had hung on the shed grinned at her en masse.

The Griswold's? Liz grabbed the deck lights and tugged, embarrassment flooding her. Happy yellow faces bounced around merrily and sagged toward the ground.

"I meant to take that down," she muttered.

But Grant didn't seem to hear as he turned and let his fingers trail through the strands of her hair. Again. Maybe he was just surprised it was loose for a change.

"I know my being here is a lot to take in," he said.

"Yes. Wow. You've no idea—"

"I'm ready, Liz. You can believe it."

"Ready for what?"

"You asked if I wanted to have sex with you," he murmured. "The short answer is, yes. I do. Very much. And, preferably, as soon as possible."

"You came all the way from Chicago to tell me *that?*"

She would have stalked away in dignified brilliance like the heroine of her own self-actualized drama, but he stopped her with a hand to her arm. "You didn't let me finish. I'd love to make love… Just as soon as we're properly engaged."

She blinked. *Oh, Dear God. Did he say…?*

And then he was sliding his hand into his pocket and sliding out a little blue velvet box. "I've been waiting," he said, "keeping you to myself, I know, not wanting to share you even with random strangers in restaurants. I've wanted you to want our relationship to move to the next level as much as I do. I think it's time, don't you?"

He opened the box, and Liz could only stare into the cool brilliance of the largest solitaire diamond she'd ever clapped eyes on. "I… I don't know what to say."

"Say you'll marry me. Say you'll be Mrs. Beacon-Blackerby."

"Beacon-Blackerby?" *Ohmigod! How had she never thought how that would sound before now?* "I— I need to think about it," she lied.

Grant blinked, his handsome features registering a moment of surprise. "Think? What's to think about? We've already discussed this. I thought—"

"I thought so, too. Now, I'm not so sure." Liz ran a hand through her hair and grimaced. It smelled like window cleaner. "I'm sorry. You've surprised me, that's all."

"Of course." Grant nodded and smoothed his sport coat. "I didn't give you any warning I was coming. You're overwhelmed. You need a few moments to take it all in." He pressed the velvet box into her palm. "Here. Take it. Think on it. It's a big step, I understand. You wouldn't be the woman for me if you didn't take the time to make sure it's the right decision. We'll discuss it over dinner." He leaned down and kissed her full on the mouth.

Liz's jaw gaped and she forgot not to swipe her lips in front of him as he walked down the front path. She found her voice as he reached his rental car. "Grant, wait!"

"I'm staying at the Sugar Falls Inn," he replied, opening the driver's door. "I'll pick you up at six."

Liz watched in dismay and disbelief as he pulled away. She couldn't have been more surprised if he'd suggested they move to Tajikistan and drink yak's milk. Engaged? He wanted to get *engaged*?

She glanced down at the velvet box and turned its cool, silky weight in her palm. Her fingers flexed around it. She didn't dare open it again. The brilliant solitaire only mocked the future she'd once thought she wanted.

CHAPTER FORTY-SIX

CARTER GRINNED AT THE goodies on the seat beside him and pressed his foot down on the accelerator. He'd had all of fifteen minutes to shower, shave and get dressed after his last job, but the flurry of activity had only fueled the buzz of energy he'd been riding all afternoon.

Sure he'd made mistakes. He'd never been perfect, but he only saw good things ahead with Liz. For once, he—impulsive, spur-of-the-moment, Carter McIntyre—had a *plan*. He would surprise Liz with endearing gifts, delight her with romantic dinners and outings then win her over by helping her achieve every item on her "Liz Never" list. His hand fisted over the deck of cards on the seat beside him.

If all went well, by tonight they'd be crossing off number three with their own private game of strip poker.

Carter pulled into Liz's drive shortly after six-thirty. Imagine him, Carter, early! After a few moments with no answer at the front door, he walked to the back slider, whistling. He knocked, a light-hearted staccato beat to match his mood.

No answer.

Perhaps she was in the shower? He tried the door. Locked. Maybe she'd gone into town with Trish or Bailey on a quick errand. *Hmm.* Maybe she'd decided to spring for some new lacy underthings? Heck, he grinned to himself, a man could dream.

He shrugged and decided it was fine Liz was out. It would give him time to plant something fun and whimsical in her front yard. Like the giant fake sunflowers he'd gotten at the lawn center earlier. She wouldn't mind. He'd fill in the holes when he was done.

He retrieved the fake flowers from the bed of his truck and laughed. For a landscaper, you'd think he'd at least have the sense to bring a shovel.

Chuckling over his own scattered wits, Carter headed to the side shed. He knew Liz had been keeping it locked, but it was his lucky day, because the door was ajar when he got there. He pushed it open and scanned the jumble of tools and debris slumping lazily against the walls and floor for a shovel.

Shed clean-up had obviously not been tops on Liz's to-do list.

Spying what looked like a shovel handle in a far corner, Carter pushed aside a half-used bag of fertilizer with his foot then muttered in annoyance as it upended.

He stooped to pick it up and paused as he noticed plastic-wrapped packages of something on the floor under a tarp. He pulled the tarp aside… and swore harshly under his breath.

What the hell?

The idiot. Some people never learned.

Carter flipped open his cell phone. Someone needed a wakeup call.

LIZ CLOSED HER EYES and imagined it over. She'd been trying to talk to Grant the whole ride to the inn, and yet here she was, sitting across from him, no closer to breaking the news than when he'd first opened the car door.

Her hand closed around the velvet box in her lap as she listened to the cool splash of wine in her goblet. She swallowed uneasily and looked across the table at Grant.

He sat confidently—stylish, composed. The height of gentlemanly demeanor and masculine chic. He was everything she'd ever wanted.

Until now.

Liz reached out to take a quick, bolstering sip from her glass then set it aside. "Grant, we need to talk."

"I agree." *Finally!*

She'd hoped to do this in private, but Grant had kept murmuring *hush* like she was a child about to spoil a surprise the entire ride over. If he only knew.

Her tongue dashed out to moisten suddenly dry lips as her gaze darted to the other diners in the room. "This is all wrong," she murmured despairingly.

"I'm sorry?"

"This... all of this." She gestured vaguely at the crisp linens and gleaming place settings.

"You don't like the restaurant?"

"No!" She buried her face in her palm for a moment as a hysterical burst of laughter threatened to overcome her, then set her shoulders. "No. That's not it. It's just... I don't know what to say, Grant. I thought... I don't know what I thought, but I never expected *this.*" She pulled the velvet box from her lap and placed it on the table.

Grant frowned and reached to cover her hand. His fingers were cool around hers. "This? This is what we've been talking about. Are you going to tell me you're having second thoughts?"

"Second thoughts? I wasn't even sure you were having *first* thoughts! I mean, just two weeks ago you were—well, I don't know what you were doing, but it didn't strike me as a business meeting. Gone for an entire weekend? I'm not that naïve." Okay, maybe she was, but that wasn't the point.

Grant pursed his lips and nodded regretfully, pulling his hand away. "No. You're right. I wasn't completely honest about that weekend."

"*A-ha!*" Liz said, oddly satisfied. If he'd cheated, too, she need not ever bring up Carter. "I didn't think so."

"Ethan and I—"

"*Ohmigod*," she breathed, choking on her Pinot Grigio. "You're having an affair with Ethan?" She sat back. "I suppose it all makes sense now. Your overt homophobia. Your willingness to wait to have sex for WAY longer than any normal—I mean straight—man would wait… "

Grant regained his power to speak. "I am *not* in a homosexual relationship with Ethan!"

"You're not?"

"And, for the record, my views on commitment ceremonies versus marriage vows do *not* make me homophobic."

"If you say so."

"Liz, I am not homosexual. I've asked you to marry me, for God's sake!"

"Then what's with you and Ethan?"

"Ethan and I…" Liz waited patiently while Grant took a breath to compose himself. Clearly it was harder to come out of the closet than he was willing to admit. "We're leaving Ames & Reed. We're opening a boutique firm of our own."

Liz gulped her wine. "I'm sorry. Did you say you were leaving the firm?"

"Yes. We've only just worked out the details, but our lawyers tell us we're free to do so as long as—"

"You've hired *lawyers*?" Her wine glass sloshed as she plunked it onto the tablecloth in disbelief.

"Yes. That was the real business behind that trip Ethan and I took. We couldn't move ahead with our plans if we'd get slapped with a non-compete and we needed to set up—"

"Wait a minute. Let me get this straight. You're telling me you're *not* having an affair?"

"No."

"With Ethan or anyone?"

"Definitely not."

"But you *have* gone behind my back, hired lawyers and decided to leave the firm we both work for?" For some reason she couldn't explain, this upset her far more than the idea of Grant having an affair, homosexual or otherwise.

He reached across the table and gripped her hand again. "Don't you see? We don't have to worry anymore! As of next month, we'll no longer be coworkers. We're free to take our relationship—"

"—to the next level," she completed dully.

"Exactly."

She shook her head, suddenly, vividly aware of how disinterested she was in taking anything to the next level with Grant. "Did it ever occur to you that I might want to be included in this decision?"

He frowned, his forehead furrowing lightly. "Included? How? This was between me and Ethan."

"You're right. At least... it is now." She looked at the velvet box then slid it across the table, amazed at how easy it was to do so. Amazed at what a few short weeks could mean in a person's life. "Thank you, Grant. Thank you for being the man you are... and for helping me see what I need to be happy."

He stared at the box, unable or unwilling to pick it up. "I don't understand."

"I'm not the person you think I am. I like sneaking mango smoothies at the gym more than running. I think it's cute for the cat to sit across from me while I have breakfast. I think smiley-face deck lights are whimsical... I'm the kind of woman that likes to wear real lipstick and sweatpants and have sex on the kitchen table even though it's wildly unsanitary... I eat *swiss cake rolls* for crying out loud!"

"You're a different person since you've been home."

"No. That's what I'm trying to tell you. I'm finally the person I always was."

"I still don't understand."

"I know. But for your sake, someday, I hope you will. For now... could you give me a ride home?"

CARTER PACED IN THE driveway. Waiting.

Damn it! This wasn't how he'd seen the evening playing out. The evening *he'd* planned was fun, surprising and most of all ended with him enjoying himself in every way imaginable.

It certainly didn't include standing around wondering when the authorities might arrive.

Carter's muscles tensed as he watched a car roll into the drive. Closing his eyes briefly, he blew out a breath and raised a hand in a casual hello.

Crap. Crap. Crap.

"Carter!" John inclined his head in greeting as he stepped from his car. "What's up?"

"Not much. Waiting for Liz."

A muscle twitched in John's cheek as he glanced behind Carter at the house. "I thought she'd gone back to Chicago already."

"She decided to stay a couple extra days."

John's eyes flicked down the drive as he pulled a cigarette from his pocket and lit it. "When is she coming back?"

"Not sure. Could be any time."

"You going out?" John's eyes slid over Carter's suit.

"That was the idea."

John chewed the corner of his lip as he held the smoke in his lungs then looked down the drive again. Exhaled.

"Expecting someone?" Carter asked.

John shrugged noncommittally. "Just a friend. Said he might be stopping by."

Before Carter could reply, another car pulled into the drive. He hadn't seen this particular vehicle for a while—not since quitting the fire department. "You still hang out with Rick Mercer?" he asked, swallowing his distaste.

"We see each other now and again," John hedged.

Rick closed his door, his eyes twitching in surprise and recognition as he spied Carter. He cocked his chin. "Hey, Carter. How's it hangin'?"

"Good." Carter flashed the easy smile he'd worked a lifetime to perfect. He didn't trust Rick as far as he could throw him, but he'd be damned if he'd walk away now. "So, what's up? You guys have plans for tonight? " *Any chance I can help you on your way?*

"Uh, I'm kind of on a schedule here, John," Rick prompted. His car keys jangled in his hand.

"Schedule's changed," John replied. "My sister's on her way."

Rick swore crudely. "I don't have—"

"Relax. We've got company." John said, his eyes glancing toward Carter.

"Him? He's cool. Could have turned me in a few months ago, couldn't you, man? Took the rap for me. He won't bother us." Rick gave Carter what he could only assume was a grateful smirk.

"But my sister—"

"Then make it fast. I need—"

"Oh crap."

Carter couldn't have expressed his own thoughts any better as Liz pulled up in an unfamiliar sedan that stopped at the end of the drive. His heart clenched in his chest as he watched her lean over and kiss the driver on the cheek, then step out.

Now who the hell was *that* guy?

She paused when she spotted him, her cheeks pink as she walked toward him.

Carter caught the end of a murmured exchange between John and Rick.

"I'm not taking it back," Rick muttered under his breath.

"I'm telling you, *it's no good*," John replied.

"And, I'm telling *you* if it's opened I can't—"

"What's going on?" Liz asked, stepping up to them.

Carter shook off any questions about the man in the car for later and focused on the moment. He had to divert Liz. *And fast.* Clearly things were getting ugly. He didn't want any of their mess to spoil his evening.

Rick glared at John. "What's this? A convention? I thought you wanted this on the Q.T., Beacon."

Carter stepped between Liz and Rick and took her arm. "John just, ah, stopped by to see the new walkways. His landlord was interested in re-doing their front walk, and he thought he might put a good word in for me. Right, John?"

"You have a new place? That's wonderful! Carter, did a beautiful job, don't you think?" Liz asked.

"Great," John said. "Thanks for showing me, Carter."

"No problem. But, if we're going to make our dinner reservation, Liz, you'll have to run and get changed."

She looked down at the skirt and cardigan she wore. "What's wrong with this?"

"It's fine, but I'm sure you'll want something fancy. Let's go have a look. Love to stay and chat, guys, but duty calls." Carter steered Liz toward the house.

"What the—?" She frowned as Carter shoved her through the door and into the house. He shut the door abruptly behind her then peeked through the transom.

"Would you mind telling me what's going on? Who's that other—? *Oh,* isn't this beautiful!"

Carter turned to see her holding the little glass bird he'd meant to surprise her with later. Its cool, clear green reminded him of a new spring leaf. Made him think of Liz. "I thought it'd look nice on your windowsill. It would remind you of home. I mean, here, when you're in Chicago."

Her eyes were bright as she smiled at him. "That's so sweet of you."

He shrugged. "I meant it for later. After."

"You mean there's more?"

He nodded, noting with relief that John and Rick were no longer standing out front. Hopefully they had the good sense to take their business elsewhere. "Yeah, there's more. Now go get changed. You can wear that purple number you wore to the reunion."

Her eyebrows lifted uncertainly even as her hand clutched the newel post. "Are you sure that's a good idea?"

"Why not? The evening can't turn out any worse than the reunion, can it? We'll make new, better memories in it."

She grinned and hurried up the stairs.

Carter looked out the transom window again then swore to himself. Their cars were still in the driveway. Which meant they were probably in the shed. Would they notice the tarp had been disturbed? He hadn't taken care to replace it, had simply left it as it had fallen not wanting to touch it again.

Damn.

"Where are we going for dinner?" Liz called from upstairs.

"It's a surprise!" he hedged as he watched yet *another* vehicle enter the drive. "No need to hurry, though. We've got time if you need to fix your hair... or makeup..."

What the heck?

"Hey, Liz, I've got to get something from the car. I'll be right back," he said.

"Okay, but when you get back, I'll need you to zip me!"

Carter blew out a quick breath of relief. *Good.* That would keep her upstairs—and out of the way for a few more minutes while he got rid of John and Rick. And, whomever had just arrived and parked on the road. What the hell was going on?

"*Bailey?*" Carter said, intercepting her on the front stoop. "What are— Is that Trish and the kids?"

"Probably," Bailey replied. "So, what's going on?"

"That's what I'd like to know!"

"Didn't Liz's mom call you, too?"

"No."

"Huh. I got a message to be here promptly at 6:45 for some big surprise."

"I'm skyping now, Mom, can't you see?" Trish bustled up the walkway, the twins fake-tripping each other, the baby swinging from her seat in the crook of Trish's arm and her tablet held out in front of her.

"Oh, this is amazing!" Liz's mom yelled from the tablet screen. "Hello, Carter! I'm a mobile hotspot!"

Carter waved at the tablet. "Hi, Mrs. Beacon."

"Is everyone here? I mean there?" Mrs. Beacon asked, craning her neck, as if she'd get a better view from her sofa in Florida.

Trish looked around. "Not quite, but we're a couple minutes early."

"Early for what?" Carter asked again.

"The big surprise!" Mrs. Beacon yelled. "*Shh!*" she said, putting a finger to her lips. "Trish! Put me somewhere I can see the apple tree! I don't want to miss a thing!"

"I can do it," Ben said. The boy stood at Trish's elbow and reached for the tablet.

Carter couldn't believe the transformation in the kid. For one, he was standing relatively still.

"Okay, but be careful! *No* running!" Trish said automatically, but Ben was already walking, albeit quickly, toward the side yard where the apple tree was.

"Is that the same kid?" Carter asked.

Trish set the baby down and rolled her shoulders as more cars entered the drive. "Yes, I'm happy to say. Hey, Aunt Claire!"

Carter's gut roiled as yet another unwanted guest arrived. Pretty soon… yup. There was Jeff Dayton, and Ted Seamans, the Fire Marshall, and… who the heck *was* that guy?

A slick-looking metro-dude stepped out of the same sedan Carter had seen dropping Liz off twenty minutes ago. The guy ran a hand through his product-enhanced hair and glanced around at all the cars. He looked nervous as he wove his way toward them.

"Excuse me," he said, approaching the cluster of people on the front walk. "Does anyone know how I might get in touch with Mrs. Beacon? Liz's mother?"

"And you are…?" Bailey asked.

"Grant Blackerby."

The interoffice-guy?

"*Grant!*" Liz said from behind Carter. She stood at the front door, gawking, the back of her dress flapping in the breeze. "What—? What is everyone doing here?"

"Liz, I'm sorry," Grant said, peering around her relatives. "I—"

"*Jeff?*" John said, rounding the corner from the side of the house. "And Ted? What are you doing here?"

"I was chatting with Ted at the station when he got a call from Carter. It sounded interesting, so I thought I might come and take a look, too." Jeff raised one dark eyebrow at Liz's brother.

"Look all you want. I haven't done anything wrong," John said.

"If things are so up and up, why is Rick here?" Jeff pressed.

"I didn't want anyone asking questions. It's a surprise. Or, was. Plans have changed."

"What's a surprise?" Liz asked from the stoop.

"It's good you're here, Officer Dayton, because this guy is trying to shaft me." Rick hooked an accusatory finger at John.

"Just return it all," John mumbled.

"They don't *take* returns," Rick shot back.

"Actually, Rick, we have some questions for you," Jeff began. "You're not in any trouble, but we—"

And, that's when they heard the cyber-screaming from the side yard.

"Mom! *Mom!*" Ben yelled, running toward the grown-ups, the tablet held in front of him as Mrs. Beacon screamed *'fire!'* hysterically from the seven inch screen.

"*Fire! Fire!*" Mrs. Beacon yelled again.

"Mom!" Trish said, grabbing the tablet from her son. "Call 9-1-1!"

"No *you* call 9-1-1!" Mrs. Beacon screamed back.

"No *you* have to!" Trish yelled at the tablet. "And, get out of the house!"

"I'm not the one that's on fire!" Mrs. Beacon yelled back.

"What?"

Everyone looked at each other for one stunned moment, and then all hell broke loose as they started babbling at once.

Carter shoved Liz toward the house and bolted for the side yard, the others hot on his heels. He skidded to a stop. Bright yellow and orange flames raced up the side of the storage shed, fueled by the dry old lumber, licking at the branches of the apple tree nearby.

"Get a hose!" someone called from behind him.

"Get back!" Carter yelled, turning and gesturing wildly as Liz's relatives poured around the corner of the house and ran around excitedly. "Get back! Get back! *John! Get them all BACK!*"

John met Carter's gaze across the yard, recognition dawning, and screamed at everyone to *run, goddammit, RUN!*

Carter charged forward as the first explosions hammered out the shed door and whizzed by his ear. A brilliant rocket of color exploded in the bushes above a black silhouette of kissing children. A second rocket flattened the silhouette as a third whizzed through where they'd been.

Screams and a handful of startled curses colored the air along with the wild explosions of dozens of fireworks let loose. They shot by him, exploding on the ground, in the trees, zinging toward the driveway and all their cars, popping all around like toy guns run amok.

He saw Jeff Dayton hunkered down by his squad car, yelling into his radio.

John screamed, "Valerie? Valerie! Get *down!*" across the yard at the same time Carter charged toward the front of the house... and ran smack into Liz.

"What the hell are you doing?" he cried, pulling her upright off the lawn.

"We need to put out the fire!" she yelled, as she stood in the grass in bare feet, her dress flapping open, working frantically to uncurl the hose from its reel.

"We need to get the hell out of here!" he hollered back as another rocket exploded mere feet from where they stood. Why the hell weren't they going off all at once, for Christ's sake? Carter grabbed her elbow and shoved her toward the front door where the others were taking refuge even as John, foolishly, bolted across the front lawn toward the driveway.

Liz stubbornly turned on the spigot anyway and started spraying around Carter at the cinders on the front lawn. She shot him in the chest.

"Liz!" He hollered again, as she tried to drown him with the hose. "Get inside! *Now!*"

"But—"

"*Inside!*"

More fireworks exploded in a shower of sparks nearby, and he heard a scream from the driveway. He turned to grab Liz, but she tripped and pitched forward, falling hard to the ground in front of him.

Carter threw his body over hers to shield her at the same moment the shed exploded like a sonic boom.

His heart pounding in his ears, he let his face sink into Liz's hair and waited for the sirens.

CHAPTER FORTY-SEVEN

"SHE'S AWAKE."

Liz heard the whispered words somewhere outside the drumming fog in her head. Her forehead throbbed, and when she tried to open her eyes, her right eye, in particular, stubbornly refused.

"She'll sport quite a shiner."

That was Aunt Claire. Liz recognized the gravely dead-pan tone, although the slight hitch at the end was unusual.

"Liz? Can you hear me? It's Trish."

A hand covered hers. Liz soaked in its warmth. She tried to open her eyes again. "Anyone catch… license… of the truck… ran me over?" she mumbled.

Her voice felt disused, raspy, and she scowled, or tried to, as the air filled with relieved, low chuckles.

"No. No one else to blame for this one," said Aunt Claire. "For such a smart girl, you'd think you'd know enough to break a fall with your hands, not your face." She was cracking a joke, but you could hear the underlying concern in her no-nonsense voice.

Slowly, as the fog began to dissipate, Liz focused her left eye on the people huddling over her. She struggled to sit up.

"*Easy*," Carter said, holding an arm behind her to steady her.

Carter?

"How many fingers am I holding up?" Bailey demanded, shoving her hand in front of Liz's face.

"Three… Plus a Snickers."

"She's okay, folks!" Bailey announced. "She's okay!"

"I don't feel okay," Liz said. "My eye—"

"Here's a boo-boo pack," Ben said, thrusting a bag of frozen vegetables at her. "For your eye."

"Thanks." Liz held the vegetables to her face, wincing as she did so. "What happened?"

"Your brother had some fireworks stored in the shed. Somehow a fire started and set them off," said Carter.

Liz rolled her eyes and then instantly regretted the motion. "Lovely," she murmured behind the peas. "Some people never learn." Her brain hurt. Among many other parts of her. "How did he get in the shed? I locked it..."

"He took the key from your purse."

Jeff Dayton knelt beside her. "We'd like to take you to Sugar Falls General if you don't mind, just to get you checked out. Or, rather, the lady in the iPad told me that's what we'd like to do."

"Oh. Sure. All right." Liz made as if to stand, but was held in place by a rock-solid forearm.

"She needs a gurney," she heard Carter say. "She's not walking anywhere until a doctor says she can."

"I'm—" she began and then saw Carter's face. "I'm sure that's wise," she murmured.

Soon, the paramedics moved her onto a gurney, wheeled her toward the ambulance and lifted her in.

"Oh, Jesus." Valerie sat on one of the seats in the ambulance already, a bloody bandage held to her wrist. "Are you serious? I have to ride with *her*?"

Liz would have turned her head away except they'd immobilized her head for the trip. "The other ambulances are out on calls. It's less than ten minutes away, Val."

Val winced, looking a little pasty under her tan. "Fine."

THEY DROVE TO THE HOSPITAL—a caravan of cars, trucks and one ambulance—as the fire department put out the last of the smoldering embers back at the house.

The paramedics unloaded Liz and wheeled her toward the E.R. entrance. John's car squealed to a stop behind them. He leapt out as Valerie was being helped from the ambulance and onto a second gurney.

"Val? Why are you on a gurney? *Why is she on a gurney?*" John demanded.

"I got dizzy," she said.

"Dizzy? Oh God, Val! *Babes!*" John grasped her hand, squeezed it and jogged next to her as they rolled the women into the E.R. "I'm sorry! *So sorry!*"

"You should be. What were you thinking?" Valerie winced. She held up her left arm and instructed the male nurse who was trying to help her with the admission paperwork to snap to it and fetch her a hospital gown so she wouldn't bleed all over her good blouse.

"I was thinking I needed to do something big... to win you back."

243

"So you blew up my hand?"

"You'll be all right, Miss," said the nurse, smoothing a hospital gown across her.

"Who asked you?"

"Don't move your head, ma'am," a paramedic warned Liz as she craned to see what was going on.

"Shh!" she told him.

"It was going to be a big display over at the lake," John continued. "Big enough for the whole town to see… big enough for *you* to see how much I want you in my life."

Valerie's eyes grew watery. "Shut up. You don't."

"I do! And, I don't care anymore what you think your chances are with Dan. I won't let you go back to him. He had his chance with you and he blew it. It's my turn now."

Val murmured her address and phone number for the nurse to write on his clipboard. "What do you mean, it's your turn?"

John stuck his hand deep in his pocket, fished around, and pulled out a little velvet box.

The room gasped. Liz nearly threw up.

"What is that?" Valerie asked, alarm creeping across her features.

"It's a ring, Val. I'm not going to sneak around anymore. You're worth more than that to me. You deserve more."

"Don't be an idiot," she said as she turned toward the nurse. "I'm allergic to Penicillin, too. Make sure you note that."

"Valerie—*look at me.*"

Val swallowed visibly and raised a shaky hand to brush the hair from her forehead. "John, we had a good thing, but it's over." She glanced around the room. "Don't make a scene."

"I love you, Val."

Her hand stopped at her temple and stayed there a moment before she let it fall to her lap. "What did you say?"

"I love you, Val. And, I want to marry you."

Val shook her head and pressed the ring box closed. "No. You don't know what you're doing. I'm no good at being married. It won't work."

"Miss…?" Valerie just kept shaking her head, tears seeping from her baby blues, John clutching her good hand, the nurse standing by the gurney, waiting. "Miss?"

John let out a sigh and put the box back in his pocket.

Val closed her eyes for a moment then turned and snapped at the nurse, "It's Ma'am to you, kiddo. You don't look a day older than my baby brother."

"Ma'am?" the man tried again.

But, Valerie wasn't listening, was just shaking her head at John. "You almost ruined everything," she whispered.

"Ma'am?" the nurse said again, clearly not moved by romantic displays as he lowered his voice. "I have to ask before we do x-rays... is there any possibility that you are, or have reason to believe you may be, pregnant?"

Valerie's eyes leaked even faster, huge tears plopping like rain onto the front of her hospital gown.

"Ma'am? I need to know—"

"I do two hundred sit-ups a day!" she blurted, rounding on the man. "*Two hundred!* Would my stomach look like this if I *weren't* pregnant!" And then she shook off John's grip, huge, ugly racking sobs shaking her as she tried to bully the nurse into wheeling her off to a private room.

He wrote something on his clipboard instead.

"Val," John whispered from her side, "is it true?"

"*No.*"

"But you just said—"

"I know what I said! Forget what I said! Isn't there such a thing as patient-doctor confidentiality anymore?"

"Ma'am, I'm not a doctor..."

"*Oh, shut up!*" Val and John said in unison.

"But you said... you said you and Dan were getting back together! I can't believe it. I can't believe you'd..." John's shoulders were shaking as he reached out and grabbed Val's arm so she'd look at him. "You were going to, weren't you? After everything we've been to each other... You were going to try and pass off *my* baby as his, weren't you? *Weren't you?*"

Valerie didn't answer, she just yanked her arm out of his hand and continued to sob.

"Don't you think he would have figured it out, Val? Huh?"

Trish popped baby Clara over her shoulder and turned to John. "How can you be so sure it's yours?"

Everyone leaned in. It *was* a valid question, after all—even if the timing was questionable.

Valerie looked up. "Dan's infertile. Old football injury."

"*Oh.*" The room said, collectively.

"*Val*—" John began.

"Can you blame me?" she shot back. "What are my options? I'm knocked up, Johnny. Just like my mom. Knocked up and... *alone!*"

"Honey. *Babes.* Don't cry," John pleaded.

"Don't tell me not to cry!" Val cried louder. "Why are you even here? Go away! Shouldn't you be running to the hills like you're so good at?"

"I'm done running," is all he said.

Val hiccupped and swiped her eyes with her good hand. "*Ha!* You left for three months—*three months!*—with barely a word! You're just like my father! Only ever was there to knock my mother up and smile at the babies... Well, I've got news for you, Johnathan Beacon, I can take care of this baby myself!"

"You won't have to," John said, tears of his own slipping onto his cheeks. But, he didn't seem to care. He gripped Val's hand in both of his and leaned down to kiss her knuckles. "I'll take care of you both. I swear."

"Stop that," Valerie croaked, tugging her hand. "Stop doing that." But, John wouldn't let go. "How are you going to take care of anything?" she demanded. "What are you going to do?"

"I'll work. I'll take care of you—of you and the baby. I promise."

"How?" Aunt Claire interjected.

"Yeah," Val said, suddenly seeming to be aware of just how big a spectacle they'd become. She pulled their joined hands up to her hair to smooth it again. "How?"

John shrugged sheepishly. "Since I finished the last of my coursework over the winter and applied for my Journeyman's license. I'm an electrician, Babe. For real. I'm sure I can find work around here. I've been saving up. Working my ass off to get in my required hours and save enough to buy you the ring you deserve. I didn't say anything before, in case..."

"In case you didn't finish?" Val whispered. John nodded. "You idiot. I've always told you you were smart enough to make something of yourself. Why won't you believe me?"

"I believe you now," he said, crouching down beside the gurney.

Val tensed again. "What are you doing?"

"I'm kneeling."

"Get up," she said. "Get up, right this moment."

"No," John said. "Not until I ask."

"I won't." Val was shaking her head, shaking her head and crying again all at the same time. "I told you. I've done this before. It's no good, Johnny..."

But John ignored her as he fished in his pants pocket a second time, a little awkwardly now that Valerie didn't seem able to let go of the death grip she had on his other hand. He managed to retrieve the box, and Trish leaned over helpfully to pop it open, tears welling up in her eyes, too.

"Valerie Mirabelle Stinson?" John began again, "Will you make me the happiest man alive by agreeing to become my wife?"

"You're an idiot," Val whispered, her eyes glued to his face.

"Maybe," he said, "but this is one idiot who will never leave you. *Ever*. I love you, Val. You're the strongest, gutsiest, smartest, most beautiful woman I know. Marry me?"

John waited, watching, the room completely silent around them.

Val sucked in a shaky breath, pressed her lips together a moment, and then rounded on the nurse. "Can someone around here stitch up my damn hand so my fiancé can put this ring on my finger?"

CHAPTER FORTY-EIGHT

Twelve years earlier…

CARTER HITCHED HIS backpack up his shoulder and high-tailed it down the hall toward the library. He was running late. Again. But, if he booked it, he'd get there in time.

He couldn't wait to see the surprise on Beth's face when he arrived at the dot of three.

He didn't see Missy Green until it was too late.

One second he was charging down the hall, the next, Missy was flat on her backside on the floor, her big brown eyes looking up at him in surprise.

"I'm so sorry!" he said, hoisting her off the floor and brushing her off. She was carrying an armful of poster-board and art supplies, and he noticed the corners were bent on a bunch of them. He bent to hastily flatten them again. "Shoot. I didn't mean—"

"It's okay," she said, "I shouldn't have tried to carry so much at a time. I couldn't see where I was going."

Carter grabbed a stack of poster-board that was slipping out of her grasp as she gazed up at him gratefully. "Here. Let me. Where are you headed? The art room?"

"Yes! Yes, I was. I was just, um, working on some decorations for the prom."

Carter started walking down the hall, in a hurry to drop the poster-board off and get to the library. "Sounds fun," he said noncommittally.

"It is," Missy said. "You should join us! There are just a few of us working today, but the drama department has some incredible displays worked up for the big night."

"Love to," he said, "but I've got to study for trig now." He laid the art supplies he'd carried on a table for Missy. "There. Hope you enjoy yourself at the prom."

He was *this close* to walking away… but then he saw the look on Missy's face.

"What's wrong?"

"Oh, nothing," she said, briskly sorting out her supplies. "I'm not actually *going* to the prom. Just, um, decorating for it."

"Not going? Why not?"

Her face grew pink. "I don't have a boyfriend. I mean, *right now*, that is."

He shrugged. "Just ask a friend."

He knew it was a mistake the moment the words left his mouth by the hopeful, starry-eyed look on Missy's face. He also knew Missy spent most afternoons watching over her younger, Down Syndrome, sister, so the fact that she was here, working on a prom she wasn't even attending seemed all the more pitiable.

And that's how he arrived fifteen minutes late for his tutoring session with Beth with an invitation to the prom from Missy Green he couldn't say 'no' to.

Beth sat in one of those heavy oak chairs in the back of the library. It had been three days since Jenny Whitmeyer's party. Three days since Carter had experienced the most amazing, mind-blowing kiss imaginable.

Three days since he'd first started thinking that Beth Beacon might, possibly, perhaps, be someone he'd like to get to know more.

"Sorry I'm late."

He strode in, repeating the same three words he'd met her with every tutoring session since September and tossed his backpack onto the table. He shrugged out of his leather jacket, because being with Beth got his blood pumping like nobody's business, tossed it atop the backpack as well and pulled out a chair next to her.

His hormones kicked into high gear as his thigh accidentally brushed hers. He didn't pull away. "It's okay," she said, her thigh soft and warm through the thin cotton skirt she wore. "Why don't we get started?"

He ducked his head down as he searched for his trig text in his backpack so she wouldn't see the devilish smile he couldn't control, then he thumped the text on the table in front of them.

He ached to smell her hair.

They reached for his text at the same time, their hands colliding.

Beth gasp-laughed and yanked her hand away, and it sounded almost like the surprised moan she'd made when he'd first touched his lips to hers.

He smiled at her at the memory and opened the book to the next lesson.

Beth licked her lips. He could almost taste Twizzler.

Carter raised one eyebrow rakishly. "Aren't we going to start?"

Beth coughed and fluttered to pull out a notebook, her face growing pink. "Yes. Of course," she said. She glanced at the page he'd opened to. "Ah, yes. Oblique triangles and law of sines. Okay. Basically all this is doing is allowing you to find…"

Thirty minutes later Carter was jiggling his knee, frowning at the notebook and glancing at the clock on the wall as Beth's face grew red with frustration.

She bit her lip, obviously trying to figure out how to salvage the tutoring session and get anything meaningful through his thick skull, but all he could do was sit there and wonder how he could get her into a dark room again.

He was going to be late for work, and Beth was clearly not happy. She couldn't even look at him!

He ran a hand through his hair. "Maybe we should try again next time."

"No! I mean, of course we can, but I know you'll get it. It's my fault for not explaining it right to begin with."

Just like Beth, always trying to make him feel better for being thick-headed.

"It's okay, Beth," he said, deciding he'd better put her out of her misery. He started to shove his text into his backpack.

"So," she said, closing her notebook. "I hear a lot of people are getting excited about the prom."

Carter fought with the zipper on his backpack. It caught, again, and he yanked it in frustration at it and himself. "The food should be good," he said. He'd heard something about Missy having a nut allergy. Or maybe it was mangoes. He wondered if she'd eat at the prom.

"The Whitmeyers sure threw a great party the other night, didn't they?" Beth was still trying to converse pleasantly, probably to make him feel better. She was nice that way.

Carter glanced at her and wondered if she'd heard what Dan had said in the hall that night. *Asshole.* He'd never forgive the guy for being such a bastard. What had Beth ever done to him? "It had its moments."

He heard her intake of breath as he stood to leave, and he turned to see her standing next to him, hands folded together, her head held high just like she'd looked when he'd opened the door at the Whitmeyers'. He looked at her lips.

"So, Carter, I, um, was wondering… if … like, as just friends… if you thought it might be fun to go, I mean, together. To the prom, I mean."

Holy. Shit. He hadn't seen *that* coming.

He couldn't breathe, couldn't even feel his heart any more, as she stood completely still, waiting for his reply. *What now?* Forty minutes ago he hadn't even given the prom a second thought and here he was with *two* girls asking him out? But there was nothing he could do. He'd already told Missy 'yes.' And here Beth was, standing in front of him a second time, completely vulnerable, and it wasn't in his power to make this turn out right. Crap. His answer would surely crush her.

Here he was, beholden to her for so much and yet she was the one laying it all on the line. His lips tilted at the irony of it as he turned to grab his jacket. "I can't. Missy Green already asked. That's why I was late." He smiled wider hoping she would see how much he enjoyed her company, too, that he'd go with her if he could, but his hands were tied… and shrugged into his jacket.

But, if she were there, too, at the prom, could Missy complain if he danced with Beth a few times? "But you don't have to have a date to go," he found himself suggesting hopefully. "There are plenty of guys going stag. Maybe I'll see you there?"

"Right," she said, her smile taut. "I'll think about it."

"Okay," he said. "See you next time."

"See ya."

But, he knew it wouldn't be at the prom. He knew by the set of her jaw and the cold disappointment in her eyes any possibility he might have had to pursue Beth Beacon had locked shut like a Brinks truck as soon as he suggested she play second fiddle. He should have known. Beth was too proud and had too much going for her to wait around for him to sort his life out.

So, he left.

CHAPTER FORTY-NINE

CARTER SAT IN THE HARD plastic chair in the E.R. waiting room and stared at the wall. His shirt stuck to his chest, he had grass-stains on his suit, and he felt guilty as hell.

He'd just gotten the call from Ted with preliminary findings from the Beacon's house. Probable cause of fire: a strand of decorative lights. *Smiley-face lights.*

He brushed a hand down his face and glanced across to where Liz's family was gathered. Ben still held the tablet with Liz's mother peering out, sipping tea and periodically asking to see something.

Bailey and Trish and Aunt Claire were entertaining the baby.

And that Grant guy was over in the far corner grimacing into his cup of vending machine coffee.

Liz walked out.

LIZ SCUFFED HER LITTLE blue disposable booties across the floor. Low, excited chatter met her reentry. Carter stood.

She felt achy, dirty and weary as hell, but grateful. He was here. Her hero! She glanced shyly at Carter, her eyes eating him up eagerly. He looked wet and rumpled and had a big smear of dirt across one thigh, but he'd never looked better to her.

She waved, a feeble attempt at looking chipper despite the large gauze bandage over her right temple and eye and the mud and grass stains across her never-wear-it-again dress.

"It looks worse than it is," she assured everyone. "The eye patch can probably come off by morning. They just want to give it a rest until the swelling goes down. I think it's more there so I don't scare people."

Bailey gave her a quick hug. "I've got a pirate hat to go with that if you like."

Liz let herself laugh at that. "I think I'll pass for now."

Trish hugged her next. "You scared the bejeebers out of me. Don't do that again!"

Aunt Claire gave her a pat on the shoulder.

Liz let her family dote on her a few moments before her eyes met Carter's across the waiting room. She walked over and gave him a small smile. He had that serious, brooding look again. Probably because he'd been worried about her. She shouldn't find it sexy, but she was injured, not dead. And, heck, she'd be fine once the bruising subsided. "Hey," she said.

"Hey." He reached up to feather-touch the bandage on her temple. She wished he'd give her a hug. "Hurt much?"

She shrugged, then winced. Okay, so being body-slammed into the ground by your One True Love isn't something she'd want to do every day. Maybe they could go home and he could help inventory her injuries. "Some," she said. "Okay, a lot. Thanks for saving me." She reached out to touch a muddy abrasion on his cheek. "You okay? I never thought to ask if you were hurt."

"I'm fine." He grimaced, and she watched his throat work as he swallowed. She dropped her hand. "Ted just called, Liz. They think they found the cause of the fire."

"Already?"

He nodded, his lips forming a taut line. "It was the lights. The ones I gave you. He thinks there must have been a short, or the plug wasn't in right, and it started a fire. That set off the fireworks. They would have all gone off at once if John hadn't tried to plan how he was going to link them together for his big show. I guess we're lucky it gave us some warning."

"The lights...," Liz repeated.

"Must have been defective." Carter blew out a breath. "I'm sorry."

"Elizabeth? Elizabeth! Did I hear her voice? Somebody pick me up so I can see my daughter!" Ben ran over to pick up the tablet with his grandmother from the chair. He held it up. "Oh, my Lord, Elizabeth! You look *awful*! I just went to get... say, where's Grant? Why am I not seeing Grant? He should be here now that you're back!"

"I'm here," Grant said, stepping into view of the tablet. "How are you, Liz?"

I've been unconscious, have one eye swollen shut and just learned I nearly blew up the man I love, but all things considered... "I'm okay."

"She's not okay!" Mrs. Beacon insisted. "She's miserable! Just look at her. Grant! Scootch in! Why are you standing so far away? I'm sure Carter won't mind if you stand next to your own fiancé, for heaven's sake!"

Carter's head snapped up. "Fiancé? Did your mother just say *fiancé*?"

Liz blanched. "Yes, but that's not important right—"

"When did he propose?"

"A couple of hours ago—"

"*A couple of hours ago?* Wow. You were just primed for takeoff, weren't you? From 'sort of' to all the way? So much for giving me six weeks. Were you going to break up with me before or after dinner?"

Liz's head began to throb. What? "No! Carter, it's not like that. I turned him down! I don't *want* to marry Grant!" She turned toward Grant. "Sorry."

Grant gave a stiff smile. "It's all right. I'm just relieved you're okay."

"*Pfft!*" Mrs. Beacon made an inelegant noise from the tablet. "Barely! No thanks to that son of mine. He nearly blew up my next grandchild with his foolishness! Where is he anyway?"

"He's in with Vamp—Valerie," Liz said.

Carter spoke to the tablet. "Don't blame John, Mrs. Beacon. The fire was my fault. Some lights I hung on the shed for Liz must have shorted out."

"Those smiley-face lights you gave Liz last week?" said Bailey. "Bummer. Those were cute."

Grant tilted his head in confusion. He looked at Liz. "I thought you said those belonged to your parents?"

Liz swallowed, a shiver of unease trickling over her. "It's really not important whose they were. I mean, thank goodness we're all okay, right? Who wants to head out? I don't know about you all, but I could use some dinner!"

Carter looked to Grant. "She told you they were her parents' lights?"

Sweat started to bead on Liz's forehead. She could feel it running into the bandage over her eye as she stepped between the two men. "I don't remember what was said. Grant was proposing, and..." She waved her hands vaguely and tried to smile through the gauze holding half her face immobile. "Does it matter now? The important thing is—"

"They aren't around to assault anyone else's sensibilities," Grant finished for her. "Liz, no one with *taste* blames you for pulling them down."

Carter stilled and looked to Liz. "Wait. *You pulled them down?*"

"I may have adjusted them," she murmured.

"A good hard *yanking* adjustment," muttered Grant.

Liz shot him a one-eyed glare.

"Why? Why would—?" Carter began, but before she could think of a reasonable reply, because, let's face it, the truth wasn't going to help the situation, his expression changed. "On second thought. Don't answer that." He turned to Grant. "She's all yours."

"What?" Liz stared at Carter's retreating back in disbelief. "Carter, wait! Let me explain!"

He stopped, turned and raised one dark eyebrow. "What's to explain, Liz? This isn't hard to figure out. *Christ!* I'm not as stupid as you think."

"What are you talking about? Who said you were stupid?"

"Stupid enough to believe we had something worthwhile going. But how could we, when nothing has changed? You still think you're better than the rest of us schmucks who never left Sugar Falls." He choked out a hard, humorless laugh. "I'm sorry I'm so far beneath you."

"*What?* You were never beneath me!"

"Oh. Right. Except for that one time you were on top," he murmured, and the cold innuendo coupled with the hurt look in his eyes had the blood rushing from her head.

He looked up and down her tattered dress and battered form. "I'm sorry I'm not good enough for the new and improved Liz Beacon. But you know what? This is *me*, Liz. I'm a college drop-out. I don't care what other people think. I don't wear fancy suits or eat organic crap or pre-plan my every move like one of your master plan to-do lists. *This* is who I am. And unlike *some* people, I'm not embarrassed by that."

"I'm not embarrassed by... I admire you!"

"*Bullshit.* You tore them down! *You* caused the fire! And what's worse is you were going to let everyone, including *me*, believe it was my fault!" He shook his head. "Fuck this. I'm sick of being everyone's fall guy. You want me to live up to my potential? How is that even possible when the first suspect for every crime committed in this goddamn town is *me?*"

"Carter, I—"

"Save it. You're no different than the rest of them."

"How can you say that? When have I judged you that way?"

His lips were a taut line. "Did you hear I'd been kicked out of the fire department? The rumors about why?"

"Well, yes, Trish may have mentioned..."

"Did you believe the rumors were true?"

Her expression must have told him the truth, because he swore again under his breath and turned toward the door again. "To be fair," she called after him, "you never did have a squeaky clean reputation. I mean, you were the high school bad boy! I saw you smoke cigarettes... You wore a *leather jacket!*"

He stopped, his back to her. "That was my father's jacket," he said so quietly she almost couldn't hear. He turned. "And maybe my reputation was less about the truth and more about what other people wanted to believe about me."

She shook her head. How dare he judge her this way! What had *she* done? "You told me yourself you used to go drinking at the quarry and skinny dipping in Miller Brook!"

"So did ninety-nine percent of the rest of the teenagers in this town."

"But they outgrew it! They became responsible adults." Okay, only some of them, but they weren't talking about Dan or John… "*You* still have beer bottles on the floor of your pickup! I mean… Dammit! What am I supposed to think?"

"That I recycle?"

"You see? When you make jokes like that, I don't think I even know you!" But then she watched him and realized with sickening awareness that he wasn't joking at all. Oh my God. He wasn't.

"No," he said. "I don't think you do."

"Then help me," she said, something hot and desperate firing inside her. "Don't shut me out…"

"Liz, you took something I gave you and *blew up your parents' house with it.* I think we're done."

"Done? Do you hear yourself? Carter, they were *just* lights…"

"And I'm just another guy that will never be perfect enough for the perfect Liz Beacon."

"I never once said you weren't perfect!"

"No, you said it in a hundred different ways. But don't worry. I'm sure there's a pill I can take to fix it."

She stared at him in shock. *This couldn't be happening!* "I never meant—"

"You know the ironic part of all this?" His mouth twisted in anything but humor. "I came to your house tonight to tell you… to tell you…"

She felt the blood rush from her head then roar back again. "That you love me?" she whispered.

She shivered, her emotions raw and exposed, battered and bruised, and the only man who had the power to make it all right stood before her. She waited and prayed he could see she wasn't trying to be perfect, wasn't trying to make *him* perfect. She was only ever trying to be good enough. But…

"*Love you?*" he asked. "Liz, love is going out of your way to make someone else happy no matter what it costs you. Love is going into a burning building knowing it might take *your* life, too." And suddenly he grabbed her arms, his fingers tight and hot on her skin. "It's throwing yourself over someone and begging a God you were never sure you believed in to protect that person, because now that you've finally found them—*again!*—you can't bear to lose them…"

Tears began to slide down her face, and her bandaged eye started to ache. Her heart pounded hard and fast and eagerly inside her. *He* did *love her!*

"But more than anything," he continued, his voice hoarse with emotion, "love is knowing yourself enough to recognize when another person knows, appreciates and accepts the *real* you…"

"Yes," she whispered. *"Yes!"*

He let her go abruptly and stepped away. "But this isn't love," he said, gesturing to the space between them.

She felt as if she'd been thrown to the ground. Again.

"I know who I am," he said. "But who's the *real* Liz Beacon? Or should I say, *Beth*? Do you even know? Because I sure as hell don't."

He shut his eyes and sucked in a long breath, his fingers flexing in his pocket.

"By the way," he said, "I bought you these."

Then he threw a package of Twizzlers at her feet. And left.

CHAPTER FIFTY

"*EW.* THEY WERE RIGHT. It does look worse the next morning."
Bailey lifted her chocolate chip cookie in salute as Liz pushed open the
kitchen door.

Liz had taken off the bulky eye patch and left it upstairs, although
she still had a couple of butterfly bandages over the gash in her eyebrow.
She touched her cheek gingerly.

In the end, she hadn't been able to face anyone after Carter walked
out. Thankfully, Bailey had whisked her away from prying eyes, probing
questions and would-be fiancés, threatening anyone who might challenge
the plan with a thwack of a Snickers bar. She'd taken Liz home, cleaned
her up, fed her take-out Chinese, and crashed on the couch without
another word except to come in every hour on the hour and ask her how
many fingers she was holding up.

Liz had lain alone in her room, staring blindly at the ceiling.
Thinking.

It had been Carter. It had been Carter all along. Valerie said the
bottle picked Dan, but Liz *knew* it was Carter in the pantry that night.
She *knew* it. Just as she *knew* he wasn't involved in any illegal drug use.

She knew, because she didn't need proof to know what was in her
heart.

She loved him.

And, he, by some miracle, loved her.

Or *did.*

Bailey gestured toward Liz's face, pulling her out of her thoughts.
"So, how does it feel?"

"How does it look?"

"Awful."

"That's how it feels." Liz pulled a mug from the cupboard and filled
it with coffee. She didn't bother with cream or sugar.

"Can I get you anything?" Bailey asked.

"Have you learned to cook?"

"No."

"Then toast will be fine."

"Do you like it burnt or raw?"

"Burnt, please."

Bailey set to work slicing bread and popping it in the toaster oven then proceeded to ignore it as she went in search of supplies in the fridge.

"Hello? Anybody home?"

Bailey met Liz's gaze over the fridge door. "You better get used to it. She's going to be your sister-in-law."

Liz groaned into her coffee. "How did life get so messed up?"

"I'm letting myself in!" Valerie announced from the front door. Her heels clicked on the floors as she made her way to the kitchen. She thumped the door open, a bright pink cast on her left arm. "I have news!"

"What happened to you?" Liz asked. "I thought you just needed stitches!"

"Oh," Val pursed her lips at her cast and shrugged, "apparently they think I fractured something, too. But, enough about that, I have news!"

"You've cast an evil spell on Liz's brother?"

Valerie sniffed. "Your toast is burning."

"*Done!*" Bailey pulled the smoking slices out and slathered them with butter.

"No," Val said, to Bailey's earlier question. She pulled some papers out of her purse. "As of fifteen minutes ago, I have a signed Purchase & Sale agreement on this house!"

"Already?" Liz asked, pulling the document forward.

"*Eh!*" Val snatched it back again. "You can't see it. Confidential and all that. But your folks are thrilled. It's just barely over their target price, but I can't promise holding out for more will pan out. They are pleased as punch with their new future daughter-in-law."

Valerie tucked the contract back into her purse. "Well, can't stay. Have an engagement ring to show off and houses to sell, so *ta-ta!*"

"Sold." Liz said dully as she took a bite of burnt toast. "Well, I guess that's that."

"What are you going to do now?" asked Bailey.

Resolutely ignoring the hollow ache in her chest, she shrugged. "Go home."

LIZ PACKED HER SUITCASE, zipped it shut and set it by the bedroom door. With the house under contract, she was done with what she'd come to do.

"Ready when you are, Eddie."

Eddie sat on the windowsill and stared at her. It had become his favorite spot.

"You'll have to find a new favorite spot, Ed. Because, we're going home."

And, home wasn't here anymore.

Half an hour later, Trish was driving her to the airport.

"I need to make a stop before we leave town," Liz said. "Take a right here."

"You'll be late for your flight."

"I'll only be a minute."

Liz directed Trish down the street and told her where to park. "Keep the car running."

She pursed her lips, squared her shoulders, prayed Carter wasn't home and knocked on his door.

Just as she was about to try and slip the envelope underneath, the door swung wide. Liz popped up.

"John?"

"Liz? What are you doing here?"

"I could ask the same thing."

John opened the door wider. "I'm helping out with some office stuff for Carter until his uncle is back on his feet. Mostly cleaning up."

"You clean?"

He laughed, looking happier and younger than she'd seen him in years. "There's a lot you don't know about me. Yes. But, I don't cook."

"Now *that* I knew."

She smiled, amazed she could have a semi-civil conversation with John without all the drama. Would wonders never cease? "Can I come in?" she asked. "I wanted to drop off a letter. For Carter."

"Heading out are you?" She nodded. "Put it in his office. It won't get lost there."

"Thanks."

Liz pushed open the door John gestured to and stepped through.

The room smelled of Carter, a mixture of fresh air and hard work and sweet rebellion she recognized now as Twizzler. The combination made her feel like crying right then and there. She pushed the feelings down and sat in the desk chair for a moment, soaking in all that was Carter before pulling the letter of apology she'd written out of her purse.

She ran a hand over the envelope to smooth it, wishing for all the world she could make things right between them but knowing that wasn't possible. She'd made too many mistakes.

He deserved more than a woman who couldn't stand behind him or stand up for him.

She opened the drawer to retrieve a pen to write his name on the outside of the letter… and saw a large manila envelope marked "Beautification League of Sugar Falls."

She frowned, feeling guilty, but the envelope wasn't *sealed*, so she pulled out the paper inside.

He hadn't submitted the bid? But the deadline was… *today!* Why wouldn't he…?

And, then, all the self-doubt she'd heard him speak over the years washed over her in a wave. He didn't think he could do it. He was afraid of making a mistake.

Well, she thought, take it from someone who has made mistakes. The only things worse than mistakes are regrets.

By the time she waved goodbye to John, she had the manila envelope tucked in her purse and was asking Trish to make one more stop…

CHAPTER FIFTY-ONE

JUST AS SHE HAD FOR THE past three years, Liz filled Eddie's dish with one precisely measured scoop of urinary-tract-health cat food then pulled a box of breakfast cereal from the kitchen cupboard.

She grimaced. It was the hemp/flax-seed/high-fiber cereal Grant had recommended a couple months ago. It tasted like cardboard with just enough organic sweeteners to make it so she didn't reflexively spit it out, and she'd tried to make herself choke down a few spoonfuls each morning before she was entirely awake, but today she shoved it aside.

She craved swiss cake rolls.

Liz looked out at the morning and tried to muster the enthusiasm to go in to the office.

Aunt Claire was right. She needed a new plan.

Eddie leapt to the table and settled bread-loaf style on the placemat in front of her. She'd worried at one point she'd need to retrain Eddie to pretend to be well-mannered. Eddie raised one leg and started to clean himself.

It depressed her knowing no one would object.

She patted his head and pushed out of her chair. She stared out the window onto the street below as she prepared coffee. How strange that just over a month ago she'd been imagining her wedding to Grant while standing in this very spot.

Now, she and Grant were kaput, Grant and Ethan were starting their own firm, and Liz had been offered Ethan's position. It represented a huge promotion. They expected her answer today.

Dum. Dum. De-dum. Dum-de-dum-de-dum-de-DUM...

Liz bit her lip. She hadn't taken her mother's calls since that night at the hospital. She hadn't wanted to face it all, hadn't wanted to try and explain what a mess her life was.

But she couldn't wallow in self-pity forever.

She sucked in a long breath, held the phone away from her ear and braced herself. "Hello?"

"Liz?"

"*Dad?*" Liz held the phone closer. "Dad? What's wrong? Is it mom? Aunt Claire?"

"*Shh.* Nothing's wrong. We're good. I'm calling to check on *you.*" He paused. "How are you, Chickie?"

Her chest felt tight and she tried to deny anything was wrong, but he'd caught her off-guard. He hadn't called her Chickie since that day so many years ago when he'd found her sobbing into her pillow because a certain boy was going to the prom with the *wrong girl.*

"Not good, Dad," she finally said. "Not good at all."

"I'm sorry, Chickie."

That's all he said. *I'm sorry, Chickie.*

I'm sorry.

When he'd said those words to her all those years ago, she'd felt fragile as glass—hurt and sad and embarrassed—but there'd been a quiet strength in her father, as if he was trying to tell her that what she felt right now wasn't going to be the way she'd always feel. The future was sure to be brighter. And, somewhere out there the right man would recognize what a wonderful, shining star she was inside and all this heartache would be a distant memory. That's what she'd heard, anyway, when he'd said it before.

Now, she recognized that all he meant was 'I'm sorry.'

"Me, too," she whispered, and then she began to cry, silently at first, trying to hold it in, trying to control the force and overwhelming wave of misery, but then the dam burst, and she sobbed out loud. Huge, gulping, ugly sobs that wracked her frame and hurt her throat. And when her dad said something like, "aw, honey," it only made her cry all the harder—uncontrollable, hiccupping tears that flooded her face and coursed over the phone as she mopped them up with a piece of paper towel she'd hastily torn from the roll.

He let her cry, silent on the other end, until she was spent, her breaths coming in long, stuttering hiccups. She mopped her eyes some more. Blew her nose.

When she was finally quiet, he said, "I love you, Chickie," his voice hoarse and strained, and she realized with an ache in her heart he'd been crying right along with her.

"I love you, too, Dad." Liz hiccupped into his ear. "Th—thanks for calling."

"I've been wanting to for days, but your mother hasn't moved more than ten feet from the phone. Just in case you called."

An image of her mother tethered by the phone cord had her almost smiling. "She really needs to get a cordless phone."

"You know she won't listen."

"I know." But *he* had. He'd listened. Even if all she'd done was cry.

Liz took another deep, cleansing breath and hugged Eddie. Crying didn't change a damn thing, but it felt good to let it out. It felt good to know he cared enough to call. "So, um, when do you close on the house?" Her dad cleared his throat. He didn't answer. "Dad?"

"That's not going to happen right away."

"Why? What do you mean?"

"They backed out. Without the shed and with the damage to the yard, they bought another place."

"But… couldn't you just adjust the purchase price? Wouldn't they renegotiate? Can't you ask Valerie—?"

"It's done. Don't worry about it."

Liz felt new tears well up. "I'm so sorry, Dad. I know this is my fault!"

"Some things are nobody's fault."

"But this…"

"It's all right. John said he'd go over and help when he can. Trish, too. I'll come home in a couple weeks to finish up. We'll make it work."

"But, won't Mom—?"

"She doesn't want to see the fire damage. You know how she is about a lush lawn. Better to leave things how she remembered them."

"I could—"

"Hush. You've done enough. You take care of *you*." He chuckled lightly. "And, for God's sake, don't let any more men chasing after you try to get your mother to help them throw a proposal party. It took me two weeks before she'd go near my laptop again. You think she was scared of technology before…"

"Don't worry. I don't know what the future holds, but I don't think I'll be having that problem anytime soon." She grimaced. "They've offered me a promotion at Ames & Reed."

"They have? That's great!"

"I haven't accepted." He was silent. "Dad?"

"You afraid, Chickie? You know you can do anything you set your mind to."

"I think I just need more time to think about it."

"Good idea. Your little yellow notebooks always seemed to help you think. Get one of those out, and you'll have a new plan in no time."

Liz let out a long, cleansing sigh. "I love you, Dad, but yellow legal pads can only take you so far."

They said their goodbyes, and Liz went to the little window over the sink and stared out at the same sliver of street she'd looked at every day for six long years. *Eesh*, she hated this apartment. Hated the ugly popcorn ceilings and the awkward floor plan. Why had she stayed? Just because it was cheap? What did she think she was saving her money *for*?

Liz looked around at the eighties-style cabinets, the box of cardboard cereal and her one-eyed cat... and half-smiled. Maybe she didn't have a fiancé, a whole heart, or a clue where she was going in life, but there was one thing she did have: a family that cared about her.

And, despite all that made them quirky and unlovable, she'd do anything for them. Because, in the end, when everything else in life had gone up in smoke and she was left craving swiss cake rolls and crying into a paper towel, they were all she had left.

This was the love Carter had been talking about. *This* was the real, unvarnished, authentic Liz she'd run away from all those years ago, because it had hurt too much to *feel*. But the alternative—a lifetime of trying to control every outcome—wasn't the answer either. She had to go home. She had to remember who she was before she'd walled herself off from her own imperfections. She had to let the old Beth back in.

Liz swiped at her aching eyes, her nose and lips swollen from crying... and whole-smiled this time.

"Hey, Eddie," she said. "How do you feel about a road trip?"

Shed Clean-up To-Do:

Collect metal recycling for transfer station

Clear out unsalvageable items and bring to dump

Collect burnt wood and ashes & put in back lot by

    old stump pile

Trim singed bushes/trees

Check for damage on house. Clean any marks.

    Touch-up paint as necessary.

Rake burntspots in lawn. Reseed as needed.

Rake over where shed was. Apply mulch.

Place birdbath in place of shed. Walking pavers?

CHAPTER FIFTY-TWO

I<small>T</small> WAS ABOUT HOUR NINE of her fourteen hour drive, as she crossed the great state of New York surviving on coffee and fast food, that Liz began to have second thoughts about her decision to drive back to Sugar Falls and clean up the shed mess herself.

She hadn't wanted to go through the trouble of flying again, didn't want the crowds or the hassle or to put Eddie through the whole ordeal, so she'd gone to work, requested an extension on their offer, told them the sad news that her Great Aunt Claire had suddenly passed away (a small fib in the scheme of things but totally believable given the tear-streaked state of her make-up,) rented an SUV and gotten the heck out of Dodge.

It was a Monday, so as she figured it, she had two days of bereavement, two days of personal time, one sick day, a weekend, and she'd have bought herself a week.

And, if she couldn't straighten her life out and fix what she'd broken in that time, she could tell herself she'd at least tried.

It was close to three in the morning when she rolled into her parents' driveway, shut off the engine… and remembered she didn't have a key.

Liz let her head fall to the steering wheel in bleary-eyed defeat, too tired to even cry, but then remembered where her dad used to keep a spare. With any luck… She stumbled up the front walkway in the dark to the garden gnome, fished way up inside with her hand and pulled out the bubble-wrapped key to the front door he'd wedged there.

She gratefully pushed the door open and flicked on the coach lights. Somehow, seeing them at this hour, when she was so incredibly tired in so many ways, made them seem all the more welcoming. To think her brother was now a bona fide electrician.

The thought brought a smile to her lips.

Then she remembered who his fiancé was.

Good Lord, life was unpredictable.

Liz turned on more lights as she made her way through the house. She'd worked in such a frenzy before, patching and painting and fending off suitors, she hadn't had a chance to take it all in before now. But now, she saw the house with new eyes.

What she saw was lovely. Truly lovely. The living room, with its soft birch walls and bright white trim, set off the warm woodwork around the fireplace beautifully. And, she'd rearranged a little, creating a cozy seating area by the fireplace, a reading nook by the window. Someone had set up the chess set on the little side table, as if there was a game in progress.

She pushed through to the dining room, its wainscot and trim were freshened with more birch white paint, but then she'd done the walls and ceiling a sky blue, causing the small plaster medallion over the light fixture to pop.

And the kitchen. She walked in, remembering how it had felt to see it for the first time. She'd never gotten around to repainting the cabinets, so they were still that peaceful celery green.

Surely a new buyer would see how charming it was and make an offer soon no matter what the state of the side yard.

After getting a drink of water, Liz unloaded the SUV, set Eddie up in the spare room and fell into bed.

She was awake again three hours later, staring at the ceiling. Thinking.

It was strange how life came full circle sometimes. She'd lain in this very bed, staring at this very ceiling, crying over the same man a decade ago.

When would she learn to stop believing in fantasy? Those stolen moments in Jenny Whitmeyer's pantry were just that—a fantasy.

Reality was the mess in the side yard, an ex-vampire as a future sister-in-law and a promotion hanging over her head like a guillotine.

Ugh. And the sooner she faced it all, the sooner she'd be able to move past it.

Liz sat up, desperately wanting a cup of coffee, but she didn't even have half and half. It'd be better to work a couple of hours, shower and go into town for food and a break.

Pulling on her ugliest sweats, she stepped out into the cool morning and stared at where the shed used to be.

Oh, my.

There wasn't much left of the shed except for the charred remains of what looked like an oversized camp fire. A handful of metal tools sat in a jumble, their handles turned to ash. The wheelbarrow was nothing but a dented black bowl. Pieces of wood and debris were scattered around, dark with soot, from where firefighters obviously worked to get to any remaining embers. All in all, a thorough disaster.

Liz pulled on her work gloves and started hauling metal recycling into a pile. Once she got that out of the way, she could buy a new shovel in town and scoop the charred wood and ashes onto a tarp and drag it all to the back lot.

Forty-five minutes into the job, covered in soot from head to toe, she needed a drink. And a shower. Liz swiped her brow, uncaring of the smears she was surely leaving behind, and stumbled. She looked down.

She'd caught her toe on the corner of what looked like an old metal toolbox under some half-charred timbers. Dragging the box out, she stepped over the charcoal and mess and was about to throw it in with the other metal recycling when she stopped. The shape was familiar.

Very familiar.

The box sat heavy in her arms, a small bit of red paint showing on the lower corner. She brushed off the top with her sleeve and stared at it. Oh, my God. She'd forgotten all about it.

She tried the latch, but it stuck, so with shaking hands, she grabbed the head of an axe and smacked the latch until it popped open. She sat back on the damp lawn.

It was still there. Everything she'd tucked away was all there— somehow, miraculously, protected from the flames and the fire hoses.

The little ceramic kitten knick-knack Uncle Marv had given her. The lucky bottle cap from the Black Cherry soda bottle she'd saved from her sixth birthday party. A real French Franc from the old woman down the hill whose husband had fought in Normandy.

And her dreams book.

She pulled off her gloves so as not to dirty the pages and pulled the thick book out, her breath light in her chest.

She ran her fingers over the cover, letting them bump over the little cut-out flowers and stars done in construction paper and glitter glue.

She eased the book open.

Using pictures from catalogs, samples of fabric, even candy wrappers, she'd recorded her vision for every room in the old farmhouse. Each space was carefully decorated—just as she'd seen done on a TV show once—with thin-lined diagrams of walls, windows and furnishings she'd then accented with glitter pens and colored pencils. Slowly, one by one, she turned the pages, the vignettes she'd dreamed up so many years ago coming to life like mini movie sets.

Her fingers slid over the page. There was the front door, a fresh, welcoming periwinkle blue. She'd glued on a tiny gold sequin for the knob and drawn little violets at the stoop. There was the dining room with its sky blue walls and white trim. Her younger self had added a bird motif in the light fixture and a delicate, pastoral mural on the wall. And then the kitchen.

Liz sucked in a breath... and began to cry.

Dear Lord, she seemed to be doing an awful lot of that lately.

Soft green cabinets, cherry-red knobs, and there, on the counter, she'd even crafted a tiny Cookie Rooster from poster-board and pasted him onto the page.

A little tan cookie with brown magic marker dots sat on the counter beside it.

Without even knowing it, a decade later, she'd recreated everything almost exactly as she'd first imagined it.

Tears slid down her face as she leafed through the rest of the book, realizing she'd done the same thing to other houses, reimagining and reinventing individual rooms and entire facades. She remembered hoarding paint samples from the local home center and begging for fabric swatches from the quilting ladies at church so she could give each room just the right touch.

When had she forgotten how much she loved to do this?

More to the point, when had her life veered so far away from where she'd dreamed she was headed?

She let out a sigh. She knew when. She'd stopped believing in dreams three days after her first kiss. The day she'd asked Carter to the prom. From that day onward, she always had a plan. She was always prepared.

Because, it hurt too much when dreams didn't come true.

Liz carried the scrapbook back to the house, set it on the kitchen table, started a pot of coffee—even though she didn't have cream—and went to shower.

Things Liz Thought she Wanted:	Not Sure	DON'T want
$$$$$$	promotion	Jail time
Big Job	home	Class reunions
GRANT		Halitosis!

CARTER

CHAPTER FIFTY-THREE

WHEN SHE CAME BACK DOWN, Trish was there.

"Does no one knock anymore?"

"I might ask you the same thing." Trish pulled a carton of half and half, God bless her, from her diaper bag. "So what are you doing here? I thought you were back in Chicago for good."

"I came to clean up the mess from the fire. Why are *you* here?"

"It's quiet." Trish rocked Clara in her bucket seat with her foot as she added cream to the coffee Liz had made. "And clean."

"It's not quiet at home?" Liz knew not to ask about the clean part.

"Not like this." Trish closed her eyes on a sigh. "I've been coming every morning after I drop the twins at preschool just to breathe. It's very peaceful. Just between you and me, I hope Mom and Dad don't sell too soon." Trish eyed Liz over the rim of her mug. "I saw the book."

Liz didn't need to ask what Trish was talking about, because it was still sitting smack in the middle of the table revealing all her secrets. She poured a mug and sat down. "I found it in the shed."

"I remember you used to spend hours on that thing. It made me jealous how good you were at it. It's like nothing you do can turn out ugly."

Liz added cream to her mug and watched it swirl in the black coffee. "Oh, I can do ugly. You've seen the side yard, haven't you? It makes me sick knowing it cost Mom and Dad the sale. Nothing to be jealous of there."

"Oh, *pish*. That buyer was looking for an excuse to pull out. They knew full well about the shed when they signed that contract, but then a week later they say they weren't informed about the 'negative impact the fire and explosives had on the landscaping?' Seriously? Like a few branches and burnt patches in the lawn aren't going to grow back? I hear they've already signed a contract on another property off of Miller Brook."

Liz swirled her coffee pensively. They drank in silence. The baby snored.

Liz fiddled with the salt and pepper shakers in front of her. "Can I ask you something? And, this may sound stupid given the fact that you were knocked up and nineteen when you married Russ, but when did you know he was 'the one?' I mean, when did you know you hadn't completely screwed up your life by getting involved with him in the first place?"

Trish raised one brow. "What makes you sure I don't still have my doubts?"

"I'm serious."

Trish took a swig of coffee, shrugged. "Seriously? I don't know. There was never an 'a-ha' moment. When I found out I was pregnant, everybody on God's green earth was talking at me. First I had Russ insisting he'd marry me, then Mom and Dad were offering to take me and the baby in—though Lord knows how that would have turned out. With John screwing up, they had nothing left to give, you know?" She trailed off, an amused tilt to her lips.

"What?"

"I'll never forget how Russ proposed. He looked me in the eye and said our chances were as good as any other couple, and why *shouldn't* we get married?"

"Romantic."

Trish shrugged. "He was right. Maybe it seemed crazy for two kids to get married, but no crazier than our being parents to begin with. Mom and Dad were convinced I was throwing my life away, but Russ got his first sales job after that, did really well, and here we are."

"Do you love him?"

Trish's features softened as she looked at the baby. "Maybe it's not the romantic life most girls dream about, but it's a good life. I get to do what I want, when I want, most of the time. And I only have to deal with Russ' dirty laundry when he's home. He's done the best he could by me and the kids. Neither one of us is perfect."

"But, do you love him?" Liz repeated, stamping down her impatience.

Trish set her mug on the table and looked Liz in the eye. "I'd be an idiot not to. And no matter what anybody says, I've never been stupid."

Liz smiled. "No, you never have."

Liz sipped her coffee.

"So what are you going to do now? What's the plan?"

Liz choked on her coffee. "You sound like Aunt Claire. I don't have a plan."

Trish pulled a yellow legal pad from under Liz's laptop case, flipped to a clean page and shoved it forward. "Then make a new one."

Liz's palms began to sweat as she stared at the blank page. "I wouldn't know where to start."

Trish stared at her a moment then yanked the notepad back across the table. She divided the page into three columns. "Okay. Here's what I see. There are the things you *thought* you wanted—financial security, professional accomplishments, a man who wears more hair product than you... *Grant*—that's all column one." She hastily jotted each item one over the other. "Column three is everything you know you *don't* want—"

"Jail time, any more class reunions..." Liz said.

"Halitosis," Trish eagerly added. Liz gave her a look. "Okay. Now here's the middle column, the things you're not sure how you feel about. That would include, and I'm only guessing because I heard you were offered a promotion but neglected to jump at the opportunity... your job..."

"...my home..." Liz sighed.

"... and the man who you refuse to discuss but we all know you're thinking about... *Carter.*" Trish wrote his name in all caps and blew a whistle through her teeth. "*Hmm.* That middle column's a doozey."

"No kidding."

Liz stared at the list... a spreadsheet of all that was wrong with her life. The problem was, the center column was her dream column—the column she'd neatly and effectively ignored for ten years of her life. She'd tucked it in that box, thrown away the key and forgotten all about it, thank you very much, until a cursed man with a wicked smile and way too much charm came waltzing back into her life and got her *thinking* again. Thinking about possibilities and kisses and youthful fantasies she had no business dreaming about again.

Damn him. Damn him and his devilish smile and his gorgeous butt and making her fall in love with him!

Liz jabbed a finger at Carter's name. "It's all *his* fault. I was perfectly content until he came along. Perfectly happy!"

"Perfectly?"

"Fine. *Almost* perfectly."

"Is that anything like being almost engaged?"

"Stop talking to Bailey." Liz shoved the pad away in disgust. "*Aargh!* What's wrong with me anyway? I had it all worked out, Trish. Everything was going along so smoothly."

"Just like you planned?"

"Yes! *No!* That's the problem, isn't it?" She flumped forward, her hands buried in her hair. "It's just like Carter said. I've got my lists and my plans, but you can't live a life that way." Liz looked up at Trish in shock. "Oh my God, I didn't! I didn't *plan* any of it. My whole life!"

"Of course you did. You're the Queen of Lists."

"That's just it. I was reacting, not acting." Liz leapt up and began to pace. "I did well in school because I spent so much time *there* instead of *here.* Professor Greeny gave me a lead for a job, because I was constantly in his office asking for extra study notes so I wouldn't end up back in Sugar Falls struggling to get by like Mom and Dad."

She whirled toward Trish. "Everything has just... *happened.* Now I don't know what's next, because, truly, I don't know how I got *here!* I don't know what I want. I just know I can't go back." Liz sucked in a breath and stared at her sister. *"I can't go back."*

"Because of this Grant guy? He's gone, Liz. *Vamoose. Adios.*"

"No. Because... I don't want to.*"* She didn't want to. She hadn't jumped at the promotion, because she didn't *want* it! "All my life, I've tried to be what I thought other people wanted me to be. I took what seemed the safe bet. But, I don't want to bury myself researching Forrester and Gartner anymore. I don't even want to explain to you what that is. I don't want to spend the rest of my life pouring over spreadsheets and timelines and watching people's eyes glaze over when I tell them what I do. It feels like... like I've been trying all this time to make everything turn out *right* instead of trying to be *happy.* Instead of being real."

"But, you're good at it."

"I'm good at a lot of things." Liz looked around. "But, I don't want to be this person anymore, Trish. I've buried the part of me that wants to explore and take chances so I could become some person I don't even recognize. Some person that's not only run away from her family and the people who cared about her but run away from herself and everything she always dreamed about.

"Do you know I've never been to Niagara Falls? How crazy is that? We're *this close* compared to most of the world, one of the greatest natural wonders on Earth, and I've never been! Or the Grand Canyon. I haven't seen *that* either! What have I been *doing* with my life?"

"Relax. There's time."

"No. That's where you're wrong. And, I've wasted too much of it."

Liz looked out at the late spring morning. The dew had burned off, and the sun was out, the small, bright green leaves on the trees shimmering in the breeze. It was so different from the dull sliver of street she'd limited herself to for the past six years.

"I need to step off this crazy treadmill I'm on and start over before it's too late. I want to see Niagara Falls, Trish. I want to try ice skating again."

"Your butt was black and blue for weeks."

"I don't care! I don't want to miss another ten years of my life! I want to live life without apology. I want to go back—back to when everything was spread out in front of me like a clean page and… and *try again.*"

A clean page.

Like a page in her scrapbook.

"I want to come home," she said.

"You are home."

"Not yet." A smile pulled at Liz's lips as she looked at her sister, as the lid to her treasure box burst open with possibilities in her mind. Pandora be damned. "What would you say if I told you *I'm* thinking of buying the house from Mom and Dad?"

"I'd say your June Cleaver obsession has finally gotten the better of you. Be serious."

"I am. I want to see it stay in the family."

Trish sat back in her chair and gaped. "Liz, moving back here isn't going to fix everything. You're disappointed, sad, a little confused. Maybe a lot. But, you've got a good job in Chicago. You're crazy if you're thinking of throwing it all away just because you're in a funk. Take a vacation. See Niagara Falls. But, don't jump off the deep end, for cryin' out loud."

"Haven't you heard a word I've said? I thought you'd be supportive."

"I would be if you were talking sense. You're in a tough spot right now, I get that, but moving back here? That's crazy. What would you *do?*"

"I'd get a job. I'm sure there are lots of businesses that could use my skills. Who knows, maybe I can get into staging houses for Valerie's clients. She seemed impressed with what I did here. I could even take some classes—see if I could get into interior design. I'm not even thirty. It's not too late."

"Liz…"

"Maybe then, maybe if I'm *here…*"

Trish smiled sympathetically. "Liz, moving back isn't going to fix what happened with Carter. Move on." She sighed. "As much as you might want to go back, you can't rewrite the past."

"I'm not trying to rewrite the past. I'm trying to rewrite my future."

Trish took another swig of coffee and shook her head. "Whatever you say, June."

CHAPTER FIFTY-FOUR

"DO *NOT* TELL ME to be understanding, Grams. I'm in no mood to understand a thing." Carter scowled into his pancakes and stabbed a blueberry with the tine of his fork. He wasn't particularly thrilled to be rehashing the whole sordid affair again, but he also hadn't been big on cooking for himself lately. "She was embarrassed by me. Embarrassed by the fact that I wasn't good enough for her. *That's* why she submitted the bid. She was trying to make me into some other guy, some guy who's up to her level. Well, she can forget it. I'm not proving myself to anyone."

He was done proving himself. Since the fire, Ted Seamans had apologized and invited Carter back to the department, but it still rankled he'd been so quick to judge in the first place.

Carter shoved his plate away and stalked to the window. He glowered at the drizzle that fell outside. Thank God he was done with the fountain project, because this weather would have put him behind for sure. And, he had *Liz* to thank for *that* headache. He'd had to work night and day to get it done in time for the dedication. Thankfully, Rick Mercer had decided he owed Carter and lent him a hand. The kid had fallen in with the wrong crowd and made some stupid choices, but if you could ignore the wise-ass attitude, he was a hard worker. Sure, the kid was a little rough around the edges, but so was Carter in his day.

He turned, the same anger that had fueled him since learning he'd won the damn bid filling him once more. "Do you know she even had the nerve to suggest I have ADHD and might want to consider medication? *And counseling?*"

Grams stuck her hands on her hips. "Would you stop being pigheaded? First of all, you do have ADHD, we can all see *that*. If you think it might help, go to a doctor and see what they can do.

"Secondly, look at things from her perspective. Liz has worked hard to make something of herself. She thought she had to be a certain person to be a success. I'm sure it's hard to let that go. It makes her vulnerable."

"How about *me*, huh? How about the guy she's supposed to—"

"*Love?*" Grams' eyes twinkled in that annoyingly knowing way that made Carter wish he were an orphan. Again. "Oh, honey, you have to know if she loves you, she's going to fight against it harder than anything."

"You must have early dementia, Grams. That makes no sense."

She poked her spatula at him. "Don't you backtalk me. Think about it. If she gets involved with you, it's like asking her to put aside everything she's worked to build over the years and jump in feet first. If she's the woman you say she is, I'd say she doesn't do impulsive. I do *not* know why you don't get this. It was a string of lights, Carter, she didn't throw an engagement ring back in your face!"

"It's what they *represented*."

"To you they represented *you*. To her, they represented the part of her she was afraid of. She was scared. Scared of putting herself out there. Scared of getting hurt. Scared of being too in love."

Love. *Ha!* He'd happily leave it to the buffoons on Grams' stupid reality TV show.

Grams wiped her hands on her apron and wrapped her arms around him. He was nearly a foot taller than she, which made him feel a little silly. Still, looking into those eyes, that had held so much compassion over the years, had seen so much, made his chest ache. He'd do anything to get rid of that ache. "I'd never hurt her," he whispered hoarsely.

Grams pursed her lips, and nodded as she patted his shoulder. "You wouldn't mean to."

She put her fingers to his lips to silence him. "I know you'd never physically harm her. *She* knows that. But that doesn't mean she's not scared of what you make her *feel*." Grams gave him another quick squeeze then returned to the stove and picked up her spatula. "The question you need to ask yourself is: is love scarier than being alone? Or, is it scarier to lose the one you love because you didn't do everything in your power to be with them?"

Carter's throat felt thick, and he let out a shaky breath. "I don't know," he said.

She glanced at him over her bifocals. "I think you do."

He bit his lip and looked outside at the rain again and let his mind roll over the memories. Liz and the grease fire. Playing chess. That kiss in Jenny Whitmeyer's pantry. Liz fighting with the cart on the way out of the hardware store. The look on her face on that first day of tutoring when she took the Twizzler from him and their fingers brushed. The feel of her hair in his hands as he cradled her beneath him on her front lawn, praying to Sweet Jesus and Mary his body would protect her...

His eyes were blurry when he looked at Grams again, his heart thudding deep and heavy in his chest. "I'm just like my mom, aren't I?"

"Oh, honey, "Grams said, reaching up and wrapping him in a tight hug. The smell of maple syrup enveloped him. "You always were. You always were…"

"I'VE CALLED THIS MEETING, ladies, because my grandson has asked for our help." Carter fought not to wince as Grams squeezed his hand with wrinkled, arthritic fingers on top of the big farmhouse table.

Maybe this was a bad idea after all, he thought with some trepidation.

Four sets of bifocals peered at him earnestly.

"He does look in bad shape," *tsked* Lydia sympathetically. "Haven't been sleeping well, have you?" For some reason he had the sense this almost delighted her.

"Serves him right for being so hard on my Liz," Claire sniffed indignantly.

"Now, now. We're not here to judge. Carter sees now he wasn't fair to Liz and he wants to make amends. He's come to us to seek our advice on how to apologize."

"Apologize?" croaked Carter.

"And win her over," Grams continued.

"Oh! What fun!" Lydia clapped her hands, silver bangles tinkling excitedly. "Do you love her terribly?"

Carter blinked back at the four eager women. "Do I have to answer that?"

"Yes," Grams insisted. "We don't help unless you're willing to be honest. True love isn't easy and usually involves a willingness to publicly humiliate yourself, so you need to tell us. Do you love her?"

Carter couldn't have felt any more on the spot if he were on national TV. He cleared his throat. "Yes."

He might have said more, but then a floral muumuu was smothering him as Lydia cried her delight into his shoulder. "I knew it! *I knew it!* The cards don't lie!" she cried exuberantly before sitting back again and mopping her eyes with a crumpled tissue.

"Moving on," Claire said with a quelling look for Lydia. "What do you want us to do?"

"I want to surprise her. I have this idea…" He cleared his throat again. "It's a bit out of the box, so I'd appreciate it if you ladies would keep open minds. But I'll need help. Can I trust you to be, uh, discreet?"

Four silver heads bobbed eagerly. "Absolutely!" they said in near unison.

Carter chewed his bottom lip then shrugged. Hell, what did he have to lose?

SUGAR FALLS FOUNDERS' DAY CELEBRATION & FOUNTAIN DEDICATION

SATURDAY, MAY 10TH
NOON
TOWN COMMON
ALL ARE WELCOME!

SPONSORED BY
SUGAR FALLS BEAUTIFICATION LEAGUE
SUGAR FALLS BOOSTERS
LUCKY'S PUB
SUGAR FALLS ROTARY CLUB
THE OLD MILL BAR & GRILL
LICK 'N DIP ICE CREAM SHOP
SECOND CHANCES CONSIGNMENTS
MEG'S SUPER STYLES

CHAPTER FIFTY-FIVE

LIZ RESOLUTELY PULLED the zipper shut on her suitcase. It was for the best, she told herself, as she set it next to the bed. Trish was right. She had no business dreaming of making a life in Sugar Falls—no business putting all the trappings of her June Cleaver fantasies into place—until she stopped letting life happen *to* her and started going after the life she wanted. And, it all started today. She had 36 hours before she had to be back in Chicago. It wasn't enough time to take away the empty ache in her heart, but it was enough to check one thing off her list.

She turned resolutely toward the door. "No more shying away from life, Eddie. By the end of the year, the 'Liz Never' list will be no more."

Eddie peered at her unblinkingly from the top of the dresser.

Her cell phone rang.

"Hello?"

"Oh, good. Glad I caught you. It's Aunt Claire. I need you to do me a favor."

"Actually, I'm leaving town earlier than expected. I was just on my way out—"

"Even better! You can give me a ride to the dedication. It starts at noon. I promised Ruth I'd be there and Trish isn't answering her phone."

"What dedication?"

"What do you mean, 'what dedication'? The fountain! The Sugar Falls Commemorative Fountain! Where have you *been*?"

"Chicago?"

"Oh. Right. Well, it's fixed now, and they're having a re-dedication. Today. At noon. I promised Ruth I'd be there."

"Aunt Claire. I don't have a car. I returned it to the rental agency yesterday. My taxi will be here within the hour, and then I'm flying—"

"Perfect timing. You can drop me off on your way through town. I'd drive myself, but I haven't been hydrating like I should and I had another dizzy spell this morning. If you *really* don't want to, I suppose I *could* try driving..."

Liz blew out a breath. "*No*. No, I'll give you a ride. Can you get home again?"

"I'm sure I'll figure something out. See you in an hour?"

"Sure. See you then."

Forty-five minutes later, Liz blinked back tears as the taxi pulled out of her driveway. She wouldn't look back, she told herself. She wouldn't second-guess herself anymore.

Anyway, it was better this way. She needed to move forward and stop thinking about what might have been. A home wasn't a place, it was a state of mind, right?

And, Elizabeth Anne Beacon intended to put her house in order.

A faint, bittersweet smile curved her lips as she stared at the passing landscape. Soft-green leaf buds dotted the stark tree limbs. Before long, the branches would grow lush and heavy with summer foliage.

She loved this time of year. Loved the carpet of maple seeds that littered lawns and sidewalks. Loved the musky scent of spring rain, the nighttime melody of peepers as they searched for mates in roadside marshes.

Loved Carter McIntyre.

Oof. It always hit her like that, smack between the eyes when she was thinking about innocuous things like peepers or maple seeds. It was a gentler ache now, the empty space where her heart used to be. More of a hollowness instead of the stabbing pain of fresh rejection. There was nothing to be done about it anyway. Like Trish said, it was over.

Liz swallowed over the thickness in her throat.

She should have trusted her own judgment, should have ignored what everyone else said about him and listened to her heart. But it was too late. Whatever feelings Carter may have had for her had been killed by her own inability to trust and accept herself and take a leap with him.

She'd left him nine messages of apology not including hang-ups. He hadn't called her back.

Liz reached out to roll down the window. Warm air blew onto her face, a sweet medley of earthy spring fragrances teasing her nostrils. Taking a deep breath, she pursed her lips. Some things were in her control. Some were not.

She glanced at the suitcase on the floor beside her and prepared to open the door for her aunt.

"DON'T ASK," LIZ WARNED as Aunt Claire eyed her luggage for the umpteenth time since leaving her driveway.

"What makes you think I was going to say anything about the suitcase on the floor? Do I *look* like the type of woman to stick my nose into my grandniece's personal affairs? Do I seem like the kind of old lady who'd stoop to being nosy about something like that? To questioning what young people knew about making smart decisions? Do I? *Hmm?*"

"In a word: Yes."

"Well, if I'm already tried and convicted... where are you going?"

"Out of town."

"I see." Claire lips flattened in disapproval.

Liz hid a smile. "I don't think you do."

"I may be old, but I see perfectly. Now that Trish and Russ have decided to buy your folks' house, you're running away again. Just like when you smacked yourself unconscious and had that fight with Carter."

"I'm not running away! This is different. If you must know, Trish is taking care of Eddie, and I'm going to New York for the weekend."

"*New York?* Whatever is in New York?"

"About twenty million people... and Niagara Falls."

"No."

Liz sighed again. "You won't change my mind—"

"I mean 'no,' as in technically Niagara Falls is only *partly* in New York. The rest is in Canada. I saw a program about it on TV last year. Did you know the falls are eroding a foot per year and in 50,000 years they'll merge into Lake Erie and cease to exist?"

"Oh, look!" Liz interrupted with relief, not wanting to get into a geography lesson which was *so* not the point at the moment. "Sorry to cut you off, but we're here. It looks like quite a crowd, so I think I'll just let you off here by the bank if you don't mind—"

"You're not going to walk me to the common?"

"Walk you?"

"What if I have heart palpitations again? I brought a bottle of water with me, but..."

Glancing at her cell to check the time, Liz blew out a quick breath. What was a few more minutes delay in the scheme of things? Asking the driver to wait, she pushed open the side door. "Ten minutes, Aunt Claire. Truly. That's all I can spare. I've got a flight to catch."

"Fine. Fine. If we just find the other gals, I'll let you go."

"Fine." Liz gripped her aunt's elbow and pushed forward through the crowd.

~~TO-DO~~ *I've never but someday hope to...*

1.) *Skinny dip—at noon*

2.) *Try a thong*

3.) *Play strip poker*

4.) *Learn to play piano*

5.) *See Niagara Falls*

6.) *Ride Space Mountain*

7.) *Hike the Grand Canyon*

8.) *Visit a Castle*

9.) *Learn to shoot an arrow*

10.) *Stand in a Fountain and Kiss My One True Love*

CHAPTER FIFTY-SIX

"I THINK I SEE LYDIA," Aunt Claire announced as she and Liz pressed through the crowd.

Liz fought the urge to roll her eyes, as this was the third time the elusive Lydia had purportedly been spotted. You'd think a woman who dressed primarily in hideous florals would be easier to find.

"Aunt Claire, I *really* have to get to the airport. My plane leaves in ninety minutes and the pre-flight—"

"Oh, for heaven's sake, this is Sugar Falls! How long will it take to put fourteen passengers through a metal detector and onto one little puddle-jumper? *There!* I'm sure that's her by the gazebo."

The air held the warm promise of summer, and Liz's heart squeezed tight in her chest. It was the time of year for lovers. For fresh beginnings.

Maybe she'd find someone new. Out of the millions of men in the world, there ought to be one or two possibilities, right?

Her heart squeezed again. She didn't want just any man. She wanted *one* man. Carter.

She squinted against the sun and told herself that's why her eyes were moist.

"*Liz.*"

She froze. *Oh God...*

Aargh! It wasn't fair! Why couldn't the Fates let her leave on her own terms? Quietly? Without conflict or confrontation? Slinking away with at least a tiny shred of her remaining dignity intact?

Liz turned and strained to remain calm even as every nerve cell in her body leapt with awareness. "Carter!" she said with false brightness.

He stood a few feet away, his dark hair ruffling lightly in the breeze. Liz wondered distractedly whether he had some official role in the dedication ceremony, because he was wearing a trim dark suit and burgundy tie that gave him the air of a high class spy. Lord, he cleaned up nicely.

"I'm glad you came," he said. His green eyes sparkled in the sun, drinking her in, or at least that's what Liz told herself, because she didn't want that glittering look to be anger.

Guilt ate at her. She'd hurt this man so deeply. To hell with her dignity.

"I'm sorry," she blurted, struggling to remain composed, resentful of the crowd chattering happily around them. Her skin tingled under his gaze, and she fidgeted, fighting the urge to bolt. "I never meant to hurt you, Carter, to imply—"

"I know."

"You were right. About so many things. But you were wrong about one thing. The *real* me was—*is*— the me I am when I'm with you. Every time. Always. And, that's the me I want to be. That's the me I plan to be from now on..."

"Glad to hear that."

"I just... I needed to tell you that." She waited and he was so quiet, the tears threatened again. She turned away. If she didn't leave *now* she'd do something to embarrass them both, like blubber all over him and beg him for another chance. In front of the marching band. And the baton twirling squad. And that guy over there in the uniform that looked way official and was looking at her like he was afraid he'd have to offer her a tissue...

"Liz—"

"I have to go. I—"

"Wait," he said, his hand reaching out to touch her arm.

She could *not* look at him! How could she face the man she'd ruined any chance of having a future with—the man she *loved*—because she'd been too scared to be herself?

"I'm *so* sorry," she whispered, intending to make a run for it, dignity be damned.

"Sorry for what?" he asked, touching her chin lightly until she looked up at him. "Loving me too much or trusting yourself too little?"

She hesitated, about to deny both, but then she saw what his easy manner couldn't quite conceal—the rhythmic tick in his jaw, the taut way he held himself.

For some reason, her answer mattered.

She swallowed, her heart hammering in her chest. Someone bumped her from behind, but she hardly felt it. The crowd, the noise, the excitement buzzing around them was nothing to the roar of her own blood in her ears.

The air felt light in her lungs as Liz gave the only answer she could—the truth. "Both," she replied, then...

Oh God! She'd just admitted she loved him! This was not *part of the plan!*

He gave a terse nod and then his eyes crinkled. "Apology accepted."

What? He was smiling at her? Hadn't she just thrown herself under the bus of emotional vulnerability? Her mouth gaped, she knew this, because she felt like a stunned guppy watching as Carter reached down and took both her hands in his like that day in Jenny Whitmeyer's pantry. He smiled, a dazzling, smile that simultaneously confused her and warmed her to her toes, and then he leaned in and claimed her lips in a hard, bone-melting kiss, which, let's be honest, she had no desire to cut short even though she knew this was, surely, goodbye. "Me, too," he whispered as he pulled away again to look at her.

"Me, too?" She stammered her words. Nothing made sense, and all she could do was drink him in and pray he got the urge to kiss her again so her brain would have time to catch up.

"You were right, Liz. I needed to step up and trust myself. I've spent too long accepting other people's opinion of me." He glanced at the fountain. "Looks good, doesn't it?"

Liz nodded, confusion warring with something else inside her. It felt like... *hope.* "Really good."

"I've already gotten three more jobs out of it."

"That's... that's wonderful. I'm so happy for you."

He brushed the hair from her temple where she knew she still sported a lingering bruise and leaned in to kiss her gently, his lips warm on her skin. "Thanks," he said.

Somewhere in the background the head of the Beautification League wrapped up her dedication speech and the fountain turned on, trumpeting into the air. The band began playing the familiar theme song of an underdog hero making a comeback, and Liz couldn't help but grin foolishly up at him.

She had no idea what it all meant, but he was smiling and kissing her and telling her she was right. Surely, as cosmic messages go, these were all very good signs.

They stood like that, grinning at one another as the music played, the spring sunshine pouring over them. Oh, sure, there were a hundred details to sort through, rough patches to smooth over, misunderstandings to make right. But in this moment, nothing could steal the smile from her face. *Nothing.*

But then Carter glanced away and swallowed, his Adam's apple bobbing, and then he slid a finger between his collar and tie... and tugged.

Liz's smile faltered.

Oh, no. Was that a *nervous* tug on his tie? Crud! Maybe *love* was more than he was looking for! Why had she blurted it out like that, anyway? Here? *Now?* Was this a 'take it to the next level' misunderstanding all over again? Maybe she shouldn't have been so honest. Maybe *his* feelings had changed and 'love' was too strong a word. Maybe 'me, too' meant something else...

Her thoughts skidded to a halt as he slid his tie over his head—and onto hers.

She ducked as the silk fabric slid onto her neck and blinked in confusion. "What—?"

But Carter simply pressed a finger to her lips... and kicked off his shoes. She stared at his bare toes on the grass. Why had she not noticed he wasn't wearing socks? And *why* wasn't he wearing socks?

Her eyes flew up again as he handed her his suit coat. She grasped it reflexively in time to watch his dress shirt slide off his shoulders.

Her tongue felt thick in her mouth as his fingers worked his belt buckle. "Uh, Carter? What are you doing?" Her eyes darted to the people beginning to take notice around them.

"You told me once I didn't know what it was like to have the whole town see my underwear. Maybe I just want to even the score as best I can." Then his pants slid to the ground and he stood before her, smiling wickedly, wearing nothing but a hideous pair of smiley-face swim trunks.

Her face flamed. "You're crazy," she breathed, acutely conscious of the murmur of interest they were drawing.

"Crazy in love with you," he whispered back.

Liz stared in stunned disbelief, the words 'crazy in love with you' tumbling deliciously over each other in her mind as Carter stepped out of his pants, walked over to the fountain... and stepped in.

The harsh, mumbled curse of surprise that hissed through his teeth sent a rumble of laughter through the crowd. Then he shook his wet hair back and turned to face her, eyes bright. "Elizabeth Beacon!" he called boomingly, despite the fact that she stood no more than fifteen feet away. "I stand here, making a complete fool of myself, because *I love you!*"

Excited chatter rippled through the crowd, and the band came to a clumsy, cacophonous halt. "I said, *I love you!*"

Liz's eyes skittered uneasily to either side of her as the crowd turned its full attention on them.

"I... love you, too," she murmured self-consciously as someone took Carter's clothes from her arms.

Carter grinned and stretched a wet hand toward her.

"No. The water must be freezing! You can't expect—"

"*Liz,*" he said. "Come here. I can't do this without you."

She stepped forward, unable to do otherwise, until her toes touched the low wall of the fountain. "You're making a spectacle of yourself," she warned him, knowing she was a part of the spectacle now, too, but beyond caring. *Crazy in love with you,* he'd said.

"I haven't even started," he assured her. Then he bowed forward, cool water splashing her lightly as he tipped an imaginary top-hat. "So, will you join me?"

Liz felt her knees go weak as awareness heated her cheeks. "You saw number ten."

His smile dazzled. "Sorry to take them out of order. We'll get to the others later. For now... *get in here.*" He reached for her again, and she shook her head, her better sense trying to deny what her body and soul had already accepted. "I'm fully dressed!" she protested even as her feet kicked off her shoes of their own accord. And then she was stepping into the cold spray, his warm hand pulling her forward.

She yelped as water sluiced down her back and over her hair. But when she glanced up again, it wasn't the water that stopped the breath in her lungs. It was the look in Carter's eyes.

"You came," he said.

"Did I have a choice?"

"Yes." He smiled and cupped her face in his hands. His thumb brushed her cheek. "I love you. So much," he whispered—only for her this time—then his lips dipped to hers.

Her mouth curved under his, and despite the cool water soaking her to the skin, heat swirled through her. "I love you, too. But I th—"

"Good," he said, cutting her off with a kiss. "That's all that matters." And then he knelt before her, the water making his hair darken, his skin glisten, and her world tilt as the unreality of it all hit her in full force. Devilish green eyes found hers, and her heart stuttered even as his hands cupped and warmed hers.

"Elizabeth Anne Beacon," he asked softly, "would you do me the honor... of becoming my wife?" And then he arched one of those damned eyebrows and she was a goner.

Liz swayed. No longer certain whether it was the water from the fountain, the brilliant spring sunshine or tears of joy blurring her vision, she nodded and gave the only answer she could. "*Yes!*"

She laughed as a cheer rose from the crowd. Then Carter swung her into his arms and kissed her soundly as the band resumed their triumphant theme song.

Water streamed from both of them, as they stepped from the fountain, but she couldn't care less. *He loved her!* She kissed him again, then pulled back, brow lightly furrowed. "Um, haven't you forgotten something?"

"Forgotten something?"

"Don't I get an engagement ring?"

"Ah, you want a ring, do you?" His lips brushed her ear. "It's in my pocket."

Liz blushed, thinking of the swim trunks plastered to his lean hips. "You don't have any pockets."

One green eye winked wickedly as Carter slid her down his body. She stood unsteadily.

He laughed then, a robust sound, and stooped to retrieve his dress pants. "Crossing off numbers one through nine will be more fun than I thought."

Liz caught her lip between her teeth as he slid the ring on her finger. Small, twinkling diamonds flanked a clear, lavender amethyst.

"It made me think of you in your purple dress. I know it's not a huge rock, but I'm hoping to finally buy out my uncle, and—"

"It's perfect," she interrupted with feeling. "*You're* perfect."

"Far from it, but I'm glad you think so."

"Perfect for me, then," she corrected. "I'm glad you're taking this step. I know you'll do great."

His grin tilted. "Not without a little help. But, maybe a certain business analyst would be interested in helping me get started?"

Liz grinned. "I know she's thinking of making some career changes, but I'll talk to her. I hear she has a soft spot for sexy college drop-outs with potential. I'm sure you two can work something out."

"Potential, eh?"

"Loads of it," she grinned again, her knees growing weak under his hot, knowing gaze.

"Are you two going to canoodle all day? You'll miss your flight!"

Liz blanched as Aunt Claire's words broke into her thoughts. *Her flight!* Oh my God! She'd forgotten all about it!

Carter turned to Liz. "Going somewhere?"

"Okay, here's the thing," she hedged, palms beginning to sweat. "I was going to New York. To see Niagara Falls actually, but that was before—"

"Okay, Carter, your bag is in the taxi with Liz's, your dry clothes are on the seat, and I'll take your suit to the cleaners tomorrow. Anything else before you leave?" Jim jiggled the baby in her carrier and looked at them expectantly.

"Before you leave?" Liz asked in confusion.

"I'm coming with you," Carter replied as he grasped her elbow and propelled her toward the taxi. "And we'd better hurry or we'll miss our flight."

"*Our* flight?"

Carter turned and winked at the ladies standing by the taxi. He opened the door for Liz. "You didn't think I'd let you cross off number five on your own, did you?"

But she stopped, dripping, hands on hips, and contemplated the innocent expressions of four elderly ladies standing by the taxi. God love them.

She stepped forward and kissed each woman soundly on the cheek. "You are *so* getting the kitschiest souvenirs I can find," she warned them. Then she laughed, slid into the taxi and yanked Carter firmly behind her.

"The airport, please," she managed before Carter's kiss prevented any further speech. She didn't care that they were soaked to their underwear. Didn't care about anything except the fact that she'd been given a second chance to start over and do things right this time.

Start a new chapter on a clean page.

Long, delicious minutes later, she pulled back with a sigh, her head falling against Carter's shoulder.

She was engaged! Not almost-engaged this time, but publicly, completely, publish-it-in-the-paper, shout-it-from-the-rooftops engaged! And, more importantly, *to the right man!*

Just because she could, she leaned in for another kiss. "I can't wait to cross off number eleven."

"Number eleven? What number eleven?"

She leaned closer, her words whispering against the sensitive flesh of his ear. Then she laughed silkily, delightedly, as his eyes widened and his breath hissed through his teeth.

"I *love* a woman who's good at math," he murmured appreciatively. Then he pulled her into his arms and proved it.

THE END

Dear Reader,

I hope you enjoyed Liz and Carter's love story! I love that they each needed a bit of the other's personality to balance themselves out, and aren't the best relationships like that? You might have guessed, I have a special place in my heart for those with ADHD. What they lack in punctuality and focus, they make up for in energy, creativity and spontaneity and life with them is never, ever dull.

If you enjoyed meeting Bailey in *Stacking the Deck* you won't want to miss my next 'Betting on Romance' novel, *All or Nothing,* where Bailey and Carter's brother, Ian, find their own happily ever after in the most unlikely and public way.

Be sure to sign up for my mailing list at www.cheriallan.com to receive invites to exclusive contests and info on new releases.

Sweet regards from Sugar Falls!

~ *Cheri*

About the Author

Cheri Allan lives in a charming fixer-upper in rural New Hampshire with her husband, two children, two dogs, four cats and an excessive amount of optimism. She's a firm believer in do-it-yourself, new beginnings and happily-ever-afters, so after years of wearing suits, she's grateful to finally put her English degree to good use writing romance. When not writing, you might find her whizzing down the slopes of a nearby mountain or inadvertently killing perennials in her garden.

Cheri loves to hear from readers!
E-mail her at cheri@cheriallan.com.
Like or Friend her at facebook.com/cheriallanbooks and facebook.com/cheriallanauthor.
Or, visit her website and blog at www.cheriallan.com.

If you enjoyed this book, please consider telling other readers by writing and sharing a review.

Cheri looks forward to continuing her 'Betting on Romance' series with *All or Nothing* (coming spring 2015) because—after all—every woman deserves to get lucky.

Be sure to start where it all began, with Jim and Kate, in Book One of the 'Betting on Romance' Series:

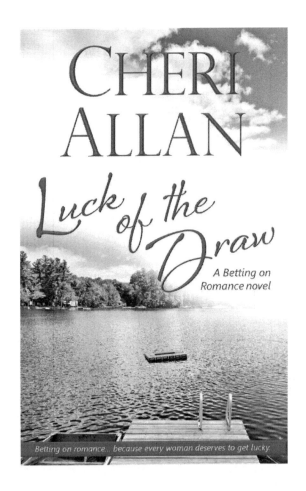

LUCK OF THE DRAW

Available now in print and e-book!

If only life had a refresh button...

Kate Mitchell never planned to be a 31 year-old widowed single mom, but when her soon-to-be-EX husband up and dies, her dreams of finishing college and starting over are thrown in the air like a game of 52 pick-up. When she's given a leave of absence from work and told to "quit or recommit," Kate retreats to idyllic Sugar Falls, New Hampshire, to figure out whether she can discover her passion and pay the bills. Cue the fresh air, summer sunshine and one sexy local contractor.

Tall, dark, and handy...

Volunteer fireman and all-around hunky guy in a toolbelt, Jim Pearson has sworn off complicated women with messy baggage. They cling to his nice-guy stability and skills with a power saw just long enough to straighten out their lives and move on... but then he meets the cute single mom staying at Grams' lake house for the summer.

While a sizzling attraction draws them together, Jim's distrust of complicated women and Kate's incredibly complicated life threaten to pull them apart. But forces beyond their control—match-making grandmothers, the lazy backdrop of summer, and their own reckoning with the past—conspire to make them risk it all... and bet on love.

Also, look for Book Three of the
'Betting on Romance' Series:

ALL OR NOTHING

Coming Spring 2015!

When finding Mrs. Right goes, oh, so wrong...

Self-made millionaire Ian McIntyre has suffered through a reality dating show only to return home to Sugar Falls empty-handed, swarmed by paparazzi, and hounded by a TV producer determined to get her *Happily Ever After.* But then his home is accosted by a sexy and snarky cleaning lady staging it for the season finale, and Ian finds himself more interested in the scrappy hometown girl dusting off his action figures than the audience's favorite southern belle...

21298499R00176

Made in the USA
Middletown, DE
25 June 2015